A WHITER SHADE OF PALE

DAVID L. GOLEMON

DLG PRESS

A Whiter Shade of Pale

ISBN: 978-0692572436

Cover art © 2015 by J. Kent Holloway

Published by DLG Press
Printed in the United States of America

For my family, for my fans.

THE PLAYERS

SAM DALHART ....PRIVATE DICK

JOHN RAINBIRD.....................THE PARTNER

CONSTANCE VALE........THE GIRL WITH THE GAMS

STEVIE KRAZENHEIMER.....................THE KID

CHARLIE CHAPLIN.................THE LITTLE TRAMP

DOUGLAS FAIRBANKS..................THE LOST SOUL

CARL VON RAILING.....................THE GERMAN

WITH SPECIAL CAMEOS BY:

CLARK GABLE

CAROLE LOMBARD

MARY PICKFORD

HUMPHREY BOGART

CAROL LANDIS

LAUREN BACALL

GARY COOPER

ADOLPH MENJOU

AND INTRODUCING

KARL VERNHOFFEN........AS THE BEAST

PART 1

THE COLORS OF LIFE, DRAINED TO GRAY, THEN WHITE

❧ PROLOGUE ❧

The man knew the cellar door almost as intimately as his very own at home because he had seen it every night for the past five months. Often times he would remove the rusting lock from the hasp and would actually raise the old brass latch, and at that point would just as often turn and run from the old mansion. There was never any rhyme or reason to what course the nightmare would take. Tonight it was the door. He watched helplessly as his hand reached out and removed the open, rusty lock and raised the steel latch away from its seat and as he did, as it did every time the dream went this way, the huge door would slide open so freely that it seemed as if it had been gently nudged from the other side.

As always happens, he stepped back fully anticipating that horrid smell from the basement. The smell of rotting wood, mildewed basement things and something he couldn't quite place, slammed him in the face like a sledge hammer. He would then reach for the pull-string that would light the bare bulb that hung from the rafters above his head. As the darkness was pushed back he would always get the same feeling of dread as his eyes would invariably lock on the descending basement stairs before him. He knew fully anticipated from his other trips to the basement just what it what it was he would see when he finished the long trek down into hell—a dank room clogged with old furniture—some covered with yellowing sheets while other pieces were left to fall to the ravages of time, but most would succumb under the onslaught of termites and rats.

The basement was as large as the grand dining room it sat beneath. As he slowly descended step by creaky step he knew the stairs would end and then just a few feet away, past the moldy and crumbling furniture, he would be facing another door. It was this door that led to the subbasement in which some long-ago movie mogul had thought would make an excellent wine cellar. This was the door, the very gateway to his nightmare proper. As in his previous nightmares he would contemplate the depth of that subbasement. Tonight however, it was there, not twenty feet further down as the stairs. It was if whoever controlled the nightmare couldn't wait the extra seconds for him to creep down the darkened steps. There was no expanse of concrete flooring, no furniture, just the door.

He swallowed and looked down. The lock securing the door was as ancient as the one above in the kitchen. He waited. First, the door rattled in its frame. He swallowed. It rattled softly once again and then the cut-glass knob slowly turned. He braced himself for the sweet, sickening smell that advanced on him like an unstoppable army. Only one thing in the world could make that horrible stench, rotting human flesh. This time it was a stench that promised a differing turn in the dream.

"Oh lord," he mumbled as he closed his eyes against the darkness of the basement and stairwell beyond the heavy door.

"You flatter me, Red Man, as always," the deep voice said in its aggravatingly low tone.

The thing's words emanated from the room's darkest recesses. It was the same as always—calm, assured, chuckling in obscene amusement. The man knew he would take the first step, and then the second…then suddenly the barren dirt floor of the subbasement was there before him.

This was something new in his nightly sufferings. Never before had he been skipped forward to this point like a record being jammed ahead, scratching the vinyl as it slid across the grooves. The candles placed on the dirt floor along the walls flickered; some even went out as if he had actually blown them out with his rapid passage down the long flight of stairs. He jumped as the door above him slammed shut, and then he heard a more distant slam as the kitchen door two stories up closed with a viciousness that had never been in the dream before.

He faced front, knowing exactly what was in the earthen room with him. He felt their cold, whitish and very dead eyes upon him. He could smell the creosote used to saturate the timbers of the rafters above him and the oil sprayed on the dirt floor to keep the dust in place. He always found that bit of his dream amazing—to smell the chemical odors of oil and creosote over the stench of the dead, the three mixing together like some sickening joke.

He took a step forward and that was when he heard the shuffling of the girls as they awoke and knew they had living company. They would soon be close enough to touch him. His fear, his very horror at that moment was usually enough to jolt him to wakefulness. But this time things were different and he knew it. Tonight the fear was palpable that he might not get out—not ever.

"Shaman, why are you here?" The voice from the shadows was deep and soft and was said as if the author was truly concerned.

"The young girls, the children, the ones here with you," he said with his eyes squeezed shut. "I think that's why I'm here."

Another soft chuckle and the heavy step of something large emanated from the far reaches of the subbasement as whatever it was he was conversing with changed its position—perhaps to see him better in the pitch blackness deep inside the basement. The candles closest to him once again fluttered, indicating movement somewhere close. The sound of coins being rustled came to his ears as the thing in the darkness moved closer. It was if someone were shaking a change purse with many heavy coins inside.

"I have had many brave men visit me, Shaman. All powerful men, but they have always come during their waking hours, thinking they have that one advantage over me, but they soon learn differently. But this visit, as with your other nocturnal wanderings, has vexed me to no end, Shaman. For me not to understand how you are capable of invading my home, is unsettling to say the least."

The first of the deathly white faces of the lost girls appeared as she entered the small circle of light cast by the candles. The dark haired girl tilted her head and smiled. The hair was matted and dirt encrusted, and the man as he always did, wanted to gag as he noticed the almost fluorescent white shapes of maggots as they worked inside one of the jagged wounds along her hairline. Her nylons were ripped, with the right one gathered around her ankle. Her once blue dress was torn and filthy.

He looked at her black eyes and he half-turned. The left side of her face looked partially caved in, as if she had been struck a devastating blow. Then he looked up and saw the second girl. She was sprawled on the floor. Her white sleeveless blouse was unbuttoned and her bra slid through the dirt, actually pushing some of the foul earth ahead like a strange bulldozer. He saw her twisted legs and knew she had once worn a pair of the discarded leg braces he had seen here before as bent and twisted as her legs; unlike the braces before, the child was a new addition to his nightmare.

He knew the other girls weren't far behind these two, and for some reason in this dream, on this night he felt he would be unable to escape them because this experience was becoming far more real and threatening than ever before.

The man turned and started to make for the stairs behind him, but as he did the steps faded and then came back into focus, and when they did, they seemed further away. He raised his foot to take the first of the five or six steps needed to reach the stairs and that was when he felt the hand on his ankle. One of the girls had him. He pulled and felt his shoe come free. He was loose and he ran for the stairs. That was when the girls screamed and he heard the Beast start forward. He wanted to turn—had to turn. As he tried to accomplish this the candles just didn't flicker out, they faded out, slowly and with terrifying intent.

He felt the heavy footfalls and knew he was about to join the girls who had been so anxious to welcome him. He fought for the rickety stairs as he heard the last few wine bottles that were left by the former owner go crashing to the fetid ground. The hiss of the girls sounded as their master came on through the darkness, and the yelp of one as the creature from the black void kicked her dead corpse aside. He heard the sickening sound as her rotted flesh struck the old wall of the subbasement and with that terrifying picture in his head he actually started making better progress toward the stairs. With the greatest of effort he had managed to gain the fourth step when he heard his host laugh out loud and then he felt the burning agony as one of the beast's long, yellowed claws reached out and raked down his back as he forced himself out of its grasp. It was still enough to make him scream in abject terror as the touch and the smell of death exuding from the foul creature reached out and took him just as assuredly as if he was in his foul clutches. He started to scream for the first time in his life. He screamed for all those times as a boy he had wanted to but had to show how brave he was for his father's sake. Yes, in this particular nightmare he knew the Beast was real and it had actually touched him. The clawed fingers were not meant to capture or kill—they were meant to frighten—or was it something else? He screamed again as he flew up the stairs, but the noise of his footsteps and the screams themselves could never drown out the sound of the laughter coming from the darkness below.

The man sat bolt upright in bed. He tore his left hand through his thick black hair and tried to concentrate on breathing. The nightmare had come again. Only he didn't consider it that anymore, he thought it more his nightly warning.

The cellar and the young women reaching for him with their cold hands and dead eyes, the way in which his feet refused to work right when he knew his only escape was to get free of their grip and out of that dank pit, could only be compared with what he thought was the lowest depths of hell.

He rubbed his chest, trying in vain to slow his beating heart before it tore itself loose from its mountings. He stood and made his way to the bathroom, fumbling for the button in the darkness. He finally hit the switch and the small tiled room came into harsh eye-hurting clarity. He stumbled to the sink and turned on the cold water and quickly splashed two handfuls onto his hot face. He stood at the sink for a moment and gathered his thoughts. Every night for the past few months, to one degree or another, the dream had come. It was always the same, starting with the girls with their reaching hands and pleading dead eyes.

Doll's eyes he called them. He shuddered, still trying to shake the feeling that he was being watched by something in the darkness of the cellar. Tonight's dream made everything that had come before clear—if the dream continued he would finally meet whatever was down there and he would be as lost as those dead girls were. As he focused on his own haunted features in the bathroom mirror he thought that tonight's dream had also given him something he could work with—certain things were becoming clearer as if he were cleaning a dirty window; he could see more of what was outside. That was what it was like. The new things had always been there, but now he was seeing them far more clearly. The dream was slowly becoming real.

The man concentrated on the face that stared back at him and the eyes that screamed for the needed sleep he had lost the last few months. He turned the knob and shut off the flowing water and reached for a hand towel and dried his face and as he did he saw his hands were shaking violently and he closed them both into fists. He stared, trying to still them but they were shaking enough that the towel flapped like a flag in the wind. He looked from his hands to the haunted eyes that stared back at him. He would have to tell Sam. This was beginning to affect his work as he was finding it hard to concentrate during the blessedly bright daylight hours. But how did you begin to tell the only man you considered a true friend that you believed you were going insane. Or worse, that you believed something was coming their way and that *something* had *teeth*. And most importantly, how do you tell him you have involved him?

He threw the towel against the wall and watched as the dampness held it firm against the paint for a moment and then it slowly crept down the wall and hit the floor. He slammed the push-button light switch off and slowly moved back to his bed—for the moment the darkness was no longer the terror it had been. He quickly prayed for relief from the continuing dream or warning, and then climbed into bed. As he watched the dark ceiling he couldn't help the feeling that he was still being watched. Suddenly his eyes widened in realization and he violently threw the covers off. He was now fully awake as he sprang from the bed. Again he felt his chest and he finally realized he was wearing a white shirt that was wet and stinking of that nightmare basement. He quickly pulled it from his body and looked at the tear down the backside. His eyes widened as they traveled from the torn and stinking shirt down to his filthy pants, and then he saw his feet. He had one dirt covered brown shoe on. The other was missing, exposing a filth covered sock.

He went to his knees and threw his face into his hands and tried in vain to concentrate on his prayer to his ancestors as he had been taught as a child, but as always the good spirits wouldn't answer. All he heard was the echo of laughter from the thing in the basement.

ONE

Hollywood, California,
October, 1939

A strong gust of wind caught the girl's umbrella and immediately turned it inside-out, presenting its skeletal frame and flimsy fabric to the rain. She struggled with it hurriedly, shaking it, hoping it would magically right itself before she became completely soaked. She shook the umbrella once while turning her small body into the wind with her suitcase heavy in her left hand. She shook it again and as her luck would have it, a third time, and indeed this third time was the proverbial charm—it slipped from her grasp and went straight into the raging water that had filled the gutter. She watched as it quickly disappeared into a large storm drain, the handle acting like the stern of a sinking vessel, pausing for a brief moment in the air and then sliding into oblivion.

"Damn, oh, damn!" she cursed, stomping her right heel onto the sidewalk while staring disbelievingly at the spot where her umbrella had disappeared.

She placed the heavy suitcase down on the sidewalk with a splat and then pulled her hat down harder onto her red hair and immediately felt and heard the brim partially tear away through the force of her action. She closed her eyes tightly for a moment and tried not to cry. The hat had belonged to her sister before she had stolen it to bring on her trip. The girl had loved the hat since she had first laid eyes on it when her sister had put it on for the first time before they went to church back in Davenport, Iowa five weeks before. She thought it made her older sister look just like Myrna Loy, and if it made *her* look like Myrna, it had to do the same for herself, because everyone in their small town always said she was the spitting image of her older sister. That was how she had justified the small theft to herself—the whole trip out here was the best thing possible for her *and* the hat.

After she had arrived at the bus stop not more than an hour and a half ago, she had inquired about the rooming house she had read about in a story from the *Los Angeles Times*. It was a character piece about an old actress from the silent era who knew the dangers for young actresses being swept away by all the glitz and glamour of Hollywood. The story went on to say this woman had started an eighteen-room boardinghouse that catered to single women who had come to Tinsel Town hoping to get that first big break. She had called months ago hoping for one of the rooms, but had been told that they were booked solid for months to come, so she started to form an alternate plan in her head on how to live once she went out west but had come up with absolutely nothing. As luck would have it, she received a call from the rooming house a few days ago (luckily her sister wasn't home at the time) saying that not only one room had suddenly opened up, but two. She had made her escape plan at the spur of the moment and had left Davenport on Wednesday afternoon before the start of school. That would give her a full eight hours head start on her sis, even more if she worked late.

After being told by the very weary bus driver that the boardinghouse was down on Orange Street close to the Chinese theater, she had beamed.

How many times had she seen the venerable old theater in her *Photoplay* magazines, a thousand? *Oh, it had to be more,* she thought to herself, not hearing the bus driver speaking a warning about how far the boarding house was and how this rain wasn't going to let up. She was just too thrilled at having a chance to live so close to one of the really big landmarks of tinsel-town. *That had to be a good omen,* she thought, therefore negating the tales people in Iowa espoused about the odds of a young lady making it in Hollywood. She wasn't as dumb as her age—her friends said if she attempted to do the impossible she would come back home with a broken heart and smashed dreams as her only reward for this grand adventure. But she pushed those negative thoughts from her mind almost as hard as she had pushed aside the recriminations from her sister about those very same dreams.

She foolishly hadn't listened to the bus driver when he told her the buses and trolley were no longer running at this time of night, along with the warning that she shouldn't walk anywhere in this town alone. She had waited for a taxicab for a while but grew concerned about how late it was getting, so she had started off on foot with her umbrella keeping her dry. And now, here she was standing on the sidewalk getting soaked to the bone minus one umbrella. Her sister's beautiful wide-brimmed hat was probably a ruin, and that was the only hat she had thought about taking in her haste to leave the farm and Iowa behind forever.

She stomped her right foot down again on the wet pavement in frustration and felt the heel snap as her ankle twisted. As a small twinge of pain announced itself as it traveled up her ankle to her leg, she looked down at the expensive high-heels and gasped. God, what was happening? Was everything she borrowed from her sister going to tear or break or decide to go boating down the curb?

She started to cry. She looked around for someone, anyone, just some sign of life that told her Hollywood was real and not just a made-up place put in magazines for the benefit of dreamy-eyed young girls. That all the buildings weren't false-fronted props like the sets of Tara and Atlanta she had seen in the *Hollywood Confidential* articles about *'Gone with the Wind.'* But as she looked up and down Hollywood Boulevard she saw not one vehicle or person along the street. Tinsel town was an empty and scary place at three-fifteen in the morning. She looked up with her tears mixing with the rain water and watched the timed stop and go signals raise and lower along the street—their small bell clanging as they did, playing as they were to an empty house.

She just knew that the eye make-up, also borrowed from her sister's bedroom make-up case, was streaming down her cheeks. And with the hot tears added to the cold rain hitting her she knew she had to be a mess. As she wallowed in her own sorrow, suddenly the surrounding sidewalk and buildings were lit-up, as if a giant flashbulb had exploded. She was startled as lightning struck somewhere close by and thunder immediately boomed like a thousand fourth of July cannons. She nearly jumped out of her skin. She quickly picked up her suitcase from the sidewalk and started limping along on her broken heel. The rain was coming down much harder now as she spied a small awning up ahead and made for it. The noise of her broken heel was accompanied by that of her left shoe and both made a *click-swish* sound as she hurried along, trying to make the windblown awning before a lightning strike could end her dreams of stardom in one bright flash guilty justice.

As she approached the sanctuary of the awning, the girl noticed it was the entranceway to a jewelry store with a small alcove on both sides that housed glassed-in enclosures filled with sparkling pieces. She hurried under the protective cover of the awning and stepped into the alcove, allowing the heavy suitcase slam to the tiled entrance. As if on a queue from some hidden director and just as she was safely under the shelter, another lightning bolt snaked across the black sky and thunder ripped the clouds above Los Angeles. She gave a small yelp and held her ears with her hands as the glass in both display cases bulged and shook; seemingly ready to explode outward to shower her with sharp, penetrating shards.

In the afterglow of the lightning bolt the girl opened her eyes and uncovered her ears and peered out and across Hollywood Boulevard and was amazed to see a familiar sight. There, as big as life was the darkened silhouette of the Egyptian Theater. She recognized the gaudy props out in front and she smiled, not because she was seeing the theater, but because she knew that *Sid Graumann's* other, and far more famous theater, was right down the block on the opposite side of the street from the Egyptian. Around the corner from *Graumann's* and down two blocks was the boardinghouse on Orange Street. Her mood brightened as she realized she was almost to Miss Hannigan's room and board. If she could just get through this storm nothing could stop her. She would show everyone back in Davenport, including her *sister*, that she was made-up of the right sand to make it in Hollywood.

She reached down to pick up her suitcase and as she did she was again silhouetted inside glowing lights. But this time it was the headlights of an automobile and not lightning that framed her in the entranceway to the jewelry store. Forgetting the suitcase she watched as the car was turning right, out of a small alley beside the *Egyptian* when its lights caught her. The girl's heart raced faster as a long black Hudson cut across Hollywood Boulevard and pulled up in front of the store, its chrome bumper facing the wrong way. The huge whitewall tires splashed through the raging water of the gutter sending a small wave across the sidewalk, so much in fact that the girl had to step further back under the awning of the jewelry store to keep from having the rainwater wash over her feet. She angrily watched the water as it flowed back into the gutter and then she quickly looked up at the idling Hudson. The windows were shaded black except for the drivers' side glass and the man behind the wheel didn't even look her way, he just stared straight ahead. The young girl swallowed, and with her eyes never leaving the car she reached down and retrieved the heavy suitcase and placed it in front of her, ready to throw it at a would be masher if need be. Just to be even safer the girl slid out of her damaged heels, thinking to hell with her sister's nylon's, she wouldn't let heels and her only hose slow her down if she had to run. As she lifted her case her small handbag, also borrowed from her sister, slipped from her grasp and landed at her feet unnoticed.

The rear left window of the Hudson slowly went down, revealing a darkened void beyond.

"Well, aren't you the proverbial drowned rat my dear. I think there may better times to sightsee," said a voice from the darkness beyond the window frame.

The girl lowered her head and tried to see who was talking, but the falling rain coupled with the distance made it impossible to see anything other than the deep blackness of the interior.

"I'm…I'm not sightseeing, I'm waiting on my friend to come and pick me up," she lied.

There was a moment when she didn't think the man in the backseat of the Hudson was going to respond, and she was starting to feel uncomfortable as the silence grew to what seemed a full minute, all the while she could *feel* the stranger's eyes on her. The girl started wondering if he somehow knew she was lying about the ride she was waiting on. She decided that the suitcase would have to be set down also; *she may have to run very fast*, she thought.

"I see. This friend is very irresponsible leaving such a beautiful young woman as you obviously are out in the wind and rain," the voice finally said, "delicate flowers need not so much water, even aspiring young actresses."

As she watched, not knowing what to say or even if she should respond at all to the strange compliment, the man slid down the seat and appeared in the open window. She exhaled the breath she had been holding in relief; she had been starting to imagine all kinds of horrors sitting in that dark interior. Something out of one of those old *Universal* pictures maybe. She was grateful to see a blond and very handsome man smile at her.

The girl smiled and stepped forward, knocking her forgotten suitcase over. She quickly reached down and set it upright. "Actually, he was supposed to pick me up in front of the Chinese theater. I just stepped in here to get out of the rain," she said as she slid the case to her side.

"If I judge correctly, maybe you both should have had your rendezvous at the train, or perhaps the bus station," the man smiled and then reached into his coat pocket and retrieved a gold cigarette case and opened it. He removed a cigarette and replaced the case and then placed the cigarette into a long black holder and then placed it in his mouth and lit it with an expensive gold lighter. He exhaled smoke and then smiled at the young girl. "I am right, am I not?" he asked through the open window, "you are here to try your hand at being an actress?"

The girl suddenly became embarrassed. She didn't know if he was being condescending like her sister had been at the mere mention of Hollywood, or if he was being sincere. She looked away, glimpsing her dark reflection in the jewelry store window, and asked herself why she should be embarrassed by this question since after all, that was exactly what she was here to do.

"I'm not here just to try mister," she said, almost huffing out her small chest, "I'm here to be an actress, something I was meant to do my entire life."

The man again smiled and nodded his head, and removed the long cigarette holder. "My name is Von Railing, and I believe you will be just what you want to be my dear," he was still smiling as he faced forward and took a long drag off his cigarette and then slowly exhaled. He looked her way again. "This is one of the worst nights I've been witness to since my arrival in Los Angeles, I like yourself, am new to this area, only myself being from much further away."

"Really?" she said, relaxing somewhat. "I'm from Davenport, Iowa."

"Davenport, Iowa, to Hollywood, California—now that my dear is the bravest thing I think I have ever heard from a young woman. To brave such a trek as that so you can act upon the silver screen."

The girl could barely hear his words over the thrumming of the rain on both the jewelry store awning and the metal hood and roof of the Hudson. But she heard enough.

"You're just teasing me now," she said, raising her voice.

"Not at all," he answered, craning his neck to look out of the rear window for a moment, and then turning to face her once again. "With that kind of determination I expect you will do very well here. I would even go so far as to say, as you just said, that you were meant to be here."

She could feel herself blushing again and knew he was right because she had thought the very same thing a thousand times. "Thank you," she said, looking away from his eyes which had locked on her own.

"I will not insult your integrity my dear by this stranger offering you a ride, you look much too intelligent for that kind of foolishness. So, if you brave just a little more of these uncommon California elements, you will find your theater and *possibly* the man you came here to meet, about three minutes fast walk to your right."

She was actually shocked he wasn't offering her ride, isn't that what men did out here with young women?

"Well, uh, thank you…for the directions," she said, stumbling over the words.

"Not at all my dear, I wish you all the luck in the world, and if your friend isn't there when you arrive, just go into the covered courtyard and wait where it is dry. Now you hurry and stay out of trouble," the man started to roll up his window, and then paused while it was still half down. "Dear?"

The girl was leaning down to pick up her suitcase when she looked at the man again, noticing his smile was even wider than it had been. "Yes?" she said.

"I think you'll not have a care in the world after this dreary and bleak morning is behind you. You may soon meet many very important men in this town, possibly maybe sooner than even you expected, so when the time comes, be yourself and make the experience last a lifetime." With that said and not waiting for further comment to his bizarre statement, the widow went up and the car pulled away from the curb.

"Well, that was optimistic, at least he wasn't a basher," she said to herself, allowing her own voice to keep her company and feeling better for it.

She retrieved her suitcase and started to place the high-heels back on her small feet, then thought better of it and decided that a pair of nylon's would be a cheap price to pay for not breaking her ankle, after all, she would buy herself a new pair tomorrow, thanks to the feed money she had also lifted from her sister's drawer. With her shoes and suitcase in her hands and her small purse left forgotten under the alcove awning, she briskly stepped from the safety of the jewelry store and started walking.

She didn't see the Hudson slow down and pull to the curb further up on Hollywood Boulevard in the opposite direction of her walk, nor did she notice the headlights and taillights go dark as the engine was shut off. She only noticed the distant lightning and thunder and the pounding rain that seemed to be swirling in one giant circle above Hollywood.

As she walked along, she wished she did have a beau out here that would pick her up and take her to a nice warm room where she could dry herself and relax, but she had never had time for things like boyfriends. Between the farm and school and not even counting all the stolen hours of acting on her high school stage, she never thought about boys at all. They thought about her, she knew that, but the thought of staying in Davenport never entered her way of thinking. The only chicken she ever wanted to see again would be the Chicken Kiev served her at the Brown Derby, the restaurant of the stars. Her future was here.

As she splashed up the sidewalk she saw what she had dreamed of seeing for the last six years of her life. All the pictures of world premieres she had seen in *Photoplay*, all the stars lined up to walk the red carpet, and now there it was. Through the darkness and rain she could make out the large pagodas and Chinese woodwork of the most famous theater in all of

Hollywood—Graumann's Chinese Theater. Even though she was soaked through to the bone the girl let out a loud giggle and started running toward the historic theater.

The marquee was dark of course and the rain was falling so hard she couldn't make out what was playing. She saw the penguin on the *Refrigerated for your Comfort'* banner flapping in the blowing wind under the marquee and she walked quickly into the courtyard past the free standing box-office in the front. The girl was grateful for the shelter as she set down her suitcase and tossed her shoes on the famous concrete entranceway. Her wet feet made marks just like the more famous prints embedded in the cement stretched out before her.

She walked from cement block to cement block not noticing the lightning and thunder any longer while she looked at all the famous people who had put their mark for all their fans to come and gush over. She found Myrna Loy and almost fainted. God, she thought, all those *Thin Man* movies, and *she* had placed her feet and hands in wet cement right here where she was standing. She pulled her hat down and actually jumped up in the air in her pure joy of having arrived. As she landed with an accompaniment of a lightning bolt over Hollywood, she suddenly felt as if she weren't alone. The thunder cracked overhead and she swallowed nervously—all thoughts of Myrna Loy and the *Thin Man* movies now gone.

She looked around her. Along the walls were small poster cases with movies that were *'coming soon.'* Her eyes traveled down the length of these advertisements until she was sure no one was there, hidden in the darkness behind the row of ads. Again, lightning flashed overhead and thunder rumbled immediately and it was during the flash that she thought she saw movement by the free-standing box office at the front of the theater. She reached for her suitcase, forgetting the shoes that she had so carelessly tossed next to it.

"Is someone there?" she asked, her voice hitching with fear. "Mister Von Railing, is that you?" she called into the pouring rain.

She saw another blur of motion out of the corner of her eye and she quickly turned to her left. Nothing. She stepped toward the front of the courtyard peering as hard as she could through the rain pelting the box-office. Then she saw it. She dropped her suitcase as she looked up into the falling rain, she tried to scream but her voice failed her. Another streak of lightning ripped the sky wide open and revealed the figure perched atop the ornate pagoda-style box-office. This time the girl managed to scream, but it was thoroughly drowned out by the crash of thunder that shook the glass in the coming attraction cases. Whatever it was, tilted its massive head and looked down upon the girl as if her scream was no more than a curiosity.

Jeannie Yale of Davenport, Iowa, USA, wanted to be an actress in the worst way and she would have done anything in the world to reach that goal. But now, all thoughts of stardom and fighting her way onto that screen that attracted so many were blotted from her mind forever as the thing jumped from the box-office roof and landed in front of her. As large as it was it should have shook the very foundation they stood upon, but instead of hitting with a thump, it seemed as if it floated down to the concrete in front of her. Again, lightning flashed further in the distance, backlighting the creature from behind.

The figure was standing motionless in the falling rain. She watched the raindrops strike its wet and shiny skin and splash off. Again it tilted its head while looking her over. Jeannie held up her suitcase, hoping it would be a sort of talisman against this nightmare that was standing in her way of escaping. Once more distant lightning flashed illuminating the eyes if her visitor. They were bright yellow. When it blinked it was as if an interior light had been shut off from the inside they were so bright. It started walking toward her. As it came closer she saw its face clearly for the first time and the suitcase fell from her hands, the brass corner hitting the concrete, chipping the middle finger of W.C. Fields left handprint. As it came closer she saw the leather string around its thick, gruesome neck.

Tied to the string was a small leather pouch and Jennie could hear the rattle of metal from the inside as it walked.

The thing saw this and stopped. It stood in front of her breathing deeply as it reached out. Jeannie was now frozen in place with terror as four long and curved claws, light brown and stained ivory in color, reached out and removed the hat. It was pulled away so gently that the stitching that had ripped earlier didn't pop a thread. The thing before her let her hat fall to the ground. It looked at her, tilting its head to the right, and then left, the yellow eyes moving over her as if taking in every nuance of her form. The thing standing to her front knew many things, and foremost among them was the fact that the last thing the young, never-would-be actress would see would be the ancient reason why mankind had feared the dark throughout history.

As she was lifted slowly off the ground a surreal sense of peace overcame her and she welcomed the darkness that embraced her body and soul. Her small hand came up and gently stroked the hideous face in front of her. She felt free, warm, and very safe because she was now doing what had always been written for her to do; she had indeed made the acquaintance of a very important man in Hollywood. As her life ended, Jeannie was finally happy. She had fulfilled her part the way she always thought she would.

As the dark figure drained the very life force of the girl, the gentleness remained as it lowered her and placed its arms under her still form. Her body swayed in his right arm as her blank stare looked into the falling rain. A single clawed finger came up and gently wiped the rain from her features as it turned and started walking into the storm, holding the small body close to its own, protecting what was now his as much as the leather sack tied around its neck.

✥ TWO ✥

Stevie Kratzenheimer ran along Sunset Boulevard and dodged a rather large woman with an ample bosom and even more imposing frame and it was that latter item that was almost his undoing. The large woman immediately grabbed for the dangling black purse that was hung on her puffy left arm with a gloved right hand, thinking the boy a masher or purse snatcher. Stevie saw the collision coming with the woman and quickly swerved right, almost hitting a man carrying a briefcase from behind. As he righted the large sack he was balancing he half-turned to see the heavyset woman shoot him a dirty look, but also looking relieved and grateful her purse was still attached to her fat arm as the man with the briefcase shouted for him to *"watch it kid."*

Stevie was dressed as nattily as he usually was day in and day out—dull green corduroys, black tennis shoes and the ever-present old fashioned golf cap turned backwards on his head of red hair. His pullover sweater, once a proud black had been reduced to a light bluish-gray by too many washing's in hot water.

As he dodged an early morning newsboy hawking the first edition of the *Times*, shouting *"Japs angered at trade embargo, send special envoy to Washington,"* the bag he was carrying tipped off balance and was in danger of spilling its contents along the sidewalk. He again shifted the sack and righted the coffee inside. He slowed his pace, knowing that at least for this morning he was early, his wind-up alarm beside his bed was feeling none too good having being thrown against the wall like it had been, but in its last act of defiance, it had indeed awakened him enough to realize he had a chance to surprise everyone and be early at the office. As he ran along Sunset the change in his pockets jingled and with any sort of luck at all John Rainbird would forget all about giving him a *fin* for the coffee, or maybe if he did remember he would let him keep the change from the five dollar bill for being early on a Monday.

He slowed even further as he saw the flat steel and canvas awning of the *Alhambra Building* up ahead. The large old English 'A' was placed on the three sides of the awning, one facing the street and the other two facing the sidewalk in both directions. As he slowed Stevie wiped the sweat from his brow with the over-long sleeve of his sweater and thinking as he did he should have worn something else as the bad weather of the last few weeks had finally departed the LA area and had been replaced since yesterday with a true southern California fall. He thought the world was coming along just fine, at least his world; he tried not to think about what was going on in Europe with Nazi's picking fights with everyone. But he figured Frankie D. Roosevelt knew how to handle things without asking him for advice just as his mother admonished him about every time he came in with news of yet another Nazi triumph.

He quickly turned under the large awning and stopped in front of the large door with the leaded glass running down its center. The brass door latch gleamed in the early morning sun as he took a deep breath and reached for the handle, opened the door and stepped into the building. To his left was a small antique dealer known to peddle old movie props that he occasionally passed off as valuable to naïve tourists. To his right was Thomas C. Watts, CPA's office—Watts was evidently a good guy as he was actually trusted enough to handle the agency's books. He was also apparently the only man in the world that made John Rainbird nervous.

Stevie started for the large staircase, foregoing the elevator in the well-appointed lobby. He took the stairs two at a time in his haste. Stevie knew the elevator was faster, but being from Brooklyn and forever used to the stairs in the old run-down buildings in Red Hook where he and his Ma had lived. Besides he never trusted the things with their greasy cables and the loud rumbling beneath your feet they produced. He was raised with stairs and he would continue to utilize them. The boy lived in fear of the truth coming out that he was afraid of all things mechanical, and he dreaded the day the rest of the agency found out about this little flaw in his character. He would just die because the only thing he wanted in the whole world was to be a detective like the fella's upstairs. Not a cop, but a private Dick. The movies had convinced him that was the way to go; the dames, the bad guys always beating you at the start and then you getting them in the end.

Man, that was the way to live he thought, even though he knew most of the work was tedious and that you didn't get a whole lot of thanks in the end and usually the only dames you ran across in this business were the ones trying to catch their husbands cheating, so they really weren't in the market for other men in their lives.

Stevie finally reached the sixth floor landing, which was the uppermost floor of the *Alhambra*, with only the front of the bag stained with coffee. He looked left, then right, and then walked to the only office on the entire floor. The double doors were wide and inset with opaque glass in the center that almost ran down to the green tiled floor. On the left door was written in nice block letters; *SUNSET DETECTIVE AGENCY,* in a half circle. Below that was a simplified image of an eye, a symbolic message that even Stevie understood—*we're watching.* On the right side door was a more colorful image of a sun that was half-set behind a line of blue ocean, below that, bold black letters proclaimed; *Samuel S. Dalhart, Pres.*, and under Sam's name, *John Rainbird, Associate.*

Stevie stopped before the doors and again took a deep breath. He pushed the thumb-latch down and opened the door quickly, knowing he was early enough that no one would be in the reception area but Tess the agency clerk and secretary.

"Surprise, Stevie's on the job," he said loudly, and then froze in the open doorway.

The clacking of the typewriter stopped, the people waiting to be interviewed in the waiting area lowered their *Look* and *Saturday Evening Post's* and *New York* and *Los Angeles Times* and were staring at Stevie who was perfectly framed in the doorway. Stevie swallowed and grimaced as it was so quiet you could hear a pin drop. Elizabeth Wheeler, the office manager, or the Wicked Witch of the East, as Stevie thought of her, was sitting behind her big desk to the far left of the reception area with her brows raised. The receptionist, Tess Adams, a nineteen year-old like himself was seated in the middle of the room, she blew a big pink bubble with her ever present gum but was smart enough not to let it burst. She just let the air out and pulled the gun back into her mouth as she smiled at Stevie, knowing he was going to get it good from Liz.

He was caught half in and half out of the door, hesitating, knowing he had to go in and face the music eventually. He slowly and quietly took a step forward into the office and closed the door. He was thinking that his alarm clock got the last laugh after all. After the door clicked shut with an extremely loud *click*, Liz was just about to say something when he was saved by a loud buzz coming from her desk. She bent to answer her intercom as Stevie looked to his right and the five people waiting to be seen. They were still looking at him as if he were some sort of bug that had appeared at the door. He swallowed and stepped toward the large desk just as Liz clicked the small switch on her intercom.

"Yes, Mr. Dalhart?" she said formally into the intercom for the benefit of the clients in the reception area. But she was still looking at Stevie with her left eyebrow arched.

"Was that the learned voice of Mr. Kratzenheimer we all heard?"

"As a matter of fact it was," she answered, again depressing the switch on the two-foot by two foot brown box.

"Tell him to come and *surprise* us with the coffee he was supposed to have here an hour ago, please."

"I will forward the message," she answered, pulling out her large chair and sitting. Elizabeth was attractive in that bookish way that Stevie knew from his school days. He would have had a crush on her as a student if he hadn't know her to be a stern task master at running the day to day operations of the most successful detective agency in Hollywood. Her pointy-framed glasses hung around her neck on a thin gold chain. She placed them on her slender nose and then she reached up and swept a strand of her black hair back into place behind her ear. The rest of her hair was done up neatly in a bun that virtually warned men she was unavailable. She was looking at something on her desk blotter as she pointed for Stevie to stand before her. A few snickers were heard from the waiting area and from the receptionist. Stevie looked her way and raised his upper lip in his best scary face. She just smiled and accidentally popped a bubble.

"Well, you managed one more time to be an embarrassment to this company Mr. Kratzenheimer."

Stevie stood before her, the coffee hot against his chest. She looked up at him, meeting his mournful stare. Then her eyes rose to his hat which he quickly snatched from his head with his free left hand.

"My alarm clock, it….it…," he stopped when Liz held up her right hand, her red painted fingernails shining in the overhead fluorescents.

"We'll discuss this after you're finished in the conference room and after you have run your errand to *Newbury's* to replace the coffee urn you burned up last week, is that clear?"

"I...I wasn't the one—"

"They are waiting for their coffee, and Mr. Rainbird will discuss the urn with you later," she said, once again cutting him off. "And Stevie?"

"Yes, Ma'am?" he said, his eyes looking at the plush beige carpeting.

"He hasn't been sleeping that well and he's not in the best of moods."

"Great," was all he said as he opened the door to the long hallway and the offices beyond.

Liz watched him go and then looked around the reception area. When she saw no one was watching her she smiled and took Stevie's time sheet and marked it in that he had been on time and not an hour late. She did this at least once a week to avoid the official paperwork that would tell the accountant to report that he was far beyond the limits of company policy. She was protecting him because she knew that Stevie and his mother were barely scraping by on what she made as a wash lady and he as, well, whatever it was he did here.

Tess Adams smiled as she watched Stevie leave the room and was about to blow another bubble when Liz cleared her throat. The girl looked over at Liz and swallowed her gum when she saw Liz pointing to a spot in front of her desk. The meaning was clear and Stevie would have been happy if he had known the girl was toeing the line in front of the office's queen bee.

Stevie turned once he was through the door to close it behind him, trying to be as quiet as possible with the conference room only five feet away down the hall. He shut it gently and turned abruptly into a small man who backed up a step when Stevie bumped into him.

"Hey, what is this?" the man said, wiping the few drops of coffee from his expensive light blue suit jacket. The smallish man held his hands in front of him with the fingers pointing down in his famous loose wrist stance. He then half-raised his right hand in a striking gesture he made famous in film. "Why I ought'a," he said, his Brooklyn accent far more pronounced than Stevie's own.

Stevie's eyes widened when he finally saw the reddish-blonde hair and those sparkling eyes. His one film idol was James Cagney and here he was standing right in front of him.

"Ah...oh...uh, jeeze, I'm sorry Mr. Cagney, let me get that for ya's," Stevie stammered as he reached out with his sweater sleeve and was just inches from wiping Cagney's lapel with the stained and dirty sleeve he had wrapped in his palm. "Why you...when was the last time you'z washed that sweater? When Hoover was president?" Cagney asked, backing up a step.

"Jeeze Louise, Mr. Cagney, that hurts," he said; only it came out sounding like '*hoits.*'

"Yeah, I'll give ya somthin' that hoits, ya little squirt," he said, "my meetin's over punk, and Rainbird promised me coffee, and where's was my coffee?" Cagney said over pronouncing his accent for the benefit of the kid.

Stevie looked from the carpet to Cagney who stood just exactly the same size as Stevie himself. After seeing the actor's face he lowered his gaze to the floor. Then Cagney playfully slapped him on the side of the head.

"Go, on, I didn't want any coffee anyways. Besides, it's that damn big Indian you'z better worry about kid, not me," he said as he reached for the door handle and then stopped when he thought of something and turned back to face Stevie. "Hey, Rainbird said you had a hand in recovering my stamp collection. Thanks, kid," he said, tapping Stevie on the shoulder. This time his false tough guy accent and persona was nowhere to be seen or heard as it was well known in certain circles that he was one of the most articulate men in Hollywood when he wanted to be. "Now you better get in there before that Indian lifts your hair."

"Yes, sir, thank you, Mr. Cagney," Stevie answered dodging by him and heading for Rainbird's office.

As he walked quickly down the hallway he heard voices coming from the conference room as he passed it. He was wondering who was in there when Rainbird's office door at the end of the hallway opened suddenly and there he was. Dressed neatly in a blue Halgren suit made special in New York for him, the six foot-six inch John Rainbird stepped out and faced Stevie. His black hair was cut short and it was oiled and parted neatly in the middle. He never knew it but most women who met him secretly wished to know the man in more intricate *and* intimate detail. But everyone at the agency knew John had someone special he never spoke of and the agency had yet to meet. As he held Stevie's gaze with his deep brown eyes, he placed his arms through his suit jacket and straightened it on his large frame. He pulled down the blue vest he had on underneath and adjusted his watch chain—never breaking eye contact with Stevie.

"If you don't have my change from that five I gave you on Friday for the coffee I'm going to throw you out of the conference room widow," John stated as he quickly brushed by the unmoving Stevie.

"Damn," he said under his breath, "this ain't my day."

He followed Rainbird to the conference room and through the open door. They stepped into what looked like a very serious meeting with the rest of the detectives of the agency including Sam Dalhart. Sam sat at the head of the long conference table and acknowledged Rainbird who took a seat beside Sam. Dalhart only briefly looked at Stevie, who thought it best to start passing out the coffee he had brought. He started with the detectives first as he knew they would be giving him the hardest time later on. He gave one to Talbot Leonard, resplendent in his ever present bow-tie and white suit. Then came Frank Wiechek. Frank was a second generation Polish-American who had turned the occasionally-necessary second-story job into an art form. The only men missing from the group were Pete Sanchez who Stevie knew to be home in bed, and Willis Jackson, also probably home sleeping since they had both been up all night working a stake-out at Charlie's house again.

Stevie turned with the four remaining coffee's and looked at Sam; he raised an eyebrow and nodded toward their guest at the far end of the table. Stevie walked to the far end and offered one of the large paper containers of 'Joe' to a man dressed in a white suit. The entire ensemble was white, save for the light-blue handkerchief sticking out of the left jacket pocket that matched the only other nonwhite article, his tie. A white hat lay on the conference table in front of the brown haired man. Stevie offered the coffee, holding it out for the man who only looked at it but said nothing. Stevie noticed that underneath the man's jacket were two shoulder-holstered, nickel plated Colt .45's.

"I guess our friend from…where are you from again, the Purvis Detective Agency? Well, I guess he isn't a morning coffee man Stevie, but I am, bring it down here," Sam said, staring at the man who was now looking down the table at the head of the Sunset Detective Agency.

Talbot Leonard stifled a laugh as Stevie set coffee in front of Rainbird and then Sam. Stevie turned and started to leave with two coffee containers still in the bag.

"You can stay Stevie; you may have to give your little report in a moment," Sam said, stopping the boy in his tracks.

Stevie swallowed and dropped his hat, then bent to pick it up. As he straightened he saw the man he knew from old crime photos glaring at him. He shuffled over and sat in the far corner, just behind Rainbird who looked at him for a moment and then turned his attention back to the visitor in the white suit.

"Mr. Purvis, this is the head of our field teams here at Sunset, John Rainbird," Sam said, gesturing to his partner. Then Sam stood and as he did he pulled tightly down on his black vest. The white shirt he wore was pure pearl and starched and he was dressed, as always, to the nines with his gold and blue turquoise inlaid cufflinks.

Rainbird was the only man in the room to notice how fast Sam had stood after the ex-G-man ignored his introduction. John knew that few things made Sam as furious as people refusing to speak to his partner because of their racial prejudices. Rainbird had stopped caring about such people years before and John knew because of Sam's over-protectiveness over his partner he might have to step in here because Sam didn't need to offend Purvis or his old master, Mr. Hoover.

"As I was saying, Mr. Dalhart, any information you may deem important enough to forward to Director Hoover through my agency would be of great help to our investigation, and it would also be seen as a personal favor to myself and Mr. Hoover."

Sam paced to the window and looked out over Sunset Boulevard. The street was coming alive with people on their way to work and those that were here to sightsee. He turned and smiled, but Rainbird knew the signs—when Sam's smile never touches his eyes, you better watch out.

"Again I'll repeat, everything we do here is of a confidential nature to our clients," he held up a hand when the famous Melvin Purvis, the killer of John Dillinger, started to protest. "We cooperate with the local police and the federal boys when we feel a crime has been, or will soon be committed. There has been no crime here, Mr. Purvis. Mr. Chaplin has been a model guest of the United States for the past six months with our current case and the last two years with cases he has initiated himself."

"If he has been so model a guest, why did Miss Pickford and Mr. Fairbanks hire your agency to, how should I say this, get the goods on him?"

"Without disclosing anything of a confidential nature, Mr. Purvis," Sam said, again taking his seat, "I will say this; it was at Miss Pickford's doing and not Mr. Fairbanks. Since their divorce in '36 he has little or no say in the business, and all she wanted was to ensure Mr. Chaplin was not doing anything that would be harmful to the success of *United Artists*, their joint venture. He hasn't and that's the conclusion that will be presented in our report to our client, Miss Pickford."

Melvin Purvis held Sam's gaze and then looked over at Rainbird. "Your conclusions as well?" he asked.

Rainbird sipped from his coffee and then looked at the former FBI agent. He knew Purvis was not only famous for the Dillinger killing, but also for ruthlessly tracking down bank robbers in the last decade and for using way and means that sometimes were outside the law he was sworn to uphold. He was also famous for making many undertakers very happy. John slowly set the coffee down on the polished table and then turned to Stevie.

"This coffee is cold," he stated, then turned back and looked at Purvis. "Mr. Purvis, Charlie has made many mistakes in the past, enough so that you make him out to be an evil man, for what reasons we don't know, maybe your boss can tell you. We assure you Mr. Chaplin is not a bad man; in all of our surveillance we discovered he's a just man, an extremely funny one and a genius to boot, but in the end just a man."

"You have no knowledge of him seeking young below age women to bed down?" Purvis asked.

The four detectives around the conference table looked from one to another. Talbot was tapping the lip of his coffee container. Frank was busily working on his dental work with a toothpick and John had his eyes closed. Then he opened them and looked at Sam and he in turn held John's gaze for a moment and then leaned on the top of the table with his knuckles bearing his weight.

"They didn't teach him any manners at the FBI, did they?" Sam asked of Rainbird who just shook his head. Sam looked straight at Purvis. "Again, if he had committed a crime we would have notified the *local* authorities, not the FBI or one of its former agents turned detective."

Melvin Purvis reached out and gathered up his white hat and then stood.

"Mr. Hoover will be very disappointed at your lack of cooperation in assisting my agency Mr. Dalhart. Do you know one of the girls we suspect Mr. Chaplin of being with was a nineteen year old cripple, an innocent girl who all of a sudden just up and disappeared? But you wouldn't know anything about that, would you?" he said smugly and with a final sneer, looking from Sam to Rainbird, who had suddenly perked his head up at the mention of crippled girl. "Good day to you," Purvis finally said, then turned for the door.

They all watched him leave with a joint sigh of relief.

"And they call us dicks," Frank Wiechek remarked, making Talbot almost spit out his coffee.

Sam smiled at Frank and then turned to Stevie.

"Before I turn you over to John for your torture session for being late, what did you find out at the school on Friday?"

Stevie didn't know if he should stand or not. He was still holding the bag of coffee and looked around for a place to put it.

"Well?" Rainbird asked without turning in his chair.

Sam saw the redness in the whites of John's eyes. He looked as if he still wasn't sleeping. Sam needed to find out what had his partner so rattled.

Stevie stood, looked straight ahead and closed his eyes.

"I….I was….there when school let out at….uh, three, uh, fifteen—"

"Oh man, oh man, this is going to be a clear and precise report," Frank said, looking out of the window.

"Was he there kid?" Talbot asked, sipping his coffee and then placing his pipe in his mouth.

"Uh, yes, sir, he showed up at about three-twenty. He waited and the girl did eventually come to his car."

"Oh, boy" Frank said, returning his attention back from the window to Stevie.

Sam looked at Frank and held up a finger. "Go on Stevie, finish."

"Well, I got as close as I could get to the car, I didn't want that big chauffeur fella seeing me like the last time and come out chasin' me, so I comes up from behind," he said, still recounting the events with his eyes closed. "Mr. Chaplin, he was hugging the girl, I saw, but I had to duck below the rear window of the car or I would 'a been seen in the mirror."

"Shit, Sam, he's doing exactly what Hoover thinks he's doing," Frank said shaking his head.

Again Sam looked at the boy who had opened his eyes. "Go on Stevie," he encouraged.

"No, sir—uh, no, Mr. Wiechek, that's not it at all," he protested.

Sam had a hunch about how the kid was going to explain the situation but let him do the talking.

"It was the girl's birthday; I saw a few of her friends givin' her presents right after school before the car arrived. He was there to give her *his* present," Stevie said, looking at Frank, then Sam, and then cowering a little when Rainbird looked at him.

"I can imagine what kind of present the little tramp was going to give her," Frank said, snickering until he saw Sam look his way. He lowered his eyes to the table and laughed to himself at his smart little joke.

Suddenly Stevie opened his eyes and said; "She's his daughter, Mr. Dalhart. I think it's a secret, but I'm sure I heard her call him Daddy, I'm sure of it."

"Okay, kid, okay. Good report," he said as he slapped Rainbird on the shoulder. "I told you," he said smiling.

"Yeah, yeah, heap big detective," John said mockingly.

"You knew about this?" Talbot Leonard asked, tamping tobacco into his pipe.

"Call it a hunch. I've seen pictures of the girl and there was a small resemblance to Chaplin to be sure, but I made a few calls and found out that Charlie had once fallen for a young actress who he cared for deeply, so he had an affair. It was a secret that they both kept because they were more friends than serious lovers. I learned of the affair from Charlie himself. He would bring her up once in a while and speak of her like she was an angel, but he'd never mention her name. It didn't take a lot of work to find out who the woman was, and the child was a just guess, but it fit. And to be honest with you gentlemen, I refuse to involve this innocent teenage girl in a scandal that bastard in Washington is hoping to capitalize on."

"Here, here," Talbot said, lighting his pipe.

Stevie started to sit, the bag still holding the coffee was shaking as he slowly lowered to the chair.

"Kid," Rainbird said, freezing him before his butt could be planted. He slowly straightened up and looked at John. "I must admit, that was a good job."

Stevie's eyes widened as this was the first time he had ever received praise from John Rainbird.

"But I still want my damn change from that fin I gave you Friday."

The conference room was cleared; Frank disappeared into the lobby to discuss something with Liz, and Talbot, wanting a real cup of coffee, left for the *Bird of Paradise Diner* across the street. Stevie had quickly left, asking no questions and waiting for none after giving Rainbird the change from his five spot. Liz had handed him ten dollars from petty cash and he left for *Newbury's* department store to buy a replacement coffee urn. John Rainbird lagged behind while Sam filled out the rest of his notes about the meeting with Purvis. Sam wrote fast, his pen sliding along the paper with ease as he waited for John to speak. He knew the man well enough that he never wasted time on idle banter. Something was on his friend's mind and he suspected that whatever it was, it was the cause for his bloodshot eyes.

"Have you heard anything from your contacts at the police department about any missing people, missing girls, in particular?" John asked, staring down at the legal pad in front of him and fanning the corner of it like a deck of cards.

Sam kept writing. "Haven't heard anything outside of the Chaplin case," he answered. "How did the meeting with Cagney go?" he asked.

"Hmm?" John uttered, still flipping the pages of his legal pad.

"You know, James Cagney, stolen stamp collection, was he pleased?"

"Oh, yeah, yeah, very happy. I informed him that Frank and Stevie saw it in his maid's house during their nocturnal visit to her place. He wasn't happy about the maid lifting it but was grateful to know where it could be found," John answered, not really looking at Sam. I offered our services in recovering it but he said he would handle it himself.

Sam stopped writing and laid his pen down and looked at his friend. He watched him as the big man absent mindedly played with his note pad.

"Does this missing girl thing have anything to do with you not sleeping?"

"Is it that obvious?" John asked, forcing his hands to be still as he looked into the deep blue eyes of his partner and friend.

Sam smiled and leaned back in his chair. "Only to me, the only other person that I'm sure has noticed some kind of change may be Stevie. You've been riding him pretty hard lately."

Rainbird shook his head and looked up at the ceiling. "You know, the kid has busted his ass doing everything he can for us, or more so—me." He looked back at Sam. "He's been trying to please me. I guess I need to talk to him and make it up to him somehow, I didn't realize—"

"What's wrong, John?" Sam asked, cutting him off.

John looked away as if he were deep in thought and then slowly smiled, an embarrassed sort of look that never really connected to the rest of his tired features.

"Remember the fishing trip we took to Montana a few years back, and I took you to the reservation on our way back?"

The question caught Sam off guard in a way he wasn't used to. He prided himself on being able to read people, especially his best friend.

"Yeah, I finally got to meet your mother and sisters," Sam said, wondering now just where this was going to lead to.

"Remember how my mother had—"

"Told me about Frankie Brill? Yeah, how could I forget?" Sam said, looking away for a moment.

Frankie Brill had been a small time-hood specializing in kidnapping for cash and also had a long rap sheet for b & e. Sam, while still a lieutenant on the police force, was the man responsible for tracking Frankie Brill down after a botched child kidnapping. The kid's father—a prominent Hollywood producer had been beat up pretty badly in the attempted kidnapping, but had managed to delay Frankie long enough that sirens in the distance scared him off. Sam was given the case and knew exactly who had been responsible as soon as he took the description. Sam hit every dive from San Pedro to Riverside and finally managed to shake loose information that sent him north. He found Frankie in Santa Barbara actually stalking another celebrity, this time a big time actress and her three children.

Frankie got thirty years, finding out the hard way that he should have stuck to breaking and entering. Sam got a two-week vacation. He headed for Montana with Rainbird—a sergeant on the force at that time. It was on the way home after the fishing trip that John surprised him by asking if he minded stopping off so he could visit his mother and two sisters. His father had run off when he had been ten and he had been raised by his mom alone, keeping him on the straight and narrow and actually saving enough for his education so he wouldn't have to attend some Indian school the federal government was so fond of. And she did all this on a secretary's salary working for the tribal council.

His mother was a very smart woman and his sisters made John blush with all the stories they told of his growing-up. While they were telling tales of his misspent youth, John went outside with his Ma. It wasn't until later that Sam realized the two of them were actually gone quite a long time.

Just before they left, Rainbird said, "Sam, my ma wants to say something to you." With that he placed his hat on his head, bent very low to kiss his mother, and then started out of the door.

"Where are you going?"

"She needs to talk to you white man, not me," John answered.

Sam sat for ten minutes listening to John's mother speak in a curious monotone. She spoke haltingly about Frankie Brill, even going as far as describing the man. She said that he was now loose, even though Sam assured her he wasn't and he even told her about the telegram he had received in Montana two days back confirming that Brill' had been sentenced to Alcatraz. The white-haired woman shook her head.

"He waits for you," she said.

"Ma'am, I don't know what you think you know, but Frankie Brill's gone away and he won't be back for a long, long time."

Her face was grim as she said,   "I know what I know. If you won't believe me, at least promise me that you'll be careful."

Sam nodded out of politeness and, sensing that the conversation was over, picked up his hat and joined Rainbird in the car.

As they drove away, Rainbird listened as Sam recounted the strange conversation. Rainbird offered no comments about his mother's prediction and said very little on the long trip back to LA.

When they arrived home it took almost an hour for Sam to convince Rainbird that he would be fine. He remembered looking in the car's rearview mirror as he drove off and seeing the big Indian shaking his head on his front porch step. When he arrived at his apartment on Flower Street in LA, he was immediately apprehensive when he found a note had been slid between the front door and jamb. It was from his captain explaining that Frankie Brill had escaped from the county jail only an hour before his scheduled trip up north to San Francisco and that little hide-a-way in the bay known as *The Rock*.

He was just pushing the door open when he was hit hard from behind and shoved into his darkened apartment. His head exploded in a burst of light and stars as he hit the carpeted entrance hall. He tried to reach for his gun which John had been able to talk him into putting on, but his reflexes were off and a foot had come down hard on his wrist and the gun was quickly pulled out of his hand.

"You thought I would just go away without saying goodbye flatfoot?"

The voice had that strange echo of dreams. Sam tried to open his eyes but found even the smallest effort hurt him. He was on his side and rolled over, causing more pain. He heard the apartment door close and then the room was filled with a sudden brilliant light that penetrated his eyelids with a sharp jab of pain. He tried to open his eyes but his brain told him through a nauseating assault of agony that it would be best to keep them closed.

Sam was picked up and held in place. He was minutely aware of something running down his cheek from his scalp in a pretty good flow.

"Well, I'll go as soon as I know you won't be tracking me. Your career as a gumshoe is over," the voice said.

"Hey, Frankie," Sam mumbled.

"Shut up," Brill said, as he moved him through the living room and toward the bathroom.

He managed to open his eyes to slits as he saw the door to his bathroom come ever closer. It was kicked open and the light came on. He was pushed to the floor and he hit hard with his right arm going into the bathtub and his body striking the tile at its base. Sam shook his head and tried to clear it. His eyes fluttered open and there in front of him stood the diminutive frame of Frankie Brill as he looked down on him with barely controlled fury.

"Not so tough now, huh? I'll teach you to mess with me," Brill hissed.

Sam had pulled himself up from the floor using the arm that had landed in the large, claw-footed tub, he leveraged and he finally found himself sitting on its edge. He placed his hand to the side of his head and pulled it away smeared with blood. Frankie had whacked him a pretty good one with his revolver, which was now pointing at him. Frankie turned, and that was when Sam noticed that the apartment's front door stood ajar, he could have sworn through his pain and foggy head that he heard the thing slammed shut after he had his gun taken away. Frankie, not noticing the front door as Sam had, closed the bathroom door without turning around and turned to face the man he was about to murder. Sam could have sworn that in the split second before the bathroom door was closed he had seen a shadow as it passed through the living room.

"This is it, *copper*," Frankie said wrapping one of Sam's hand towels around the barrel of the gun to mute the noise, and then he pointed it at Sam's head.

"Sam, take a bath!" a voice yelled through the bathroom door.

Without thinking, Sam let his body do what it wanted to do all along. Collapse. He fell straight back into the tub. Even before he felt the coolness of the enamel, he heard the gunshots as someone started firing through the bathroom door. One bullet hit the porcelain tile above his prone body, sending sharp little shards flying, some striking him and burying themselves in his skin and others chips pinging off the tubs bottom. Another hit the outside of the tub and the white enamel shattered and flew away, pushed out by the huge dent that was made by a bullet striking the iron beneath. Sam's vision blurred a moment, and then his eyes focused and he heard a loud crash and splintering wood. As he was wondering what the hell was happening to him, he was again pulled up and out of the bathtub by extremely strong hands.

"You all right?" he was asked. "Here, you better have a seat."

He was placed on the toilet and then he heard the water running. A cold rag was placed on his head and he was torn by the experience of pleasure at having something cool placed on his gash and one of pain at having anything at all touching the deep wound. But he had managed to clear his vision enough to see the sprawled out body of Frankie Brill. He had at least two large and ugly bullet holes in him, one in his side, hit as he turned toward the door and one his chest as he finally faced it, and now Brill was staring blankly at the bathroom ceiling.

"Sorry about shooting through the door that way, but if I went to break it down he would have had plenty of time to introduce you to a bullet, or more on a personal note, to turn and put one in me. So, I'm glad you understood what I said and dove backward into that tub," said the voice of John Rainbird.

Sam took over the task of holding the wet rag to his head and tried to look up. "You have to…" Sam paused and grimaced at the pain in his scalp, "quit mothering me."

John looked at the body of Frankie Brill and nodded his head. "I think you better be glad someone was mothering you, my friend. And I think you better make a call to Montana and thank the one who did it."

Sam knew he would have been three years in the grave if not for Rainbird's mother's warning. Now, what did that have to do with Rainbird's red eyes? His friend was still staring down at the legal pad on the table before him.

"That vision she had warning her of Brill and you, Sam, two men who she had never met in her life, well, I think I'm experiencing something like that."

"Visions?" Sam asked.

"No," he said, looking up. "Visions come when you're awake, Ma's came in the form of dreams; mine seems to be coming in the form of nightmares—nightmares about lost girls."

"Lost girls?" Sam tilted his head and half smiled, really not wanting to offend his friend. "I'm not really following, everyone has bad dreams from time to time you know that."

Rainbird slid his chair back and stood and walked to the same window Sam had been at earlier and looked out and saw Stevie just crossing Sunset, heading out on an errand. He watched him disappear after bumping into a man delivering ice. He saw the kid say something to the large man and then suddenly turn and run when the fellow lunged at him.

"I've been having these…these nightmares for the last six months," he said, ignoring the incident in the street. "First they came once or twice a week, but lately it's been every damn night."

"You're joking?" Sam said turning to look at John's back.

Rainbird stared through the window, not seeing his own reflection but the faces of all those young girls. "I wish I were," he answered, finally tuning around. "It's the kind of thing that runs in our family."

"Visions of the future?"

"The future, the present, who knows, remember Ma wasn't looking into the future with her dreams of you and Brill, it was the present she saw."

"Well, is there something you want to do about it?" Sam asked. Not really knowing what anyone could do.

Rainbird once again took his chair and looked at his friend. "It's bad Sam, I can't sleep anymore, and it's as if I'm being asked for help by these young girls, or maybe even warned," he embarrassingly looked at his partner. "Can you find out if there are any more missing girls around here than what's usual for LA.? And maybe check and see if any were…," he hesitated using the word. "Crippled, you know, like Purvis said. Like, the ones who wear leg braces for walking."

"Yeah, I can make some calls, maybe shake a few trees and see what falls out."

Rainbird exhaled, looking relieved. "I thought you would think I was nuts," he said.

"Look, I don't really know what happened that night three years ago. But I'll say this with all honesty, I believe *you* believe it. And I still owe your Ma for that night and I also still owe *you* my life."

Rainbird just nodded his head once. Sam was a hard man to convince about something he couldn't see, feel or read in an official report, but his answer of *shaking a few trees* was good enough for John.

They were interrupted by the buzz of the intercom. Sam hesitated, then reached out and held the switch down. "Yes."

"Sorry to interrupt, but Mister Chaplin is here and he's not happy, he ran into that ex-G-Man in the lobby downstairs, and there was a loud argument about something," Liz said.

Sam looked at John and they both said at the same time, "Oh, shit," and together they stood, again one man mirroring the other and started thinking how to handle damage control, because there was never anything small about the *Little Tramp*.

The task of phoning his contacts about lost girls was set aside for the time being because it had taken nearly a full hour for Sam and Rainbird to get Charlie Chaplin calmed enough to hear why Melvin Purvis had paid the agency a visit. Chaplin sat in a leather chair in front of Sam's desk with his hands propped upon a walking stick that he used for pure show. His light gray suit was impeccably pressed and his naturally curly hair waxed to full attention.

Rainbird noticed from his seat to Charlie's right that the 'little tramp' had developed a small twitch in his right cheek which might be an indicator that Chaplin was close to some sort of breakdown. *But then again*, thought John, *he wasn't a shrink.*

"So you see, the FBI is still looking for ways of kicking your butt right out of here, Charlie," Sam said almost out of breath for his lengthy explanation. "It's not their jurisdiction, right now, so they hired a former FBI goon of theirs to hound you into making a mistake."

"Well, that clarifies why the man who killed John Dillinger was here seeking information about poor Charlie, but now you may want to explain another, more sinister plot against me. You Samuel, and you also my fine Indian friend, have not been quite honest with me on another matter, now have you?" Chaplin asked.

Sam hated being called Samuel, not even his mother called him that. And Rainbird cringed every time Charlie called him his *fine Indian friend.*

"And what's that Charlie?" Sam asked, knowing full well Chaplin had his spies everywhere and knowing Mary Pickford, had probably let it be known that her partner in United Artists was being watched. For such a small woman she sure liked throwing her weight around. *If the public knew what a shrewd business woman she was, she would be known as something other than America's Little Sweetheart,* Sam thought. He could see why poor Douglass divorced her three years earlier.

"You know damn well you're working with the Wicked Witch of Westwood to get the goods on poor old Charlie," he said, looking first at Sam, then turning and raising an eyebrow at John. "Now gentlemen, let's all come clean in this sorted little matter, shall we?"

Sam looked at Rainbird and he in turn shook his head. "What makes you say that Charlie?"

"Because I have my spies also," he answered with a trace of acted-out indignity. "And my spy is the crème d' la crème of all spies you might say," he added in his haughty and entirely British accent.

"And what has your good friend and Miss Pickford's ex-husband, Mr. Douglass Fairbanks, told you?" Rainbird asked as straight-faced as he could. It was a very well-known fact that the two stars were the best of friends and they were both terrified of Mary Pickford.

"Why…why….what makes you think he would be my confidant, why I never—"

"If she had hired us Charlie, and I'm not at all saying that she did, she would have done so only because she doesn't want any bad light shining on U.A., Douglas should have told you that, as I suspect he or his new wife did."

Chaplin lowered his head to the point that it rested lightly on his hands atop the cane. He inhaled and let out his breath slowly. Then he looked up and his eyes were moist with tears.

"Gentlemen, I'm tired. Everyone thinks me a cad of the first order. Why, if it weren't for me, we wouldn't have half the freedoms we do in this little valley," he looked up at the ceiling. "You would think the federal gentlemen would have other priorities with Hitler planning to steal half the world, and the Jap's snatching the other half—instead they hound me. Me!"

Sam leaned forward and placed his hands on his desk. He gently slapped a blue, white and silver box of Kleenex across the desk until it stopped in front of Charlie.

"You bring it on yourself, Charlie. You never learned the meaning of confidential and that will be your downfall. They fear you because you have power they can only dream about. They envy you because the common man thinks you're a hero, and may I say I believe that also," Sam said, holding the tramps gaze.

Chaplin pulled a Kleenex from the box and that was when Sam and Rainbird knew that this time the Little Tramp wasn't acting. He was actually hurt over the federal government's actions against him.

"What can I say gentlemen, my heart is on my sleeve as always," he said as he dabbed at his eyes. "I am lately resistant to the charms of—of younger women, but I found that some people in power won't let me forget the mistakes of my past."

"Charlie, Melvin Purvis and his former boss in Washington don't have anything on you; if you stay clean they can't touch you. Hell, I even understand Roosevelt told Hoover to move on to more important things, and from what I understand you and a chosen few are going to be hosting the president when he visits, that true?"

"Yes, it will be a gala evening," he said perking up. Then he tilted his head. "The President actually said that, for Hoover to leave me be, really, you're not just pulling the tramp's proverbial leg are you?"

"No, Charlie he isn't," Rainbird answered.

Chaplin sighed and looked at the two men a moment, then said; "It's not just the Bureau Boys…even the local police are asking embarrassing questions, if this keeps up it's bound to get out."

"What questions?" Sam asked.

"It seems a woman—," he caught himself, "well, she was but a girl, but of legal age mind you. Well, I met her at a nice little party in Pasadena, it was one of those charity things for polio, she was an unfortunate victim of that terrible disorder you see, we talked and I'm afraid several guests at the party noticed this fact. Well, it seems this young lady turned up missing later that week. The police actually had the gall to ask if I had been with her, you know, in *that way*, and then asked if I knew of her whereabouts. Can you imagine?"

Rainbird closed his eyes for a moment and then opened them and looked at Sam. The meaning of what had been said didn't go unnoticed by him either.

"How old was she Charlie, do you remember?" John asked.

Chaplin looked closely at John. "For a red chap, you certainly just lost some of your color," he said, then looked at Sam.

"Answer the question Charlie," Sam said.

"Wait a minute gentlemen, I assure you that I would never—"

"We know that, just tell us her age Charlie, for crying out loud," Rainbird said standing and rubbing a hand through his hair.

"Well, I seem to remember her saying she was nineteen. I don't know about the other two they asked about because I never had the pleasure of their company or even meeting them in the least."

"Other two? What other two? Do you mean two other girls?" John asked, slowly sitting again and placing his large hand on Chaplin's knee.

"From what these two detectives said, they were her roommates," he answered, looking worried at the expression on John's face. "I must say, your behavior at this moment is quite unsettling my large Indian friend."

"Charlie, this girl at the fundraiser, was she wearing leg braces or was she in a wheelchair?" Sam asked.

"Leg braces I believe."

Sam stood up and held out his hand to Chaplin.

"Charlie, I think Mr. Hoover will start looking at someone else to pick on for a while. I want you to keep your nose clean, okay my friend?" Sam said sincerely.

Chaplin took his hand and shook, still looking at Rainbird. "Yes, yes of course," he released Sam's hand and slowly walked around his chair, glancing now and then at Rainbird. Then he snapped the fingers of his right hand. "I almost forgot the reason I came here," he looked at Sam. "You are aware of my party tonight, are you not?"

Sam didn't show it on his face, but he had completely forgotten about the invitation to join Chaplin and the Hollywood *who's who* at Charlie's house for drinks and to take part in welcoming someone or other from Europe.

"Sam, you didn't forget did you? After all, it was your agency that assisted me in getting their visas; they will want to meet you and John both."

"Uh, no, of course I didn't forget," he lied.

"I suppose you won't be bringing a special someone for me to drool over?" Charlie asked, winking.

"No, I'll be alone, as usual."

"Well, I'm sure you'll enjoy meeting the Count and Countess, after all, they were smart enough to get away from Il Duce before the world comes down on him, and the German fellow. He's brilliant and very anti-Hitler.

After all he went through to escape that horrid Reich, he just might gain that respect you are so slow in handing out."

Sam was looking at Chaplin but was also watching Rainbird out of the corner of his eye. He hadn't moved since he heard about the girls that Charlie had mentioned. He sat with his right index finger to his lips thinking, not paying attention to the conversation going on right next to him.

"Well, I guess I'll meet him and the Count and Countess and see you tonight at...?"

"Nine o'clock, Samuel. Nine sharp," Charlie reminded him as he started to leave. He turned and looked at Rainbird for the briefest of moments, then at Sam again. "If you're a good boy I'll introduce you to *real* detectives, Nick and Nora Charles, William Powell and Myrna Loy, of those fabulous *Thin Man* films, they would undoubtedly love to meet the real thing," he said as he laughed, then with one last look at Rainbird, left whistling.

Sam sat back down and looked at Rainbird who was still far off in thought. Instead of saying anything he pushed down the switch to the intercom, it buzzed briefly.

"Yes, Mr. Dalhart," Liz's voice answered.

"Liz, get Frank in here will ya? I need him to run down to police headquarters for me."

"Okay, I'll check his office," Liz said as Sam leaned back in his chair. He looked over at the silent Rainbird who was lost in deep thought.

Out in the reception area, Liz took a deep breath and moved Frank's hand from her shoulder. She swiveled around in her chair and looked the man in his green eyes. She almost weakened when she saw him smile, looking for all the world like the actor, John Payne, only a smaller version, but knew that there were eyes watching them from the reception area.

"You know Sam isn't dumb. He knew you were out here or he would have just called your office."

The smile disappeared from Frank's face. "Hmm, didn't think of that."

Frank opened Sam's door and poked his head through.

"You wanted to see me Boss?" he asked.

"Yeah, c'mon in here. I want you to grab Talbot and start doing some snooping around. You go to the police department and I'll make a few calls and someone will help you find what we're looking for. Tell Talbot to get on the horn to his newspaper friends and find out if anyone's working on any stories concerning missing girls, you're going to do the same at police headquarters."

"Missing girls, boss? When did we start doing missing persons cases?" Frank asked.

"We don't do missing persons, but we're doing this as a personal favor for a friend," Sam said.

"You got it boss," Frank said, starting to close the office door.

"Frank?" Sam called out.

The door opened again. "Yeah?"

"Tell Liz the next time you go out for one of your visits to her, to call Pete and Willis and tell them to stay home tonight and get some more sleep and get to know their wives again. I'm pulling the surveillance off of Chaplin."

Frank was almost to the reception area door before he realized what Sam had said about his clandestine visits to the front of the office. Liz was right, that man did pay attention.

❧ THREE ❧

The man sat and read the *Los Angeles Times*. He shook his head in wonder; the world was still blind, or at least the British were, to the ultimate plans of the madman across the water.

"Adolph's luck is still holding I see," the man mumbled as he reached out and stubbed the cigarette out in the ashtray sitting on the small table to his right. He blew air through the cigarette holder, clearing it, and then placed into his satin robe.

"Excuse me, Sir, I didn't catch that," his valet said in his thick Scottish brogue as he placed a fresh whiskey and water next to the ashtray which he immediately removed. He walked over to the small waste canister and dumped the lone butt. Then after wiping it clean he placed the crystal ashtray back onto the table.

"The man has been given the blueprint for victory and he damn well better follow it."

Ralls McDougall placed his large hands on his hips and looked down at his employer. He wore a long-sleeved white shirt under a satiny black vest.

"If you ask me I don't understand why the Master placed such faith in that moronic man in the first place. You know he will never be able to control the army, not with certain General's knowing about who is responsible for that little fool, I suspect they may even send out assassins to try and bring an end to Hitler's association with—"

"If the arrogant bastards in the Wehrmacht did they would meet a very unfortunate and horrible end as so many others have come to in the past." Von Railing half turned in his chair and looked at his manservant. "And to answer your question about why our little Austrian friend was chosen for this is because our dear little Fuhrer has a very rare gift, he can lie large forever and he will be believed by those slathering masses that want and need to be led."

"Then, sir, I still fail to see what we can do here to facilitate *his* plans for Europe. How can these….these actor people be of use to us?"

Von Railing turned the newspaper around so that his manservant could read the headlines—*Roosevelt Arrives to Court Hollywood Royalty.*

"The answer to that question is not yours, nor mine to ponder. I think this visit is our Master's first move in this country. No matter what it is, we will do *his* bidding and let the chips fall where they may, as the Americans are so fond of saying. Thankfully thus far the only talk concerning us in this magnificent town is our miraculous escape from the clutches of Evil, with a capital *E*," he again lowered the paper.

McDougall smiled and then half bowed and turned to leave.

"Shall I have the car ready at the same time tonight, Sir?" he asked reaching the wide-doubled doors of the library.

"Don't you remember? I have to be at that horrid little comedian's official welcoming party tonight, so we won't be going out until very late."

"Yes, sir," McDougall said.

Karl Von Railing was looking and smiling at the headline and then carefully folded the paper and laid it in his lap and then reached for his drink. As his hand touched the cold glass a thought entered his mind unbidden. He cocked his head in uncertainty of the word that was embedded just as a deep seated memory would have been; *Dalhart*. He lifted his whiskey and water from the table and watched as a single drop of condensation worked its way slowly down the side of the glass blazing a trail as it picked up more water along the way until finally falling from the glass and landing on the dust-laden tabletop. *Dalhart*, was it a place or a person perhaps? As he thought about the question he sipped his drink and as he did so another thought was sent to him and he lowered the glass and cocked his head as the word was sent to him; *Shaman*. That was a word that was no mystery to him. It was a word that could only mean trouble. Could these *words* stand between the Master and the President?

"Ralls," Von Railing rose and stepped into the hallway.

McDougall appeared from the dining area, wiping his hands on a small towel. He actually had to stoop to get through the doorway of the formal dining room. He stood looking at his employer while still chewing whatever it was he had been eating when called. Von Railing grimaced in disgust. He didn't want to think about McDougall's dietary habits.

"I'll be in the basement for an hour or so. Be sure I'm not disturbed."

The strongly-built Scotsman nodded his head and turned back to the dining room.

As Von Railing started down the hall the words that had forced their way into his mind dizzied him. He set himself down hard in one of the filthy old overstuffed chairs that flanked the library doors to try to get control of his swirling, whirling thoughts. *Shaman, Dalhart, Dalhart, Shaman*, he felt the whiskey rise in his gorge as the two words drowned out the world. He placed his palms to his eyes and leaned forward.

"Stop it, stop it, *STOP IT!*" he screamed. It was as if a needle had been jolted by a scratch in a phonograph record. It skipped and jumped to the end with nothing but the gentle swish of clear air. The silence was merciful.

"Are you all right, sir?" McDougall asked, his face a mask of bland of forced curiosity.

"You know damn well I'm not at all," he answered. "If your brain was capable of understanding you would see for yourself the pain I'm in, but I guess you were chosen for your," he paused for a moment, "other attributes. Now go back to gorging yourself on whatever fine delicacy you have waiting on you."

A look of disdain etched McDougall's features. He loathed the weak and seeing Von Railing collapse like this made him despise the German.

Von Railing took a few deep breaths as he watched McDougall disappear then he stood slowly, pulling the belt of his lounging robe tighter and using his hand to comb back his blond hair. He watched the entranceway to the dining room for a brief instant and then when he was satisfied McDougall was once again eating he turned and made for the back of the huge house. As he passed moving boxes that Ralls had yet to put away in their new home he was disgusted by the state of the house. His black Italian hand-made shoes made crunching noises on the thick pile carpet that ran the length of the hallway between the foyer and the large kitchen in the back. He shook his head. As he passed through the kitchen with a pile of dirty dishes stacked on the counter next to the pearl enamel sink, he paused for a moment when the cellar door came into his view next to the walk-in refrigerator. The door was thick, being the only renovation done thus far to the thirty-plus room mansion in the months they had been there. The workmen who had installed it were amazed that someone would want to install an eight-inch thick oak door that would protect nothing but an old basement and below that a dank and very dark wine cellar that had been carved out of the very dirt the mansion sat upon.

Von Railing stopped in front of the door and waited. He swallowed and then looked around him. The faucet over the sink was dripping steadily into a pan that had filled with water, making a *tinkle-plop* sound that was most unnerving. He pulled an old-fashioned skeleton key from his robe pocket, a key that had been old when this house was new. The lock was the only thing that was old on the new door. The German closed his eyes a moment, and after a few seconds he opened them and then he inserted the key in the large lock which was hooked through an impressive wooden latch. The lock clicked open and Von Railing pulled the locks loop through the handles. The heavy padlock he turned and placed on the filthy stainless-steel counter. He turned back and looked at the door a moment before pulling it open. Suddenly a pressure change from somewhere down below pushed the heavy door outward and while not opening it, it did force the mustiness and wet smell though the gap at the bottom and it hit him in the face along with a chilling draft that made the skin on his arms crawl.

"Damn," he said under his breath as he half turned away from the smell emanating from below.

Beneath the odor of mold and mildew coming from the bowels of the house was an underlying smell that once again made his gorge rise. The undead odors snaked their way through the door to find escape through the small gap in the frame and microscopic imperfections of the wood. He took a step back and placed an arm over his mouth and nose and then he turned away for a moment. His eyes roamed the kitchen taking in the filth with his eyes but not registering it in his mind. His total concentration was on the cellar.

He stepped forward and pulled the heavy door open wide, so wide it slammed into a small stainless steel counter. An oil lamp fell and broke on the floor but Von Railing never noticed. He strode into the darkness to the bowels of old redwood mansion.

Von Railing had moved down through the darkness past the rotting furniture and then through the landing leading down until he stood at the foot of the second set of stairs that would lead him to the deepest part of the property—the subbasement. The candles that were almost constantly lit at this, the closest end of the dank hole in the ground, were out. He closed his eyes and then quickly opened them. His eyes penetrated the darkness and he saw many sets of feet lining the wall. The girls were there, rotting away and unmoving, at least for the moment. That meant the Master was in a more contemplative state of mind.

"You cause considerable pain when you insist on invading my mind. You need not push as hard as you do, I am not your average man."

There was only silence from the back of the subbasement. The air was still but the smell palpable. Von Railing shifted from one foot to the other and waited. He didn't have to wait long.

"I am not concerned with that. I had a visitor again last night," said the deep and rasping voice in a language that only Von Railing understood. He had been versed on the tongue over many years and understood it just as readily as his own German language.

"The same dream?" Von Railing asked in the Aramaic tongue and immediately regretted his question.

"*Dream*! I don't have dreams you fool!"

The German took a step back as he felt the dirt floor beneath his feet move with a sudden shudder as if something large had been dropped on the very foundations of the house.

"It was a poor choice of words, my Lord," he said, more than humbled by the voice out of the darkness.

"The red man has the ability to invade my dark times; this has never been possible by anyone! And this name he clings to, this Dalhart, it leaves a death taste in my mouth upon uttering the word."

Von Railing looked up and into the blackness, unsure of the meaning of what had just been said. The Master was up, he sensed at least that much, and the feeling of the beast's agitation was rampant in the odiferous atmosphere.

"That name my Lord, I have seen it written upon paper before."

There was a moment when the German felt a sudden shift in the air. Then the voice was there, only feet from him in the darkness and he quickly lowered his eyes and for all his weakness wanted to turn and flee.

He heard the shifting of the sack around the beast's neck and the jingle the objects inside made as it moved.

"Explain this rather bold statement, German," the deep voice said close to his face.

Von Railing couldn't open his eyes as he heard his master sniffing him for the stink of untruth. "Our benefactor, this boorish fool of an actor, he used this man, this Dalhart to supply us with added security while awaiting our temporary visas. But he was not needed in the end."

"He was to be a protector of ME?"

"If we felt unsafe in this new country, being refugees, he would have been contracted for our security yes; however it was for securing the property my Lord, not you."

The air changed again as he felt the creature shift his position in the cellar. With the candles out Von Railing had a hard time knowing for sure, but he felt his master was by the wall looking at his collection of newspaper clippings supplied by himself for its study.

"So, we have a link, the red man and I. This Shaman has a master himself, this Dalhart."

"If I'm not mistaken, this man should be present tonight at the fool's house."

"This may be helpful. We may indeed need his protection as we may need to use this Dalhart and his Shaman for many things." Now, his Master reached out to Von Railing, touching him and when his Master's clawed hand closed around his arm it made Von Railing shrink. "Learn what you can. I want to know what kind of man he is. We may turn this strange visitation by the red man to our advantage. I must dwell on this more. Leave me."

As Von Railing was released he had to use all of his will power not to turn and run back up the stairs. The jingle of coin was loud as the beast moved off into the darkness. He swallowed and with a will power few men had turned slowly and started back up the stairs. He felt the yellow eyes momentarily on his back as he climbed a step at a time, thinking about another task set before him. A task that put him between his benefactor and the only two mortals he'd ever felt made the master of the darkness afraid.

The Sunset Detective Agency

As evening started to shade the late afternoon out of her way, Sam sat in his office and finished the final report for Mary Pickford. He didn't know what the final tally would be but the agency had spent a total of two hundred and twenty man hours on her case with most of that coming in the form of Pete and Willis' overnight surveillance. A pitiful waste of manpower and time for a wild goose chase, especially after Miss Pickford had been warned by him personally several times that he thought Charlie was on the up and up. But in the end he said he would do it because Pickford and Fairbanks both had placed a lot of trust in him a few years back when he started the agency. But Sam was never one to like spying on a man he considered a friend, and Charlie was just that—a friend.

As he started placing the paperwork back into the United Artist file for transcription later by Liz, his intercom buzzed for what seemed the hundredth time that day.

"Yes."

"Sam, Frank is on line one," Liz said.

"Got it," he said, picking up the heavy handset and pressing a black button on the phone that read '1'. "Frank, that took a while," he said as he leaned back into his chair, allowing his back to stretch out for the first time in what seemed like hours.

"Yeah, well you know cops, boss. They think everyone on the private side is trying to steal their thunder," Frank answered.

"Did you find anything significant?"

"It's strange, boss, nobody'll say nothin.' Finally, an old Sarge I know let me look at the main blotter for the last two months and when his captain caught me looking through the book he almost slammed my nose through the top of the desk. He told me that if anything outta that leaks to the press he would personally haul my ass in for a rubber hose session."

Sam knew all too well about the department's treatment of prisoners inside the city's jails; it was one of the reasons he didn't want to be a part of the system any longer, and the main reason for the Sunset Agency's existence.

"So, did you come across anything that would justify this captain being so nervous?"

'Sam, from what I saw in the short time I was looking at the blotter there were over seventy reports filed about missing girls between the ages of fifteen and twenty-five. And you know there will be some whose families don't even know they're missing, which means they haven't filed any reports, so that number actually has to be higher."

"What does the department have to say about this?" Sam asked, sitting up in his chair, the cramp in his hand forgotten.

"That's the strange part, I started asking some of the guys around the station about it and they all said it's no more than usual for Los Angeles. But I dunno, it just doesn't feel right and I don't think it feels right to my old Sarge either. He never tipped me before and I think the only reason he did this time was 'cause something ain't kosher here." Frank paused, "how's this feel to you, boss?"

"I'm not buying it," Sam said after only a moment's pause. "I don't remember ever having that many missing persons reports filed in that amount of time when I was on the force, ever. And yes, some of them will be found eventually raising a pack of kids and kissing husbands goodbye in the morning, but not that many," Sam said, writing the number *seventy* down in a small green notebook, and beside it, *February and March?*

"Sam, I have to get out of here. The uniforms are looking at me like they're fitting me for a snitch jacket or something else nasty. It's strange, I never felt this way around cops before."

"How do you mean strange?"

"It's like they have a secret and they know I know it." Frank said, lowering his voice.

"Yeah, get out of there and go on home."

Sam hung up the phone and stared at the numbers and the dates he had been told. *Seventy girls*, that's just too damn many, even for a city known for losing people as easy as they lose loose change. And from what Frank was telling him the police were aware of it. He was thinking when a knock sounded at the office door.

"Yeah," he said.

The door opened and Stevie stepped in carrying his two suits and his tuxedo from the Chinaman's place down the street.

"Where ya want these Mr. Dalhart," he asked, removing his cap quickly.

"Hang'em up in the closet, kid."

"Big doin's tonight, huh?" Stevie asked, opening the small closet and hanging up the three garments next to three others.

Sam grunted as leaned back in his chair. He was finding it hard to believe the line John was handing him about his nightmares, but old college educated and sensible John believed and Sam believed in John. Looking at the numbers he had written on his notepad he was feeling that old gut wrench he got when he was faced with a conclusion he didn't really care for but had to act on.

"Well, I guess I'll check outta' here if ya's don't need me no more Mr. Dalhart," Stevie said, closing the closet door thinking Sam was mad at him when he didn't answer him right away.

"Kid?" Sam asked,

"Yeah, Mr. Dalhart?" he answered quickly while swallowing and kneading his golf cap in front of him as he waited for the worst. It had to be Sam's contribution for him being late; he must have heard that Rainbird hadn't got around to browbeating him for his screw-up this morning.

"You live out on Iris Street, pretty close to Flower, not real far from me, right?"

He didn't know if he should feel relief or not. After all, Sam was a smart one; he could be laying a trap about how it shouldn't take him that long to get into work.

"Yes, Sir, 357 Iris, upstairs walk-up apartment 35 B," he rattled off quickly.

Sam raised his brows wondering if the kid had had too much of his own strong coffee from that new urn he had just bought. He briefly smiled and then shook off his wandering thoughts.

"Have you heard anything from your neighborhood about missing kids?"

Stevie looked at Sam a moment, totally taken back by the question; he moved his weight from one foot to the other. "You mean like children?"

"Girls, teenagers, maybe a little older," Sam said as he finally looked up at Stevie, tearing his eyes away from the staggering number on the notepad.

Stevie looked toward the ceiling and then at his shoes, then bit his lower lip and then started to place his hat back on, and then lowered it again, "Nah, I ain't heard nuttin' like dat, Mr. Dalhart," he answered, still twisting his hat and shifting his weight. Then he brightened. "Unless you's count Mary Sheffield, she lived in the basement apartment in my building, she's what you might call missin,' jeez, I wonder why I didn't tink of dat foirst off," he said by way of Brooklyn accented explanation.

"How old was she?" Sam asked, picking up his pen.

Stevie looked to the ceiling again and squeezed his eyes shut in thought once more. "I think she was twenty, yeah, I'm pretty sure she was twenty," he finally answered as if unsure. He opened his eyes.

Sam wrote the girls name, age and address down under the other disturbing words on the paper.

Stevie bit his lower lip and looked off into space; he looked as if he was deciding if he should add something.

"But, she was…," he paused a moment, trying to find a word that kept fluttering around, bouncing off the walls of his brain, "She was what you would kind of call, loose, Mr. Dalhart, you'z know what I mean?"

"She enjoyed the company of men?" Sam asked, sort of enjoying the way Stevie stumbled around for words as he did when anything embarrassing came up.

Stevie smiled and shook his head. "Dat's it, boy, you sure know how to use words better'n me, Mr. Dalhart," he smiled and looked down at his black tennis shoes and then just as quickly back at Sam. "The landlady, Miss Leach seems to tink she ran off wit' one of those Mexican zoot-suit fellas. She hung around them quite a bit," he added. "It's really amazin' when ya's tink about it."

"What's so amazing?"

"Her bein' in a wheelchair an' all, sometimes she wore dose leg walkin' ting's."

"Anyone else, anyone at all?" Sam asked while writing the information on the girl down.

"Nah, dat's it, Mr. Dalhart," Stevie said, now disappointed he couldn't give any more information to help his employer out.

Sam finished writing and looked up, tapping his pen on the notebook. He lightly tossed the pen down and seemed to go off in thought. Stevie watched him for a moment not knowing if he was finished with him or not, so he just stood in front of the large desk feeling uneasy. Sam was now leaning back in his chair looking off at the far wall.

"You did well on the Chaplin case kid," he said, still staring off, focused on nothing in particular.

"Why thanks Mr. Dal—"

"I want you to keep your ears open out there about people who come up missing," Sam interrupted before Stevie could finish and moved his eyes to fix the kid's own. "And if you're late again, Liz won't be able to hide the fact on your time sheet like she's been doing," he added, his stern gaze not wavering a bit as his blue eyes were drilling into the eyes of the younger man making Stevie feel like he wanted to shrink into the carpet and disappear. "I'll ask you to come to my office all nice and all and then I'll throw you out of this window, is that understood kid?"

Stevie swallowed, his Adam's apple noticeably moving his green sweater up and down. "Yes, Mr. Dalhart, I understand poifectly."

"If you wanna' keep working with us and eventually work your way up, you start acting more professional, and you never, ever take advantage of people like Liz who are looking out for you." He paused to make sure that Stevie had gotten the message and then suddenly barked, "Now get out of here and keep your ears open, and I better damn well see you on time in the morning."

"Yes, sir…I'll…I'll be here," Stevie assured his boss, putting his hat on and quickly exiting the office.

The kid moved fast down the hallway, not sparing one glance back at the office door.

Jeez, he thought, *how can a man make you feel so good about yourself one minute, then have you thanking god for sparing your life the next?* He was halfway down the hallway when he realized that Sam had said Liz had been covering for his lateness all this time. Stevie shook his head. Sam Dalhart was a man like no other Stevie had ever met in his young life and he wanted to be just like him—him and Mister Rainbird.

Now Sam had actually given him another task, a real task, and he would surely do it. For the first time in the two years that he had been hanging around at the agency and in the year since he had started to work for them, he had a feeling he would someday be accepted by the only people outside of his mother that he ever trusted, and trust came hard to a kid like Stevie Kratzenheimer.

✌ FOUR ✌

ainbird stood at his office window and continued looking out at Sunset. He had been standing there for the past forty-five minutes and had counted at least three, possibly four young girls who looked as if they had just stepped off the bus from places with homey names like Granville, Oklahoma, or Pleasanton, Oregon. They struggled with suitcases that were for the most part larger than themselves. And for reasons he didn't quite understand yet, he wanted to go out there and in the middle of Sunset Boulevard and start shaking each and every one of them until they got some sense rattled into their star-struck heads. Maybe one or two of them might turn around and climb right back onto the busses and trains that brought them here and that would be one or two saved from whatever was out there.

As he stood at the window he wondered if Sam had had the same impulse this morning—to try to shake some sense into *him*. Rainbird knew that people who viewed life from the skin out had no idea what was under that skin. That was where things really happened according to his people. Rainbird knew Sam would never be easy with the fact that he came from a place where it was no stranger for his future to be told than it was for him to pick up the morning paper nowadays to see if it was going to rain. But he knew Sam would accept whatever he told him. Now, if he could only figure out why he was the one who'd been chosen to receive this message. A knock sounded at the glass door, temporarily bringing him out of his troubled state.

"How you doing?" Sam asked leaning through the opening.

Rainbird noticed Sam's tuxedo and then quickly looked at his watch. It was almost eight o'clock. He turned back to his window and saw that the sun had set while he was still staring at the street below and he hadn't even noticed.

"Lost track of time," he said, turning and then sitting in his chair. He looked up at Sam with an uneasy smile on his lips. "Well, don't we look dapper?" he said smirking at his friend.

"Yeah, dapper, you bet. I take it you're passing on the party—again?"

Rainbird looked down at his desk and smiled. Sam never understood about these things with whites and Indians, or whites and blacks, or whites and Hispanics for the matter, maybe that's why Rainbird called him a friend, because Sam just didn't see the bad in people when it came to prejudice.

"Nah, I would be just a square rock in a field of round boulders," Rainbird answered. "Besides, if I don't get some sleep soon I'm not going to be any good at all the rest of this week and if you've looked at our workload, it's one hell of a busy one."

Sam looked at Rainbird without commenting and then stepped into the office. His black tuxedo jacket was unbuttoned and he pulled up his trousers slightly when he sat in the chair in front of the desk. He reached into the jacket's inner pocket and removed a small bottle and tossed it to John who caught it and looked at it. The bottle was brown and was half-full of an amber liquid.

"I know you don't like things like this but I figured you could be persuaded this once. Just put three drops into a glass of water and drink it; nothing should be able to wake you for a full eight hours."

Rainbird looked from the bottle to Sam and then placed it on his desk. "Is this the same bottle we juiced Tallulah's gin and tonic with?"

"You bet," Sam said with his famous smile stretching across his face.

Rainbird had to smile again, remembering the night they had been contracted to keep an eye on Tallulah Bankhead who had just had a not so secret liaison with a man reputed to be a mobster from New York. Well, she had picked that one glorious night to break it off with the mobster and he had gone a little wild and started to smack her around. That was when Sam and John had to make their presence known and bounced the mobster around the parking lot of the Brown Derby restaurant. By the time it was all over and they got Miss Bankhead home she had already sworn vengeance on the smallish man from the Bronx and was on her way back out her front door with a gun. It had taken several minutes to calm her down, talking her into a drink first before blowing the guy to pieces. It was then that they were able to give her the *'Mickey Finn'* from the very same bottle that Sam had tossed to John.

While she was out they *convinced* this gangster that he would live much longer breathing the air of the Hudson River than smelling the exotic perfumes of Hollywood and its famous dry river.

"I think maybe I'll pass, Sam," he finally said.

"Look, this thing that you're going through, I may not understand it but it's obviously getting a good hold on you," Sam said, leaning forward for his next point. "I told you I would check things out."

"No, I think I need to be able to wake up if I have to. You don't know how bad and how...*real* these dreams are."

"Look John, I need you fresh, the feedback I'm getting from Frank and Talbot, well, there just may be something happening here."

"You mean there are girl's miss—"

Sam held up his hand as Rainbird leaned forward quickly.

"John, there are always women missing in LA, you know that. But we may have had a few too many lately."

Rainbird leaned back in his chair and waited, his eyes never leaving Sam's. The question didn't have to be spoken out loud.

"Maybe seventy," Sam said, looking away.

John didn't say anything, he just swallowed and stood up and walked back to his window and looked down into the street again and the night that had already fallen heavily onto Sunset Boulevard.

"Sam, you're the boss, if you tell me to leave it alone I will. I know we wouldn't be getting paid for anything, I mean no one has contacted us about missing persons, but….," he trailed off and searched for words that wouldn't come.

Sam watched his friend as a look almost resembling one of panic took hold of him. John attempted to hide it by looking out of the window but Sam saw the tension in the big man's shoulders.

"I figured we can put off the MGM and Jack Warner cases for a week or so. I can even speak to Mr. Meyer tonight at the party; I'll give him some excuse. But I think we can throw some time at this case of yours."

Sam watched as his partner took a deep breath and reached out and touched the glass window pane.

"Thanks Sam," he said without turning around.

The more Sam saw of the mansions up on Summit drive, the more he thought the world had gone mad. He shook his head as he passed *Pickfair*, the monstrosity of a house Mary Pickford and Douglass Fairbanks used to share in royal splendor as they surveyed the Hollywood they had virtually created along with Chaplin, their British born neighbor down the street. He understood that in America the tradition of Kings had been ousted a long time ago, but it seemed that subconsciously the country had swapped one monarchy for another here in Hollywood.

As Sam pulled his 1937 Chevrolet into the long tree lined road at 1143 Summit Drive he was amazed at the maze of vehicles the valets were busy parking. Well, Charlie had been working hard on his new film due out soon, so Sam thought it was good that he put on a spread for those refugees from Europe. At least it would keep Chaplin's mind off of other things. He pulled up to the front of the huge house and put his car in neutral and pulled the parking brake as a valet ran for the back door of his modest Chevy.

"Sorry buddy, only me," he said stepping from the car and tossing the valet his keys.

"I'm sorry, sir, I thought—"

"Don't sweat it kid, there are still a few people like you and me that work for a living, huh?"

The red-coated valet closed the back door and smiled at Sam, probably the first real person he had met all night. "Yes, sir," he answered as he gave Sam a ticket for his car and received a dollar in return.

Sam walked up the wide stairs and started for the door, it opened just as he reached for the ornate handle. A butler stood there and held it open for him as he ambled in. Another servant dressed in tails held out his hand and Sam shrugged out of his black overcoat and removed his new fedora and handed them over.

"Thank you, Sir," the short man said, handing him another ticket.

Sam shook his head hoping he didn't get all these claim tickets mixed up.

"Samuel! You did come! You have made the evening for me, my dearest friend," a voice said coming up from behind him.

Sam turned and saw Charlie, resplendent in his white tuxedo jacket and black bow-tie.

"You know I would have rather have burned all my good hats than not be here."

Charlie looked far more tired than he had just that morning in his office. He took Sam by the arm and steered him toward the bar.

"Always the joker, Samuel."

Sam let himself be led to the long bar set up inside the patio near what seemed like twenty French style doors that stood open so all of his guests could view the Italian marble balcony just above the Olympic sized pool and the expanse of sloping manicured lawn beyond. As they walked Sam was studying Chaplin until they stepped up to the bar and then Sam couldn't stop the question.

"Charlie, what's wrong?"

Chaplin pretended not hear as he lightly tapped his palm against the rich mahogany of the bar-top. One of the three bartenders turned and gave a slight bow to the host and his guest.

"Give Mr. Dalhart a whiskey and water and, well, maybe just a ginger ale for me," Charlie said looking around as he tried to avoid the knowing eyes of the detective.

"Again I ask Charlie, what's got you so spooked?"

Chaplin leaned closer, almost conspiratorially and pointed a finger against Sam's chest, only the manicured finger wavered a moment then slid to the right. Sam followed the direction of the finger and when he saw what Chaplin was pointing at he couldn't help but be slightly amazed. There, standing not fifty feet away was Melvin Purvis and there by his side was his former boss, J. Edgar Hoover. Purvis was in a white tuxedo and red bow-tie, Hoover in black. They were apparently chatting and star watching. As Sam studied the two men, Tallulah Bankhead slid by Hoover and Purvis and sneered, swaying and spilling a little of her drink as she did.

"They actually crashed your party?" Sam asked, accepting his drink from the bar.

"Well, I uh, well I sort of invited them," Chaplin said, lowering his head and sipping his ginger ale and grimacing.

"What in God's name did you do that for?"

"I'll not be intimidated in my town, Samuel, not even by him," he said, momentarily showing a little fire. Then he lowered his eyes again. "Well, I thought it would be the thing to do to get them off my back and show them I'm human," he looked up again at Sam, his large and expressive eyes wide and serious. "But Sam, I'm scared now," he croaked in a whisper. "It was a mistake, I just know it."

"Well, there's nothing you can do but make the best of it now. So just go about your business Charlie, and do what you do best. Keep your guests entertained. If I have to, I'll run some backfield interference for you."

The actor immediately looked relieved as he puffed out his chest and placed his drink on the bar. Then he looked at Sam and shook his head.

"You're too damn good to me Samuel," he said as he turned away and then looked back with a smile. "I'll personally make sure that the dragon lady pays your bill promptly," he said as he half bowed and then held his hand up to wave goodbye.

Sam nodded in gratitude, not wanting to burst Charlie's power bubble, but Mary Pickford always paid him in cash and on time. Sam watched as his host turned just in time to greet Carole Lombard, grabbing her hand and kissing it, making a big fuss over the beautiful starlet. He shook his head as he watched Charlie continue to charm Miss Lombard until her date for the evening pried Charlie off of her. Chaplin looked indignant momentarily until he saw it was Clark Gable who was looking down at him sternly and shaking a finger in Chaplin's face. Gable was apparently running some interference of his own. Sam smiled and turned back to the bar and took a long drink of his whiskey and water.

"Our little British tramp is very tired," a voice said beside Sam.

He turned and saw that it was the small and austere figure of Douglass Fairbanks. He was holding his glass of gin and looking at Charlie as he ambled off to greet yet another beautiful woman.

"Mr. Fairbanks, how are you?" Sam said, holding out his hand.

Fairbanks set his drink on the bar and took his time wiping his hands on a rather garish red handkerchief he had pulled from his tuxedo jacket. Done, he daintily let the silk kerchief float to the floor. Then he took Sam's hand lightly and bowed.

"Samuel Dalhart, I must insist you call me Doug, you are in *our* realm now and I say it is all right for you to do so," he said in a slow, deep and over stated near-do-well drawl, belying the fact the man was born in Denver, Colorado when that town was still mostly frontier.

"Alright, Doug," he said, "If I call you Doug then I must insist you call me Sam and not Samuel, I get that enough from our friend the little tramp," finally releasing the soft grip of Hollywood's once-upon-a-time greatest action star, "But I do agree Charlie looks like he's been hitting it a little too hard."

Fairbanks turned to the bar and picked up his drink and drained the glass and then tapped the empty on the bar and watched as another gin was immediately placed before him as if he had standing orders for the bartenders to keep his iced reverie going at all times. Sam watched as Fairbanks half drained the drink and then Fairbanks closed his eyes and sighed. Douglas had gotten noticeably thinner since the last time the two men had seen each other only a few months before. Again he set his glass down and looked at the taller Dalhart.

"It's that motion picture my boy. *The Great Dictator* or whatever he plans on calling it. He's at it night and day, day and night. Why, he's even forgone our ritual tennis match, not that the little heathen could ever best me."

Sam didn't comment as he took in Fairbanks and his painfully obvious failing health. He decided to get off the subject of who was looking bad.

"So, have you met the guests of honor yet?"

"Why yes my boy, I have indeed. Two of them are your typical European waste, and the other is a supposed former Nazi that wore out his welcome in 'za Fazerland," he said as he mock bowed like the perfect German soldier, even clicking his polished heels together, then grimaced and then drained the remainder of his drink. "Don't tell Charles I said that old boy, please. He thinks he's doing something marvelous by helping them evade something they *probably* had a hand in starting."

"Well, I have yet to meet them. Charlie actually hoodwinked me into signing on as their security if they need it, but I'm sure they can't be that bad, after all Mr. Hoover is right there, and he would know if they were the slightest bit hinkey," Sam said.

"My boy, is that even a word—*hinkey?*" Fairbanks said grimacing as if he had tasted a bad olive. "Please Sam, use proper English when in my presence; and they say I have difficulty since talkies came into the world. Besides, our esteemed Mr. Hoover wouldn't know an enemy of the state if it came and crawled into his bed, that is if there would be room in there of course," he said raising his eyebrows up and down and curling the end of his thin moustache. "I've heard the talk, even out here in dreamland," he stated, again slapping the glass on the bar and again it was immediately replaced. "Charlie is trying way too hard to show he's a good, upstanding citizen. He didn't have to do this for these people, nor did he have to invite that boorish G-Man either."

Again Sam didn't respond to the remark about the Europeans or the dangerous homosexual rumors about Hoover. Besides, he had spied the ex-Mrs. Fairbanks, Mary Pickford, winding her way through the guests having set her sights on Fairbanks. She politely smiled and nodded to the greetings called her way as she crossed the room as a royal queen would do, but she didn't stop to chat politely because she was on a mission. Sam coughed and cleared his throat in warning to Douglas, rolling his eyes in the direction of the fast approaching Miss Pickford. The venerable actor straightened, focusing as well as his eyes would allow. He nervously and too quickly placed his drink on the very edge of the bar. Before Sam could react to catch it, the now half full glass fell to the floor with a loud crash. Sam quickly stepped backwards and motioned for the barkeep. Douglas Fairbanks cringed as Pickford smiled at Sam and then turned to face her ex-husband.

"Darling, I'm sure you have had enough, at least until you get some food into you," she said as softly and politely as she could, tastefully ignoring the mess on the floor. "I'm sure Mr. Dalhart will excuse you to do just that," she said, half turning to Sam and nodding.

Fairbanks straightened, trying to make himself taller as he stood ramrod straight.

"Sam Dalhart, my *mother* has informed me I can no longer play with you. Therefore I shall abruptly leave this area and report for a hearty meal where my mother will undoubtedly apply my napkin around my neck."

"Oh, you stop being silly," Mary said slapping Fairbanks arm only slightly, then again turning and smiling at Sam. "He's so—"

"Drunk," Fairbanks finished for her still looking straight ahead.

"Yes, he is that isn't he?" she said, taking his stiff arm. "Sam," she said, nodding her head again in farewell as she steered Douglass away.

"I must protest this treatment, I will inform Mister Hoover, who is by the way in our company this very evening," Fairbanks said loudly waving his right index finger high in the air as he was led away. "And say that I am being manhandled by America's Sweetheart! And just what will my new wife say?"

Sam laughed as he would have loved to have heard her response to the threat of J. Edgar. Odds are she wouldn't have batted an eye as she would no doubt verbally assault the Director of the FBI also, possibly sending *him* away in tears. For a silent film star she was very capable of making a sailor shudder. As Sam turned and got his smile down to a mere grin, he had to admit, Mary Pickford did dearly love Fairbanks, even though they were no longer man and wife. He also knew the truth that she was probably one of the only people in this town who was truly untouchable, by Hoover or anyone else.

"Mister Chaplin, that man inhabiting the area of the bar furthest from the slightest of human contact, who is he?" the dark haired woman asked.

Charlie, who was busy staring at the heart shaped figure of the woman's behind, barely heard the question. His lack of response made her turn slightly to face him. The tall woman placed her long slender fingers under Chaplin's left cheek and swiveled his head up from the view of her bottom half.

"What was that my dear?" he said, batting his long lashes at her, blinking himself out of his entranced state.

"The gorgeous man leaning his frame up against the bar, who is he? He seems to be out of place."

Chaplin looked over in the direction where the woman had indicated, and then he suddenly understood her comment.

"Ah, he my dear, most certainly is out of place among us phonies. That is a very good friend of mine, Mr. Samuel Dalhart, the very man who applied his name to your visa documents so you could arrive on these golden shores. He is here if you feel the need to be protected," he looked back at the woman with a smirk. "He is what we call in America, a *private dick*," he said with a flourish of Britishness.

The woman wore an evening gown of dark blue sequins with aquamarine accents. Her jewelry was spectacular even among the bangles and baubles of the Hollywood royalty. The dress, the jewels and the light combined to make her sparkle, casting blue and green lights dancing onto Chaplin's face.

"I'm beginning to believe you are a most crude little man, Mr. Chaplin," she said, understanding the double entendre as he had intended her to do. "If you don't mind, while my loving husband is trying to seduce Miss Bankhead, I should like to meet this man."

"It shall be done then," Chaplin answered, gently taking her by her right arm. He led her through the crowd while avoiding a few couples heading to the small dance floor. Sam was talking with one of the bartenders and didn't notice Chaplin and his guest step up behind him. The bartender saw them and stepped away.

Chaplin cleared his throat.

"Samuel, I must insist you speak with someone other than the help this evening," he said. "And what better way to step out of the gutter than to greet one of my guests of honor this evening."

Sam turned to face Charlie, and when he did he didn't even see the little man, so taken was he by the sight of one of the most beautiful women he had ever seen. He couldn't help but stare. Placing his drink on the bar he swiftly looked the woman over, taking in her form from head to toe. He saw immediately she wasn't just one of the two thousand Hollywood types he had known in his career. This woman was elegant in a way that acting and etiquette coaches just couldn't teach.

Charlie's voice seemed to come from a great distance, "Samuel, may I present the Countess Francesca D'Sarcuni, recently of Milan, Italy, now a lowly and lost child who refused to be exploited by *Il Ducé*."

Sam took the Countess' extended hand as he frantically tried to remember the protocol for meeting a titled woman. He took her hand, paused a moment, then lightly brushed his lips to the back of her hand.

"Countess, Samuel Dalhart, Esquire," Chaplin finished.

"Signore Dalhart, it is a pleasure," she said in good English. Her voice was deep and rich, piercing Sam soul like a sensual perfume.

"Countess, it's a pleasure, Ma'am," Sam said, releasing the woman's hand.

She looked deeply into Dalhart's blue eyes. It was as if she were studying him, trying to figure out how he fit into the scheme of things here among the Hollywood elite.

"You are an actor, a director perhaps?" she asked, knowing already he was not.

Charlie snorted out laughter before he could contain it. Sam looked at him and he straightened and stifled the laughter. The countess seemed taken back.

"You must excuse me my dear, Countess, but the thought of Samuel here as an actor, well, I just couldn't contain the hilarity. Why, it would be like placing our revered Mr. Barrymore in the company of the Three Stooges," Charlie said, straining to contain the laughter from welling up again.

Sam just glared at Chaplin, feeling somewhat uncomfortable as well as a bit annoyed. The Countess also stood in silence until Chaplin finally looked up and noticed no one was joining him in his moment of comedic genius.

"Uh, hum. I believe I hear a sour note emanating from the stringed quartet, thus if you will excuse me I will attend to that," he said, bowing and backing away.

"Such a strange little man, but funny to many in the world I imagine," the Countess ventured, watching Chaplin walk away with several backward glances.

"Charlie's a good Joe, he just doesn't know when to be serious sometimes, but he's harmless enough," Sam said as he turned back to face her.

"I must apologize to you Mr. Dalhart, Mr. Chaplin informed me of your profession before we intruded upon you, so I was brought here under false pretenses. I just wanted to make your acquaintance and to thank you for assisting in guaranteeing our safety and to ease the mind of your government." Her eyes sought his and held them. "Now, I have read many American and British mystery novels, Mr. Dalhart, from my understanding a 'Private Dick' refers to a detective of sorts, am I correct?" the countess asked.

"Well, yes, but I'm afraid it's not all glamour and glitz as the writers of such books claim. It's mostly made up of long and very boring hours watching people go through their just as equally boring lives."

She placed her slender fingers on Sam's arm. "I'm sure you are selling yourself short, Mr. Dalhart." He noted this little gesture and decided to steer the conversation away from his work.

"So, you have decided to grace our country with your lovely presence. Are things getting that bad in Italy?" Sam asked, even though he was well versed on foreign affairs and held many of the same opinions as some of the most unpopular of public figures; that the Unites States was bound to get into a fight with one part, if not the entire Axis sooner or later.

"*Il Ducé*, I'm afraid has become far too dangerous a character for my tastes. Power has such a terrible influence on the weak minded, don't you agree, Mr. Dalhart?"

"I'm afraid the national policies of Mr. Mussolini have been lost on me. After all, I'm just your ordinary working man, like most Americans," Sam said.

"But alas, it is just that same working man who will be called into service to bring this unscrupulous element to its knees," a voice said from beside Sam. "*Cara mia*, will you introduce me to this learned gentleman?"

Sam turned to see a dark rotund man with a pencil thin moustache standing not far away. With his immaculate black tuxedo he wore a bright scarlet sash that went from his right shoulder crossing his barrel chest to rest on his left hip, a gold Papal medallion was at its center. His splendid costume did little to take away the ugliness of his face; a bad case of chickenpox sometime back, or so Sam assumed, had left tell-tell pockmarks on his cheeks. He took the countess by the arm and half bowed to her. She smiled sweetly at him, acknowledging the bow. The man had been escorted over by Gary Cooper, who stood beside the newcomer with his famous *little boy lost* look on his face.

"Let me do the honors. Sam Dalhart, may I introduce Count Orlando D'Sarcuni, the Countess' husband," Cooper said smiling as if this would be a great shock to Sam.

Sam looked at Cooper a moment and then offered his hand to the count.

"I'm very honored and pleased to meet you, sir. We were just discussing a little friendly politics, and the reasons for you're leaving your beloved homeland," Sam said taking Count D'Sarcuni's hand and half bowing. Sam watched Cooper as he eyed the countess, doing nothing short of openly lusting after her.

The private detective knew Cooper well and it was obvious he was up to something concerning the beautiful countess. The world had yet to discover that Gary Cooper was one of the true wolves of Hollywood. On screen he was the quiet and unassuming guy all women loved to see and most men aspired to be. Even bashful some would call him, but in real life he never met a woman he didn't love. And Cooper loved a lot. He used that embarrassed and boyishly harmless way of his to seduce every woman he came into contact with, and now he had his *Joe American* sights set on the countess. The outcome of this particular pursuit would be interesting indeed, however Sam decided he would bow out of this before Cooper turned this into an international incident.

"Yeah, the Count and I were over there wondering just what you two were talking about," Cooper was saying in his halting style of speech. "Sam, it's an amazing story of how they found themselves here in America, just amazing! You really need to hear this one, it's just fascinating. Why don't you listen to it and I will take the Countess to the faraway land of the dance floor, with your permission of course, sir," he said bowing to the count.

"By all means, Mr. Cooper, my wife is an excellent dancer," the Count said, extending his arm in the direction of the dance floor.

Cooper looked at Sam and raised his eyebrows up and down twice as he slid by him and offered his arm to the countess. She gracefully accepted, all the while holding her gaze on Sam's blue eyes. Sam watched Cooper lead her away and then looked down at the smiling Count, who stood watching his wife with his hands clasped behind his back.

"A true gentleman, I have seen many of his moving pictures," the count said.

Sam turned to the bar and his long forgotten drink. "Yeah, a real gentleman," he mumbled.

"So, Mr. Dalhart, Mr. Cooper was kind enough to inform me of your occupation. It must be very exciting with all the women and hooligans you must come in contact with."

Sam chuckled and was about to comment when another man stepped up and spoke.

"He's just another city policeman who decided the streets were a little too rough for him," the voice said.

Sam turned and took in the bulldog features of J. Edgar Hoover who stood with one hand planted in the right coat pocket of his tuxedo. His black eyes were staring at Sam and ignoring the Count. *What was this*, Sam asked himself, *the most popular side of the bar? Was he wearing a sign that said come and talk to me, I'm different?*

"Ah, the famous Mr. Hoover, I am so—"

"Take a powder Count; I have some words I would like to say to Mr. Dalhart here.

"Well I never!" D'Sarcuni said loudly.

Hoover turned to face the Count, his right hand coming free of his coat pocket.

"Listen, I said take a walk before I start looking into your immigration case *Count*," Hoover said, saying the word like it left a bad taste in his mouth. "We at the Bureau are curious about why it took you so long to figure out what that fascist Duchy was up to before you decided it was going to get a little hot around there," he said, stepping closer to the Count, "along with Mussolini being such a close friend and all, I won't even go into the visits you made to Germany since 1933."

Sam almost started laughing at Hoover's pronunciation of the Ducé, but decided discretion was indeed the better part of valor. He watched the reddened face of the Count as he turned and stormed away, sure he was going to have a stroke over Hoover's words. But Sam thought maybe the head of the FBI wasn't too far off the mark this time. He had had a strange feeling while in the presence of D'Sarcuni and the Countess that maybe they weren't all they were represented to be. It was that old gut feeling he got when speaking to people with a past, or a present that didn't quite measure up. It was as if they were perhaps shading the truth as to the reasons they were here in America. If Rainbird had been here he would have had a better opinion on the two Italians.

Hoover watched the Count storm away looking for Chaplin. Then he turned to face Sam as Melvin Purvis joined the two men. Purvis waved the bartender off when approached.

"You know who I am I assume?" Hoover asked.

"I know who you are."

"You must be a very stupid man, Mr. Dalhart."

Sam smiled and shrugged his shoulders. "Some people would say just that, so your reputation is intact, Mr. Hoover, you are an astute judge of character," Sam said, taking a large swallow from his glass.

"Your humor is lost on me. You failed to give Mr. Purvis here adequate information on the nocturnal activities of Mr. Chaplin."

"I'm going to say it just the way I said it to your organ-grinder monkey here," Sam said, all the while watching Purvis take a step toward him. Hoover gestured with his fingers for him to step back. "Chaplin is not the man you think he is and anything beyond that is not going to be discussed as its privileged information."

"I believe you may be covering up a crime—"

"Several maybe," Purvis said, cutting off his former boss.

Hoover stared at Melvin Purvis for a moment. It was a look that said *you are an ass for interrupting me like that.* Sam knew Hoover didn't really care for Purvis because a few years back he had tried to steal most of the glory from the director during the times when Dillinger, Machine Gun Kelly, Baby Face Nelson and others roamed the Midwest, using the newspapers to show the country he alone was winning the war on crime. Thus Hoover forced Purvis to get out of the FBI racket in '36.

Purvis held Hoover's glare for a moment and then looked at Sam. He turned and left, staring at Chaplin who stood by the dance floor with the Count looking at the exchange at the bar. Purvis purposely swerved out of his way, barely grazing Chaplin with his shoulder. Charlie merely looked at his retreating form for a moment, and then turned back to the exchange between Sam and Hoover.

"If I had evidence of a crime I'm obliged to report it to the police. If you have evidence of a crime that Mr. Chaplin may have committed get a warrant and arrest him, if not, get evidence or leave my client alone," Sam said, putting his drink down and walking away, leaving the director of the FBI standing alone and fuming in frustration.

Chaplin watched Hoover clench his fist several times and then turn and storm out of the ballroom, carefully stepping around Clark Gable who the Director of the FBI knew not to offend. Charlie excused himself from D'Sarcuni and quickly followed Sam out to the balcony.

"Thank you again, Samuel," Chaplin said coming up behind Sam as the detective lit a cigarette.

Sam didn't turn to face Charlie; he just looked out over the expanse of lawn toward the tennis courts.

"For what Charlie?"

Chaplin took a step forward and placed his hand on Sam's shoulder and squeezed. "For defending this old fool against an ogre of a man—and for believing that I had nothing to do with any missing girl."

Sam took a drag off his cigarette and tossed it over the marble balcony.

"I can't stand people who think this is their own private country and allow only who they want to come in, or to live the way *they* think they should live."

"I'm afraid he made my new friends a tad uncomfortable," Chaplin ventured.

"He did do that," Sam said. Then he looked at Charlie. "How is it you came to be involved in their coming here? I mean, they really aren't your normal acquaintances—royalty Charlie, really?"

"That, I'm afraid is complicated. I guess you could say they were just part of the package," Charlie said as he stepped to the edge of the balcony and leaned on the marble railing that wound its way around it. "I was actually helping out an agency that smuggles people out of Germany, you know, Jew's and other German undesirables," he said leaning into Sam conspiratorially, "Well, one was a very well-placed man who was close to their officials in the German government and old naïve Charlie thought he could bring this man to this country and be the big hero. To, you know, maybe help Roosevelt wake this bloody country up a little by having this German chap explain what's really happening in Germany and the Count and Countess in Italy. But then this Hoover thing started up and I've yet to do anything but throw this elaborate welcome party."

"I swear Charlie; you come up with the most ridiculous bullshit schemes I have ever heard of in my life, and don't think I didn't notice that you hoodwinked me and told me they were going to be here temporarily. You knew I would never agree to their security for their damn visas."

Chaplin turned and smiled at Sam. "I've always had a vivid imagination Samuel, you know that. If I had told you the truth you never would have signed that agreement," he said sadly. "I just wanted to do my part in this insanity that has gripped Europe. I don't know if my film *The Great Dictator* is enough. Oh bloody hell Sam; I just wanted to make a difference."

"Smuggling former Nazis out was your idea of helping? Charlie, I hate those guys. And I am amazed Hoover didn't add that little tidbit in there with this missing girl thing," Sam said shaking his head. "Do me a favor; don't do anything like this again until you run it by me, clear? I'm sure Mr. Churchill can manage fine without you. And let the President bring the people around, saving a former Nazi may not be the best way to do it."

Charlie patted Sam on the back.

"Thank you anyway for getting in between me and super G-man, Sam; I would be lost without you." Charlie turned and started walking back into the house.

"Charlie?" Sam called.

He turned and looked back.

"Anything you can remember about that missing girl, you'll let me know?"

"I will do just that Samuel. I really do hope they find her unhurt," he said rubbing his hands together in nervousness.

Sam watched as Charlie slowly walked back into the party and his no doubt quickly thought-up excuses and apology to the Count D'Sarcuni.

Sam was taking in the beautiful night. The moon was at one quarter and the rains of the previous month past had left the lawns in LA particularly lush and full, unlike the dreaded summer recently departed when the reservoirs in the area were taxed to their limits even with the new improvements to the LA River bed it had been miserable.

Sam accepted a drink from a waiter who had been sent out by Charlie. He took a swallow and watched as the waiter went to the far corner of the balcony and in the shadows bent over as if he were delivering another order or taking one. Sam watched the exchange, and then as the waiter walked away he let the tray dangle to his side, indicating to him that a drink had indeed been delivered.

"Great Sam boy, you just solved the mystery of the delivered drink," Dalhart said under his breath.

He was just getting ready to walk back into the house when a momentary flair of light from the same corner illuminated that area of the patio. A man had just lit a cigarette.

"I must make my apologies for not making my presence known, I assure you the conversation between our host and yourself was not overheard," the voice said, and then a soft glow emanated from the corner as the hidden man inhaled smoke from his cigarette.

Sam didn't respond as he stood where he was and was ready to re-enter the house without comment. Then he saw a dark shadow stand and stride toward him. The man was Sam's size and again the tuxedo was far newer than his own. It was simpler than the Count's had been but there was one noticeable difference Sam saw as the man drew closer and into the soft light of the balcony. The man had no bow-tie. His shirt was entirely white and had a very high starched collar that was open in the front to a square of about five inches and a beautiful blue ascot with a diamond stick-pin was the only thing adorning the neck between the two collar halves.

"I've got to stop buying my clothes through the Sears and Roebuck catalogue," Sam said as the man approached. "Between you and the Count D'Sarcuni I feel positively underdressed," Sam joked.

"Ah, then you have met my two traveling companions?" the blonde man said as he stepped up to Sam.

The two men were standing almost toe to toe and both were instantly sizing the other up.

"Traveling companions?" Sam asked.

The stranger took a sip of his cocktail but his eyes never left Sam's. He lowered his glass and smiled. "Yes, the Count and his lovely wife, we journeyed here together."

"So, may I deduce you are the third part of the European triumvirate that Mr. Chaplin is honoring tonight?" Sam asked.

"Why indeed I am. My name is Karl Von Railing, former Colonel of intelligence for the German Wehrmacht."

Sam raised his chin and just said, "Ah." *Where was Hoover when you needed him*, he thought.

Von Railing bowed, then straightened and finally held out his right hand. Sam took a moment then switched his drink to his left hand and then took the German's hand and shook.

"Sam Dalhart," he said.

Sam felt a momentary slowing of the handshake and a slight stiffness come into Von Railing's fingers, but it was so slight he thought he may have imagined it.

"A name among so many here, I am sorry to say, I have never heard of you before," the blonde man lied.

The comment momentarily threw Sam off, and then he quickly understood what the man meant. "No, I'm not one of them; I leave the acting to others that have studied it. I have found I'm not very good at it."

The man released Sam's hand and looked him in the eye. "Yes, deception of the masses is an art," he said, taking another sip from his glass.

"You had better come up with a better way of phrasing it Mac or they'll eat you alive here in Hollywood. They take this acting thing pretty serious out here."

"Ah, but of course they do. But I sense you are a man of a, how should I put this, more serious nature and profession?"

"Well, I guess it's not as serious as being an intelligence agent for the German Army, and as for a serious nature, nah, I'm easy going."

Von Railing seemed momentarily lost for words. "I'm afraid I have worn out my welcome in the Fatherland. I have many enemies that would like to see me, how do your American gangsters say it, *wearing the cement boots?*"

"Yep, that's just how they say it," Sam said in all seriousness.

The German nodded his head and turned to look toward the tennis courts.

"What is it you do in this sparkling city?" Von Railing asked.

Sam had heard Los Angeles called many things before, but sparkling wasn't one of them, but he none-the-less turned and smiled. "I am a private detective, Colonel, one who actually played a very minor role in your arrival in the States. I'm at your service for any security matters that may arise since the German consulate will not guarantee your safety here."

The man cocked his head.

"Well in that case, I at least owe you a drink," he turned to waive a waiter over but Sam stopped him.

"I've still got a full tank of ethyl here, Colonel."

The German tuned back to Sam and looked at his drink and then smiled.

"Ethyl, you mean gasoline? Yes," he chuckled, "I, as you say, get it, very good."

Sam just smiled as if pleased beyond measure that the Kraut *got it*.

"Now, I am familiar with detectives as you say, but how do you mean private?" Then recognition dawned on his features. "Ah, I understand, like the very exciting tales of Mr. Hammett I have enjoyed," Von Railing said, overjoyed.

Sam swore someday he was going to get Dashiell Hammett and shake him until he told everyone who ever read his books that Sam Spade was a character and not a very accurate character at that. Hammett had once been a Pinkerton agent and so Sam knew that the writer knew better.

"That's it, just like that."

"Amazing, you must have very exciting adventures," Von Railing said, watching Sam closely.

"Um, huh, very," Sam said. "So, you have taken up residence in our town, it must be kind of boring compared to the excitement happening in Germany nowadays."

Von railing took a deep breath and sighed and then drained his glass and turned to face Sam.

"We tried to warn the fool," he started, then caught himself. "I was not in favor of many things that happened in my homeland, Mr. Dalhart. Hitler and the thugs he has surrounded himself with will pay a dear price for what they have brought to Europe, it would help somewhat if you Americans awoke to the real world around you and not so much at what car style will be available next year. Do you even have an opinion on what's happening, if I may ask of course?"

Sam was still looking him dead in the eye. He didn't know why but he was getting the same feeling he had when he spoke with the D'Sarcuni's. Was it a deception on their part or was it that he just didn't care for Germans and Italians lately, so much so that it affected his judgment?

"I think you," Sam caught himself, "excuse me; the Germans, have pushed Great Britain and France into a corner, and let me tell you, they're neither Austria nor Czechoslovakia, they are going fight, just like Poland did; only they may have a little bit more of a punch."

"Mr. Dalhart…may I call you Sam?" he waited for an answer, but Sam stayed quiet, he just gave him a slight nod of his head. "I think you may be under a false impression of me. I am here in your country because Adolph Hitler is my enemy. The man has not a humane bone about him, and I am afraid he is going to eventually lead Germany to such a ruin as has never been seen before on this planet," he said as he saw other faces watching and listening to his words and people from the party started filtering out onto the veranda. "Eventually you Americans will awaken to the fact that you can no longer hide your heads in the sand, and if my being here will help that along so be it. Please don't take me for one of those foolish German caricatures that have so recently sprung up in your motion pictures," Von Railing didn't seem to notice that a shock of his blonde hair had fallen in front of his eyes as he spoke. "You cannot fathom what Hitler is capable of; he will not stop until men, women and children are shoved into the flames that he himself has started burning."

Sam reached out and put a hand on the Germans shoulder. "Easy there Von Railing, don't get your hackles up, I think maybe you *should* talk to a few folks in Washington. Let them know how things are over there."

Von Railing timidly smiled and managed to look momentarily embarrassed. He swallowed and pulled down on his tuxedo jacket and then ran his hand through his blonde hair, inwardly pleased by his performance. He turned and acted as if he had just noticed that several of the guests were standing at the French doors and were looking at him along with those few who had ventured outside. Then suddenly one man, then another, then a woman started clapping their hands. They were soon joined by others who had heard the pre-prepared outrage and anger of his speech.

Sam nodded his head and gestured at Von Railing, patting him on the back as actors and actresses applauded the man for his comments. Sam watched the German closely as he took a step forward and half bowed. *The funny thing,* he thought, *he suspected that Von Railing was sincere in his indignant response to Hitler's aggression. But was he truly indignant about that aggression or jealous that he was no longer a part of it?* He didn't get a good feeling from this guy at all.

Charlie stepped outside and gestured for Von Railing to join the other guests inside. But before he did, the German turned and faced Sam. The look was one of an adversary, not that of a friend. Then the German abruptly smiled, and shook Sam's hand.

"Sam Dalhart, I very much hope we shall meet again."

"Look forward to it, Colonel," Sam said, gripping the man's hand a little tighter than he normally would have.

He watched him follow Charlie back into the house and onto more adulation, while Chaplin half turned and mouthed the words, *what happened?'*

Well, Sam thought, *I managed to make an enemy tonight and he didn't even know why.* He had never taken a disliking to someone so fast in his life. He shook his head trying to clear it a little as he was approached by Chaplin's former live-in girlfriend, Paulette Goddard. Her small frame and dark hair was a sight Sam saw as a godsend after the company he had been keeping since he had arrived at the party. Paulette came up to Sam and placed her arm around him and started steering the stunned detective back to the party.

"If I may ask Sam, weren't you aware that he was shouting at you? It actually looked as though you two were about to punch it out. I saw your fists balling at your sides."

Sam hadn't realized any of this. Why would he have not noticed, he was always so careful never to allow outsiders to know his thoughts or feelings. He didn't like the way things had turned out this evening, first Hoover, and then this confrontation with Von Railing and with the latter it felt like he had lost round one in a set up fight, and lost badly. For some reason Von Railing had used him. He turned and looked at Paulette.

"I guess I pushed a button, huh?"

Paulette Goddard laughed and patted Sam on the shoulder.

"Only Charlie, or a close friend of Charlie's could make a bunch of isolationists, *actors* to boot, and studio head Jews stand up and cheer a Nazi, that's a real talent you have there, Sam."

An hour later Sam was on his fourth whiskey and still wondering why the German picked him for his little performance out on the back veranda. Why not some other poor slob here? At least someone with a little more influence than what he himself wielded.

"It wasn't as bad as all that, Sam," Goddard said, leaning against the bar with him, her long dress hanging far below that of the high legged-stool in which she sat.

"Listen Paulette, it was like he intentionally baited me so he could show these people he was on the up and up about the reasons he was here."

"And you being the big detective, have a gut feeling it's for a far more sinister reason, is that it?" she said, lifting her glass of champagne. "Here's a flash, Sam Dalhart, maybe he is here because he didn't like what was happening over there."

"Yeah, you're probably right," he said, sliding his half empty glass away from him. "Hey, Paulette, someone taking you home tonight, I mean, you're not going anywhere alone are you?"

"I'm a big girl, Sam."

"I know that," he said, patting her on the knee. "It's just—"

"If I can survive Charlie for all that time, I can make it home without a white knight protecting me."

Sam looked at her and pursed his lips and nodded his head. "I know you can Paulette. Just be careful out there."

"Okay, it's not just Fritz over there, you actually seem to be worried about something, so what gives?" she asked, sitting her glass down and locking eyes with him.

Sam took a deep breath and held her gaze. "Nothing, I just worry about...things I guess," he said while trying his best to smile.

"Is it about that girl the police have been asking Charlie about?"

Sam looked taken back by her comment and he knew it.

"Do you think anything that happens in this town that involves Charlie escapes my attention? I can't live with the man Sam, but I do love him."

"I know you do, Paulette," he said, looking away and trying to focus on anything other than the beautiful woman before him.

"Anyway, Charlie had nothing to do with that girl's disappearance, it's not his style," she said, sliding out of the chair and reaching for her purse. She lightly touched Sam on the temple and then ran her fingers through his hair. "Sam, all those times you brought Charlie home for me after his binges with Douglass, I want you to know that I thank god for you every night."

"I'm glad someone here likes me," he said trying again to smile and lighten the moment.

"One question before I go home and curl up and read about a real detective, Sam Spade," she said watching Sam for his famous reaction to Hollywood detectives by shaking his head. "How come you never once made a pass at me, Doug and Coop did all the time, why not you, Sam?"

Sam straightened and looked almost hurt as he looked her in the eye as she had almost compared him to the philandering of Gary Cooper and Doug Fairbanks.

"Because Charlie's my friend, why would I do that?" he asked her in an actual innocent voice.

She smiled and again placed her hand on the side of his face.

"I just wanted you to know Mr. Boy scout, you may have had a chance."

Sam smiled, "Really?"

"Yes, until tonight that is," she started to turn and walk away, then said over her shoulder, "Until you picked on that nice Nazi man, I could never fall for a brute."

"Smartass, you know I never liked you much," Sam said back, watching her go with the nice little wiggle she had. She held up her hand and waved. Sam smiled and shook his head. "What a dame," he said.

❦ FIVE ❧

Rainbird knew the dream was upon him, but once more he knew this night was going to be as different as the night before. He knew beforehand that this time there would be no last minute reprieve, no momentary burst of will power that would set him free of the nightmare and send him up the stairs. There would be a hard intent by the beast to keep him in place. The drug that Sam had given him to take made him a prisoner of his mind just as he suspected that it might. The small amount he had taken coupled with the fact he was physically exhausted fixed him to his sweat soaked sheets as if he were chained.

He had become accustomed to the gloomy interior of the house, its musky and wild odor that lingered in the way the smell of rotted meat would linger in a refrigerator long after it had been disposed of. Only John knew that the rotting meat he smelled had never been taken away. It waited for him a few feet beyond that cellar door. Once again he was compelled to reach out and touch the old fashioned latch and the lock that held it in place.

"I was hoping you would come to me tonight, Shaman."

John's hand fell away from the door and he quickly took a step back, so quickly he bumped into a large wooden butcher's block. He turned and saw that there was about two pounds of raw sausage links coiled neatly on top. He swallowed and turned back to the door. The voice from the cellar had never spoken to him before his entrance through the basement and into the subbasement. This was shaping up different than all the other visits he had been forced to endure.

"I sense…I sense more of you than usual," came the deep voice through the door way. It had the echoing quality of depth.

Whatever was down there was right. For some reason John felt more physically *here* than he ever had before. It must be the sleeping drops he had used. His mind was more susceptible to this outrage than ever before. He closed his eyes and willed himself to think. He knew he couldn't do as he had done before. The smell below would be stronger; the cold touch of all those young girls would be more than he could bear.

He looked around the old kitchen. The twin stove and ovens were the same as his many other visits with the dirty dishes in the sink and even the flies buzzing around them. Then he saw what it was, the bare lights in the overhead fixture of the kitchen, they had dimmed when before in his other dreams they had been bright. When he had closed his eyes they had been brighter as before and now they had only half the illumination they once had. He tried to push himself away from the butcher block but found he was frozen with fear and couldn't move.

"Dalhart, why does that name run through your mind? You use it like a talisman, like a weak minded fool with a rosary. Who is this Dalhart, your benefactor perhaps?"

Rainbird looked around frantically. The voice, though unseen was moving *upward!* *Oh god*, he thought, it was coming up the bottom most stairs. He sensed the girls down there and without actually seeing them he knew they were afraid—so afraid they had scattered to the far corners of the dirt floored wine cellar, cringing in dead horror at the *thing* that passed by them, the very creature that had ended their existence and the same horrible beast they so longed for, lusted for, would kill for. John felt helpless and foolish. His only protection it seemed was when he thought about his friends at the agency, Sam in particular. At that moment he felt, no, he sensed the movement up the stairs stop. He felt he could see the thing pause on the upper landing on the lowest set of stairs before it entered the basement immediately below the kitchen. The basement filled with antiques left behind by the previous owner.

"Come to me Shaman, Red Man, RAINBIRD! Yes, that is your name! And your Christian name? Ah yes…John," The voice said soothingly. *"John Rainbird."*

The voice now sounded as if it were just the other side of the door and although the statement wasn't shouted the voice and power of the creature rattled the few dishes in their cabinets, shook the grime covered windows and made one of the cast iron oven doors fall open, revealing a pan filled with aged and crusted food of some kind. John flinched and tried to turn away and this time his head moved easily and his eyes fell on the large door.

"Stay out of my head!" he managed to scream.

"But your mind is so warm and inviting, unlike many I have visited lo these many years, Rainbird."

"God!" John grabbed his temples and pushed.

"You are a treasure trove of anger. The names that were once used on you as boy and man alike were so harsh and, yes, so…so…true. These names course through your memory like blood through your arteries my friend. The names are true in your mind, aren't they Rainbird. The names you were called as a boy, you heard them so much you came to believe them. Embrace them. You used them for your own protection. If you failed in anything, you had those names to fall back on, after all, what could be expected of a savage, an Injun', a Red Niggar, but failure in one's self?"

"Fuck you!" he shouted, still holding his pounding head where the thing in the cellar probed him.

Rainbird sensed another change. This time he felt the girls, moaning and moving as one to the stairs, dragging bare feet, socked feet, nylon-covered feet through the damp earth toward the stairs. The thing was no longer there, he was sure of it. He knew he was trapped. Knew he would be an easy target for the doll eyed girls.

He turned away from the door and pressed himself into the butchers block. He shook his head, trying in vain to clear it of the vision of the young girls moving up the stairs, the ones capable of it, walking, the others crawling, moving past the point where the thing had stood on the lower landing, following the last straight line of stairs to the kitchen door. Rainbird pushed at the heavy butcher's block, moving it an inch or two. He pushed again, but this time there was nothing. Then he heard it, the small thump against the door, then another, and another.

"God, help me!" he cried over and over.

It wasn't just the fact that he was going to see those dead girls again, but somewhere in his induced sleep he had come to the realization that the creature that ruled the darkness below was using the girls to keep him occupied until he could find him in the waking world, find him in bed where he was actually sleeping. There would be no dream meeting, the creature was using his own mind as a homing beacon to find him and meet face to face. He knew he had to awaken before that happened or he would forever be locked in this horrid dream world—or worse, the real world of the house where the beast dwelled.

The door was slowly opening as the lights dimmed even further. John forced himself to turn around. In life he was brave. Nothing scared him but the specter of failure—failure at not measuring up, for not being what he wanted to be. Fear of being his father, his uncles. Fear of being what most people thought Indians were; dead inside, never wanting anything more than to be left alone and pitied. But now he was terrified beyond words at the hand that snaked around the door. Then more white hands with broken and cracked nails, bloodied fingers pushing open wider that barrier that held the yawning hell hole of a cellar at bay. He knew they would hold him until the beast found him, alone in his bed, sweating, even aware of the thing's presence. Oh, he knew the creature would allow him the presence of mind to be there when they were formally introduced.

The first of the dead girls smiled at him. She saw his fear and frowned and held out a bloodied hand. John screamed, coming close to losing his mind. Another girl, this one with the left side of her throat torn out also smiled and reached for him, actually coming into contact with his face.

"Ahhh!"

Suddenly hands were pulling him over the butcher block; he was screaming and knew that somehow they had gotten behind him. He thrashed about but he was in a death grip by something he couldn't see. He heard his name being screamed over and over. Then he felt a slap to his face. It felt wonderful, almost cooling to his hot skin. Then he realized why, it was human contact, it didn't matter that it was a brutal strike, it was human and it felt great.

"John wake up, goddamn it!" Sam yelled.

Rainbird reached up from his nightmare and struck Sam across the cheek, then his other hand hit him in the mouth, drawing blood and knocking Sam backward. He rebounded with purpose and went to the sleeping man once again, determined to wake him.

"John!" Sam slapped him as hard as he could across the face. Then he slapped again and he actually saw his friend smile in the throes of his terror. "Wake up, wake up!" he screamed.

Rainbird's eyes fluttered and then they flew open. He saw Sam upside down and he panicked. He threw himself up from the bed, actually striking Sam again on the chin, knocking him once more backward against the headboard. He jumped from the bed and ran to the window and raised the blinds and looked around the front courtyard of his apartment complex. He looked left and then right. He quickly reached down to the small night table never taking his eyes off the darkness outside and opened the drawer and without looking pulled out a snub nosed thirty-eight revolver.

"Whoa there partner," Sam said as he dove over the bed quickly, bouncing upon it and quickly reached for the gun and wrestled it from Rainbird's hand.

John turned slightly from the window and didn't notice he didn't have the gun. He just kept looking out of the window with that terrified look on his face.

As Sam watched, Rainbird's breathing slowed to normal and then he leaned against the widow frame and slowly reached up and pulled the blind down.

"You enjoyed hitting me didn't you?" he said without turning.

Sam closed his eyes and turned away.

"I figured it may be the one time I could get away with it and not get hit back," he wiped blood from his mouth, "but I guess I was wrong," he said turning back to face John.

Rainbird turned and looked at his friend. "Sorry, ooh, looks like I whacked you a good one."

"Yeah," Sam said as he tossed John his thirty-eight.

Rainbird took a deep breath. He sighed deeply as if catching his first real breath in ages, and then sat on the edge of the bed. He picked up the bottle of sleep drops and tossed them over to Sam who caught it and shook his head.

"Not a good idea, huh?"

"Nope," John answered as he rubbed his temples after placing the gun on the nightstand. "But you're forgiven since you more than likely saved my life."

"What do you mean?" Sam asked as he headed for the small bathroom.

"Something was on its way here," he looked at Sam who had stopped in the bathroom doorway. "No joke, I think it was coming here to kill me and it was using my nightmare to home in on where I lived."

Sam didn't say a word as he turned and moved toward the sink and turned on the cold water. He removed his tuxedo jacket and tossed it on the toilet lid. He gently rubbed cold water on his face and then spit out blood. Then he looked in the mirror. He didn't know what to say to his friend but he knew John truly believed he was going to be visited by whatever was haunting his dreams.

"Sam?"

"Yeah," he said as he reached for a towel.

"I think whatever this thing is, it knows about you. It seems fixated in some way on your name."

"Oh, this is good, thanks buddy," Sam said smiling in the doorway. Then he tossed the damp towel at Rainbird who caught it easily. "Now I've got former Nazis and dream monsters for enemies, really, thanks."

"Hey, what are friends for."

The mental connection between itself and Rainbird was suddenly cut off. The creature was sitting atop the Roosevelt Hotel and it angrily growled and swung its long arms in an arc, knocking loose a steel vent that led down to the exclusive hotel's laundry room. Its yellow eyes focused outward toward Elysian Park and it growled. It had been sure the Shaman was not able to awaken on his own; something would have had to interfere, bringing his dream state to a sudden close.

The beast closed its eyes and concentrated. It sensed that single word; Dalhart! Why was its mind so concerned with that name? It had feared no man in its long history. They had never been a threat to its existence. Why now? Why this man and his shaman?

Phaltazar climbed the neon lined Roosevelt sign and examined the distant sidewalk below. A few people scurried here and there, but it picked up nothing of interest. The anger it had felt was tempered by the fact that it knew the name of both of its possible antagonists; John Rainbird and Samuel Dalhart. With this knowledge it might be able to use the men to its advantage, if not, it now knew it could easily have Von Railing find them with the connection of that court jester, Chaplin.

It swung backward from the girder work of the sign and landed easily on the gravel covered roof of the hotel. Its cloven hoofed feet tossing small pebbles up in the air like a splash of water. It then slowly ran along the edge and leaped easily over to the next building. It repeated its movement time and again, working its way toward the darkness of Elysian Park and something it sensed there.

The girl heard the tapping at the window, a little too loud and far too insistent. She cringed at the thought of her father walking in just as she was halfway out of her bedroom window.

"You better tell that stupid boy to be quiet, if Papa catches you—"

The fourteen year old girl lightly slapped at her twelve year old sister.

"Shhh," she hissed.

The smaller girl sat up in the bed she shared with her sister.

"I'm just saying there are better ways to do this, dummy."

Angela looked at her younger sister and wondered where she got her smarts from, she never remembered being that bright two years ago. As a matter of fact she thought her younger sister Adria was far too bright for *any* age.

"You just shush and let me worry about Albert and Papa," she said as she finally slipped out of bed. She was fully clothed in her Catholic school skirt and white blouse. She didn't bother with a coat as the night had turned warm after the early fall rains had left the valley. She eased herself toward the window and pulled aside the curtain. She smiled when she saw Albert standing beside the Elephant Ear plants, smiling. His gold tooth sparkled in the front porch light. *"Damn,"* she whispered, *Papa left the light on!*

Adria sat up and smiled. Papa wasn't as dumb as Angela thought he was, and if he caught her sister and her eighteen year old boyfriend, eighteen would be the last number of years in life he ever reached.

Little Adria thought the boy was a creepo of the first order and hated the fact that her older sister couldn't see that. As she watched from the bed, Angela eased the window up and with a last look at her, eased her leg up and through the window frame. Then the heavy wooden window eased back down.

Adria looked quickly from the closed window to her bedroom door and then tossed the bed covers aside. She too was fully clothed under her nightgown. It had taken all of her skill to lie in bed next to Angela and not give away that fact by accidentally rubbing up against her, and in their small bed that was amazing in and of itself that her leg braces had gone unnoticed. She quickly pulled her white nightgown off and tossed it on the edge of the bed and then used the bed and wall as a crutch, swinging her legs in an awkward duck-walk to the window, the steel leg braces making it impossible to bend her knees. She eased the curtain back and peeked. *Yechhh,* she thought, Angela was actually kissing that creep!

Angela broke the kiss and pushed Albert Calderon away.

"I told you not to make any noise, do you know how light a sleeper my father is?" she whispered angrily.

"Come on baby, if he came out here I would just have to take care of him," the skinny eighteen year old said patting his back pocket where the familiar outline of his knife comforted him.

"Yeah right, all hundred and twenty pounds of you against the meanest father in Los Angeles, I'd like to see that," she said taking his hand and quickly pulling him away from the small house. They ran across the street and straight into the darkness that was Elysian Park.

Adria made her way easily along the palmetto bushes that lined the outer edges of the park, using her braces and hand crutches as only a lifelong recipient of polio could have. It was easy keeping track of her sister by the loud laughing footfalls through the grass. Adria grimaced as she swung her nonfunctional legs out and then back on the support of the crutches. She didn't like disobeying her sister, but Angela couldn't be expected to look out for herself, she barely made C's and D's in school so shouldn't be expected to know much, not that Adria condemned her for it, as a straight A student, that didn't stop her from adoring her older sister.

She finally had to break free of the bushes when she heard the two veer off into the center of the park toward the picnic tables and small playground. She should be able to stay out of sight if she kept herself in line with the row of brick restrooms the city had just installed. Besides, the park was so dark after the surrounding lights went out at twelve midnight that you could barely see your hand in front of your face.

Angela let Albert go as far as she ever did, stopping him just short of allowing his hand to drift into her panties. Feeling on the outside was alright, she never really considered feeling cotton a sin. Her breasts didn't count, as small as they were she figured the lord would look the other way.

"Oh come on, all you do is tease, I knew I shouldn't have hung out with a broad that was so damn young!" Albert said in his best acting language.

"I am not a tease, you take that back!"

"No, what have you done to make me feel like a man, nothing! You have nothing up there," he said as he lightly slapped her chest, making her wince. "And you won't let me in there," he said coming up short of slapping her crotch. "I should have been with Rosy tonight, she's a woman and would have given me anything."

"I'm only fourteen, what do you want me to do?"

"Hey, fourteen is fourteen, it's plenty old enough," he said as he quickly reached out and snatched at her plaid dress.

Angela closed her legs and tried to slip quickly off of the picnic table but Albert caught her and eased her back onto to it and then partially lay on top of her.

"See how easy it is?" he said as his hand shot up her leg.

"Stop it!" Angela said.

"You don't know it yet, but you're going to thank me for—"

That was as far as he got as two small hands cupped his ears in a double slap from behind. He yelped as the pressure and noise almost burst his eardrums.

"She's only fourteen creepo!" Adria screamed as she started pulling his greasy hair.

Angela quickly rolled out from under him and then tried to get her sister off Albert's back, but it was too late. He reached back and grabbed the small girl by her long hair and pulled her around to face him.

"You little bitch!" he said as he slapped her hard on her cheek. Angela flew into a fury as she watched her little sister strike the bench and fall to the ground, her leg braces clattering on the cement and her crutches flying off her wrists.

"You son of a bitch!" she screamed as she flew at Albert slapping and swinging for all she was worth. She couldn't believe how this was turning out; she thought Albert was the one for her. He picked her out of all the other girls in the neighborhood.

Albert easily pushed her back onto the table top and slapped her twice in quick succession, stunning her. Adria was crying and trying to sit up on the cool grass when Albert placed his foot on her chest and pushed her back down. He pulled the switchblade from his back pocket and the seven inches of steel popped free. He held it in front of Angela's terrified face with his left hand and with his right he quickly punched her with a closed fist, bringing a spurt of blood. He bit his lower lip and bobbed his head up and down twice.

"I'm like my father; I don't like it when I'm disrespected by a woman," he said and then reached up her skirt.

Suddenly he was just not there anymore. Angela felt his hand as it slid roughly up her thigh, and then it was gone. She had felt only a brush of air.

The fallen one, the betrayer of man, had watched the exchange between the girl and boy with mild curiosity. It hadn't moved for the longest time as the scene was played out before him. Its hiding place was high in a palm tree that lined the street and was only a few feet from the house it had seen the three young people leave from. But it hadn't been the two older children that caught its attention; it was the younger one that followed. It tilted its head and sniffed the air. It listened as the leg braces made small, almost imperceptible clicking noises as she hurried along the parks outer edge. It sensed a high degree of intelligence, but also a naiveté about the real world that could be most helpful to its cause.

The beast paced in front of Albert, towering over the boy as its hooves sank into the soft grass around the newly constructed restrooms. It had taken him to the far side and away from the girls. It tilted its large head and looked the boy over. The large lips curled back from its yellowed and brown teeth as it took him in. The ever present pouch hung around its neck and swayed when the beast moved from side to side.

Albert sat and held the small knife out like it could protect him from the evil that paced the ground in front of him. He could swear he could hear the grass sigh and collapse with every step the beast took. His breathing was in automatic and the hardness in his pants all but a distant memory.

Phaltazar turned away and looked toward the sky. The stars were shining bright and it was momentarily distracted by them. It reached up with a hand that spread to a foot and a half across and held it in place as it watched the night sky and the twinkling of the distant worlds that filled it.

Albert slowly moved to his right, sliding on his butt and holding the pitiful knife outward as if it were talisman against the evil that had come to him in the night. The creature merely looked down at him for the briefest of moments and then back toward the distant stars. Then it easily and quickly reached out toward the boy and pinned him in place with a sharp, black cloven hoof, with the movement causing the jingle of metal inside of the pouch. Albert couldn't bring voice to the pain he felt as the hoof cut deeply into his calf. The knife slipped from his hand as he reached toward the searing pain in his leg.

It was at that very moment that the two young girls came around the corner of the restrooms and straight into the nightmare Albert had become the star attraction in. They had originally thought the restrooms would be a point of safety from him, and now they stood wide-eyed at the thing before them.

Phaltazar's head turned from the sky but its massive frame stayed over the prone form of the struggling boy. In the darkness the girls could only see the height of the beast and the searing yellow eyes that held them frozen in place. The long gray hair of the creature was silverish in the starlight as the beast smiled. Both of the girls stood rooted before it, almost assured by the smile and heroic depth the monster placed into their susceptible minds.

"Get…help," Albert whispered in pain, lightly tapping his fist against the hoof that held him pinned to the wet grass.

Angela and Adria ignored him and kept their young eyes on the being before them. They knew it had been this creature, this angel, who had saved them from Albert.

"It's Frankenstein," Adria whispered, blinking her eyes and allowing her smile to truly break free.

"No, it's not a monster…its, it's an…angel," Angela said as the smile on the creature grew as it knew that its power had fooled both girls into believing it was something it was not. The small one however was seeing something different than her older sister and this intrigued the beast beyond measure.

Albert moved and the creature reached down and dug its yellowish-brown claws into his shoulder and lifted him up to a level facing it. It partially opened its mouth and Albert had to turn away as its teeth came into full view. The two large front teeth hung down much further that the rest and they actually curved inward toward each other. The nose was flat and wide and the lips large with the upper drawing itself downward toward the large chin. Albert could feel the heat coming off the beast in waves, but what made him want to scream was the fact that he could see the raw skin of the creature underneath green scales when it moved. He could see faint moonlight filtering through the white and silver hair of his assailant. It coursed down its back and was tied off with a piece of old, brittle leather, forming a long braided pigtail. Then he really felt his mind slipping when the creature chuckled and reached out with its free hand and pulled the two girls toward it, actually patting Adria on the head and nodding at Angela, as if the large beast was consoling her.

The two girls were still smiling twenty minutes later after the quick screams of pain and terror had ended and the creature had finished feeding. Adria had surfaced for a moment in her delusion of safety to know what she had witnessed was a wrong that was fundamentally damning, but the soft lullaby of the beast had pulled her back down into the abyss where it was warm, safe and nothing could ever hurt them again.

Enrique Rodriguez was awakened at four AM by the soft charm of his youngest daughter Adria who had the softest and sweetest voice in the world. He smiled as he opened his eyes, then he quickly realized something was wrong as his wife started screaming from somewhere inside their small house. The soft singing was coming from the darkness outside of his bedroom window and then fading away even further than that as he realized it had all been a dream in his sleeping hours. In his dream he remembered his daughters had come...no, that wasn't right, they had been allowed to come and say goodbye and Adria had sang to him her favorite song.

He started crying, the feeling of immense loss settling in as if a black blanket had been pulled over his soul. He found he had no strength to move as his wife continued to scream from the girl's empty bedroom.

❧ SIX ❧

Von Railing sat in the backseat of the large black Hudson in silence. He noticed every few minutes that the foolish Scotsman would look in the mirror, seemingly studying him to find out his mood.

"The reception was fruitful?" McDougal finally asked.

Von Railing was tempted to let the not so innocent inquiry go unanswered, but decided it wasn't worth the trouble.

"It seems I was fated to meet the very man I was supposed to find. The Master was right on that point."

McDougal looked quickly into the mirror, easily controlling the large car through his peripheral vision.

"This man you sought was at the reception?"

"He signed some papers, typical immigration red tape that allowed us to forego our consulate's security and uneasy questions that would have been asked by their state department, so he being there did not come as a surprise. I even had a rather heated conversation with him about the fool in Germany. But I'm in a quandary as to how this man and his agency have infiltrated the Masters thoughts."

"What kind of man—"

"He's a detective, a contractual policeman," Von Railing answered, cutting off the obvious concerned questions. "He has no real power here, but it is curious that his job would entail the gathering of information, that is the only concern I can possibly think of that would interfere with our visit here. I don't know how *He* plans on using this to our advantage. I sense danger with this man."

"The answer is simple; we remove him if he is that much of a concern."

The German looked at the eyes of the manservant as he watched him through the rearview mirror and shook his head, knowing the Scotsman was probing him for information, for what reason other than cowardly self-preservation he did not know.

"I was told to find out about him, I did. As for killing this man when orders haven't been given to that effect, well, are you prepared to make that decision?"

McDougal turned his attention to the road. No, he wasn't prepared go beyond his orders, just as he knew Von Railing would not either.

"He just may be a curiosity to the Master, possibly something to be used to his advantage in the coming days."

The Hudson drove along Highland Avenue until they came to the private road. The massive car drove between two large eucalyptus trees and entered the twenty-five acre estate of the late silent movie director, D.W. Griffith. The wooden mansion had been empty for ten years and even before that was used only to seal deals for the moving motion picture giant when the need arose for impressing those he needed to finance his projects. The one mile long drive was lined on both sides by juniper and eucalyptus trees that had basically gone bad from neglect. The once finely trimmed lawn had grown old and yellow over the years until the property became so rundown realtors stopped showing it. The giant Redwood mansion was finally purchased by an overseas investor from London three years ago and had only hosted its newest tenants for the past eleven months.

The Hudson's headlights outlined the gravel drive that wound its way in a large upside-down 'U' shape that ran past the front porch and then back toward the mile long drive back out to Highland Avenue. The front porch was massive and lined with very old and crumbling wicker chairs and tables where the once rich and famous silent stars of the twenties sat about drinking and laughing in the summer nights. Now the ghosts of that laughter seemed to echo in the darkness as the Hudson pulled to a stop.

"I'll park the car and…," he started and then stopped just as suddenly.

"What is it?" Von Railing asked as McDougal's eyes locked on the mirror.

"We have company," he said as he reached out and opened the glove compartment and removed a Luger pistol.

"Don't be too hasty with that thing, I'm very capable of handling anything that may arise," the German said as he opened his own door and stepped out.

He waited by the rear fender as a small MG sports car came up the drive. The expensive sport's car crunched through the gravel and came to a stop. The top was down. McDougal had exited the Hudson and stood behind Von Railing with his hands behind his back, hiding the weapon he held there.

As the headlights shut off, Von Railing saw the woman; her black hair was covered with a brightly colored blue scarf to match her dress. She sat for a moment and stared at both men. Von Railing made no move toward the small car; instead he reached up and untied his black tie and the top button of his shirt.

The woman's laughter touched the sudden darkness around them.

"Does that fool of a manservant of yours intend to shoot me?" the Countess Francesca D'Sarcuni asked as she opened her door outward and placed first one beautifully formed leg and then slowly placed the other firmly on the ground and then demurely held her hand out.

Von Railing said; "Put the car away and check on things."

McDougal sneered and turned and tossed the Luger into the open car door and then followed it and moved the car away toward the back of the house. Von Railing stepped forward and looked at the woman a moment and then took her hand and yanked her up unceremoniously.

"Oooh, so rough," she said as she landed hard against his chest.

"Did you enjoy yourself tonight my dear?" he asked, looking into her bright and unnaturally green eyes. They looked at him with an inner fire, as if they were back lighted.

"I haven't danced so much in a lifetime. Why, were you jealous?" she asked as she raised her right hand and ran a finger along his strong jaw line.

"With that fool of a husband watching you like a falcon you succeeded nicely in making a whore's spectacle out of yourself," he said raising his left brow and quickly pulling her probing fingers away.

"We are European, it is expected that we have rather...advanced morals," she said as she again raised her fingers and ran them along his lips. "Besides, wasn't it you who practically ordered me to be friendly to these stupid people?"

"Not to the extent that you cause gossip where your loving husband is concerned," again he brushed her fingers away. "Speaking of that fat little fool, where did you leave him?"

This time Francesca took a step backward and looked at him angrily, her eyes growing brighter for a split-second before they calmed. Von Railing's blue eyes were holding at a steady, barely subdued brightness of their own.

"I left him in the capable hands of three Los Angeles police captains and three deputy sheriffs of the County, at least I believe that's what they are called, you would know better than I."

"Then he is making the final payments to the officialdom of this city and county?"

"Yes," she said as she held his eyes.

Von Railing stepped forward and slapped her hard across the face, not once, but twice. She turned her head back and looked at him with no emotion, but her breathing came in ever increasingly hard, short gasps.

"And not a single indignant protest my dear?"

"I am assuming you will give me your reason in your own time," she said as a woman would after being stroked someplace other than her face. She wiped her mouth with the fingers of her gloved right hand and then looked at the smear of blood on the satin. She closed her eyes as she removed the gloves and tossed them inside the car. Then she wiped her mouth again, taking away more blood from the fast healing wound.

"This Dalhart, I don't believe in coincidence. There is a factor here we don't understand, and what's unnerving me is the fact that I don't believe the Master understands the connection either. And you pick that exact moment to show him your whorish ways with the help of that actor, Mr. Cooper."

"My whorish ways being?" she asked calmly.

"The way—"

"Go ahead; say it you fool, the way I looked at him."

"Steer clear of this Dalhart. Seduce all the actors you wish, but stay away from the detective, is that clear? We were just supposed to find him and observe. I will handle any conceived threat," he looked toward the house, "or *He* will."

The Countess looked at the darkened and rundown mansion. Just knowing *He* was in there made her cringe. She lowered her eyes.

Von Railing watched her and then slowly raised her right hand to his mouth and kissed her fingers, lightly smearing the blood she had wiped from her mouth over his lips. Then he grabbed her shoulders and kissed her mouth, sucking her lips and kissing her. She reciprocated and grabbed his hair and pulled him in even harder. His polished shoes scraped through the gravel and then first his feet, and then the Countesses, lightly lifted free of the ground. Her blue sequined dress brushed against the open door of the small sports scar as they rose to five feet, and then he pulled back and they settled to the ground once more. He roughly grabbed her left breast and she hissed as pleasure shot through her body.

Von Railing kissed her neck and bit, drawing a small amount of blood. Then he yanked hard on her hair, freeing it from the pins restraining it. It flowed down to the center of her back as she leaned away, allowing him to take what was needed from her.

A moment later they heard footsteps as McDougal approached from the back of the house. Von Railing closed his eyes and pulled the Countess toward him, practically hiding her body in front of him.

"What is it?" he asked, angered at being disturbed.

"The outside cellar door was open."

The German let go of the Countess. She stumbled away against the car, weakened from his embrace. She held a hand to her forehead until the dizziness went away.

"He went out? What about the girls?" he asked.

"I don't know, and I'm bloody well not about to go down there and find out either," McDougal answered in his Scottish brogue.

"You fool, if they get out they will attract attention," he hissed as he quickly turned and ran up the broad wooden steps and to the large double doors at the front of the house. He turned the ornate glass knob and quickly entered.

McDougal's eyes went from Von Railing's retreating form to that of the Countess.

"Interrupt something, did I?" he asked.

Francesca had placed the scarf over her loosened hair and had mostly recovered from the feeding of Von Railing.

"Careful my little maggot, someday you will surely overstep your bounds," she said as she took a menacing step toward the tall and powerfully built Scotsman. Then she suddenly opened her mouth and hissed, exposing teeth that had grown overly large and sharp. The suddenness of the threat making McDougal stumble backward. He recovered quickly and then turned and ran for the back of the house.

The Countess Francesca D'Sarcuni laughed as she brought her feelings *and* fangs back under control. She watched him round the corner of the house, and then she turned back to face the front door where Von Railing had disappeared inside. She cringed at the thought of following him in there. She never envied the German's liaisons with Phaltazar; nothing could make her do that, the power *He* allowed Von Railing was not worth the horror of being that close to it.

She knew it would get her killed if she was ever observed doing it, but she crossed herself with the catholic triumvirate anyway and then turned and entered the MG and quickly left the property.

Von Railing waited at the subbasement door. He had sent McDougal to his quarters on the first floor. It was well past three AM when he heard the outer basement door close and the heavy footsteps on the wooden stairs. He swallowed and listened.

"I know you are there, German," sounded the deep voice through the door. The beast spoke in Aramaic, the dead tongue.

Von Railing took an involuntary step backward. He turned and wanted to retrace his steps back up the basement stairs, but caught himself.

"This Dalhart, I met him tonight," he said instead of running.

Suddenly the door opened as if it had never been closed. Von Railing took another step back until his polished shoes struck the first step of the basement stairs. He steeled himself against the death smell from below and stepped forward through the door and into the blackness beyond. He again used his left hand to guide himself down the steps, as he went his unnatural eyesight adjusted to the darkness of the subbasement until what he was seeing was a horrid shade of green and grays, near to the vision of a cat. His mind eased as he finally caught sight of the earthen floor below. Thankfully none of the Master's girls were in sight.

"It truly must mean that I am destined to meet this man in some manner," the voice said from deep in the basement. "What of the Indian?"

"He wasn't present at the reception, just Dalhart."

"Tell me of him."

"He is but a man," he said as he advanced slowly into the basement, but stopped when he saw the legs of the first of the girls. He needed not to see the rest of the poor thing. She was sitting on the dirt, he could see her hands playing with the hem of her torn dress and he averted his eyes quickly.

"I was close to finding the red man this night, but he awoke and I lost him. I suspect Dalhart interfered somehow. As a curiosity, I must know why this man is so intriguing to me. And just what role he will play in the days ahead."

"Does it not worry my Lord that this savage acquaintance of Dalhart's has the ability to come unbidden to your home? And you spoke of using this man somehow, I believe it is—"

"YOU BELIEVE? It is what I believe that is of greater importance! Has your once-upon-a-time kind ever been a threat to me? No, it is this Red Man that holds this Dalhart in high regard, not I. I could easily destroy them both. But I find the nightly visitations by this American Shaman to be most amusing. He is a delightful linguist and actually challenges me. He fears me, the unknown, but is not afraid."

"This Dalhart is a detective, not a policeman, whom by the way we will not have any trouble from thanks to our donations."

"Excellent, the Italian and his wife is worth the treasure we waste on them then?"

"Yes, the authorities all have dreams of Avarice here; there is enough greed to go around. But this Dalhart and his friend the Indian, it concerns me. American's have a firm belief in heroes and this detective strikes me as such, at least morally speaking."

Laughter split the darkness in two and Von Railing felt the air part before him as the creature made its way toward the spot where he was standing with the jangling of coin in the pouch, a sound that always brought chills to the German. He was soon looking up into the yellow eyes of Phaltazar.

"He is a man, yes?" the beast asked as he lowered his head until it was eye to eye with Von Railing. The smell of blood and death was expelled in a hot invisible mist.

"Yes, my Lord."

"You did not sense the ancient ones in him, the Arch's?"

"No," Von Railing said as he flinched away from those eyes and that smell.

"A man, a hero, the two words have no meaning in the context in which you use them, unless he is schooled in the ways of the ancients, he could never be a threat to me."

The German placed his hand over his mouth until his gorge settled and then turned to face his master.

"If not he, the Indian?" he managed to ask.

"He is a curiosity as I said, nothing more," it said as it reached out a large hand toward Von Railing. It pulled his arm down away from his mouth and stared into his eyes. "Do I still frighten you my old friend?"

"You are my Master and I obey, and…of course you frighten me," he answered as arrogantly as he could.

"Good, still, maybe you need reminding from time to time why I rule the night on this world," it said as it patted Von Railing on the shoulder, the long claws cold through his tuxedo jacket. "I need the Scotsman to bring down food and water…no, not water, milk and make the food something a girl child of this country would like. I have finally found the last piece of the puzzle, our time here is nearly finished and then we can return home."

"I don't—"

"YOU never need understand; you need to follow instructions."

"Yes, my lord," he said as he turned away.

He climbed three steps and then was stopped by a small, melodic voice from somewhere in the deep blackness of the basement.

"Jesus loves the little children, all little children of the world..."

Von Railing hesitated for the briefest of moments as the soft singing voice of a small child sent chills up his spine, then he quickly went up the stairs and with every step he took he felt his masters yellow eyes on him, following him with amusement.

Phaltazar watched the German leave, its yellow eyes never leaving his back as he retreated up the stairs. Meanwhile it tilted its head and listened to the melodic voice of the girl as she sang and the beast smiled. She was undoubtedly singing to her older sister, but she wasn't hearing anything any longer. The King of Darkness turned back toward the end of the cellar and watched as his girls all stood as one and crowded around it. He placed loving hands on them and watched as they in turn caressed his legs and held his large hands. He brushed hair away from dead eyes and smiled, baring teeth that were filthy and yellowed with age. All the while the small child sang as she looked closely at the blank stare of her dead sister. Tears stung her eyes as she wiped first one and then the other. Deep in her dream state she knew her older sister wasn't hearing her favorite song and the fact she would never hear anything again.

SEVEN

The conference room was quiet as Stevie passed around the morning's first cups of coffee. Pete Sanchez and Willis Jackson were the only ones that were wide-eyed and well rested on this early Saturday morning. Talbot Leonard was dreary faced because he had hooked up with some old columnist friends of his and had a late night. Stevie had been bumming around the strip and had gotten chased by zoot-suiters who hadn't taken too kindly to him when he insulted their clothing choice and hadn't made it back to his block until three that morning. Frank Wiechek had fallen asleep on Liz Wheeler's front steps after begging to be let in most of the night. Sam watched Rainbird yawn, knowing full well his drug-induced sleep of the night before hadn't done him one ounce of good.

"Okay, so everyone has their notes and where they'll start. At this point I want nothing set aside, even the obvious runaways that have already shown up back at home. I want them called and questioned about anything untoward that may have happened during their time in Los Angeles and Hollywood. Talbot, was there anything on the morning press wire?"

Talbot Leonard stood and rubbed his temple with his right hand and then opened a large manila folder that sat before him. His usual impeccable bow tie was askew.

"There is this one item out of Elysian Park. Late last night it was reported that two young girls were taken from their home at approximately one thirty AM. A police report was filed by the girl's parents. Also it seems there was a homicide in the park last night at about the same time as the girl's disappearance. Don't know yet if there's a link. Elysian Park as you know has always been a favorite dumping ground for the recently departed," he said as he tapped his pipe stem on the yellow note he had written down in the file.

Sam waited for Talbot to sit down.

"Pete, Willis, after you get done checking the blotters at the precincts I want you to take a run out to Elysian Park and check it out, see if maybe you can get in and talk with the parents," he looked at Talbot, "Rodriguez was the name?"

Talbot nodded his head slowly affirming the last name of the parents. "Be delicate Pete, but see if there's anything that could help us, the younger of the two sisters was a polio victim," Talbot said as he shook his head.

Willis and Pete both wrote the name in their notebooks.

Sam was watching Rainbird who was staring at the table top. Then he wrote something quickly on his note pad and slid it over to Sam.

In my dream, one of the newer elements were I stumbled over several sets of leg braces in that black hell hole.

Sam looked from the note to John, and then looked up at Pete and Willis.

"I know you may not make it out there before dark, but get it done. Now, we'll create a big board here in the conference room, Stevie, if he can add and subtract correctly will keep tabs on what's found out. We'll begin to get a handle on what's happening numbers-wise. Stevie get a map of the city and start marking the areas where the girls are disappearing from, or where they were last seen, the boys will be phoning in their findings from the police precincts, also—"

The phone buzzed. Rainbird seemed to come out of his stupor and reached down and depressed the switch. "Yes," he said with his eyes closed.

"Mr. Rainbird, Adolph Menjou is insisting on seeing either you or Sam," Liz subdued voice said over the intercom.

"Give us just a moment, Liz," Rainbird said and then switched off the intercom.

"Okay, let's find something out so our friend here can get some sleep, and be careful, we don't know what we're dealing with."

The others stood to go and Rainbird stood and removed his suit jacket from the rack behind him and put it on. Sam stood and walked to the door and heard arguing outside. He quickly opened the door and saw Liz physically holding back a smallish man with a pencil thin moustache. Sam recognized him from a hundred different movies. Adolph Menjou was a highly sought after character actor of the first order. Always playing the feisty manager or newspaper editor or sidekick, but right now it looked as if he were just plain feisty. Liz was having a hard time holding him at bay.

"I told you, they will call when they are ready to see you," she said as she tugged on his arm. Behind them a woman stood by the inner office door twisting her small handbag into knots.

"Whoa, it's alright Liz, let him come in," Sam said as he straightened his coat. He looked from the small actor to the simply dressed woman behind him. His eyes lingered on her for a split-second longer than he wanted and it looked as if she noticed and took offense.

Menjou shot Liz a quick and dismissive dirty look and straightened his coat, then he looked at Sam and started asking rapid fire questions.

"You Dalhart?"

"Yes I am, this is my partner, John Rainbird," Sam said quickly.

"Yep, you're the one. I was told you had an Indian for a partner, no offense young man, I have nothing against Indians mind you," he said holding his hand up to John.

"No offense taken," John said as he held the conference room door open.

"Names, Menjou, Adolph Menjou, and I am not unheard of in this town, perhaps I am familiar to you?" he asked as he quickly brushed passed them and into the conference room.

The woman smiled and nodded, but found the effort too great and ceased immediately as she followed Menjou into the conference room. Sam looked at Rainbird and lightly shook his head.

"Yes, sir, I've enjoyed many of your movies," Sam said as he pulled out a chair for the young woman.

"That just thrills me to no end young man, I'm happy I make you happy," he said shaking his head. "Gentleman, I must apologize, in my anger and excitement I have been unbearably rude, may I introduce Miss Constance Yale, of Davenport, Iowa, I believe she likes to be called Connie, but then again I could be wrong I just met her yesterday."

The brunette blinked and nodded her head. Sam looked at her and smiled and Rainbird creased his brow, he was getting a sense from her that he couldn't pin down, it wasn't shyness, it was outrage, not for anything happening here, but general outrage at some circumstance or another.

"What can we do for you?" Sam asked as he sat at the head of the table. "May we offer you some coffee?"

"No time Dalhart, no time. Look, you come highly recommended by…well, by folks in town that make far more money than myself, not that I'm poor mind you. They said if you have a problem go to the Sunset Detective Agency. Well, here we are, we have a problem and the goddamn police don't seem very damn concerned about it."

Sam pulled over a yellow legal pad and took his fountain pen out and unscrewed the cap.

"Now, before we hear what you have to say, I must inform the both of you that we have a rather lengthy case pending that we're handling at the moment and may not be able to offer assistance to you as fast as you may like," John said, looking from Menjou, the woman and then finally at Sam. He felt pressed to keep his friend on track about what was currently important.

"Well, surprise, surprise," Menjou said glaring at Rainbird. "Exactly what the damned police said, I should have known better," he suddenly stood and reached for Miss Yale's arm. "Come on Connie, I guess these jokers are as unconcerned about missing girls as the coppers are."

"Girls?" Rainbird asked quickly, half-rising from his chair but then settling back as he tried to gain a measure of control.

"Yes, my sister and Mr. Menjou's niece, a week apart," Constance Yale said, in her country voice while gently easing Adolph Menjou's hand free of her arm.

"Mr. Menjou, please sit back down," Sam said, eyeing John.

"Then you'll at least hear what we have to say before you tell us not to be too worried like the cop's did?" he asked while easing himself back into his seat.

"Are you two related in some way?" Sam asked.

"Related?" Menjou asked, then he looked at Miss Yale, "Oh, you mean us? No, we met yesterday at the Hollywood precinct, where we tried in vain to make out missing person's reports."

"And they wouldn't take your reports?" John asked.

"Didn't I already say that, we're wasting time here gentlemen, I'm missing my young niece and Connie here is missing a sister, and the Los Angeles Police Department, the LA County Sheriff, nor the Beverly Hills Police seem to give a damn about it," Menjou said and then reached out and took the young woman's hand. "And we're worried that something's happened to them, Dalhart, Gable say's you fella's are the ones to see, I hope to God he's right."

Sam didn't respond, he looked at Constance Yale and then at Menjou, he leaned over and wrote on his legal pad while Rainbird watched him.

"We'll accept your case as we're working on a similar file," he looked up at John, "for a friend."

Rainbird smiled and pulled his own writing pad over and wrote down the names of their new clients, grateful Sam was willing to throw their case in with the rest.

Sam reached out and pushed the large button on the intercom.

"Yes," Liz's electronic voice asked from the reception area.

"Liz, draw up two Pro Bono case contracts for a Miss Constance Yale and Mr. Menjou please."

"Yes, Sam."

"Listen here Dalhart, I'm no charity case, I will render expenses for both Miss Yale and myself and a sizable bonus for any results garnered from your investigation," Menjou said indignantly.

"If indeed you have heard of our agency Mr. Menjou, you would know we never take missing persons cases, but this…this is something special as we do investigate crimes against children and we never charge our standard fee for those cases, no matter what the wealth is of the initiating party," Rainbird said as he stood and went to get more coffee. "Now, as soon as our office manager joins us, we will need a complete and detailed report on your niece and Miss Yale's sister, everything, habits, good and bad, problems of any kind, even their deepest secrets if you know them."

"You mentioned that you were working on a similar case, may I ask if it involves a young woman?" Constance asked.

When no answer came immediately she stood and walked over to the small table where Stevie usually sat and poured herself a glass of water and before taking a drink she closed her eyes and without turning asked; "These things don't usually turn out very well do they? I mean even if they're alive," she lowered her head, "They could still be in trouble, I mean, serious trouble?"

Sam laid his pen down and looked at the woman's back. He knew exactly what she was asking. Young girls who came up missing sometimes disappeared because expectations weren't met in the way that they had hoped, and they may have fallen in with the wrong people with prostitution and blue movies being two of the many pitfalls for young women in Los Angeles. But how could he tell this woman or Menjou that at the moment, even those awful scenarios was wishful thinking. The statistics from the past year was proof enough to himself, even without Rainbird's strange stories about nightly visitations that something out of the ordinary was happening in the city. But all he could do was stand and place his arm around Connie Yale and lead her back to her chair. He sat on the table just to her right and looked at her until her eyes met his own. He smiled.

"I promise you, if she's in this town we'll find her," he looked over at Menjou, "your niece also, I have the best detectives in Los Angeles here and they get results."

Menjou swallowed and finally removed his hat. "Thank you, Sally is my only niece and she's been missing for three weeks."

"Jeannie, that's my sister's name, she's headstrong, like me I guess," Connie said sipping from the glass of water. "She never wanted to stay at home and tend to the farm, I guess I never really did either, but it seemed the longer we worked at it, the longer I could keep her near me," she sat the glass down and accepted the handkerchief from Sam. "I despise women who cry over spilt milk, but it was like I pushed her right out the goddamn door."

"We all wish we had certain things we could get a second chance at, but what I need you to do is make sure you tell Miss Wheeler everything, okay?" he said patting her on the shoulder.

Liz entered the conference room right on cue and smiled and gave Sam the two contracts, the smile never reached her eyes because they were busy asking how she was supposed to run this office if they turned away clients and gave everyone who walked in a Pro Bono free ride. When Sam smiled back she gave up on her silent accusation and sat down and started taking the two statements.

Sam walked over and stood next to Rainbird as he was looking out at the overcast morning. People on Sunset were again busily going on their way without a care in the world outside of their normal lives.

"Look, I need you fresh and bright-eyed in the next few days, so why don't you head to your office and get some sleep."

Rainbird watched a young girl below with a suitcase struggle with it while crossing the street, he wanted to slide the window up and yell at the top of his lungs to get the hell back to where she came from, that Los Angeles was no place for decent girls, but instead he shrugged his shoulders and turned away and made his apologies to the two new clients and left the conference room.

Sam took a deep breath and continued to look out at the morning rush. He listened to Menjou describe his niece to the dictating Liz but it was just a drone. He finally tuned and was taken back when he noticed Miss Yale looking at him. He watched as she stood and walked toward him.

"Now that I have gotten that womanly cry out of my system, I want you to know that I'm not like others who fall to pieces over every little happening that doesn't correspond to my daily routine."

"I would say a missing sister is enough of a happening for you to let out a little emotion, hell, we all do it, some in that way—"

"I don't cry, I just wanted you to know that," she said, cutting him off. "Now, would you like to volunteer the reasons why you and your quiet partner are so concerned about my sis and Mr. Menjou's niece?" she asked. "I'm no ditzy farm girl, Mr. Dalhart. I graduated from Columbia University with a degree in journalism. I only came home after my parents were killed to raise my little sister, so I know how to read between, beneath and around the lies and half-truths of newspapers, so just how many girls are missing in this damnable town?"

Sam tried not to show his surprise at how easily this woman had read Rainbird and himself or how easily the curse cruised from between those set lips. Obviously she was far beyond that of a woman who fed chickens, slapped the asses of cows and repaired fences for a living.

"Just be sure to give Miss Wheeler all the information you can about…Jeannie, wasn't it?"

The left eyebrow of Constance Yale went up and she stared at Sam for the briefest of moments and then quickly turned away and returned to her chair. She didn't look back up, but Sam saw her jaw muscles working beneath her beautiful face. He would have to be careful as he suspected this woman was very resourceful and that required respect as he didn't need relatives getting in the way of what was beginning to look like a very strange case.

Stevie was talking in hushed tones with Tess who was listening absent mindedly while typing up Pete and Willis's final report on the Chaplin surveillance. Her chewing gum bubbles grew larger by the second as Stevie was blathering on about how he needed more excitement in his day to day routine. He shushed and straightened when Adolph Menjou exited the office area with his hat in his hand and acted as though the two weren't even there as he headed for the double doors.

"Boy, he looks just like he does in the movies," Tess said as she placed her head on both hands and watched as Menjou left.

"Yeah, I never pays no attention to stuff like dat," Stevie said.

"Don't you have something you should be doing? If the dragon lady comes out here, then we've both had it."

"Me? You's bet I have things to do, Mr. Dalhart and Mr. Rainboyd, they have me checkin' out the neighborhood, you's know, snoopin' around, seein' if anybody seen anythin' suspicious like."

"Then you better go about it then, and you may want to pick up a dictionary on your way out, you's nose, to like learn how's ta talk," Tess said mockingly and then blowing an even larger bubble and then allowing it to pop in Stevie's face.

Stevie pushed his cap forward on his head and looked long and hard at the receptionist and then made for the door.

"I's tink I has pretty good dictionary as it is, no's body else seem's to be complainin.'"

Tess watched him leave and smiled. Despite the way he spoke and the ridiculous way he idolized Rainbird and Sam, he was alright, she knew if the chips were down she would rather be with him than any other boy their age.

Stevie closed the door and looked back through the opaque glass. He heard Tess start typing again. He stood and listened for a moment and then shoved his hands into his pockets and turned for the stairs. He knew he could never impress her enough for her to want to see a movie with him, but he kept hoping. Her words always stung him more than he let on. He decided right then he would stop and get a dictionary, that would show her, or at least he could carry it around with him in her presence to show he was trying.

He reached the stairs and started down while whistling a Benny Goodman tune he would never really know the name of, as he did, a tall man stepped from the shadows of the empty office across the way. The stranger had used the ornate doorway for concealment. When he was sure the clump of Stevie's tennis shoes was not hesitating on the way down, he looked at the door that marked the Sunset Detective Agency. He wrote down the suite number just under the address he had written down earlier. Thus far he had counted at least nine employees of the agency, not counting two others that may or may not be clients.

Ralls McDougal closed his black notebook and started for the stairs himself. Von Railing had ordered him to find out where the Sunset Detective Agency was and how many agents were in Dalhart's employ. When McDougal asked why this was so important the German watched the shade of the overcast morning turn lighter from his upstairs bedroom. He turned away when a momentary flicker of sun appeared above the low lying mountains before it was swallowed by the dark clouds that smothered the valley. He looked at the servant and said simply; "Know thy enemy."

∾ EIGHT ∾

The girls hadn't come for him as they had the other hundreds of times he had entered the subbasement, but of course he had never ventured into the dreamscape during daylight hours. As he stood there in the darkness that seemed to enter through the very pores of his skin—invading and corrupting his soul like a cancerous residue—he realized inside the dream that he never took afternoon naps. That is until today. He remembered lying down on the couch in his office, falsely promising himself that he would only close his eyes for a moment and then stop shamming and join his field agents in their search for information on these very girls he now saw sitting, lining the dank walls of the basement. Their lifeless legs sprawled outward in the fine powder of the dirt floor. But as they say, the best laid plans of mice and Indian's. He assumed he was sound and deeply asleep on his office sofa, undoubtedly snoring.

Rainbird closed his eyes and tried to will himself awake. When he opened them he saw the girls, still sitting motionless, but still looking right at him. The smell was getting worse if that was at all possible. It seemed even more death had been added to the collection already in the basement as the smell of fresh blood mixed with that of the old, and overpowering all was the odor of rotting flesh.

As he looked to his right and the lit candles that seemed to be placed before the flapping newspaper articles as sort of an altar to god knows what, he saw that another, even larger headline had been added to the group already there. He took a tentative step toward the wall and the scraps of flapping paper as the thought struck him that these may be a key, possibly something that could shed light on what was happening to him and the city.

"This is an unusual time for a visit Red Man."

Rainbird again closed his eyes but couldn't help the soft moan that escaped his mouth. His right foot was still inches off the floor and all thought of investigating the makeshift scrapbook on the wall flew from his mind.

He forced open his eyes when he heard the singing. The Sunday school song had been taught to him back home on the reservation, as had almost every kid in the country. It had once been a favorite of the young naïve Indian child that had been Johnny Rainbird, but now the song seemed distant and dark, almost as dark as the ground he found himself on. The child's voice was very melodic and he felt his consciousness slip deeper into the nightmare or, day-mare as this instance was proving to be.

"You never cease to surprise me Shaman. Is it the fact I have," he paused looking for the right word, "difficulties in the light of God's sun, or was your coming here pure chance?"

Rainbird felt light footsteps through the soles of his own shoes. The packed earthen floor transmitted the footsteps even though he knew it was normally impossible to do so. As he looked into the blackness of the subbasement he saw a figure of a young girl, and then a smaller shape emerged from the darkened corner to join the first. This child was the one softly singing *Jesus Loves the Little Children*. The taller of the two had her hand on the child's shoulder and was either being led, or guiding her toward the dim candle light. They stopped just four feet from John as the child continued singing. He looked them over and was surprised to see that they weren't in the same condition as the others that were dead and decaying around them. The small girl was actually smiling. It was a warm smile and for it being there in such a cold place amazed Rainbird. The older girl, young woman actually, seemed to have an injury to her lower neck but other than that bruised and reddened mark she seemed unhurt. She was also smiling softly as she pulled the young girl closer to her, making the child almost stumble due to the awkward leg braces she was wearing. They were both alive but their minds were on vacation as he took in both lovely girls.

"The girl child has a heavenly voice does she not, Red Man? I'm afraid her older sister's heart could not stand the shock of truth and has joined my other girls in oblivious slumber. But this one is strong and will act as her protector while they are in my house. At least until she truly awakens to her reality."

"Protector?" John forced the question past his lips while watching the taller of the two girls looking at him with an almost imperceptible gleam of hope in her eyes. Her arm stayed around the young Spanish girl, but John could see her blue eyes dart left and right every few seconds as if her trance, or was it transformation, were somehow incomplete.

"The others, Shaman, you know their touch, even this small one's sister will come for her if she is not watched and protected. The older woman child I took in the rain, one of those lost children the world has no time for. She has a strong mind, good stock I believe you would call her lineage; I may free her with the child."

"Why are they alive, why are they different?"

"The answer is one you could never understand, so do not attempt to question. Does the taller, older child seem familiar to you...Rainbird?" the voice asked, saying John's name for the first time.

He looked closely at the young woman. Her torn dress, the nylons that had been torn and had run's traveling the length of her long legs, her

Auburn hair, unkempt but still in some semblance of organization. But it was the girl's eyes, the shape of her face. *Yes*, he thought, *she was familiar. Did he know this young woman?*

"Your hesitation is indeed answer enough Shaman. It is a curious thing, when I took this one on a rainy night not many days ago, I sensed something in her, a road perhaps, as if her journey and mine own would be linked in some way. The same feeling that brought you to me undoubtedly."

"I feel as if you kidnap me every night. I've no desire to be here."

"But that is not the truth. Perhaps at first your feelings were of that mind, but now you seek information. I believe you and your supposed savior Dalhart are planning to make war upon me?" the voice laughed and as it did Rainbird felt the creature come closer, standing just outside of the flickering candle light as it moved with the clinging of metal from the pouch hanging from its thick neck. *"I will warn you my native friend, I have been made war upon many times in my many years, but I have yet to be harmed, does your Dalhart have the mettle? Do you?"*

"Why have you taken these girls?" he finally asked.

"Because that is what I do Shaman, it is my curse if you will."

"Why are you cursed?"

"Do not bother with your meager attempt to understand the mind and works of God; he most assuredly doesn't care for that, and his ways are far beyond your understanding. Just be it known I have set in motion in other parts of the world His children's downfall. The age of reason will soon be at an end, Shaman."

Rainbird felt the smaller child as she struggled forward on her leg braces with the help of the older girl. She stepped up to him and lightly touched his leg. The older girl took his large hand in hers.

"You seem a beacon to my two children. Should I be jealous, or at the very least, envious, I wonder?"

"Can I take these girls away from here?" John asked, watching the darkness but pulling the two girls in closer to his cold body.

There was silence for a full minute and John could swear the darkness swirled before his eyes.

"*I must ponder this offer,*" the creature said as it came closer, enough so that for the first time Rainbird got a sense of its size. It towered over him as it pushed the fetid air aside.

Suddenly the girls lining the wet and mildewed walls started standing, some had a hard time making the attempt and fell over as their bones and rotted flesh were not giving them the support they needed. Others started crawling. The young child at John's side stopped singing but continued humming the familiar Sunday school song, then she stopped completely as her head turned and saw the horrid shapes starting to gain their feet. The older girl actually took a step to John's left and shied away from the dead girls now eyeing all three of them hungrily.

"*Ah, my two conscious children, they sense protection from you, Red Man, I am truly jealous. My other children are so very hard to control, and as you saw fit to visit me in the sunlit hours, I have so little power over them.*"

John felt his feet grow heavy, actually feeling his Florsheim shoes sinking into the hard packed dirt. He knew for some reason that he couldn't understand that he wouldn't be able to move. He gently eased the two girls behind him and then gave them both a gentle shove. They went wordlessly to the far wall with the taller girl assisting the smaller one in a step and then stop motion, while John alone faced the horror coming their way.

"*You must know I have no power to harm you in your dream state, but if you believe I can't reach you, my Red niggar, you are very mistaken. I have killed, and killed, until I've had to lie down tired from the killing. Spilling the blood of innocents and so fatigued by the taking of their lives. Now it is time to show you some of my power!*"

John closed his eyes as the dead girls started reaching for him. He then opened his eyes and tried to push the first of them away but found the weight on his arms were like that of barbells. His arms couldn't rise above his belt as the girls grabbed him and started pawing at his clothing.

"*Now to let Dalhart and yourself know that the task before you will not be an easy one, I want you to scream Red Man—Scream!*"

John had the smell of the decomposing girls curling into his nostrils, invading his mouth. He actually felt the skin on one young woman's fingers slide away as she grabbed for his belt and missed, then she reached with white, shining bone and curled the fingers through the black leather and pulled. Another reached for his face as others grabbed his legs and held him even more firmly in place.

"Scream! I want Dalhart to wake you, Shaman. Scream you accursed man!"

Sam was holding the door open for Connie as she and Liz stood before him. He had promised to update her twice a day about anything they found out about her little sister.

"You're staying at the Roosevelt?" he asked.

"Yes, room 404," she said searching his eyes as she spoke, "You can reach me anytime, Mr. Dalhart, *anytime*," she said again with emphasis as she held out her hand.

Sam smiled and took her small hand in his own. Liz was curious to see her boss's eyes take in the young woman and stay there for a moment longer than was necessary. She was starting to turn away when the reception room door opened and Charlie Chaplin burst in quickly. He was soon followed by a winded Douglas Fairbanks. They were both dressed in tennis whites consisting of long pants and white shoes. Even without his famous moustache to identify him, Connie's mouth fell open with recognition of Chaplin. Her hand actually squeezed Sam's hard at the sudden appearance of Hollywood's most familiar face.

"Mr. Chaplin, you know the rules of this office, you have to—"

Chaplin held a hand up toward Liz cutting her words short of their inevitable destination of office policy.

"Sam, that monster that calls himself a Special Agent, or private investigator, that Purvis fellow, he came to Doug's house, *his house,* and accused me of the most awful, horrible acts!"

"Charlie, hold on," Sam said, finally releasing Connie's hand, "slow down," then he saw the way Doug Fairbanks was leaning against the wall, he was sweating and he was trying to loosen the top button on his white shirt. "Doug, are you alright?" he asked as he pushed by Chaplin and took the elder actor by the arm.

"Oh my, Douglas!" Charlie said as he finally noticed the condition of his friend. He too went to his friend's aid.

"Gentlemen, please, there are women present. I am fine I assure you," Fairbanks replied as he stood straighter but looked none the better.

"Liz get some water," Sam said as he started to lead the former silent star toward the conference room. As he did the most horrible, gut wrenching scream anyone of them had ever heard froze them all in place.

Liz dropped her steno pad and Connie brought her hands up to her mouth. Fairbanks grabbed Charlie and Charlie likewise took a firmer hold on Fairbanks. Sam immediately shot through the gathered circle of people and ran down the hall toward Rainbird's office. Frank Wiechek, having heard the commotion from the reception area raced through the door and was pushed forward by Liz.

"Go with Sam," she ordered loudly.

Sam reached the door and turned the brass knob and pushed. Rainbird was still screaming as if he were on fire inside of the office. Sam started through the door when it suddenly sprung back on him, tossing him into the hallway where he struck the wall and fell to the floor. As he slid down the wall he would have sworn in a court of law he saw a large shadow through the opaque glass that held the gold lettering that spelled out; *John Rainbird-Lead Investigator.* Frank Wiechek went to his knees and helped Sam to his feet.

"What in the hell is going on in there, boss?" he asked with his eyes wide.

Sam acted as though he hadn't heard the question as he quickly rose and reached for the door handle once more, grabbing it before he came all the way upright. He turned the knob again and pushed, this time the door only gave an inch or two before he felt a wood-cracking impact against it, and then the door slammed closed once again, this time amidst John's screaming both men heard a deep laugh emanate from the interior of the office.

"Help me damn it," he shouted at Frank.

Chaplin, seeing his friend's predicament and hearing those horrible screams, released Fairbanks and ran to help open the door. He reached out just as Sam and Frank succeeded in pushing it open a foot. Charlie added his weight behind theirs and the door opened wider. Just as it did Sam was able to get a partial glimpse inside the office. He saw Rainbird laying prone on his leather sofa, but what was amazing in the brief glimpse was the fact that he was fighting to get up and off of his back, and Sam could actually see his white shirt being pulled this way and that as if something, or someone unseen were holding him in place.

"What the hell?" Sam said loudly as the door started to close against their best efforts.

"Oh my goodness, there is something in there with him!" Chaplin said loudly as he stepped backward, bumping into the white faced Douglass Fairbanks, who despite his obvious illness came to assist the three men in their attempts to gain access to the room.

As the door slowly closed against the best efforts of Sam and Frank, they both looked up in time to see the same shadow that Sam had seen a moment before. It was enormous in size and misshapen in ways neither man could guess at.

"John, wake up!" Sam shouted through the open space.

Another scream of not frustration, but of pure terror emanated from the office.

"Come gentlemen, we must double the effort to gain entry," Fairbanks shouted. His words were heard and they immediately rammed the door again, opening it to three feet. "Again gentlemen," Doug said loudly, taking charge just like he had in his old swashbuckling days of silent film adventure.

Just as they pushed at the door with renewed effort, the window at the doors center smashed outward, striking the four men. A large piece of glass sliced nicely into Sam's cheek and another three inch piece struck Frank between his two dark eyebrows and stuck there. Each and every man cringed when an animalistic roar reverberated through the small office shaking the photographs hanging on the wall outside the enclosed space. Then as they cowered, a basketball sized hole appeared in the wall about three feet in front of the two women who had started forward when they had seen the glass explode outward. Plaster and slatted wood shot across the hallway and struck the other wall, knocking down a photo of the large, rotund actor, Sidney Greenstreet. Then another animalistic roar burst forth from John's office and then just as quickly faded away to nothing. Sam stood up and watched as Rainbird's door slowly opened without as much as a creaking of its hinges. The last piece of opaque glass gave up its hold on its frame and fell free, making Charlie jump back even further.

"John!" Sam said as he ran through the opening.

Rainbird was half on and half off the couch. His white shirt was torn in many places and his black hair was hanging in front of his face.

"He's hurt, Mr. Dalhart," Constance said as she pushed her way past the men at the open door and then by the stunned detective.

Dalhart blinked and then saw Connie, and then for the first time saw blood seeping through John's undershirt as it started to blotch his dress shirt.

"Miss Wheeler, do you have a first aid kit?" Connie asked Liz as she used her right hand to raise Rainbird's face from his chest. His haunted eyes met hers and stayed that way for a moment.

Liz, who was trying to pull the piece of glass from Frank's face, acknowledged over her shoulder that yes, she did have a first aid kit. "Stop fidgeting you baby, it's not mortal!" she said as Frank was trying desperately to get away from the further pain she was causing him.

John whispered something as Connie quickly removed her coat and handed it to Sam as he finally joined her at the couch.

"What was that?" she asked Rainbird as she tried to look at his wounds.

He mumbled again but she still didn't understand him.

Connie patted his right cheek lightly a few times until his eyes focused on her face.

"Come on, let's get this shirt off, you've got some bad scratches here," she said as she started tugging on John's sleeves to remove his torn shirt. "Please remove his tie, Mr. Dalhart," she said.

Sam dropped her coat onto the top of Rainbird's desk and first loosened and then removed John's tie. As he did, Charlie and Douglass entered the office and moved to the opposite side and watched.

John whispered again as he was truly drained from his dream state ordeal.

"I'm sorry?" Connie said as she leaned down and looked into John's face.

"He said he knows you," Sam said as he tossed Rainbird's tie.

"Did…you come out of that house with me?"

Connie Yale looked from John to Sam with a questioning look on her face. Sam just shook his head.

"John, this is Miss Yale, she's a new client, you met her earlier, her sister is…," he paused and then looked at Connie, "missing."

John lightly shook his head and carefully looked from Connie to Sam and then back to the young woman who couldn't have been more than twenty-five. He tried in vain to smile.

"She's not missing," he said looking at Connie's face closely as if studying her. "Not anymore," he took Connie's hand and squeezed it. "She's alive and looks just like you."

Constance Yale straightened from the couch as she looked at John as he muttered the amazing statement. She felt her knees go weak and was angry for it. She took a step back and felt she was going to faint out of joy at Rainbird's words. She started to fall back, but it was Sam who stopped her fall by taking her in his arms.

Twenty minutes later the rain was still falling out on Sunset Boulevard. Charlie, Fairbanks, and Frank Wiechek sat on the couch where Rainbird had thrashed about earlier. Their faces were blank and none of the three had commented on what had happened. They listened as Rainbird told his story from the very beginning. Sam had just nodded his head that it was alright to share it with all present as everything that had happened involved them somehow. His voice was a monotone as he sat at his desk chair with his head back and his eyes closed as he told them all about the nightmares he had been having and the strange creature that had enveloped him in the lunacy they all now found themselves a part of.

The two women, Liz Wheeler and Connie Yale, hadn't said a word. Not one question was asked as they cleaned and dressed the long, deep scratches on John's chest, arms and legs. Even when he told them in a dream-like voice about the young girls who had held him in place as the beast was loose in the Alhambra building.

Sam stood at the window and looked out on the alley adjacent to the building and smoked, listening to his friend and partner. His sleeves were rolled up and his vest unbuttoned. His hair was still uncombed from their fight to get into the office. He turned and looked at the long deep scratches that marred the woodwork on the inside of the office door. He shook his head as he knew there had been absolutely no one on the other side of that door keeping them out. But the nail, no, that wasn't what they were, not fingernail marks, they were claw marks, were there for all to see. Charlie had run his fingers along and then into one of the longest gouges and his fingers came away with a smell of decay and rot, forcing him to wrinkle his nose when he smelled them.

Connie used iodine and cleaned the last of the scratches on John's chest. She smiled as he opened his eyes and looked down at her. She could see sadness in his dark features that gave her the impression that he thought she wouldn't believe him or his outrageous story.

Sam waited without comment. There were no questions after Rainbird had fallen silent, so he turned and stubbed his cigarette out in the ashtray on the desk and then watched as John started putting on a fresh shirt Liz had retrieved for him from his coat closet.

"Charlie, you said that Melvin Purvis was harassing you again, what about exactly?" Sam asked looking directly at the Little Tramp.

Chaplin closed his eyes and shuddered, clearly unable to get past the earlier terror filled moments.

"Well Samuel, that awful man had two Los Angeles police detectives in tow and came upon Doug and myself as we readied ourselves at Pickfair, hoping to get in a game before the rain started in earnest, and actually accused me of being in either one of two places last night, Redondo Beach or Elysian Park, and he informed me that young girls had been kidnapped from those areas. They wanted my alibi he said."

"And I told that man Charlie was with myself and Mary last evening playing bridge late after the party, of course I lied, but obviously Charlie had nothing to do with something as dastardly as the police were implying," Fairbanks stated with his self-taught cultured voice. He was still looking pale as he sipped some water.

"So Charlie," Frank asked from his spot next to him on the couch, "Where were you last night?"

"I was at my own home, alone, well, maybe with a few guests, you know leftovers from the party."

"Did you explain that to Purvis, even he wouldn't think you can be at three places at once," Sam asked leaning on the desk.

"I…I froze, Samuel, I couldn't say anything, that man terrifies me," he said as he placed his head in his hands and let his graying hair fall forward.

"Charlie, that stupid bastard doesn't have a thing on you. He's trying to rattle your cage and watch your reaction, and you obviously acted just the way he thought you would; guilty," Sam said as Chaplin's head shot up. Sam stilled his protest by holding his hand up. "We know you're not Charlie, the only reason I brought it up is because I want to know what he had to say about the girl's in Redondo and the park."

"He didn't elaborate, Samuel, he just accused our Little Tramp of practically ripping them from their parent's arms," Fairbanks volunteered for Charlie, "very sordid and uncomely if you ask me."

Charlie looked at Constance Yale as she was looking at him.

"Madam, I can assure you that I have no pedophilic tendencies," he said embarrassingly, "Only a few….minor indiscretions."

"John, are you sure the two girls you saw in your dream were alive? Not like the rest that you have described?"

Rainbird looked at Sam and then at Jeannie Yale's older sister. "They were warm," he said and again tried to smile but failed. "They were alive, Sam."

"Could you see…see what my sister was wearing?" Connie's voice and the gleam of hope in her eyes told everyone in the office that no matter how strange the tale John had recited to them was, she had believed every word of it.

"Not really, the…the…*thing* inside the basement won't ever let me see too much."

Hope momentarily ebbed from Connie's features and Liz quickly helped her to one of the chairs John had lining the wall of the office. She was careful to seat her away from where the hole had been punched through the thick plaster.

"Thoughts, John?" Sam asked, again sitting on the edge of Rainbird's desk.

"That thing is playing with us. By us I mean me and you," John said as he stood and tucked in the new white shirt into his gray pants. "He says I am, or," he stopped all movement and looked at Sam, "That *we* are just a curiosity to it."

"What in God's name do you think you've crossed paths with my Indian friend?" Chaplin asked, his large eyes taking in John.

Rainbird just shook his head. "I don't know Charlie, but I know it likes causing pain…," John's words drifted off as he relaxed for a moment in thought. "Sam, I remember now, it was going to release one of the girls, the smaller one I think."

Sam stood suddenly, knowing full well this could be a break.

"If the girls were still alive, they would have to have been taken recently, don't you think?" he asked.

"I don't know. Miss Yale's sis was alive and she disappeared…when?" he asked.

"Almost two weeks ago," Connie answered, her brows raised in the hope it would be Jeannie set free. "Look, can't we go to the police and tell them this?"

"We don't have anything to go on but John's dreams, they would look at us all like we were crazy," Frank said and immediately received a quick look of disapproval from Liz. "Well, they would."

"He's right. Besides, they seem lost in Shangri-La when the subject of missing girls comes up. No, we have to pursue this case ourselves. Whatever it is John's dealing with may have made its first mistake by telling John one of them may be released. We just have to narrow down which one. We have all the known addresses of local girls that have been taken," Sam started to say, and then all in the room watched as he quickly deflated. "Damn! That's too much ground to cover."

"Sam," John said as he placed a large hand to his mouth, "How young was the youngest one on our list of the missing?"

Sam pulled out his list from his vest pocket and scanned it. "Sixteen," he said, quickly rereading it again to make sure.

"Listen, the young girl who was singing Jesus Loves the Little Children, she couldn't have been no more than eleven, maybe twelve."

"Sam, the girls from last night, they're not on your list. The boys just called that in this morning, their ages I mean," Liz said as she rummaged in John's wastepaper basket and brought out the morning edition of the *Times*. She hurried through the pages until she found the same article. "Here," she said handing him the paper.

"I forgot all about that, Pete and Willis...," he quickly looked at his watch, "they may be on their way there now to the home of the two sisters from Elysian Park," Sam quickly went through the door and out into the hallway. John followed as did the rest.

"Sam, I remember now, you said the younger sister had leg braces, she had them on in my dream, it's her, I know it," John called out.

Sam heard John and didn't hesitate.

"Liz, get the parents of those two girls on the line and inform them that Pete and Willis will be there soon to ask a few questions, and if they arrive at the house before we get there have Pete call the office, you'll explain to them to stand guard over that house until Rainbird and myself arrive, tell them to go in armed." The office manager stood rooted to the spot as everything started moving too fast. "Liz, do it now!"

"I'm coming along too boss," Frank said as he followed Sam into his office and removed the gauze bandage from his forehead as he watched Sam pull his thirty-eight from his top drawer.

"I think Doug and myself will stay with Liz...just in case," Charlie volunteered with Fairbanks agreeing beside him in the hallway by nodding his head and pursing his lips.

Connie grabbed her coat and then looked at Sam, "I'm coming, if it's not that child it may be Jeannie. If it is, I want to be there."

"Absolutely...," Sam started to say angrily.

"Fuck you, Mr. Dalhart, I am *absolutely* going!"

Sam looked perplexed, but saw in her eyes that indeed, she was coming. Instead of protesting further he gave her a half-smile.

"Careful Miss Yale, your country girl shyness is showing through."

"Sam, look outside," John said as he took a second revolver from Sam's desk and made sure it was loaded.

Dalhart turned and looked out of the window," he couldn't tell if the rain had stopped or not...then he realized why—it was dark.

"The light's gone; it's that *thing's* time. It went out of its way to tell me that."

Sam grimaced and then closed the cylinder on his thirty-eight Police Special just as Stevie Krazenheimer stepped through the reception room door. His eyes immediately widened when he noticed Sam, Frank and Rainbird put their shoulder holsters on. Then he watched as they slid the sleek, black weapons into them. His eyes went from there to the shattered glass in the hallway and then back to the crowded office.

"Boy, what did I miss?" the kid asked and then screwed up his face in pain as John pulled him by the ear until he moved out of their way.

"You stay with Liz, Charlie, and Mr. Fairbanks, we're not sure, but you may have company."

Sam went to his closet and removed another thirty-eight from the top shelf and tossed it to Fairbanks. "I assume from your films you can at least point and shoot that?"

Douglass Fairbanks looked at the gun and then swallowed, then put on a brave front he surely didn't feel. "Of course!"

"Good, Liz has a weapon also. Stevie and Charlie...well, do what you can if anyone we don't know comes in while we're gone."

"Just what do you think is coming?" Liz asked worriedly as Charlie's eyes grew wide.

Sam stopped at the doorway and turned toward the staring and worried faces.

"I don't think that anything is coming here, at least with John gone. But what we really need to talk about is what this thing really is. *My* hunch is that this is something old world." He started to turn and then stopped. "What we know from John is that it enjoys what it does, that it's arrogant and afraid of nothing. We know that it stays underground in the daylight and," he sniffed at the hand that he'd rubbed in the scratches, "whatever he touches stinks of blood and death." He patted John on the back and waved him toward the door. "What does that sound like to you guys?"

John turned around to stare at the group. When no one spoke, Sam said, "Maybe I've been watching too many movies, and maybe I spent too much time reading the pulps when I was a kid, but this is starting to feel a little familiar to me." He hesitated, looking embarrassed, and then said what he was thinking. "This thing lives for the night, loves pain and blood. It lives underground surrounded by its dead and the only link we have is that it likes to invade the dreams of my partner, and the kicker here is we know there are missing girls in this city that will never be found. Do any of you watch movies at all?"

"My motion picture history was steeped in adventure, Sam, but I do realize what you're driving at, and I must say that your theory, while scary enough to fit what happened here today, is a rather outlandish one," Fairbanks remarked.

"Wait, as a comedian I rarely get to watch the genre of other efforts in this business, so may I ask just what in the bloody hell you two gentlemen are driving at so recklessly?" Chaplin said as he watched Sam grab a box of .38 shells from the desk drawer.

"It all adds up to something that couldn't possibly exist Charles," Fairbanks answered as he too watched the two detectives. "Our good friend, our very down to earth detective, Samuel Dalhart has just described—a vampire."

With that Sam pulled John out the office door. The group left inside the office heard the reception room door close. Charlie looked from face to startled face. If Sam hadn't been the most down to earth man any of them had ever met, they would have been laughing hysterically. But it was Chaplin, the comedian who finally asked the question.

"Is he bloody fucking kidding?"

While the Countess paced, her husband just stood motionless at the filth covered window and looked out at the darkening skies. The rain was somewhat lighter than it had been in the city but was still a dank drizzle that clung to a person like a cobweb. Von Railing sat silently in one of the few easy chairs that were dust free and smoked a cigar. He was watching the Countess and his eyes told his story. Every time she crossed the room in her black dress the slit up its left side opened and introduced one beautifully shaped leg to the filth covered den.

"Honestly Karl, why don't you have that ghoul of a manservant clean this place," she ran a finger along one of the lower bookshelves that sat empty. "Do you ever have thoughts of entertaining again?"

Von Railing watched her rub her fingers together and frown. He rolled the cigar at his lips and then looked over at the Count D'Sarcuni who hadn't moved from the spot at the window since their arrival fifteen minutes before. He smiled and then looked at the Countess who had turned to face him.

"Entertain? Who, these American's? I would sooner invite a Pole or a Jew in for company."

She shook her head. "I find the Americans quite charming, and I don't mean these hollow movie stars, but the real people of this town are quite…engaging."

"Ah, but I suspect that you're referring to one American in particular, my dear?"

"What's this?" the Count asked as he finally turned away from the window.

The Countess cast a nasty look at Von Railing who immediately rose to the challenge.

"It seems your lovely wife was quite captivated by that private detective she met at the court jester's party."

The Count's groomed right eyebrow rose and his thick lips turned south, bringing his pencil thin moustache down with it and the frown didn't do anything to help hide his heavy jowls.

"Don't you listen to him Orlando, darling, he's being a bastard again," Francesca explained as she stepped up to her husband and lightly touched his cheek.

"She always had a soft spot for the peasantry of any country," he said as he smiled and accepted her reasoning. "Now, there is no reason you are aware of that the Master called us here, I mean, our resources for getting him out of Germany were to his liking, were they not?"

Von Railing took a long pull on his cigar and smiled as the smoke hid his features for a moment.

"I have no thoughts on the matter, nor do I care to guess as to why he summoned the two of you here. But I do have another thought for you to worry about."

"And that is?" the Countess asked, forgetting all about her husbands concerns about her flirtations.

"If you didn't cover our tracks well, you know those fool generals will track us here, and despite the fear and devotion they have for their little paperhanging corporal, they have delusions of themselves still having honor, they may attempt to thwart the Master's plans."

"Even if they knew where we were, the army would never take a chance and challenge Hitler's orders for our safe return home after our task is complete, much less challenge *Him*," Francesca said nodding her gorgeous head toward the basement.

"While the German army lacks the will power to challenge Hitler at the height of his popularity, don't underestimate their ability and pleasure ordering those under them to their deaths to foil his plans in Europe, by stopping him here in America. They know Hitler would be lost very soon without the Master's guidance. If they attempt to slay what can't be slain, that is all well and good, they will die horribly, but one thing both of you must consider, while failing to harm the Master, they may just harm the three of us, and as I'm sure you're aware we are not quite as indestructible as Phaltazar."

"If those German malcontent pigs show themselves to me, I will show them just how hard I can fight!" the count said, his face turning red.

Von Railing smiled and put his cigar down.

"Calm yourself little man, if they are stupid enough to show themselves here, the Master can handle them, even if they send a thousand. If they do, the old-timers in the German army will meet their maker at the end of a rope. Herr Hitler would be quite put out knowing that his own army was stabbing him in the back."

"I just want to finish what we came here to do and go back to Europe," the Count said.

"I think I see the final solution to our American problem. I believe that the Master will take care of our small dilemma very quickly." He smiled and stood and walked to the bar and poured himself a drink.

"Why doesn't he just take care of things without so much intrigue? Why not just do what needs doing and quit playing this infernal game of cat and mouse?" the Count asked turning on Von Railing.

The tall German took a sip of his whiskey and then turned and looked at them both.

"*He* has formed…an infatuation with two young girls. He has had them, one for a full night and the older one for several weeks. She may be brain dead by this time, but the fact remains he has not killed them. And his unhealthy attitude with this Dalhart and his Red Indian friend, I think I see it, and maybe understand it just a little. He will use them to get close to…,"

"Have you really seen it? Francesca asked, cutting Von Railing off. "His plan for dealing with these Americans, or have you merely sensed a weakness in the Master?" Francesca asked.

Von Railing and the Count both cringed. The German sat his glass down on the bar so hard he cracked it. "Keep your mouth shut. Don't even think of anything like that while you are within three kilometers of this house, you stupid bitch."

"Yes, my dear, he is right, absolutely right. He may have heard you and all we need is for him to think we are not loyal," the Count said taking the woman's hands into his own.

Von Railing had taken a menacing step forward when the den's door opened and froze him in his place. He closed his eyes and the Countess actually let out a small yelp of terror. The Count was the first one to see it was Ralls McDougal. He slowly closed the door while balancing a tray in his right hand. On the tray were the remains of hamburgers and a partially eaten hotdog.

"The Master wishes for the Count, Countess and you to join him below," McDougal said as he placed the tray down on the bar and reached for the same decanter of whiskey Von Railing had just used.

The Countess closed her eyes and straightened her dress. The Count ran a thick hand over his balding head, but what little hair was there was already pasted down with oil.

"The children have been fed I presume?" the German asked.

"Yes," McDougal said just before he downed about three inches of whiskey. "As disgusting as it was, yes, they ate," he said as he poured another drink. His strained nerves made the glass rattle as the decanter lightly tapped it. "I believe that's what he wants you for, *them* too," he sloshed his drink at the Count and Countess, "He seems angry about something. While I was in there, he took three of his girls and crushed their heads. Didn't say a word mind you, he was just squatting in the corner listening to that little bitch sing and then suddenly squish, like something just came to him. And there were four more dead ones mauled in the corner lying near him from sometime earlier. God, I had to get out of there before he turned on me."

"You bloody fool, you make no sense!" Von Railing said as he snatched the glass decanter out of his hand.

"He's been angry all bloody day; he must have felt something earlier because he told you to get them two over here! Then when he thought about whatever it was again he killed more girls, it was only the singing of the little bitch that calmed him enough to wait for *their* arrival," McDougall said as he snatched the decanter back from Von Railing.

Francesca turned away from McDougal and placed her manicured fingers to her lips. Her eyes held a terror only an animal could feel while being stalked by a predator.

"What could we have done wrong?" she cried.

"Calm yourself Fran—"

"GERMAN!"

Von Railing felt his brain constrict inside of his skull. The name was called so loud in all their heads in the dead tongue of Aramaic it almost made the Count and Countess fall to their knees in pain.

McDougal, immune from the ancient telepathy took another drink and noisily placed the glass down and then retrieved his tray. "I don't think he likes being kept waiting," he said as he turned for the hallway door and scurried away like the rat Von Railing knew him to be.

The subbasement door stood before them. The Count as gallantly as he could, stood protectively before his wife but still well behind the blonde German. Von Railing reached out and opened the door and closed his eyes as the smell struck him full in the face.

"My God, what has he been—"

Von Railing turned on the Countess and she cut her words off as his blue eyes were suddenly shot through with red. His breathing became deep and deliberate.

"I have not grown so old as to cringe every time my Lord's name is taken in vain. You are far too protective, German. Please bring our friends down to my house."

The voice was soft and inviting despite the coldness of its timbre. Von Railing continued to stare at the Countess until she looked away submissively. Then he turned and quickly headed down the dark stairs. He felt the other two follow quickly behind him.

Candles were lit and lined the walls closest to the stairs of the subbasement. The girls were nowhere to be seen, but the presence of the Master was felt before they reached the bottom step. As their feet gained the bare earth they could hear soft mumbling and the quiet sobbing of one of the girls. They could tell the Master was attempting to actually console one of them with soft murmurings. Von Railing didn't interrupt; he took four quick steps to his right inside the light cast by the circle of candles and waved the D'Sarcuni's in beside him.

"Tasks. Tasks. We all have to do the work of our Masters, you, and even I," the voice said almost musically.

"You have duties for us my Lord?" Von Railing asked with head bowed.

"This small child, she has invigorated me with her voice, but alas, I may only smother that which I have come to adore. Her instruction from me is complete."

Von Railing looked up and then over at Francesca who stood quietly between him and her husband, his look was questioning at the ambiguousness of the deep, soothing voice.

"My Lord?" he asked.

"If she stays she will die, her mind is already starting to slip from her and I fear I have already lost my storyteller, she is slowly losing her way with word."

Von Railing understood. The older of the two girls, the one he took from Hollywood Boulevard on that stormy night two weeks ago, he was using her to tell him stories. She must have been well versed in motion picture lore. And the small girl, the horrors she had seen while in this place for just one night and day were starting to affect her adolescent mind, possibly her soul. Knowing the sister that had been taken with her a night ago was dead hadn't helped her situation.

"You wish me to dispose of them my Lord?"

"NO!" the air stirred in front of them and the candles flickered and several went out completely. The Master was standing just inside the total darkness of the blackest corner of the basement. At the spot where he was held at bay, the candles started to dim, allowing him to come even closer. "The child is to be taken to her home; this must be done for it serves me two purposes."

"Take the child to her home? Surely this is dangerous, my Lord?"

Silence greeted Von Railing's query. The air didn't stir but as he looked into the darkness he saw his Masters yellow eyes flaring, they didn't blink but held him dead in their gaze.

"It will be done Master."

The yellow slits widened and then the air moved once again.

"I have forewarned the Shaman the girl will be returned this night, thus Dalhart will undoubtedly accompany the Red Man to the child's home. I wish the local authorities to believe Dalhart was responsible for the recovery of the girl."

"My Lord, I think I see your plan unfolding, but I have concerns," Von Railing said and then waited for a clawed hand to seize him by the throat, but when nothing happened he looked at the Count and Countess.

"The Red Man and his ability to enter my home?" questioned the deep, soft voice.

"Exactly, there is danger there for the plan you foresee."

"Yes, I may have to silence this man's mind; I believe he may have become dangerous."

The German took a deep breath, relieved that his Master had come around to his way of thinking.

"I see my Lord."

"No, you fool, you don't see. For reasons unknown to me, people in this backward country sense themselves apart from the old world. This Dalhart and his Indian are not unique here, it's as if they and others like them are bred to protect. I must see first, learn, and then destroy them, and all those like them, or the seed we planted in the East will not flourish as long as men such as this are there to oppose it, and they will soon become aware of the dangers of a madman across the sea."

"Your will, is but my task," Von Railing said.

"These two children of the church, the Papal worshiper and his…," the deep laugh again, "lovely spouse, the Countess, I sense a divide that has become dangerous to me."

"We worship only you my Lord," Francesca said meekly and as quickly as possible.

"Woman of man, lie to me not. Your heart is still with the *Son*, even though your soul will be forever burning when your time comes, as will mine own for my treachery. Regardless of what your Papal church teaches, *He* is not *that* forgiving of either you or the Son's betrayer. Worshiping the betrayer and spurning the one true God and his only son does not forge a new key to the gates of heaven. You must choose one side or the other—in either case it is far too late for your eternal soul."

Von railing looked over and in the semi-light of the candles he saw the Count lower his head in shame. The Countess on the other hand stared into the darkness defiantly.

"The only key I wish for my Lord, is the key that allows me entrance to your house, not one that holds the weak minded at bay."

"Bravely spoken my dear," the deep voice boomed as a long and powerful hand shot out of the blackness and took the Countess by the neck and squeezed.

Von Railing threw himself back and the Count could only stare. The huge, green tinted hand relaxed, the shiny scales threw off sparkling light as the candles dimmed with the sudden movement and the jingling sound of the pouch around the beast's neck. Von Railing watched as his master ran one long talon along the left side of her flawless face. Then the hand moved down her neck to her shoulder and caressed. The Countess refused to close her eyes but also couldn't bring herself to look at the hand that smelled of human decay. The Master didn't have the same effect on her as other women, he didn't lull her into believing he was host, a protector, something that called them home to a welcoming bosom of family and the warm feel of being loved. The Countess felt the reality of her Master, a rough scaly hand and long claw of one of the three fallen ones.

"My house? I am welcomed in no house. I have been thrown from one and barred from the other. My house is one of loneliness and death. You wish for no such key as that," the hand shot back into the darkness, bringing light and life once again to the dying candles.

The countess forced herself not to reach for her neck and the dried, cold skin where the beast had touched.

"Whilst the German and I are occupied this evening, you will attend to the minions of Dalhart. I want no followers of his to impede my work here. I believe his workplace will be filled with those anxious for loved ones, even if not, kill those that dwell in the house of Dalhart."

Francesca could not voice an answer, she swallowed, forcing back tears which she had not shed for fifty years—she only bowed her head.

"Papal worshiper, your influences brought me safely to these shores and you have done well in seeing that the officialdom of this town stay clear of our activities."

Count D'Sarcuni puffed out his chest and his bottom lip came up as he bowed at the waist. He proudly reached out and took the Countess by the wrist. He failed to see the disgust in her face at being touched by him. Where she had failed moments before to register her horror at being touched by Lord Phaltazar, she succeeded in announcing her disdain at being touched by her husband. The Count was proud as he straightened; his fangs had shown themselves as he smiled.

"Now, unlike the work your lovely wife has in front of her, your task is…," again the deep laugh, "more political than it is dangerous."

"Anything my King of Kings."

"Do not ever call me that. I am the lowest of the low. I am darkness that has been cast upon the world of light. My master *was* the King of Kings."

They all heard the master as it tried to control its anger. Then the atmosphere of the basement lifted somewhat as the beast regained control.

"Arriving tonight on these shores are our former enemies. I know not of their mission to this misguided country, but it bodes ill for you and your wife. They may think they can harm me through you. They will perish here. I need you to find out where they will shelter themselves when they arrive. I dreamed of the German consulate. That is where you will watch for them."

"But my Lord, they cannot come here and try anything on American soil; the generals could never be so bold as to act in a neutral country such as this. The chance at gaining an advantage would be lost if the Americans shed their isolationist leanings."

D'Sarcuni saw the yellow eyes approach but felt no menace towards him.

"You will guarantee our safety? Then by all means my Count, my friend, the follower of the *Carpenter*, you shall stay and dine with me tonight instead of performing the task I have set before you and we will discuss your plan on keeping me safe."

Von Railing pulled Francesca out of the way roughly as a raw and dripping piece of meat was thrust out of the darkness, striking the fat Count in the face and staining his white shirt and red sash with blood. Laughter erupted from the dark space before the dismembered leg of a young woman was pulled back. Von Railing pushed Francesca toward the stairs and then reached out and grabbed the Count who was wiping his mouth of the foulness that had been thrust upon him and shoved him toward the stairs behind his wife.

"He will do as commanded, my Master," Von Railing said turning back to face whatever was in store next.

"Yes, I suspect he will," the beast said with a humorous tone. The basement suddenly grew quiet and still as the air changed; it wasn't quite so heavy almost as if a window had been opened.

Von Railing heard a splat as the piece of raw meat was tossed on the dirt covered floor. He then heard Phaltazar mumbling softly and then he heard the smallest child say; "Okay," and then out of the darkness he could see a girl of perhaps eleven or twelve step awkwardly into the light. She hesitated when she saw Von Railing and stopped and looked back into the darkness. She was having difficulty standing and that was when Von Railing saw the leg braces. Then he saw the large hand appear and give the girl a loving caress on top of her small head, the long claws and thick fingers moved easily in their caress of the girl.

"Go, you will be safe. I suspect you will be as safe with this man as any in the world if I so order it. Now go child and give joy once more to your mother and your father. Your time with me is over and will never come again. German, you will clean and perfume her before your arrival at her mother and fathers. I assume you read the ledgers, the chronicles of this town, the newspapers?"

"I have," Von Railing replied.

"Then you know of this place where she dwells, I will be there also."

The girl was actually crying and reached out for the green hand but it was gone.

"Bye Frankenstein," she said.

"Come, let's take you home girl."

The child tentatively walked toward him struggling with her legs spread wide and half-turned her head; "Goodbye Angela," she called out to her sister, but there was no answer. Then she called out; "Goodbye Jeannie."

Von Railing heard actual crying this time coming from the blackness of the basement. There was a girl sobbing back in the darkness and he shuddered to think about what she had witnessed while being down here.

"Adria, tell my sister where—"

"Silence young one," the Master ordered softly. "When breakfast arrives on the morrow, you will tell me one of your stories, maybe a tale of love this time."

Von Railing cringed at the thought of the young girl sitting before that monstrosity in her monotone voice telling it a tale of love, even while knowing itself incapable of any such emotion.

"I will be watching for Dalhart and then we will see why this Shaman holds him in such esteem. We will see how he stands up to my test. Now take the child, her work is just starting."

Von Railing felt the touch of the young girl's hand and he turned for the stairs as he heard the massive cellar door open and then slam shut. The beast was out and he was looking for blood—the blood of Samuel Dalhart's savage Indian.

"Do you want me to sing, too, mister, like I did for Frankenstein?" the girl asked as she looked up at the tall German.

"No, I want you to not speak at all, is that understood?"

The girl just lowered her head and held onto the man's hand as they climbed the stairs. Von Railing was angered at her slow progress as she carefully took one step at a time, so he reached down and snatched the thin girl into his arms. Adria felt far colder in the German's embrace than she had in the creatures. She was also confused because Frankenstein had told her she would sing to very, very important people. Then she thought of something else but the memory of her new friend's lesson wasn't clear in her head any longer. She hoped she would remember because she wanted to please Frankenstein so very much, even though it had taken her sister from her. He promised to return her, but deep down Adria knew her sister was never going to come home, even if she fulfilled her promise to *him*.

A small crowd of concerned neighbors were standing vigil outside of the small house in Elysian Park. The Rodriguez's had made themselves available to their neighbors for a few minutes to show they were grateful to them for supporting their small family at this most horrible of times. The father of Angela and Adria stayed the longest trying to calm his friends about the seemingly nonchalance the police department was showing the case. Even the murder of the young boy that was obviously connected to the girl's disappearance was being handled with even less enthusiasm than usual by the police when it came to a Hispanic. They had said there was probably no connection. No connection! Now the crowd gathered in the rain was shooting angry glances at the prowl car parked half a block away.

Pete Sanchez and Willis Jackson pulled up in Pete's '31 Dodge and were surprised to see so many people standing in the rain. Willis looked over at the park and saw that the crowd of people was spread out to its lighted fringe.

"What is this?" Pete asked.

"Anger, people take it serious when two girls are taken from their home, how would you feel?"

"I see your point. You packin'?" Willis asked.

Pete reached inside his old sweater and pulled out his snub nosed thirty-eight.

"This is Los Angeles, Willy boy; I go to church with a gun. You being a Negro here ought to let you know how both our people are treated in the city of angels."

A sudden rap at the passenger window startled Pete enough that he almost jumped into Willis' lap, the gun he had just pulled from his thick sweater fell into the black man's lap.

"Hey, it's Sam," Willis said with visible relief.

Pete straightened up and took back his gun from Willis, his embarrassment evident in the look etched across his face. He turned and rolled down his window. Sam's brown fedora was dripping water as he leaned in close.

"Took you fella's long enough to get here," he said looking from man to man.

"Damn coppers aren't in the best of moods when you ask to see their blotters, hell some wouldn't let us see them at all boss," Willis said. "We just finished up in Pomona."

"Alright, we may have a development, Rainbird has a hunch something may happen here tonight, so I want you to stay inside as long as you can, make up any excuse you want, but stay in that house, the parents may need your protection."

"What in the hell happened?" Pete asked.

"Hell boys, I can't figure it. I've never been through anything like this before, but John's somehow crossed his signals with a killer," he held up his hand when he saw both Pete and Willis start to say something. "I don't know how, but he's hard wired to him. You just get inside and stay inside and you may get to meet whoever it is. Keep alert, whatever it is may be responsible for these missing kids."

"You got it boss," Pete said.

"No matter what happens, you hang onto that piece of yours, Pete."

"My hand was wet," Pete stated embarrassingly.

"Uh, huh," Sam said with a smirk and then turned and walked away into the misting rain.

A flash of lightning lit up the surrounding area and also the large crowd of people that were standing out in the yard watching Pete's car.

"Well, let's go ask some questions and baby-sit awhile," Willis said.

Both men got out and ran hunkered over as the rain started to come down in earnest. Pete tried to see where Sam and Rainbird were parked but there were too many cars to see one in particular. As they made their way up to the small house there were a few shouted curses about the cops being incompetent, or how they just don't care as long as the girls weren't white.

Pete and Willis finally made the front porch and shook themselves free of some of the water.

"They think we're coppers," Willis said.

"I can see them thinking maybe I was, but you?"

"Ring the damn doorbell pepper-belly."

Sam watched his two men enter the house after Mr. Rodriguez had answered the door.

"Well, they made it without shooting anyone or being shot at; let's hope they get to stay for a while."

John sat quietly in the front seat with Sam. Constance Yale, who hadn't said a word on the way out to Elysian Park, sat looking in the mirror at Sam's reflection. Frank Wiechek sat next to her looking out at the angry mob of people and every once in a while he would touch the band-aid between his eyes.

"Now, this could be a long wait, so why don't you tell us what you think, John," Sam said as he removed his wet fedora and placed it on the shift lever.

"I know it's a killer Sam. I also know it thoroughly enjoys what it does, so I have to agree with the ridiculous description you ventured back at the office, and also what Doug Fairbanks said, as silly as that word sounds, but a vampire is as good a guess I can come up."

"Mr. Rainbird, why not him or he, why does it have to be something from one of those horrible novels?" Connie asked, watching Sam for a reaction also.

"Look doll, did you see those gouges in that door today, I don't think they were made by BoBo the Clown," Frank said sarcastically.

"My name is Connie, not doll, and I believe my question was directed at Mr. Rainbird."

Frank started to turn to her, but Sam said; "Frank, shut up."

Connie waited, the thrumming of the rain was louder now but John still hadn't moved. He finally turned and looked at her.

"Miss Yale, I've been around bad men all of my life, starting with my worthless father and working my way through our reservation all the way to the white man's world. This is no man. I don't even know if it ever was a man."

"But of course it is," she caught herself. "Of course *he's* a man, what else could he be?" she said with a small laugh that really didn't convey any humor. "I'm not buying the fairytale; men are entirely capable of madness and murder and doing unspeakable things to others."

"Miss Yale, did you see anything in that room with me? Do you think I punched those holes in the wall and then lay back down on the couch?" asked John.

"Mr. Rainbird, there has to be a more realistic explanation than something from one of those horrid Universal films."

Sam interrupted. "I gave up looking for logical explanations when John's mom saved my life with something she saw in a dream. She's what his people call a *dream walker*; she sees things, now John at his ripe old age sees them too."

"I read an article once about special people who can see the future, is that what you mean?"

"Don't ridicule me, Miss Yale," John said with no trace of anger in his voice.

"I'm serious; some doctors think it may one day become a science, of sorts."

Sam watched Rainbird as he relaxed somewhat. The way Connie spoke it was like a cool cloth to a warm and feverish head, even though she wasn't buying anything that they had come up with since John's attack in the office.

"They do? Enough people have claimed to have this…this ability that they write papers on it?"

"I assume you're an educated man, Mr. Rainbird, why haven't you done some research on this?" she asked.

"I thought….well, I thought it was a tribal or family thing."

"I hate to break into this fascinating conversation, but let's get back to what in the hell attacked you in your office, I'd like to know that one for starters. If someone's dream walkin' as you say, maybe you should start locking your head up at night, because whatever this thing is, it's damn hard on the doors and walls," Frank said, still half-frightened from this afternoon.

"Damn it Frank, do you think this happens all the time? This thing is invading my dreams and has the ability to track me down, maybe even to project itself into the real world, not just the dreaming one."

"Maybe? Maybe? Come on John," Frank said far more scared than he had let on.

"Okay, it *can* project itself into my real world, does that convince you that this isn't a man, or at least not a normal one?"

"Think, Mr. Rainbird, what sense do you get from *it*."

Sam smiled and turned to face the storm outside. Miss Yale said it just to concede the point to John, if it was mercy, fine, but he suspected his partner had convinced her that it wasn't a man that had taken her sister.

John was looking out at the running rivers of water on the windshield and the fogging glass before him.

"Old. It's old Miss Yale. I do sense that."

"How do you mean, John?" Sam asked.

Rainbird looked over to his friend and smiled. "The first time I had the nightmare, I prefer to call it a nightmare and not a dream, it had different connotations," he said and smiled. "I think I caught it off guard. It didn't know I was there and it didn't sense me as readily as it does now. I could swear I heard it reading from a book, or maybe just reciting it when the nightmares first started. I couldn't tell because it's pitch-black in the basement where this thing lives."

"What book, did you recognize it?" Connie asked.

"Yes, it was the bible, the old testament."

The car was quiet as they absorbed what John had just said. He turned and looked out on the house as distant lightning illuminated the hills around the park.

"What book of the bible was it, Mr. Rainbird?" she asked.

"Revelations. It had been in very good humor that first night of reading about the end of the world."

❧ NINE ❧

Stevie jumped back from the reception room window which looked out onto Sunset Boulevard. The lightning had crept close enough that it startled him. He placed his hat more squarely on his head and turned to look at Liz, Chaplin, Fairbanks, Talbot Leonard, and Gary Cooper, who had just arrived to offer Sam his apologies for cutting in on his action with that Italian Countess the night before at Charlie's place. At the moment Cooper was busy wooing Liz at her desk and Charlie and Doug Fairbanks were still sitting and talking, trying to come to terms about the events of the day. Stevie just felt better that no one had seen him jump away from the window.

"Boy, 'dat really lit up da sky," he said pulling up his pants and pushing his hat forward on his head.

Doug and Charlie looked up at Stevie and Liz ignored the comment altogether, and Cooper just gave the boy a cursory glance, then leaned over and whispered into Liz's ear.

Liz immediately closed the file she was working on and looked to her left at the lanky actor. "Mr. Cooper, I fear your reputation has preceded you, so please, feel free to work your charms and exercise your libido elsewhere. This is a business office."

"But you're such a fine figure of a woman I just can't help myself," Cooper said in his slow, halting way, putting a period to his sentence with the ever-present boyish grin he used to perfection.

Liz smiled and pulled out a perfume bottle and looked as if she were about to spray an amount on her neck but intentionally squeezed the small rubber ball at the end with too much pressure, missing her neck on purpose and spraying Cooper in the face.

"That stuff stings," he said wiping at his eyes.

"Oops, I had it pointed the wrong way."

"Hey, what was that?" Stevie asked.

"What, what did you hear my salty young fellow?" Chaplin asked as he quickly stood up and started looking around.

"Charles, quit being so melodramatic, stick to comedy, you seem to be somewhat competent at that," Fairbanks said tugging at Chaplin's sleeve to assist him sitting back down.

This time they all heard a loud thump somewhere in the building.

"What was that?" Fairbanks said as he too stood, his small stature not that much larger than the Little Tramp.

"If I didn't know better, I would say you boys are a mite jumpy tonight," Cooper said from the edge of Liz's desk as he accepted a handkerchief from Liz and wiped his eyes.

Talbot Leonard had been told about the afternoons attack in Rainbird's office. He reached into his white jacket and with a pretense of removing his own handkerchief to clean his glasses, unsnapped the gun which sat in its shoulder holster, then he smiled and brought out the handkerchief and finally did wipe and clean his glasses.

"Oh, I'm sure it was just a door slamming somewhere," Talbot said.

"It sounded like something on the floor above us, Mr. Leonard," Stevie said looking up at the ceiling. "Listen," he said.

They all cocked an ear toward the white painted ceiling. Then they heard it too, footsteps coming from the vacant office on the seventh floor. The steps were light and they seemed to travel from the Sunset Boulevard side toward the center of the room.

"Say, what are you guys so spooked about?" Cooper asked as he watched Talbot Leonard stand up from the chair he was using and follow the footsteps overhead while watching the ceiling.

"There's not supposed to be anyone up there, Coop, the entire floor is vacant, has been for a year," Talbot said as he slowly removed his pipe.

"Oh dear, I wish Samuel and Rainbird were here," Charlie said.

"I'll go up and take a look-see," Stevie said hitching up his pants again and starting for the door.

"No," they all said at once with the exception of Cooper who was looking from one upturned face to another as if everyone had lost their minds.

Just as Cooper asked one more time, "What has gotten into you guys?"

The lights suddenly went out.

"Oh come on, this is rather bad writing don't you agree old boy?" Fairbanks asked Chaplin who didn't respond. "Obviously someone is playing us for fools, possibly even Samuel himself."

"Sam doesn't play games like this," Liz said, "not today he wouldn't."

Their eyes started to adjust to the darkness and they relaxed somewhat when Stevie pulled the drapes all the way open and allowed the neon lights from Sunset to invade the conquering blackness.

The double doors flew open so hard that the left door hit the inner wall and the glass shattered, the other door hit the wall and bounced closed again, only to be knocked open by something unseen out on the landing.

Talbot raised the gun he had hidden at his side and pointed it toward the black opening.

"If you all are doing this for my benefit, I admit you got me, my heart's going at a pretty good clip," Cooper said as Liz's handkerchief slipped from his grasp and fell to the carpeted floor.

Liz reached into her top desk drawer and pulled out her small but deadly .32 automatic which she had only had to brandish once because of an irate husband who Sam had got the goods on. Copper tuned and saw the gleam of metal during a brief but very bright lightning flash. His eyes widened.

"I guess you folks aren't trying to put one over on me, huh?"

"No Coop, we're not," Leonard said stepping in front of Liz's desk while he pointed his thirty-eight at the blackness beyond the doors.

"Well, do I get a gun, she has one," Gary Cooper asked, almost with a whine in his voice.

Liz lightly pushed over a letter opener, he felt for it and picked it up; "Oh, gee, thanks."

They could hear wind as it rushed up the stairwell. As they were watching and waiting the picture plate window at the front of the room exploded inward. Stevie was pelted with flying glass as he covered his head.

"Oh, my goodness, is that boy all right, Charlie check and—"

The words had frozen in Fairbanks mouth as he saw the green eyes just above the cowering Stevie. A flash of lightning lit up the rain filled sky outside and for a brief moment they all saw it. It was pure, deathly white. Dark hair was piled high on its head with a long ponytail coursing down its back. The hair was held in place by beads of some kind with a bright object attached. The long fingers curled around Stevie's neck and they could briefly see the unnaturally long fingernails as they dug into little Stevie's flesh. The mouth was large and filled with teeth, crooked, leaning in every direction. The two front teeth were the largest and the longest and bowed inward as the thing hissed at the closest two people; Charlie and Doug.

The figure that stood hissing before them was clothed in a flowing pair of sheer black silk pants. They saw one breast slide free of an equally sheer silk blouse as the creature swayed behind the wide-eyed Stevie, the green eyes going quickly from face to face—the unvoiced challenge was clear to all, as its long nails caressed Stevie's neck.

"Good God in heaven," Chaplin said aloud.

"I don't think God has anything to do with this, old man," Fairbanks whispered as he grasped Chaplin's arm.

"Don't move Stevie," Leonard said as he turned his gun toward the intruder and took two tentative steps forward.

The creature before them hissed and snapped at the approaching Talbot. The nails dug more deeply into the boy's neck, the other hand pulling the boy closer into it. One of its legs was propped on the window frame and the other hung free. Its free hand swiped at the air in front of the advancing Talbot Leonard.

"Stevie, remember what Mr. Rainbird said about how you get to the top of our profession?" Liz called out.

The thing shot out its right arm and slashed at the air toward Liz.

"No….no Ma'am," Stevie stammered.

Stevie flinched when the thing shook him with its hand, the long, bony fingers tightening on his neck. It made a move like it was going to bite the boy, its eyes ever watchful of the people in front of it. Then it smiled.

Liz nudged Talbot with her shoe.

"He said sometimes you had to *elbow* your way to the top!" she yelled as loud as she could.

Stevie's eyes widened but did as Liz commanded. He closed his eyes and then brought his elbow out and back with everything he had. His bony elbow caught the creature in the sternum and it screamed in pain, but the elbow had created the desired result when the elongated fingers flew away from his neck and the boy hit the carpet of the reception area and the creature was left with the razor sharp nails of its right hand piercing his hat.

At that split-second of frozen time between action and reaction, Talbot Leonard fired three times from his snub nosed revolver. The muzzle flair brightly illuminated the darkened room. The first bullet was on target, striking the strange creature in the shoulder, knocking its arm away and sending Stevie's hat across the room. The second thirty-eight slug caught it in the throat, knocking it down from the window frame. The final shot went astray of his aimed point and glanced off of its upper right forehead.

Chaplin jumped so high he actually landed in Doug's arms, forcing him back into his vacated chair and sending them both over backward. Cooper was frozen; flash blinded and still holding the shiny letter opener Liz had given him. Stevie, a creature of necessity was crawling at a fantastic rate of speed toward the desk area. Liz had her small gun pointed straight at the quickly recovering abomination before them.

The beast had grabbed for its spurting throat, obviously the most serious of the three wounds. It removed the grotesque hand away and allowed the blood to spurt free onto the thick carpet. It tilted its head in curiosity at first and then looked up into the astonished eyes of its attackers and it actually smiled. As they watched the streaming blood lessened as each spurt sent out by its beating pulse slowed until there was just a small trickle of blood.

It hissed and advanced. It caught Stevie by the leg and easily tossed him five feet across the room as if he were nothing more than a rag-doll. He landed hard against the wall just below the shattered window, grunting as he lay still. Talbot fired again, catching the nightmare in the stomach, making it momentarily double over. Liz added her small amount of firepower and caught it once in its left arm and again in the thigh, eliciting a scream of pain and outrage.

The creature hissed and spat as it momentarily looked at the struggling forms of Fairbanks and Chaplin, obviously deeming them less of a threat. It then advanced one slow step at a time, its wounds no more than a hindrance as it now zeroed in on Liz, Cooper and Talbot. Cooper finally broke from his paralysis and let go of the ineffectual letter opener and picked up the heavier desk lamp from Liz's desk and attacked the beast that stood at least a foot above his tall frame.

"No Coop!" Talbot yelled.

But it was too late, Cooper swung the lamp, the cord flying behind it like a whip and smashed the creature in the face, but the effort was like hitting it with a fake movie prop. The impact sent its head reeling backward but it was as if it was placed upon a powerful and thick spring. The beast was immediately upon Cooper, hissing and snapping like a mad dog. There was no scream for help or any verbal reaction at all, but Gary Cooper was still self-aware enough to protect his throat as it seemed that was what the creature was reaching its long, thick neck toward. His elbow was planted in its neck as he tried desperately to fend it off.

With his free hand he punched it several blows in the face, at first he thought he was doing well, the thickened lips of the monstrosity looked as if they were bleeding, until Cooper realized with sickening clarity that it was a deep red lipstick and not blood that was smeared across the creature's lips.

Talbot Leonard stepped quickly up to the beast and fired point blank into its temple. The force of the bullet slammed its head to the left but that was the extent of the impact. It turned as fast as a hissing cat and struck out at Talbot, hitting him and sending the detective hard into the wall, knocking a large picture of Greta Garbo from its nail. Talbot grunted and slid slowly down to the floor, while the beast turned and continued to try and get at Coopers throat, snapping and spiting like a berserk cat out of someone' darkest nightmare.

The teeth were now only inches from the movie star's throat when an impact sent the creature sprawling away from Cooper as both Fairbanks and Chaplin had added their weight to the brawl. They rolled with the horrible thing until they ran into the legs of the unconscious Talbot Leonard, whose bow-tie was now hanging from the right side of his collar. He grunted as his belly stopped the momentum of the three combatants. Cooper tried to stand but fell from the enormous amount of energy he had expended keeping the female nightmare from reaching his throat. He collapsed as he saw Liz point and fire her small .32 automatic.

Liz screamed in frustration when she pulled the small chrome trigger and nothing happened, *'click.'* The weapon misfired. She didn't know what to do as the strange creature had gained the initiative with Fairbanks and Chaplin. Charlie was still swinging his fists for all he was worth, actually slapping as the case may be, but he was still connecting, with each blow of his open hand the creature would snap at it and Charlie would pull it back just in the nick of time and the beast would clap her enormous teeth onto empty air. But Doug Fairbanks was not in the best of shape; he meekly brought his arms up in defense but was unable to strike. He was losing all his strength, in the semi-darkness Liz could see he was fading fast, something was wrong, possibly his ailing heart.

Liz was now in a panic. Charlie's defensive strikes were slowing and the horrible entity straddling both men acted as if it were enjoying the battle with the fast weakening men.

Stevie groaned and looked up from the spot where he had come to rest and immediately saw the six of them were losing a battle they hadn't been ready for. This reminded him of the tavern his Ma used to work at in Brooklyn where they had a brawl every other night. There were people laying everywhere. Stevie stumbled to his feet in time to see Liz jump on the snapping creature and start pulling on its hair, then he saw Mr. Fairbanks struggling for air and then he quickly spied Charlie weakly slap at the creature's strange white skin, all the while the thing's form writhed and smiled at the weakening attempts to fend it off.

Stevie suddenly gathered his strength and stood and tried to run but stumbled. He came to rest beside Cooper who was trying to gain his feet and rejoin the fight. Stevie tried to stand again but his shock weakened legs gave out and he fell onto his knees and then onto his belly. His hand hit something sharp and cool to the touch. He grasped it and realized it was the letter opener that Mr. Cooper must have dropped. Stevie even remembered it was Liz's personal opener which they all had chipped in for at the office (although his contribution had only been two bits) on her birthday. It was embossed with her name and it was made of Sterling silver. He pulled it toward him and tried to stand.

He knew if he attacked with such a small weapon it would probably be taken from him and stuck into his own chest, but he had to do something, Sam would, no matter the odds he would never allow people who had come to him for protection to be harmed. Stevie steeled himself and pushed up onto his hands and then stood upright on shaky legs. He saw that Liz had lost her hold on the long hair of the beast and was now sprawled out behind the fracas.

"Ahhhh," he screamed as he jumped for the struggling group.

He tripped; Cooper had seen what he was attempting and grabbed his right tennis shoe at the last moment, bringing him up short. But an amazing thing happened that often does in warfare—a seemingly tough blow to your plans somehow works out better in the long run. If Cooper hadn't grabbed Stevie's shoe at that last critical moment in an attempt to save the kid from the foul thing before them, he would have overshot his target and plunged the letter opener deep into the now fully conscious Talbot Leonard. But luck, strange as it is, delivered the letter opener straight into the smiling creatures left temple.

The scream of pain issued out of the female mouth shook the room. They heard breaking glass throughout the building as the high-pitched wail of anguish coursed through the steel and brick of the Alhambra. The creature shot upward, striking the ceiling and staying there, trying in vain to pull the letter opener from its temple with one hand while the claws of the other dug deeply into the plaster. The scantily clad breasts swung backward and forward as the creature wrenched at the silver letter opener, but still her backside clung to the wall, the chain of beads holding its hair was shaken free where it fell onto Cooper. The hair now free of its bindings swished about as if it were under water, fanning out like that of an enraged peacock. But still the creature was pressed hard onto the ceiling, thrashing and screaming and speaking in a strange tongue. The wounded beast pulled and tugged at the silver object jutting from its head as its movement weakened. The creature slowly started floating down from the ceiling as if it were being lowered on unseen wires.

When the beast finally touched down onto the carpet, Stevie ran forward and went to his knees. He could see that the monstrosity lying before him was dying; its eyes were clenched shut as it fought with the infernal instrument that was causing its death. Stevie knew he wanted to pull it free and strike at the beast's heart, so he reached out but his hand was grabbed by the creatures, only this time it was so weak that Stevie easily shook of her grip. He reached for the letter opener.

"No Stevie, leave it in," Liz and Talbot shouted at the same time.

But it was too late, he grabbed the handle and pulled the small blade free and just as he raised it up again to strike the nightmare at its heart, it quickly scrambled to its feet, then turned and literally flew at the window and just before leaping free it turned and screeched at the shocked people witnessing what could not be happening.

"Your fate has been sealed," it hissed in English," then it jumped through the window and into the gathering storm.

Stevie ran to the window and looked, but the creature was nowhere to be seen. There was only rain and the few people below who went along their way underneath umbrellas ignorant of the life and death struggle that had just taken place not two hundred feet from them. As Stevie looked out on an oblivious world he wished he had been one of those ignorant souls whose only concern was crossing Sunset without getting their herringbone suits wet, because the safe and sane world he thought he was just now getting a grasp of, had somehow turned into a dark, menacing mystery, and that mystery had teeth.

The Count D'Sarcuni had only been in front of the German consulate on Wilshire since six o'clock this evening when the man he was sent to watch hurriedly left in his chauffeur driven Mercedes. The Master's premonition had been right; this night was seeing strange activity on a rather large scale. One of the men was the German military attaché, and he had covertly exited the embassy, obviously bypassing the SS men who undoubtedly guarded the building.

It was getting harder and harder for anyone coming and going from the German consulate to escape the surveillance that was now placed on them by the American FBI and that peasant director of theirs, Hoover. The count knew the American FBI wasn't that hard to fool. D'Sarcuni had watched the first Mercedes leave the front of the old buildings grounds about five minutes before, but he hadn't fallen for the bait, but the FBI tail had. He had had to lower himself when two cars parked not fifty feet behind his own, turned on their headlights and followed the first car. The bait had managed to pull both of the surveillance cars away from the grounds, while the real car carrying the Consulate General and the German military attaché quickly exited the grounds from the back and was going in the opposite direction. It was a standard embassy or consulate trick invented for shaking unwanted surveillance and anyone else spying on their activities.

Luckily the only way out from the back entrance brought them only feet away from where the Count had parked. If the FBI had waited only a few seconds their real targets would have presented themselves.

As D'Sarcuni's car fell in unseen behind the Mercedes, he knew he would have to report to the Ancient One that certain elements of the German diplomatic corps had joined the Generals and Field Marshall's in their quest to rid the world of *Him*.

D'Sarcuni ordered his driver to follow at a discreet distance. While they went west, he hoped his wife was having a good time dealing with Dalhart's remaining people at his office; she always seemed to get the fun and more exciting end of things.

Twenty minutes later, D'Sarcuni got an uneasy feeling as the large Mercedes turned into a small marina just outside of San Pedro Harbor. He ordered his driver to douse the car lights and go through the entrance with as much stealth as possible. There were no guards at the gate as they pulled into a parking spot two hundred feet from where the Mercedes had pulled in. As he watched with a set of binoculars, the consulate general and military liaison exited the car and waited in the falling rain with only the German consul using an umbrella. They were there only a minute when he was approached by a man who had appeared as if from nowhere. After a moment's conversation all three men turned and started walking down the rain-soaked pier. The Count watched, almost as far as the binoculars would allow until he saw them step into large motor-launch. The Count tossed the glasses on the seat beside him and regretted not bringing a bottle of Cognac along. He was always amazed he retained his appetite for such earthly things, but he figured he really never wanted to be like his Master, to him immortality would have been a boring life without the creature comforts he once knew.

The small boat chugged its way out into the choppy harbor. The consulate general was clearly starting to feel seasick. The tall colonel who'd come onboard with him knew that the crew hated the weakness of men like this. The crew was specially chosen for this mission—they were men from the elite Special Operations Department of the German Navy. The colonel had only known the Consulate General for a week and knew little about him other than he carried the smell of weakness about him as he would a briefcase, and was clearly a man who would turn his allegiance right back to the Nazis if confronted with the slightest hint of danger. As he took in these naval specialists he knew they would just as soon cut his and the consulate general's throats as follow their orders. But taking orders—even from a cowardly diplomat and his pet military attaché was part of their duty.

They traveled just outside of the harbor entrance and then the captain ordered slow-ahead. He left the small flying-bridge and shouted a few orders, but the wind and rain snatched his words away before they reached the career diplomat. Men went fore and aft and started coiling ropes and a few even removed hidden submachine guns from the three lifeboats that lined her decks on either side. The captain waved the Consul General and the German Colonel forward.

"Do you wish to see why we will win any war that madman Hitler has in store for us, even though he is as incompetent as an angry child?"

The colonel only stared at the sea captain; obviously the fool was unaware of the actual reason his commanding admirals had assigned him duties here in American waters. It wasn't to win a war, it was to stop one from ever happening, or at least shorten the one they now had.

With his gorge rising into his throat, the consul general only nodded, keeping his lips tight. The Colonel just looked away.

"Good, watch closely now," the weathered captain said pointing off to the starboard side of the small vessel.

He raised a lamp as the boat hit a heavy swell; the captain held the lamp higher and flicked the lever on its side three times, then two times in rapid succession.

The official representative of the Third Reich—the Reich of a thousand years, and his attaché watched as between two large sea swells there was an eruption of bubbles and spray from the surface of the sea. The civilian was astounded at the size of the bubbles and the amount of foam surrounding them. Then he gasped as a large pointed bow of a ship broke the surface of the water and that was quickly followed by the large conning tower of a submarine's bridge. That sight was surreally illuminated by occasional flashes of lightning further out at sea. The submarine rose in silence as the boat crew scrambled to make ready lines that would secure the U-Boat to their much smaller craft.

"*Gott in Himmel*," the consul general exclaimed aloud, lowering his umbrella and wiping his mouth with a white handkerchief.

"No, Heir Klienmann, this is courtesy of Admiral Raeder and Field Marshall Hartmann," the Army Colonel said smiling as the U-Boat surfaced completely and arrogantly inside American territorial waters.

As the smaller boat maneuvered forward, the large submarine, the U-166, sat silently but with a menacing countenance as men emerged from below decks and manned her forward 5 inch gun. There were other men dressed in black and gray commando garb that lined the forward deck. One of these men stepped forward and glanced upward into the driving rain and then he gave the captain of the submarine stationed high above on the conning tower the traditional army and navy salute, forgoing the mandated Nazi courtesy of an extended right arm. The captain returned the offered salute and the men in unison turned left as the smaller craft hit the exposed side of the larger boat's ballast tank. The men easily stepped down to the ballast tank and then further down onto the fishing boat. The Consul General counted fifteen men in all. The commandos were not as menacing and filthy looking as the German fishermen, but far more deadly in appearance.

As the last man stepped into the boat, three of the fishermen used long poles to push away from the U-166. Then the men on her deck disappeared after securing the forward gun mount and then without any fanfare slowly and silently slipped beneath the waves.

"Herr Klienmann, this is Major Paul Lansdorf, second in command of the *Black Forest Group Commando* of the Seventh German Army Corp.," the colonel stated as a big man stepped forward in the rain and saluted.

"Welcome to America, Major," he turned toward the consul general. "Would you excuse us Herr Klienmann?" he asked politely.

The consul general looked around him, the seaman were going about their business as the small boat made its way back to the marina and they paid him no mind as they worked, so he felt safe to step a few feet away and was content to try and hide his illness at the railing.

"The admiral briefed you on our strict need of tight security in this matter while you were in Buenos Aires?"

"Yes, we are not at liberty to divulge any aspect of our operation to anyone, especially the consulate staff. We are ordered not to speak with anyone other than you, our commanding officer, for as long as the mission is in place.," the major finally made direct eye contact with German military attaché. "The only incidental not discussed or mentioned in our sealed orders was the specific target of that mission."

Colonel Erich Raedal smiled and through the falling rain the Commando Major could see his eyes close and then slowly open again.

"Our unit was chosen because of certain historical quirks, Major, in as we have no love for our Fuehrer. We were segregated by certain command authority officers as an ideal unit to work for them directly," he held the Major's gaze a moment. "These gentlemen are of the same opinion as ourselves that the madman now running the lives of millions of Germans will lead us to utter destruction."

The major remained stock still and ramrod straight. He knew there were small idiosyncrasies that had caught his attention as to the make-up of their commando unit, but hadn't really questioned it until now. Through the grumblings and barely hidden threats about their new government by the men secretly selected for their unit it now made sense to him and he was silently relieved he found himself not-so alone as he had been only moments before this new revelation as to their mission.

The smile was finally returned.

"Then why aren't we at home where we can correct that situation with the man responsible for our current hostilities?"

"We are Major, we are here to kill the thing responsible for our situation in Europe, the real Furher, and I suspect this blasted nightmare will kill us all. We won't be dealing with a former paperhanger as is Hitler here. This is something entirely out of the realm of a nightmare."

The German colonel said nothing as he turned and left the foredeck just as the fishing boat got underway again. Major Lansdorf watched the most brilliant commando in the world, Colonel Erich Raedal, leave the deck and duck into the wheelhouse and then he shuddered, not because of the rain but because he was now asking himself, *just who*, or perhaps the better question to ask was, *just what was it they were here to kill?*

Elysian Park, Los Angeles

There hadn't been any conversation in the car for the past half an hour. Every few minutes Rainbird or Sam would wipe down their half of window as the heat from their bodies were creating considerable condensation. Connie had her eyes pinned to the mob of people outside of the residence Pete and Willis had entered over forty-five minutes before. The crowd of neighbors had grown by at least twenty and their attitudes had become more agitated toward the police whom had also grown by two more prowl cars. She was thinking it would be hard to see anything out of the ordinary with all these people crowding the sidewalk and the park.

Sam reached over and tugged on Rainbird's overcoat and nodded his head toward the window.

"Me and John are going to step out for a minute. Frank keep your eyes on those people, I don't like the way this is shaping up."

"Gotcha' boss."

Connie watched Sam put his fedora on and open the door, his eyes catching hers for the briefest of moments in the rearview mirror, just enough to give her a small jolt to her stomach. She squirmed in her seat and pulled her coat tighter around herself. The eye contact should have been uncomfortable with a stranger like Sam, but it wasn't. It was more of a pleasant fluttering in her stomach. She closed her eyes and just figured it was her way of acknowledging his help in trying to find her sister, nothing more than that.

Sam pulled his collar up on his raincoat and walked to the back of the car and turned and faced the house which hadn't shown much movement since Willis and Pete had gone inside. He glanced at the police cars which were sitting side by side sixty yards away. The house they were parked in front of was dark and Sam wondered if these neighbors were part of the mob currently outside. He was joined by Rainbird who stood silently next to him.

"You were awful quiet in there John. Is there something on your mind besides having a large speaking part in a Universal horror script?"

"Not really, Sam. I just have the feeling he gave me this information in the dream on purpose. I think he knew we would track him here."

"I thought that was pretty clear, otherwise why would he say he was letting one of the girls go? Since we don't know where Jeannie Yale was abducted, this is the obvious starting point. It could still be a wild goose-chase; he could release her in Ontario, or Pomona, even the damn walnut groves out toward Chino. It's just narrowing the odds a little."

"No, he wants to see us in the flesh Sam, I know he does, to size us up. Why he thinks we're a threat, I don't know."

"I want to ask you something John," Sam said as a bolt of lightning made the mob in front of them jump and move about nervously.

John placed both his hands in his raincoat and waited. Rain water cascaded from the brim of his hat, but he didn't make eye contact with his friend.

"It's you isn't it?"

Rainbird looked over after a long silent moment.

"What do you mean?"

"It was never your mother, was it?" Sam asked as he pulled out a cigarette and turned away from the slanting rain to light it.

"How did you know?" John finally asked.

"When you were talking to Miss Yale about it, I saw it in your eyes. It's like you're ashamed of that particular ability."

"It's been this way since I was a boy, Sam. The only other one that has this...this...thing is an uncle. I had no friends because I would dream about them, but only when something bad was going to happen, never anything good. I turned them against me. My Ma, god-bless her, started telling folks it was her doing the dream walking to take the heat off, but it was too late for the people on the rez," he looked at Sam, "on the reservation, I was marked, tainted. But I guess it worked out for me in the long run because after a while my Ma figured it was time for me to go and she arranged my schooling for me, and ta-da," he removed his hands from his pockets and held them out like a magician, "here I am today, a sleepless detective that's not worth a good goddamn to anyone."

"Yeah, worthless," Sam said as he took a drag from his cigarette and then flipped it into the running gutter. "Well, I suspect you're right about this maniac's intentions, I think he'll be here, but he's only going to see you three, if he shows, I'll be nearby, he only knows you, is attracted to you, maybe we can use that little bit of knowledge to our advantage."

"How so?"

"Feel like being the bait?"

"Just as long as the fisherman doesn't forget his pole's in the water," John said with a smile.

Sam winked and patted John on the arm and then walked slowly away beside the dark house and disappeared into the open backyard. John watched him go and then decided it was time to get out of the rain.

Von Railing sat in the back seat of the black Hudson. McDougal was in his customary spot behind the wheel and little Adria sat beside him, resplendent in a new dress and new shoes. Her hair was combed and tied into a pony tail, all thanks to Francesca's steady hand and soft words she used on the girl just before the Countess went on her mission to the detective's offices.

He looked over at the small girl who was looking out of the Hudson's side window. She recognized where she was but kept her questions to herself as she knew the mean man didn't like her speaking to him. She would look out into the rain at her house and then sit back and place her hands on her lap in silence. For Von Railing, she had at least stopped humming that irritating little tune.

"I don't like being as near as we are to a crime scene, and the local constabulary only feet away from us, this is madness," McDougal offered.

"I'll be sure to pass along your concerns, peat farmer," Von Railing countered.

"Is it true the Master believes they know where we're at?" he looked in the mirror for a reaction, "I mean the German resistance, they know we're here in this country, this city?"

"That idiot Count D'Sarcuni has never been discreet has he? We don't know that the generals and admirals know anything for sure—the Master is only being cautious."

"Cautious? This is being cautious, bringing a child back to the scene of her abduction, just so the Master can lay eyes on people who couldn't in a million lifetimes cause him harm? This is madness."

Von Railing couldn't very well disagree with McDougal; after all it was the Scotsman and himself taking the ultimate risk. *My god,* he thought, *McDougal could be stopped with a fist to his jaw, and I, I could be killed by sticking a tree branch or croquet peg into my chest. Yes, it was madness.*

"Such is our lot. We have cast our futures with the Master, and we will do as he says."

"I'll tell you one thing; those goddamn bleeding hearts in Germany won't give a damn about us. If they want the Master badly enough, they will by god take him and go through us to do it."

"Would you silence yourself, the Master has just started his work in Europe, he will go back alive and well *with us,* and I'm afraid the Reich's resistance will crumble before him. Those fools will find out in no uncertain terms what it would be like to step through the front door of hell if they come for him."

McDougal fell silent. Von Railing looked at his pocket watch; it was fast approaching eight-thirty, time for the little miss to go home.

Von Railing reached over the small girl and opened the rear door. "Go home to your mother and father; hold your new raincoat up over your head so you don't get wet, and mind you do what the Master asked you to do."

Adria looked at the German. "You're not a very nice man."

Von Railing leaned as close to the small girl as he could.

"Who said I was a man at all," he allowed his incisors to show. They grew to almost four inches long and then he hissed at her, scaring her until she virtually jumped from the Hudson.

"How long do we have to stay out here, Sarge?"

Sergeant Lyle Henderson looked at his rookie partner and blew out a long trail of smoke into his face. Patrolman Henry Feeney waved at the smoke and then coughed then turned away.

"We stay put until we're called off. The captain doesn't like this crowd hanging out here."

"Ah, Sarge, they're just folks worried about their neighbor's is all."

"The Captain thinks they're trouble makers, besides there's talk around the division that say's the parents may have had something to do with the abduction."

"You're kidding?"

The Sergeant didn't answer, he sat stock still, the windows were totally fogged over and they couldn't see the patrol car next to them much less the crowd they were supposed to be watching. The sergeant unscrewed the cap off a small bottle of whiskey and took three long swallows.

"Hey, Sarge?" but suddenly the question froze in the patrolman's throat as he realized he and his partner were not the only ones in the car. He slowly turned his head and all he saw in the darkness of the patrol car were the yellow eyes.

Through the thrumming of the rain on the hood and top of the car, both policemen could hear a voice, giving soft commands. They blinked and smiled politely, nodding, understanding the silent orders that filled their heads, and then they looked at each other and nodded just once. The sergeant let the bottle of whiskey slide from his fingertips unnoticed. Each officer opened his door and stepped out into the rain without placing their hats on their heads. They removed their nightsticks from their belts, the Sarge also reached into his back pocket and withdrew a Blackjack—a lead weight filled strap of leather and hid it in the palm of his hand. They then went toward the front of the car. The rookie patrolman started striking his left hand with his nightstick and looking angrily at the crowd. For a moment the stick slowed as he had a momentary questioning of his orders, then he felt another hard hit in the brain and he began slapping the nightstick harder—hard enough that people standing ten feet away could hear it over the rain. Both men waited, smiling.

The young patrolman in the next car wiped his side window free of condensation and stared at the two policemen just standing there beside them in the rain. He was about to turn and say something to his partner when the two men waded into the crowd of people standing vigilant around the house. The patrolman's eyes widened, then he and his partner jumped out of their car and were immediately surrounded by angry members the crowd who had watched the first two policemen attack their friends without warning.

Rainbird couldn't believe what had just happened. The Los Angeles Police Department was never known for their civic kindness, but what he had just seen was blatant brutality. The first attack was a vicious blow by a patrolman against a kid who couldn't have been any more than twenty-two, and then the young officer struck a woman who'd been passing out coffee to the crowd in the face. She collapsed and then the cop struck her again. His partner had also caught an unsuspecting man off guard and immediately started raining blows down upon him. Then the rest of the gathered friends and neighbors weren't going to wait to be hit, they pounced on the two patrolmen. Then the two men in the other car, not knowing what was really happening, and who only saw their brother policemen go down, sprang quickly into the rain and started hammering away at the gathered people in a vain attempt to save them from themselves.

"What the hell? Has everyone gone nuts?" Rainbird said as he threw open his door and ran toward the expanding riot in front of the

Rodriguez's house. As he ran he knew Frank was beside him and that meant Connie was alone. Then he saw Willis look out of the window and John waved him back with both arms flailing in the rain. Willis saw this and closed the blinds and disappeared.

"What started this?" Frank asked trying to keep up with Rainbird.

John didn't answer as he got to the first mob of people who had the young officer down and were pounding him with their fists as he meekly swung his nightstick. Rainbird threw one and then another of the people off and tried in vain to reach for the policemen but the first two people were replaced by more. He was joined by Frank and they waded into the small knot of people, not trying to save the cop that instigated this whole thing, but to try and stop this thing before someone really got their head busted, this was only going to bring massive retaliation from the police department no matter who started what.

They finally managed to free the young cop, dragging him away by his limp arms, and then they made him stay put leaning against the bumper of his patrol car. Rainbird and Frank had just started moving to the next congested ball of people when John felt hands on his raincoat pulling him away. Then he heard a woman's voice rise above the din happening around them. Lightning erupted over the hills and another bolt struck close by in the darkened Elysian park, the immediate smash of thunder shaking the very ground they were on. John turned and saw Connie; she was screaming something at him and pointing toward the house. Frank saw what was happening and let go of one of the neighbors whom he had by the collar and screamed at him to go home.

"Mr. Rainbird, look!" she screamed again as she pointed. Rain had soaked her head and her hair was dangling in her face, but John followed her finger.

"I'll be damned," he said far too low for Connie or Frank to hear.

Walking as if a riot weren't taking place all around her, a small child had placed a light yellow raincoat over her head and was walking across the street toward the house. She had leg braces on but seemed to be negotiating the rain soaked sidewalk just fine. Her small crutches attached to her wrists marched time with her legs perfectly. She easily stepped around a man who had just hit the ground beside her as she turned easily up the stone walkway that started just beyond a small fence that surrounded the Rodriguez's front yard. She walked up and turned for just one moment and looked at the sky. John followed her gaze but could see nothing but falling rain. Then she walked the short distance and climbed the three steps to her door. He watched as she tried the knob and when she found it was locked, knocked. Rainbird took Connie by the arm and then he reached for a battered Frank, and then they made their way through the struggling neighbors and the three remaining but still battling policemen. They splashed up the walk and stood just off of the porch and waited. The girl turned and looked at them. She had lowered her small raincoat and they could clearly see she was clean and dressed well and warm. Connie tried to smile but failed as tears welled up in her eyes. Lightning lit the sky again and John looked up as the hairs stood up on the back of his neck. He felt as if they were being watched from somewhere high up, but he ignored the feeling and watched as the door was opened by Mr. Rodriguez.

"Ahhhh," the man screamed as he reached for his lost child. They were joined by who John thought must be the mother and right there in the middle of a riot was a homecoming all the concerned neighbors and supposed hard working policeman were missing.

John again took Connie by the arm and joined the people at the open doorway. Willis squeezed past and looked at Rainbird with a questioning look on his face.

"I don't know, Willis, let's get them inside, before those idiots out there see her," he said.

The crying and hugs went on forever, even after John was introduced by Willis and Pete. They slapped John on the back and hugged him as if he had been the one to bring her home, and they failed to hear when he denied having anything to do with their joyous reunion. He could see that the girl's parents just didn't care who brought her back as tonight everyone was a hero and they would be forever in everyone's, anyone's debt. Amidst the screams and yells and anger of the outside world they watched as everyone cried. Connie wiped her eyes, happy for the family, but crying also after realizing her sister wasn't the one freed. She was dying to talk to the small child.

"What in the hell is going on out there?" Pete asked as he pulled the blind away from the window.

"The hell if I know," John said as he eased out of his raincoat.

"Well, more cops are here, three cars full I think."

"Close the blind Pete, we don't want anyone snooping around in here just yet," Rainbird said as he also removed his wet fedora.

The lights flickered for a moment and then steadied again. The child was crying, not really knowing why her parents weren't mad at her.

"Your sister, sweetie, where is your sister?" her distraught father finally asked.

Her mother pulled the raincoat off of Adria and tossed it away, not liking something about the way it smelled.

"Angela...," a confused look crossed the girl's face. "She was sick...I think."

"Oh god, please, no," the mother said and crossed herself.

"What do you mean?" her father asked, holding her by the shoulders.

"She's with the other girl's...I think," Adria said scrunching up her face in deep thought as if she were trying her hardest to remember.

It was John who thought that maybe it was in the young girl's best interest that she wasn't able to recall the basement. It was time for him to do his job, but he didn't want to frighten the girl any more than she already was. Then he struck on an idea.

"Mr. Rodriguez, Mrs. Rodriguez, this is Miss Constance Yale, her sister is also one of those missing; can she ask your daughter a few questions?"

Connie looked at Rainbird gratefully for broaching the subject she herself hadn't known how to do.

"Si, si," the father said and quickly straightened up from where he was kneeling and moved aside, but not letting go of his daughter's hand. The mother only nodded, keeping her hands wrapped in her apron coiled at her mouth.

John looked around and the lights flickered once again after another bolt of lightning illuminated the screen covered windows. The following thunder made everyone tense. John nodded, giving an unvoiced command for Pete to move to the front door. He twisted his hand in the air, indicating he should lock the door.

"Hi," Connie said as she removed her green coat. She handed it to Rainbird who tossed it on top of his own.

"Hi," the girl said. "You look like my friend."

Connie developed a lump in her throat and was in danger of crying before she got her questions out.

"Does your friend have a name, the one that looks like me?" she stumbled with the words but finally managed to get them out of her mouth.

Frank, Pete, Willis and John watched the little girl tilt her head and then smile.

"She tells really neat stories, she knows so many stories, she told a hundred stories and we listened all day and night. Then I would sing!" she said enthusiastically.

"Honey, the one that looks like me, her name was…?

"Jeannie!" Adria said and jumped like it was a big surprise with her leg braces almost failing her when she landed. Her father steadied her, half laughing, half sobbing.

Connie lowered her eyes and collapsed to her knees. John touched her shoulder and she looked up quickly, "I'm all right," she said more for her own benefit than anyone else's.

The girl let go of her father's hand, actually twisting out of it would be a more descriptive term. She walked straight legged up to Connie and hugged her as if she had known her forever.

Connie buried her face in the girl's new smelling dress. "Is she alive?" she asked into the girl's shoulder, barely loud enough for all to hear.

"Yes, silly, she's only a little sick, not like the other girls. The others are mean now, but Frankenstein won't hurt her, he likes her stories as much as I do."

Connie cried openly now, not caring who saw her weak side. The small child patted her on the back as if consoling her as she would her older sister. She kept smiling. Adria then smiled up at Rainbird, who returned it.

Then the lights went out.

"Oops. I think he's here. He doesn't like the lights," Adria said and clapped her hands once in happiness as she backed away from Connie.

Connie stood, taking the child's hand and looked around at the now darkened house. She could still hear loud voices outside as the small riot was being brought under some kind of control.

"The lights in the park are still on, so is the house on the left. It's only this one," Pete said as he looked out of the small triangular window set high in the front door.

Rainbird and Frank pulled out their guns and Mrs. Rodriguez gave out a small shout of fear and reached for her daughter.

"Everyone stays close together," John said. "Pete, get in here, Willis, you keep an eye on that hallway, Frank you're on me."

"What are we supposed to be looking for John, for crying out loud," Pete asked nervously as he moved into the living room, stubbing his shoe on an end table as he did.

The sound hit everyone as if the words were spoken into each individual's ears.

"As you see, Shaman, I keep my word; one of the children has been brought back home."

Pete, Willis and Frank spun around as if Satan himself had tapped them on the shoulder. Their guns were out and pointing in all directions.

"The parents of this girl are grateful," was the only thing John could say. His mouth was full of cotton and his hands were shaking.

"Yes, I imagine they are, but alas, I did not do this thing for them."

"Then why," he asked, turning this way and that, trying to pinpoint where the voice was coming from, but he soon discovered it was coming from everywhere as the other three detectives could attest, as they too swung around in circles.

"Where is my sister you goddamned bastard!" Connie screamed out loud.

"Sister? Oh yes, the sister. I will keep her. She is no longer yours; after all, did you not forfeit her by chaining her to a farm?"

"I did not—"

John silenced her by placing a big hand over her mouth. She struggled at first and then relaxed, realizing she was playing into this thing's hands.

Lightning from outside illuminated the room which was quickly filled with unsettling shadows. John used the brief moment of light to quickly scan the area. Frank, Pete and Willis did the same. He saw Willis head down the hallway, opening doors as he went. Rainbird grimaced, wanting him to stay put.

"Dalhart is not among your party, Red Man?"

"He has business elsewhere," John answered.

"Then he shall meet his fate elsewhere."

Bait, the word kept going through John's mind like a runaway bowling ball. He had to force himself to stop thinking while the creature, that's what it was, he was sure of that now more than ever, was so near to him physically. He looked around in the darkness. His skin was clammy, he was shaking, just like in his dreams the air was heavy and oppressive. *The wolf was among the flock*, he remembered a reverend used to say that when he was a child about liquor being prevalent on the reservation, only this time, this particular wolf was really here and he felt like a lamb facing down the unseen threat.

"Sam's a little more resilient than even you would believe," was the only retort Rainbird could manage to utter as he moved the aim of his .38 to and fro.

"I believe you let one of your tribe wander astray Red Man," the voice boomed with a light chuckle.

Suddenly out of the darkness, lit momentarily by a streak of lightning and the crash of thunder, Willis went flying from the small hallway where he had been checking rooms. He smashed into Pete and they both crashed to the floor. Amidst the screams and yells of surprise, John thought he saw movement exit the hallway and into the living room, but the house had grown pitch black once again and his night vision had been ruined by the lightning strike outside.

"Willis?" John called out.

"He's hurt, I feel blood," Pete called out from the floor.

Connie went to her hands and knees and quickly made her way toward the sound of Pete's voice. She passed Adria and her parents who had also went to ground when Willis went flying into the room. She finally made it as far as the small table where Pete was holding the head of Willis in his arms. She quickly felt for a pulse and was happy when the steady beat of his heart could be felt.

"He's just unconscious, he's still breathing," Connie called out.

Frank joined Connie at Willis's side and handed her Willis's gun which he'd found on the floor.

"The Nubian is breathing only because I am merciful at times of initial introduction," the voice called out softly and ended with another light chuckle.

"I think it's time introductions were properly made, who are you and why are you here?" John asked as angrily as he could.

"Where are my manners?" the voice came from all around them. *"I am here to usher in my time—a time that sees not joy, but despair. Darkness, even in the light of day, the plan of a million years has finally been put into motion and I am its author."*

"El Diablo," Mr. Rodriguez mumbled.

The laughter was deep and it was mocking, dripping with the kind of venom reserved for the deepest sanitarium.

"Lucifer has no place in my world as he is a lover of man while I am mankind's butcher. In the end, he will side where he always sides, on the side of himself."

"I have come to think of you as an over the hill actor, always bellowing to say something, but never saying anything clearly enough to be understood, one who plies riddles where a simple answer would suffice," Rainbird said even as he thought *Where is Sam?*

"You mock me Red Niggar, after I make you a gift of the child?"

John didn't answer, like in his dream he felt the air swirl in front of him, he looked closely at a single spot and concentrated, then he felt a soft, nauseating wind pass him and go to his rear. The presence then left there and lightly brushed past him once again and he felt it head for the Rodriguez's in front of him. He heard the screams of the parent as Adria was snatched up and held, seemingly magically floating before them. In the darkness John could see the lightness of her dress, and to his amazement he heard the child giggle.

"Perhaps I should take back the gift of the child?"

"No, no, no," the mother cried.

"Please, not the girl, not our baby," Mr. Rodriguez said sobbing.

"There has to be a price for insolence, that is an understanding of all warriors, is this not so Shaman?"

"Warriors strike warriors, soldiers battle soldiers, they leave women and children be."

"Yes, the old way. Your understanding of the dead times, maybe that is the attraction between you and I? You have knowledge of the battles of the Old Testament?"

"Yes, they were drilled into me as a boy," John answered as he remembered each and every Sunday on the reservation, being forced to absorb the Baptist way from the white man who taught it.

"Then of course you know that the death of innocents was always our Lord's way of retribution—is this not true Shaman? Or have you turned your face from his book of history and returned to your backward ways?"

The beast was right, the death of children and other innocents was scored throughout the bible, and it seemed God never had any qualms about destroying the good along with the bad.

"For instance," the voice said as the girl was placed on the floor in front of John. Then a loud rustling was heard and then John listened as the mother screamed and start talking in Spanish, and then her words were cut off by her choking.

The girl was snatched up by Connie who had hurried forward and taken her from the floor. John couldn't actually see her do this, but knew it was her; it seemed his senses were growing a little at a time. His eyes moved to the parents, he could see the vague outline of the beast holding the woman, her small hands striking at the clawed hand holding her. The husband was in the creatures other hand, silently kicking, trying to draw a breath of air.

"There is always a price to be paid for mercy. I am merciful, but voids must be filled. The child is free and unhurt, but the barter of that mercy is an expensive one."

"You bastard, you cowardly pig," Connie screamed out and for the first time the shocked child showed an emotion other than happiness, she started crying, seeing her parent's struggling for their lives. She called to them but all was silent.

"Sister, are you willing to pay the price of my mercy?"

Connie was still holding the child close to her, protecting her the best way she could, with her own body.

"I would die a thousand times for my sister."

The beast dropped the parents of the girl and they collapsed, trying to drag air into their starving lungs. Connie then saw movement toward her in the darkness and then had a brief glimpse of the creature as it reached for her. She pushed the girl away from her and at that instant she was picked up by her arm and dangled just as the girl had been.

"My price has now risen woman, you and your sister is what I barter for the child's life!"

The riot outside had grown loud again as the police were using loud speakers to try and get the people dispersed.

Lightning illuminated the room once more and Connie's eyes widened. There in front of her was something unimaginable. The beast was at least eight feet high and stood on cloven hooves. The face was a smear of humanity with scales and incisors that reached its drooping lower lip. The upper lip curled down to the jaw-line and tapered into it. The eyes were deep yellow and they glared into hers as if they were glowing coals of hatred. From the pits of Dante's version of hell she was introduced to Phaltazar.

John gasped as he was seeing his enemy for the first time. He drew his weapon and fired three times, careful not to hit Connie who was screaming and thrashing in the extended grasp of the beast. The bullets struck the creature in the torso and it hissed in pain but didn't still it didn't drop Connie.

"Don't do that," it called out, shaking Connie as if she were a rag doll. She screamed as her arm dislocated. *"The action is not worthy of one such as you."* The beast said as it stepped forward and John watched Connie as she clenched her jaw shut against the pain. *"Now that I have your attention Red man, I will barter with you."*

John was frozen. He heard Pete somewhere behind the creature moving, or at least he thought it was Pete, or maybe Frank.

192

"The woman's life for three days of grace, and then we will face each other in the old way. Your champion, Dalhart, yourself and the foolish men that follow you, will come to me, do we have a bargain?"

"Hey, green boy, drop the dame!"

John recognized Sam's voice but couldn't see where he was.

The beast swung around and Connie trailed its quick movement with a loud scream of agonizing pain. Everyone in the room heard what sounded like water being splashed and the smell of gasoline filled the living room and then the sound of a lighter opening.

"Jesus, Sam!" Rainbird cried out and snatched the child up quickly and then he drove through the darkness where he could barely make out Connie's dangling form.

"Dalhart!" the beast roared as it took a step toward the man in front of it.

Sam kicked Pete, indicating for him and Frank to move Willis out of the way and then struck the lighter. The room filled with the flare of the lighters wick catching and the full view of the beast was there for all to see. John bade the child to stay and then quickly stood and grabbed for Connie, he snatched her dangling right arm and pulled, making her scream out in pain as she was ripped free of the clawed hand, taking three inches of her skin as he did. Sam saw his moment and tossed the lighter.

"I was hoping you would—"

That was as far as the beast got in its greeting as the room suddenly erupted with a *whump*. The creature screamed in shock as the gasoline driven flames swirled around its huge frame. It swung out blindly, missing Sam by only inches, then the pain of the flames became too unbearable and it roared in anger and shock. It leaped from the floor and attached itself to the ceiling and then fell down again to the flaming carpet. It regained its balance and on its large hooves charged toward the plate glass window of the living room and launched itself from the window and into the strengthening storm.

Outside the riot was just being brought under control as neighbors and friends were lined face down on the sidewalk as the reinforced police were trying to restore order. They all turned as one when Phaltazar crashed through the window in flames. The beast stood frozen in time as it hit the wet lawn and roared again, shaking the very ground all were standing and lying upon. The police also froze but the friends and neighbors of the Rodriguez's saw their chance. They gained their feet and fled, not wanting to know what had just exited their friend's house.

The creature roared again and made a fantastic leap toward a giant palm tree, just one of the many that lined Elysian Park. It hit the palm fronds and they exploded upward and outward like a bomb in the heavily falling rain. Then the beast leaped again and hit the grass of the park and rolled, extinguishing the flames in the rain-soaked grass.

While the police were watching the spectacle before them in horrified fascination, Sam quickly led his small band of survivors out of the house, sending Frank and Pete with Willis between them to the right and their car, and to the left went he, John, the injured Connie, the child and her parents, as they were trying to make Sam's car before anyone even knew they were there.

Across the street in a giant pepper tree the creature watched. Its breath was coming in deep, rattling heaps. A bolt of lightning again wrenched the night sky and through the falling rain the yellow, hate-filled eyes of the beast locked on the small band that was making its way free of the house which was now starting to burn in earnest. The eyes followed them to the car, and then it roared as loud as a train, its eyes focused on the man in the lead—Dalhart. The beast saw the policemen staring at it and payoffs or no payoffs to their watch commanders and other officials, they were reaching for their guns, not that the weapons worried it any, but being seen did. It hissed and then leaped two hundred feet away into the night and the harsh storm covering Los Angeles.

Sam drove away as slowly as possible as not to call attention to their escape. The only sounds in the car were Connie moaning quietly and the child crying between her sobbing parents.

"What in the hell made you think of gasoline?" John asked, holding onto Connie.

"I guess I got a good look at that thing's mug before you did while I was in the back yard as it entered the house. It didn't look like bullets would slow it down much. You know I do go to movies too you know," he said as he turned the corner and then sped up, passing even more police and fire vehicles as he did.

"What do you mean?" John said as he adjusted Connie's head, trying not to touch her arm.

"I think we're dealing with somewhat of a legend here, John."

"Goddamn it Sam, spill it okay, I'm not following."

"He means he knows for sure it's a vampire," Connie hissed through the pain. "Mr. Dalhart guessed fire was the only thing that would stop it short of a stake through the heart."

John didn't say anything, he just stared at his partner.

"That's why it took me so long to show up. I had to wade out through that damn riot and siphon a coffee can full of gas from the damn car. My being slow to catch on to what we were really dealing with almost cost Connie and that girl's parents their lives."

"But you saved us," Connie said, trying to sit up, but the pain in her shoulder kept her down.

"In case you didn't know it, that shoulder's going to have to be popped back in," Sam said quickly, taking his eyes off the wet road for a moment.

"Don't call me that again," Connie hissed and put her face deeper into John's arm.

"What?" Sam asked.

"You called her a dame, I don't think she likes that," John said with a small grin.

Sam didn't say anything, he just looked at Connie's form and then smiled as the car sped away toward the city below.

✀ TEN ✀

am had decided the office would be the safest place to hold up for now. It could accommodate more people and he figured with the entity they were dealing with they had better keep everyone together, and the only place large enough was the office.

Sam assisted Connie, following John through the back door of the *Alhambra*. Frank and Pete had Willis between them, following close behind. Willis had finally come around after his ordeal and asked where the truck was that smacked into him and that was enough to make Pete Sanchez laugh. Sam could see that the old man needed the humorous moment as he was close to going over the edge.

As they entered the building accompanied by a flash of lightening, Sam saw with not just a small bit of trepidation that the lights in the stairwell were out. The darkness beyond looked like a large mouth just waiting for them to venture inside. He decided quickly to try the elevator. John and the Rodriguez's brought up the rear through the downpour of rain. Young Adria was asleep in her father's arms. After securing the *Alhambra's* front doors, John motioned the exhausted couple into the elevator and then he stepped in after them. He quickly withdrew his thirty-eight police special and kept it low at his side. Sam saw that he felt uneasy about the elevator as much as himself.

"John, when we get inside I want you to get hold of Doc Goodwin in Century City and see if he can come in and look at Willis and Miss Yale, it also wouldn't hurt to have the girl checked out either."

"You got it," John said.

"Look, Sam, you saved me from getting torn limb from limb, so why don't you just call me Connie, huh?" she said as the bell chimed for the sixth floor. "I allow anyone who saves my life that particular peccadillo."

"Look, I'm sorry—," he started and then stopped just as quickly when the elevator doors slid open.

Connie gasped and the others became immediately on guard as they saw the glass on the landing and the smashed front doors that led into the office of the Sunset Detective Agency.

Sam let go of Connie, letting Mrs. Rodriguez take her, and then drew out his own thirty-eight. John and he stepped quickly from the elevator and saw that the lights were on in the office but they couldn't see anyone inside the reception area. The two were joined by Frank, who also had his gun out. Sam could see that Frank was anxious about Liz, enough so that he would make mistakes. The taller Sam took his arm and shook his head slowly back and forth, wanting him to calm down and think. Frank took a deep breath and nodded. They both turned when they heard footsteps on the stairs coming from the floor above. John had moved quickly to the wall and reached out and hit the landings push button switch plate.

"Hey, don't shoot Mister Rainboyd," Stevie said, throwing his hands over his head.

"Damn it, what were you doing up there?" John asked, looking from Stevie to the area behind him on the stairs.

"I had to find the circuit breakers for the upper three floors, they're up on seven, thas' all, I swear to ya's."

"What in the hell happened here?" Sam asked, "Is everyone alright?"

"We were attacked by..."

Sam watched Stevie as his answer trailed away to nothing. He was looking at Willis and Connie leaning against the Rodriguez's, Pete and the back wall of the elevator.

"Stevie!" Sam said loudly, trying to get the boys attention back on the moment.

The kid looked over at Sam with wide eyes.

"We's were attacked by…by somethin,' we've got some pretty shook up people in there. The Doc's here lookin' at Mr. Leonard, he took a pretty good one on the chops," Stevie said nervously, moving from tennis shoe to tennis shoe.

Sam turned and entered the reception room.

"Stevie, help Mr. and Mrs. Rodriguez, and Pete get Miss Yale and Willis inside the office."

"Yes, Sir Mr. Dalhart. The others are in the conference room, we figured they'd be safer in there…less windows," he said nervously looking from Sam toward John, hoping they wouldn't ask about the windows comment. They didn't.

Sam, followed closely by John went through the reception doorway and into the office area. The conference room door was open and they heard voices. Not trusting the word of anyone right then, they burst through the open door with guns pointed.

The sight that met them was one that made them lower their guns and just stare. Doc Goodwin was tending to Talbot Leonard's head. The older detective was prone on the conference room table. Charlie Chaplin and Doug Fairbanks were in the far corner with Charlie wiping a cold cloth over the face of a ghostly white faced Fairbanks. Liz and Gary Cooper were beside the wet bar having a drink. All faces turned to them as they entered.

"What in all hell happened here?" Sam asked, holstering his gun.

"Stevie—where's Stevie? I sent him out to turn the breakers on?" Liz quickly asked as her eyes went wide and full of worry.

"Easy, take it easy, he's helping Connie inside," Sam answered while looking at Talbot.

"Helping Connie? What happened to her?" Liz asked, putting her drink on the table by Talbot's head who reached and took it and tried to sit up, but the Doctor removed the glass just as quickly and pushed him back down all in one smooth motion.

Sam didn't answer, he instead turned from Talbot and walked over and checked on Douglas.

"Hey old boy, how are you doing?" he asked.

"Samuel, it is good to see you my boy, we had a visitor after you left, a rather nasty woman, even more so than the ones Charles here sees from time to time, hell, even worse than my darling Mary."

"You take it easy Doug old chap; you still don't have the pallor of a healthy individual," Charlie said with genuine concern for his best friend.

"That's because his heart fails to beat every other time it's supposed to. No matter what he thinks, he's had a minor heart attack, so leave him be, and if I see one more person reach for a glass of whiskey I walk right out of here and you can look after yourselves!"

Everyone looked at Doc Goodwin as if he had gone mad. Then they went back to what they were doing.

"You there, ruffian, put that young lady into the chair over there," the Doctor said when he saw Stevie enter with Connie. "And you, put him on the other end of this table, lay him down gently, it looks like he's got one hell of a head wound. Get some ice on it until I can look at it."

"Yes, sir," Pete said as he placed a shaking Willis on the end of the table.

"I would say that whatever happened, we came out on the losing end," Liz said as she finally saw Frank enter the conference room. To the others the secretary visibly relaxed.

"Who did this?" Sam asked as he surveyed the damage to the office and his people.

"I would tell you, but that would make me have to visualize it while I explained, and I don't want to do that," Cooper said ignoring the Doctor's orders and taking a stiff drink anyway. He poured another and then saw Sam standing next to him and poured him one also. Sam took it and he too swallowed the offered shot.

"Okay, Coop, you've had your drink and I've had mine, now who did this?"

Cooper poured another and then looked at Sam.

"Looked like a vampire to me," he said looking from face to face, "I don't know, Sam, who am I to say, I don't even care for horror parts, won't do them, always left 'em to Lon Chaney, I always thought that they were just too unbelievable."

"Liz," Sam said, "You want to pinch hit for blabbermouth here?"

"Well, if it wasn't a vampire it sure would have passed for one, but who knows for sure, let's just say it wasn't entirely human. Also let me say that it was not the Bela Lugosi type either," Liz answered with Frank following her toward the bar. She took the glass from Cooper's hand just as he lifted it to his lips and drank it down, and then she noticed the small child with the leg braces standing in the conference room doorway and immediately walked over and picked her up. "Don't tell me this is the missing girl?

Sam just nodded his head.

Liz smiled at the two people waiting in the hallway. They looked horrible. The parents had been through so much that her heart ached for them.

"Hey, you want a soda pop?" Liz asked Adria.

The girl gave her a half-hearted smile and nodded.

"And I bet you two could use some coffee," she said to Mr. and Mrs. Rodriguez.

They both just nodded their heads.

Sam watched them leave the office area and told Stevie to follow them, then called him back and tossed over his revolver.

"It's loaded."

"Yes, Sir, Mister Dalhart, yes, Sir!" he said and practically ran from the room.

"Doc, you wanna' stay and hear this?" Sam asked.

Goodwin held up his hands and Talbot yelped when the gauze he was wrapping around his head pulled far too tight.

"You want me to leave while these people still need attention?"

"Okay, but after tonight we may be fugitives of some sort," Sam said as he tossed his wet hat over toward the wet bar where Cooper caught it after a short juggle.

"What's the difference, I would still bill you the same so say what you have to say."

"Okay, Doc," Sam said as he looked at the faces around the room. Connie half smiled while she held her arm at the elbow and Sam winked at her, and despite her pain, she received that school girl shot of butterflies in her stomach again. He locked eyes with John and then looked at the injured people in the room.

"Look, I don't know if you people do this sort of thing all the time or what, personally, I always thought you just spied on fella's like me, but I can see now that it may go somewhat deeper than that, but what we had in here tonight was something out of a damn nightmare," Gary Cooper said as he not too gently smashed Sam's hat onto the bar.

"Vampire, that's what you said a minute ago, Coop, a Vampire," Sam said looking at him with a hardness Cooper wasn't used to.

Gary Cooper just nodded and shook his head up and down. "If that's what I said, I guess that was the first thing that came to mind. She came in here and just attacked us. I admit she reminded me of a few Midwestern women I've dated, but it was definitely a woman...like...thing."

"She had breasts, worse thing since Garbo," Talbot said from his prone position.

"Well," Sam said, "our encounter didn't include breasts, but it was large and ugly as hell."

"Wait a minute, Samuel; are you saying you ran into one of those, those things?" Charlie asked, letting the damp rag fall into Doug's lap.

"Yes, Charlie, that's what I'm saying," Sam said and then went to one knee and looked into Connie's eyes. "Doc, when you're done with Mr. Hollywood there, Connie seems to be in a lot of pain."

Goodwin handed the ball of gauze to the prone Talbot and left him there holding the bandage. Leonard looked about with a dumbfounded countenance.

"Let's see here, young lady," he said as he felt along her shoulder. Connie closed her eyes and grimaced but didn't say anything as the doctor probed her shoulder and arm. "Well, you have a dislocation at the shoulder and a severe sprain of your forearm, it may even be broken, I can't tell without an x-ray."

"Just fix the dislocation, Doctor, my arms not bothering me," Connie said.

Sam looked at her and then at the doc and pursed his lips.

"How about *I* tell *you* what we're going to do, alright young lady?"

Connie didn't respond, she took Sam's hand in her right and then with a lot of pain she held out her left arm and waited for the Doctor. Sam shook his head and held her hand without comment. Charlie turned away and looked elsewhere. Cooper thought she was as nuts as everyone here, and Pete and Willis were busy talking quietly not noticing what was happening on the medical front. Rainbird walked over to the window and pulled the blinds and stared out at the wet street below. The rain had stopped and people were again filling Sunset and going about their nighttime business just as if the world had not turned upside down.

Goodwin took Connie's arm and looked at Sam. "Hold her Sam, take your other hand and wrap your arm around her at the waist and don't allow her to move."

Sam did as he was told; he kept her hand in his as she buried her face in his side as he pulled her close and held her. The doc started putting a steady strain on her arm by pulling it from the wrist and forearm, gently at first and then with building power. Connie let out a small gasp of air as the arm popped back in. Sam held her hand and felt the pain she was feeling as she grasped his hand with tremendous strength for a woman. The doc lowered her arm easily and patted her head.

"There you are brave girl; you'll be as good as new before you know it," the Doc said as he adjusted his glasses.

Connie kept her head buried in Sam's side. Rainbird turned and looked. He smiled and nodded his head. Sam squeezed her hand again.

"Hey, you alright?" he asked.

She raised her head and gave him a half-hearted smile. "Not bad for having been pulled on like saltwater taffy."

Sam watched as the doc wrapped a white bandage around her arm and secured it to her chest.

"Keep this arm immobile for a day or so, but you're still going to be sore," he said and then looked at Sam. "Keep her out of harm's way for a while, Sam, you should know better than to take ladies out in your world."

Sam didn't retort, but Connie did.

"I'll be my own decision maker here. Where he goes, I'm going, at least until I get my sister back."

The doctor nodded and then moved past Talbot who sitting up on the table, still holding the roll of gauze and watched the Doc ignore him as he walked over to attend Willis.

John turned from the window and walked over to Sam and tapped him on the shoulder.

"I smell cops," he whispered.

Sam didn't respond. He smiled at Connie and patted her hand and then straightened and nodded for Rainbird to follow him as he moved from the conference room. They went through the reception area where Liz was holding Adria on her lap. He saw that Mrs. Rodriguez was holding a bottle of soda with a straw, allowing the girl to sip. Frank was talking in low tones to Mr. Rodriguez and Little Stevie was at the window twirling the thirty-eight like a gunslinger as Sam grabbed a dry hat from the many on the hat rack.

"Easy there Hopalong, you'll blow your foot off," Sam said as he placed the dry hat on his head.

Rainbird shot the kid a look that froze him in place.

Sam took the stairs two at a time with John on his heels. They gained the ground floor and saw a figure waiting by the door. Sam looked at Rainbird and they walked to the door and John unlocked it, but instead of allowing Melvin Purvis inside, he held the door for Sam and then joined him, stepping out under the *Alhambra's* awning.

"Well, fancy bumping into you agent Purvis," Sam said, "Just heading out for a cup of Joe, want to join us?"

"I wouldn't care to do that, window peeper," Purvis snarled hoping the private detective smear hit home.

John looked at the ex-FBI man and his eyes were on fire. After what they had went through tonight he wasn't in the mood. This man just wasn't that damn scary to him.

"Just thought I'd ask, have a good night," Sam said as he adjusted the fedora and started to walk away.

"Our conversation at the party last night gumshoe, I'm still gonna get that little bastard."

Sam stopped and turned. He stepped back and looked at Purvis, "And that little bastard being?"

"Chaplin, you know damn good and well who I mean."

"Charlie again, you're just a broken record aren't you agent Purvis?"

"Let's just say I'm a record stuck on a sour note, and that note is Chaplin, my former boss wants him and I'm going to get him."

"Then I wish you luck in your pursuit of the evil Chaplin, good evening."

"Wait a minute, where is he, you know so tell me," Purvis said as menacingly as he could, "You can't hide the little pervert forever. Mr.

Hoover knows about his presentation to the President tomorrow night and doesn't want that pedophile anywhere near Mr. Roosevelt."

"Then tell Hoover to tell the president what to do, not us."

John walked past him, brushing against him and making him step back.

"Goodnight," Sam said.

They walked until they knew that Purvis had left. They watched as he made a screaming 'U' turn on Sunset and sped away.

"He's going to be a problem," Sam said.

"Maybe we ought to bring him in on it, introduce him to our new friend out in Elysian Park."

Sam laughed as he watched the taillights recede into the dark night.

"Yeah, wouldn't that be something. But then again, he does work for Hoover, might not be that much of a change."

"Now look chaps, I saw what I saw, but really, all I know about vampires is what I've learned by seeing what that mad Hungarian did in *Dracula*. Other than that little educational experience, where I might add the brute force of the being that assaulted us tonight most definitely was not dressed in a fashionable tuxedo. As I said, other than that, I couldn't tell you what attacked us," Chaplin said, again applying a wet cloth to Fairbanks forehead and hoping his ramblings about Bela Lugosi was understood.

"Here, here," Doug said from his prone position in Chaplin's lap. "Even the name is so melodramatic—*Vampire*, are we to believe in such things?"

"Then you obviously have an explanation for what it was that came to visit us tonight in this very office?" Liz said as she adjusted the child's makeshift pillow consisting of her overcoat. She had just laid the sleeping girl down between two chairs she had pulled together. Her parents sat vigilant over her as they listened to the others in the office talk.

"Drugs—pure and simple—I mean I have seen some wild things done by people hooked on drugs," Willis offered from his seat at the conference table.

Sam was watching Cooper, who hadn't offered any comments since he and Rainbird had returned from their small confrontation with Purvis. He had shed his suit coat and was playing with something in his hand.

"You say it was a woman because she had breasts, is there anything you can add to that, Coop?" Sam asked, watching his right hand.

Cooper looked surprised Sam had called on him. "Me? Uh, no, well..."

"Why were you here tonight?" Sam asked.

"Well, I uh, came by to say I was sorry for last night," he said as he opened his palm and looked at the item he held.

"What about last night?" Sam asked.

"The Countess, I felt bad in case you were, you know, making a play for her and then I came along and stepped on your toes."

Connie sipped her coffee and looked at Sam, for some reason he didn't look like the Countess chasing type. She was interested in hearing his response.

"What've you got Coop, you find something?" John asked, obviously catching a twitch of Cooper's hand and eyes just as Sam had.

"Maybe a coincidence," he said almost looking ashamed. "No, it's not, I mean she was there at Charlie's party, and she does have a strange European way about her....," he stumbled, barely being heard by the others.

"Coop, concentrate here, you're not making a lot of sense," Sam said, standing up from the conference table and walking over to Cooper and removing the item from his hand.

"A rosary?"

"It was in that things hair, you know, a kind of fancy hair-tie," Cooper said twirling his fingers in the air while looking from face to face.

"I don't think that thing looked as if she goes to mass on a regular basis," Charlie said.

"How would you know what someone who goes to church would look like," Doug said as he sat up and looked at what Sam was holding.

Sam let the beads slide through his fingers and looked at the cross.

"Silver?" Pete asked as he looked over Sam's shoulder.

"No, something else, nickel maybe," he said as he turned the crucifix over in his hand. Then he looked at Cooper who hung his head and placed his hands in his pockets.

"I'm not a big believer in coincidence, Coop," he said as he turned from Copper and fixed Chaplin with a look.

"What? What is it Samuel?"

Sam held the rosary out to Charlie who at first didn't want to touch the dangling necklace. He tilted his head and tried to read what was inscribed on the back but gave up and took it from Sam's hand. He read the name and then let the crucifix fall from his hand where Sam caught it.

"Well, are you going to keep your audience waiting all night, old boy?" Doug asked.

"For invaluable service, Pope Pius XI – The Countess of Venice D'Palacia – Francesca Annamarie Lochenzza D'Sarcuni," Sam said as he tossed the rosary over to Rainbird.

"And this is?" Liz asked.

"Charlie, I think you can account better than I or Coop," Sam said. "Would you care to enlighten those who don't know?"

Chaplin was still speechless. He stood and walked over and poured a shot of whiskey and downed it without making a sour face.

"Perhaps from the beginning, Charles, that's always an excellent place to start a tale," Fairbanks said.

"Senator Emil Farnsworth, you know, the same politician that arranged the benefit for the president tomorrow night, he introduced me to the refugee program, *Americans for Freedom*. He said that sponsoring royalty, scientist's and artists, you know, to help financially to smuggle them away from the Nazis and Fascists, that it would look good for…well, it would look good for me," he said as he hung his head. Then he looked up at Sam and Sam alone. "To maybe take the heat off of all this deportment nonsense by helping those help themselves, to show I can be a good American," he looked at Sam, "I didn't know, Samuel, I swear to you, I've only known her and the Count D'Sarcuni for maybe a month."

"This woman was the, the creature that was here?" Liz asked standing with her hands on her hips and looking at Cooper.

"I swear, I didn't know, you know me and women, there's usually not a lot of talk between us."

"We know what you mean, Coop," Sam said, stopping his lurid explanation of his womanizing.

"Could it have been the husband, I mean, he is a bloody Count," Charlie said excitedly remembering that Dracula from the movie had been a Count.

"For some reason I don't think a five foot two inch Count turned into what we ran into tonight in Elysian Park," Sam said. "The other man you sponsored, Charlie, the one I had words with last night at your party, this German fella, Von what's-his-name?"

"Railing," Chaplin said. "I know very little about him. He was more or less a package deal with the D'Sarcuni's. I believe he had to leave because he was on one of Herr Hitler's little lists of undesirables."

Sam looked at John and he shrugged his shoulders. "Ring's no bells," he said. "None of those names has ever been mentioned in any of my dreams."

"All I do know is that the D'Sarcuni's were also on a list. They were visiting Germany when a warrant was issued for their arrest and from what I understand it was signed by Il Duce, Mussolini himself," Charlie said looking down. "Or so they said at any rate."

"Charles, inform me next time you try and think on your own old boy, you seem to get mixed up with the most sordid characters," Fairbanks said as he took the freshly poured glass of whiskey from Chaplin who stood and watched him quickly down it.

"Did they say what they had done for them to need asylum? I'm sure you inquired," Connie asked, stepping in front of the same question Sam was about to ask. The hardened detective looked at her and raised his brows. "Sorry," she said wincing when she shrugged her shoulders.

"Well," Sam asked, "Did they?"

"No, they didn't, Samuel," Charlie answered. "All I know is that they were regular visitors to the Vatican and it was my understanding the Countess had something to do with the Vatican archives, or something to that effect."

"And this Von Railing, what's his story?" Sam asked, giving Connie a split-second look, thinking she was going to cut him off with the same question again.

"Fell out of favor over something or other. I really don't have a good memory for these things Samuel, you know that," Chaplin said.

"This girl that Purvis and the police keep asking about?"

Chaplin suddenly looked up, the dawning of where Sam was going finally slashing its way through the fog that was blocking his thoughts.

"Why, she was with me at the formal greeting for the D'Sarcuni's and Von Railing at the Senator's office, as a matter of fact, this German chap was speaking with her for the longest time because she was there for the Foundation of Polio Victims that the senator was sponsoring, she was supposed to meet the president."

"That coincidence thing again, Sam," Rainbird said with a raised brow.

"Don't tell me that these people are going to meet the president?" Sam asked.

"Oh, my goodness no, they're not on the list for the reception, they only met the girl because their meeting ran over with the polio people."

"Okay, Coop, Charlie and Doug, you fellas don't lose sight of one another for the next couple of days, you were seen with us so you may now be a target, for what, I don't know, but I suggest you become roomies for a while."

"I'm afraid Mary would never go for that, old boy—Mr. Cooper she may allow in, but Charlie under our roof? I assure you that she would rather have Lois B. Meyer stay over."

"She feels that strongly about me?" Charlie asked with a hurt look.

"Not now," Sam said heading off Chaplin's *poor me* routine. "It's either at Pickfair, or at Charlie's joint. I know Coop's place, well, let's just say I don't think you or Mary could handle that little piece of Hollywood bachelor's paradise."

"Hey, what's that supposed to mean?" Cooper protested.

"It means if you would keep your hands off of your maids they may get a chance to clean your bungalow once in a while, now you listen to Sam and do as he says," Liz said standing over them with that stern school teachers look only Frank and Stevie knew intimately.

They all three nodded.

"Now, the rest of us have work to do, if you three want to come in and handle the phones, you can still be informed, Liz may have other work to do, we have a lot to accomplish before more girls come up missing."

"Sam? What about the child and her parents?" Talbot Leonard asked, still holding the gauze that the doctor had seemed to have forgotten about.

Fairbanks stood and approached Sam.

"Samuel, it may be just the thing, Mary would love to have her and her parents over for a few days, and it just may take some of the heat off of having Charles creeping about underfoot, after I explain a few things first. You may have to intercede for us; a phone call would help in the morning old boy."

"Okay, Liz you go with them in case America's Little Sweetheart doesn't buy the camouflage."

"Got it boss," Liz said.

"Willis, Pete, Frank and Talbot, you may want to take time to think about this, we've never dealt with anything like this before," Sam stated looking from man to man. "You too Stevie, maybe this is a good time to stick around the house and help your mother."

"That hoits, Mr. Dalhart, what did I do ta' deserve that crack? You think I would leave ya and Mr. Rainboyd, high and dry facin' somethin' like dat alone? I ought'a quit and let's ya's," Stevie said as tough as he could.

"Yeah, what he said," Frank offered, knocking a big fist into Stevie's arm, making him fall back three feet.

Talbot, Pete and Willis nodded their agreement.

"What that thing has done to those girls since it's arrived here, it's like it's been doing it for centuries, maybe longer," Sam said. "No one would believe what's really going on even if we told them. Chances are we're already being sought by the cops, who may or may not already be aware of this bastard being here. This isn't an angry husband or a mad studio exec. There's real danger here and we all might not make it out alive. But it's here for a reason and I don't think it's just to murder young girls, it does that anyway, for fun or because it has to. It tried to bargain for time with John and I don't think that's the creature's style, to bargain. It needs time for something and can't afford for us to interfere with it. We have to find out what it is."

"Damn, that sounded like you were trying to scare us off," Willis said with a smirk.

"Yeah, are you trying to get out of paying us or what?" Frank chimed in.

Sam looked at John and smiled.

"What did I say when we hired these mugs?"

John looked at the four detectives and with a straight face answered Sam.

"That they looked just stupid enough to work for us."

An hour later, with everyone going to their appointed destinations, Sam and John were on the way to his apartment. Connie didn't like it, but Sam had ordered her to go along with Liz to Pickfair to drop off Adria and Mr. and Mrs. Rodriguez and then go over to Liz's apartment and wait. The two women were now were heavily armed and would be joined there by Frank in an hour.

They drove through the quieting city where the streets were finally draining of their small rivers of rain water. The stop signals cast long red and green splashes of light that reflected eerily off the macadam as the long stop and go markers dinged and moved up and down.

Throughout the ride John was quiet, and then for no reason Sam could fathom his partner started laughing. Sam smiled but didn't say anything at first. He knew John had to have a release of some kind after a day like this, but he really thought it would have come some other way.

"You going to let me in on it, pal?"

John stopped laughing and then looked over at Sam and then he suddenly let loose laughing once again. He was out of control, so much so that Sam thought he was going to bash his head on the steel dashboard.

"Hey, don't go south on me now partner."

John slowly wound down. He removed his hat and tossed it in the back seat.

"A vampire Sam, are you kidding me? A vampire? Have we lost our damn minds? There's no such thing as vampires and we both know that."

Sam didn't answer, he just looked straight ahead at the light flow of traffic. Flower Street was just about empty tonight as most of the tenants there were business related rather than residential. Sam slowed and pulled the car over to the sidewalk and then he set the parking brake but kept the car running. He took a deep breath and looked at John closely, the merriment he had found earlier seemingly from an untapped source Sam had never been aware of was gone and in its place was a haunted look, as if he himself had been responsible for bringing whatever that thing was into this world.

"John, you're not responsible for anything that's happened. I really don't know what it is you've tapped into but you're not responsible. For the sake of argument we're calling it a vampire. Is it something that runs around dressed in evening clothes and bites women on the neck? No, I don't think so. I think it's much more, so much more that maybe there is no name for it."

"Do you think it's the Devil?" John asked, slightly turning his head toward Sam and holding his partners eyes with his own.

"No, I don't think so. I think it has contempt for any side of religion, *any*. I didn't hear as much as you in that house, but I do know it's killed young women at a rate I can't begin to get a handle on. What we did learn tonight is that it's a trickster and a liar. But is it Satan, Lucifer or old Scratch, whatever name you choose to use? No, maybe it's a close relative, but I really don't think so."

"But why are we, the two most grounded guys' in LA so ready to believe in something like this? You especially, as for me at least my heritage is full of superstition. My people's past is haunted by our dreams and nightmares, but you, white man, what's your excuse?"

"You think you native's folks have cornered the market on backward beliefs? Come on, my Grandmother used to tell us bedtime stories about werewolves running around France. They sell a million books a year of Grimm's Fairy Tales, have you ever sat down and read those damn things? They make the imaginings of these Hollywood types pale in comparison. I don't know how kids ever go to sleep. So let's not bring race or heritage into it fella."

"I see what you mean," John said shaking his head. "So, what do you think we're dealing with, a giant green Mother Goose, or a really pissed off Hansel and Gretel?"

Von Railing and McDougal had just pulled up at the old wooden mansion after doing their ordered delivery work out in Elysian Park. As he sat in the backseat of the Hudson he closed his eyes and tried to get a sense of the goings-on in Los Angeles. Strangely, his mind was a whirlwind of non-clarity. First he could picture nothing but blackness and then anger, and then confusion. Was he picking up the thoughts of the Master? He couldn't be sure. Sometimes Phaltazar was able to block his probing completely, but most times he was allowed to view what he was up to. Tonight was a swirl of confusing visions. Suddenly he opened his eyes as red, orange a blue flame erupted and he tensed. His vision had been blocked by a wall of flame. He closed his eyes again but there was nothing as he was now unable to concentrate enough to break through the powerful mind of the ancient one.

"What in the hell are they doing?" McDougal asked loudly as he watched something in his rearview mirror. He started to open his door when the Mercedes he had spied careened off the Hudson's rear fender and then sliced into the old and very much dead flower bed lining the house. The front bumper hit the redwood siding and wood flew in all directions.

"That crazy bastard could have killed me," the Scotsman said as he threw his door open.

Count D'Sarcuni opened his driver's door and fell out of the front seat. He gasped and cried for McDougal to help him. Von Railing opened the rear door of the Hudson and stood there, momentarily frozen at the comical gesturing by the Count.

"Have you lost your fucking mind you stupid Wop?" McDougal screamed as he helped the Count to his feet.

D'Sarcuni pushed him away, "Not me you bloody fool, my wife, she's hurt badly. I found her upon my return home."

Von Railing hurried forward and looked into the rear seating compartment of the Mercedes. His eyes widened when he saw Francesca, or what he thought was her. She was sprawled un-lady-like on the backseat, her mouth was moving as she cried silent tears. She was caught half in and half out of her transformation. Her fangs worked as her lips couldn't cover them any longer. Her skin was sallow and her hair was completely silver in color. Gone was her beauty and in its place was an abomination Von Railing could no longer look at.

"What happened to her?" he asked through clenched teeth as he backed away from the car.

"Please, please, help her, she's dying!"

Von Railing let his fangs out and suddenly pulled the fat little Italian toward him by his lapels. Then he slowly brought his right hand up and clenched the Count's throat and lifted. He threw him against the car and then slid him toward the trunk, his small legs kicking dents in the side of the expensive Mercedes.

"I will not ask twice!" he said menacingly, his eyes turning red and his mouth widening unnaturally.

D'Sarcuni was battling for air as he started hitting Von Railing's ever tightening grip with his chubby fists.

"I found her like this, in our bedroom."

Von Railing loosened his grip only momentarily. "Take one more breath and explain what happened, Papist," he ordered coldly.

As the breath of blessed air coursed down the Count's throat he opened his eyes and looked into the red one of the German. He was prepared to kill him and he could see it in his eyes. No matter what the

Master's wishes would be to the contrary, Von Railing was prepared to suffer any consequences for his murder.

"I...returned from...the Consulate, and found her in our room, something had happened at that detectives...office, my driver had gone and—"

Von Railing suddenly let go of D'Sarcuni and he fell to the gravel, the impact cutting his explanation short. The large German pushed the staring McDougal aside and opened the door and gently pulled Francesca out. Her features were twisted into a mask of horror. The face had sunk in to her bones, the cheeks so prominent that they appeared almost ready to burst through the paper thin skin. The hair, as silver as it was couldn't hide the wound or the blood that coursed down her head.

"She has been struck by a silver weapon, she is poisoned. How did they know to use silver on her?" he asked no one as he turned for the front porch. "Assist that fool inside; I've not finished with him."

McDougal gestured for the Count to follow Von Railing. His eyebrows were arched.

"It is probably best you come inside Count," he said with disdain lacing his voice.

Von Railing was kneeling beside the Countess and lightly touching her face. He spoke to her in Latin as she groaned. She had been pleading for Von Railing to end her suffering, for him to end the life she had once held so dear. He smiled and slowly explained that her affliction was but a temporary one. The wound wasn't fatal, at least for their kind; it had been just deep enough to cause much pain and disfigurement that wouldn't last the night. Still, he whispered into her ear and she heard what he had to say and the elongated fingers rose and gently touched his cheek. The long and now crooked nails lightly scraped his face as she hadn't the strength to keep her arm poised. As she lay still, her red eyes closed and she braced herself for what was coming.

The silver weapon that had been used on her left microscopic traces of the metal in the wound and was festering inside which would retard her healing. Von Railing placed his thumb and fingers around the bubbling wound and then squeezed down and under the suppurating cut, lifting the skin of her temple. Puss and watered down blood shot outward, barely missing the German's face. He squeezed again and this time the Countess couldn't withhold the scream inside of her. The shriek was like that of a wounded bird. More puss and infection exited under even more pressure. Blood ran along his fingers and he could feel even now the powerful effects of the minute traces of silver. As it irritated his skin he realized that the weapon that had been used must have been silver plate and not solid. If the weapon had been left in for any amount of time the silver contamination would have quickly spread through her blood system until it struck her heart and seized it. As it was, he thought she had had the quickness of thought to remove the weapon quickly, before any real damage had been done. The silver was as abhorrent to their kind as the poisons of the green and growing things of the world were to human kind.

Finally he eased up on the wound and tried to reassure Francesca that she would be alright. Her eyes fluttered and he could see that the deep wrinkles of her face were starting to flatten out and the smell of disease he had smelled upon her earlier was subsiding. He leaned over and kissed her on the forehead.

The Count stood at the bar and tried to swallow some whiskey, but winced as the burning liquid hit his throat, he touched the area where Von Railing's cold dead hands had locked on his neck. The blood was still apparent where the German's yellowed nails had dug small grooves on both sides of his throat.

"She will live. If you would not have panicked you would have known this upon examination. You are becoming too careless, what if you had drawn authorities here to this place, men whom we have no influence over? Your fool actions could have cost far more than your beautiful wife!" he said as he easily laid Francesca's hand on her heaving chest and stood to face the Italian.

D'Sarcuni, pain or not quickly downed the whiskey and tried to set the glass on the bar but missed and it crashed to the filthy carpet.

Von Railing sighed and closed his eyes.

"I need to find out what happened, how Dalhart or his people knew how to stop Francesca."

"Maybe it was a fluke, maybe they didn't actually know silver was a danger to her," the Count ventured now that he didn't believe Von Railing was going to kill him.

"That's a possibility, but if not, we have to reevaluate our mortal friends, because if they know the secret of silver, then we may face other, more harmful ways of the ancients."

He wasn't able to finish his speculative thought. The house shook and windows broke in several rooms, upstairs and down. The roar of pain and anguish shook them all to their very unnatural cores. The Count went to his knees and hid his face. Von Railing turned toward the study doors and his eyes widened. He had never in his many, many years of long life heard what was continuing to be the most anguished cry he had ever encountered. Even Francesca started screaming, hopelessly crying in her delirium for the pain that was being thrust upon them from somewhere below. McDougal started shaking and he quickly turned for the door and then thought better of it and turned back and just stood with his hands at his large ears. If it had been the Master returning, he had not just entered the house, he had crashed through the three inch thick oak doors that led to the basement below.

Von Railing pushed McDougal aside but found the Count had reached out and grabbed his pants leg from where he was kneeling and crying.

"No, don't go, the Master's hurt, maybe it was the Germans!" he cried, burying his face into Von Railing's leg.

The house shook again as a scream of pain and anger coursed through the very floor they stood upon. They could hear muffled screams from below and thumping that vibrated up the walls and resounded through the first floor support beams.

"What are you talking about? I left the Master at the home of that wretched child!"

"But I saw them, many German soldiers, they came from the sea," he said as he still held his face against the German's leg.

"Don't be a fool," Von Railing snapped. "There was no time for our European enemies to coordinate." Von Railing turned away from the door in thought. He turned and looked through McDougal at empty space. "It seems that we have underestimated our foe here in America."

Von Railing turned suddenly and went through the door without further comment. He hadn't known how to react to the anger and pain emanating from below because the Master had only been hurt a very few times during his long service to him, and never as much as it sounded now.

"Come fool," he said half turning toward McDougal.

The subbasement had mercifully grown quiet as they hurried down the stairs. Von Railing tried not to show his fear at opening that last lock that lead down to the subbasement. He dropped the keys and had to take a deep breath before reaching for them; McDougal retrieved them before he could and handed them over, but held Von Railing's hand for a moment.

"The Master can't die, can he? You told me that many times," his eyes were almost pleading.

"There's not a weapon in existence that could kill him, he's been hurt, that's all," he said as he turned and inserted the key and pulled the lock free and entered.

The stairs were totally dark and it took a moment for Von Railing's vision to adjust. The familiar green scope of the stairs took shape in his unnatural night vision and he started down.

"Master, are you hurt?" he called out.

A loud moan greeted him and sent chills down his spine as he finally reached the last step and planted his feet on the dirt flooring. The smell of blood struck him, but instead of making him desirous of the red flow of man, he was sickened. The blood was not fresh, but tainted and it had been spilled with no concern as to its waste.

"My Lord?" he called out again as he entered the subbasement and started through the carnage.

As Von Railing looked around the mess that had been delivered upon the filthy floor he could see the torn bodies of the Masters young girls. They were torn to pieces and he felt as if he had stepped into a slaughter house. The Master had returned and destroyed them all. As he approached the far wall, he saw the only survivor kneeling next to a dark shape that was Phaltazar. He was in the corner of the subbasement and had buried himself in the blackened, maggot filled dirt that had been their constant companion no matter where they traveled. He was buried all the way to his neck and was doing something Von Railing had never before witnessed—the Ancient hunter of man was crying, he could even see the tears running like bands of silver down its cheeks. The girl, the storyteller he believed it was, kneeled before Phaltazar, silently rubbing the black soil onto its face and neck. Von Railing gasped, McDougal stayed well back of the German, shaking and nearing collapse.

"I am burned," it said in the ancient tongue of Aramaic. It had its eyes closed tightly. "My punishment continues—how much, oh Father, can I endure?" it cried, raising its head toward the rafters above.

"My lord, how could this have happened?"

The girl whispered softly as she gently caressed the sour earth against the beast's scaled face. The creature leaned into her hand and Von Railing could see the healing actually taking place. The green peeling skin that had been red and blackened from burns was slowly returning to its normal color as the rich, maggot filled dirt fell away. The Master's breathing slowed and it actually raised one of its giant claws from the dirt and ran its index finger down the pale skin of the girl. The touch of her calmed the frightened countenance of the oldest animal on the planet.

"Dalhart, I could not see him, he burned me. ME!" Phaltazar said in strong English.

Von Railing took a step back as the yellow eyes flared open and then slowly closed as more tears ran free from the creature before him.

"My Lord, the Countess, she is also injured by these….these people."

The yellow eyes slowly opened again and looked up and into the damned soul of Von Railing.

"The bitch was careless!" it cried out with more fury than a moment before.

"I am sure no more so than yourself, my Lord," Von Railing said and then immediately regretted his words as the yellow eyes fixed on him.

"Careful German, as you may see, I am in no mood for your pretend bravado," the eyes closed as the girl continued to sooth his stale skin with soil. The tears had stopped flowing.

The German steeled himself.

"I mean no insult Master, but there is much more here than we know. I have never seen you injured like this, and the Countess is as ruthless as I, but still she was taken off guard by an attack with silver, as you were by fire. Truly you think these not a coincidence?"

A soft growl came from the corner of the basement.

"I was enjoying my moment of clarity with the Red Man, somehow he must have clouded my thoughts as to this…this rat in the walls, *this*

Dalhart. I must dwell on this. There has been no change as to our goal other than that stupid bitch's failure with Dalhart's people?"

"No, my Lord, the president is arriving by train tomorrow," Von Railing answered and then hesitated before broaching the next subject considering his Masters mood.

"What is it? I am impatient with all things this night," Phaltazar said slowly, as if he were drifting to some place Von Railing couldn't follow. But one thing was for sure, the ancient and foul earth that the girl rubbed upon him and he lay in was doing its healing magic.

"The Count, he has proven himself at least useful with his little dog's nose, he has reported that German soldiers have arrived by sea this night, thus I fear the resistance may try and foil us here in America, so we must assume that—"

The slow penetrating laugh stopped Von Railing from finishing.

"Then we will send the cowardly enemies of Hitler a message; let them come, let them find I am not one to have my plans thwarted by the likes of cowards. Their Fuhrer has been set upon the path I wish him to be on, and now I will retard any response or interference from the new world to act against him."

"And Dalhart and his people, will you just let this night's arrogance pass without punishment?"

Von Railing grabbed his head as the door to his rear slammed shut, closing out the vision of McDougal's widening eyes. The beast's anger was present inside the German's head with such agonizing clarity that he was nearly brought to his knees. But as quickly as the pain had come it passed, allowing him to straighten. Despite his relief, he kept his eyes lowered.

"Inform the scribes of this town of the rescue by Dalhart of the young child. Let the people know his celebrity. Then I wish to speak to our friend in the senate to discuss arrangements, is this understood?"

"Yes my Lord."

"Now leave me alone with the child."

A moment later the beast opened its eyes and watched the girl for a moment. She smiled at it and continued to rub the cool and dank earth on his cheeks and neck. He hadn't killed her because he knew he would need this one. Despite his desire to hear more of her stories, he also needed the link she could so very easily provide it.

"Your sister, she has luck and power about her," he gently touched the girl's smiling lips with one curved and yellowed claw. "And you look so much like her; it is almost as unnatural as I."

The girl batted her eyes, making them look almost well. The dark circles were easily overlooked when she smiled in that manner. She leaned forward and grabbed another handful of the soil and started to reach out. The beast caught sight of the dangling gold chain around her neck and took it in his hand.

"A beautiful cross, is this talisman yours my child?"

Jeannie almost reached up and pulled the chain from its clawed hand, but then just smiled and demurely shook her head, the matted hair moving as one strand as it was mud caked and filthy.

"Then it is your sister's, perhaps?" it asked as its eyes went from the small gold cross to the girl's filthy features.

She smiled wider and nodded her head, seeming embarrassed that she had stolen her sisters cross.

"You will make me a gift of this?" it asked the girl.

The girl actually giggled and held a filthy hand to her once red lips. She nodded again, her insanity was almost complete.

With a smile that raised his thick upper lip toward the brown and crooked elongated front teeth, the beast easily snapped the small links of the chain and held the cross up.

"It is a beautiful thing, is it not?" it said almost sleepily, its yellow night eyes closing.

The girl again reached for dirt and gently rubbed it on the side of Phaltazar's rough face. "Beautiful," she repeated in a dream-like voice.

"Yes, I feel your sister even now. Tell me young one, tell me a story of your sister. Is she strong willed?" he placed a giant hand around her face and lifted her head. "Come my lovely child, tell me of her."

"Connie, dear Connie, she must be ever so angry at me, but I love her so, it won't matter that I took all of her nice things will it?"

"How could the mere trinkets you have compare with the love of the flesh? No child, she is not angry. She has traveled a great distance to receive the help of a masterful man, she loves you in return, so tell me of her and maybe I will let you see her."

As the girl eased the dwindling pain of her new Master, she started talking softly, smiling brightly as she thought about her sister.

The coarse and scaly brow of the beast arched as it listened; the smile had disappeared completely as the ancient one slowly closed its eyes and held on tightly to the gold cross. Its road to the woman, and then to Dalhart and his men would be open to it very soon.

✤ ELEVEN ✤

Liz tossed Frank a blanket and pointed to the couch. He tried to look hurt but was secretly thrilled she hadn't just tossed him out on the street after he followed the two women back to Liz's apartment just off of Rose Street. Frank smiled and raised his brows.

"Don't even think about it Chilly Willy, I have a gun and I will shoot the first Goddamn thing that comes through my door. I haven't had the best day," she said as she turned her attention to Connie who was just swallowing the water and aspirin powder Liz had given her.

Frank was about to protest when there came a soft knocking on the front door. Frank tossed the blanket on the couch and looked at the two women and raised an index finger to his lips. He then crossed the small living room and placed an ear to the door and a foot at its base.

"Who is it?" he asked, easily pulling his gun free of its shoulder-holster.

"Stevie, let me in."

"Why ain't you at home kid?" Frank said as he removed the chain and unlocked the apartment's door, but still keeping the gun up and ready.

Stevie was standing there with his hands in his front pockets, his hat sitting crooked on his head; he wasn't facing the door but looking behind him down the long hallway. He finally turned and looked at Frank sheepishly.

"I uh, my Ma's not home and I thought..."

Frank could see the unease in the boy's face as he placed his weight on one foot and then the other and then Liz slipped between Frank and the door and raised her eyebrow.

"Just what are you doing here?" she asked, placing her hands on her hips.

"I thought, well, maybes' you and Miss Yale, could use a little...,"

Liz could see what Frank had just noticed, the boy was terrified. Obviously his mother was out and he couldn't stay at home alone. And God knows she couldn't blame him, because after all she herself would never look at the night the same way ever again.

"To tell you the truth, the more people surrounding us the better, but you have to use the floor or sleep with Frank on the couch," she turned and glanced at Frank. "I recommend the floor myself."

Frank sneered and walked toward the couch. Liz stepped aside and let Stevie in and then she closed and locked them all inside.

"Come on, Miss Yale, the cavalry here will watch over us, such as it is," she said as she didn't spare Stevie or Frank another look.

"Would everyone please just call me Connie, I feel like my mother," she said as she placed her empty water glass on the kitchen counter.

"Yeah, sure, I can call ya's Connie," Stevie offered as he removed his coat and tried to sneak Frank's blanket, which was snapped away quickly.

Liz smiled and guided Connie down the hallway.

"I mean what I said about any visitors, I'll shoot the first bastard that comes through that door," she said over her shoulder.

Frank watched Liz go and shook his head. He wondered when she would lighten up. It was like she enjoyed being mean most times, while at others it was like they were meant to be together. He took a deep breath and placed his thirty-eight on the coffee table in front of the couch. He looked at Stevie who was already lying on the floor with his jacket as a pillow. His hat was pulled down over his face. Frank smiled and reached for his blanket but thought a moment and then tossed it to Stevie who was startled enough that he sat bolt upright.

"Cover up kid, from what Liz told me, you did real well tonight."

Stevie looked from the blanket to Frank who sat hard into the couch.

"Jeez, tank's Mr. Wiechek, tank's a lot."

"Call me Frank kid; anyone who's my new partner can call me by my first name."

Stevie's eyes widened and he smiled, then he threw the blanket back at the detective who caught it and looked bewildered, "You's sleep, Frank, I'll takes the foist watch."

"You bet kid, my gun's on the table."

"It's all right Frank, Mr. Dalhart and Mr. Rainboyd gave me a gat already," he said as he pulled the old thirty-eight out of his waistband and waggled it so Frank could see.

Frank didn't say anything, he just smiled. But he was terror stricken to know that the kid from Brooklyn had a gun and that he was actually going to be sleeping with him in the same room.

"Great kid, that's great," Frank said as he lay down. He didn't fall to sleep for a very long time.

McDougal wasn't happy about having to drive the Count and Countess back to their hotel. He refused to even step out of the car to assist with Francesca who was almost back to normal, but still she felt the need to have her cloak's hood covering her head. McDougal watched as the doorman for the Westerly Hotel held the door open for the couple then he quickly sped away.

Outside the hotel two men sat in a parked car. The driver's side window rolled down and the driver waved a car that was parked behind them forward. The black sedan sped into the road in pursuit of the Hudson. As the two figures inside the car watched their companions follow the car that had just dropped off their targets, they exited the car and walked underneath the portico. The doorman was most understanding of the two men and their situation and for a modest gratuity of a fin, opted to give them the information they requested on the Count and Countess. The two men turned as one and strode quickly back to their car. The doorman watched as they sat motionless in the darkened interior. They were there until he was relieved at six the next morning. As he left he gave a short and quick tip of his hat, but the men just looked right through him. The driver, the one he had noticed having a large scar that ran down his right cheek, looked at him like he was a bug that had just crawled out from under his breakfast plate. As he lowered his hand he was thinking he wouldn't like to meet up with those two gents in a dark alley.

Sam looked in on Rainbird. He was sleeping quietly and didn't move as the door opened. Sam knew it had been a quiet night for John. Did it have something to with that creature being injured and not wanting his company? He wasn't sure, but the big man hadn't stirred in the three hours he had been in his guestroom.

Sam closed the door silently and finished buttoning his white shirt. He heard a soft rap on his front door and he turned and opened it without using his peep hole. Pete and Willis were standing there looking tired. Sam nodded as the two men came in. He knew they were tired, but so were they all. They didn't have the luxury of taking time to rest, they needed answers and they needed them fast. Besides the strangeness of their predicament, Sam had a deep hidden feeling that there was more than just a supernatural situation happening, there seemed, at least in his dark recesses of thought, that there was more to this. He couldn't put his finger on it, but he really didn't believe they, or John, were this creature's only target. He had lain awake most of his time on the couch trying to figure out what the thing could be after. He was sure that there was something in play here and it wasn't them, but he wasn't sure of anything else.

He grabbed his tie and made sure his thirty-eight was tucked neatly into his shoulder-holster. He frowned because he hadn't had the need in the last few years to walk around armed, but until they had a handle on what was happening, he figured it was better to go around with a little extra weight. He also shoved twenty more bullets into his pockets.

"John's sleeping soundly so let him go as long as possible. We need him fit, boys. But if he starts getting restless or looks scared do whatever you have to do to wake him up. I don't know much about what's going on, but I figure things are going to get worse before they get better."

"It's already started to get worse boss," Pete said as he held out the morning edition of the *Times*.

Sam scanned the headlines and closed his eyes. "That's all we need right now."

In the car on the drive over to Westwood, his thoughts turned inward at the vision of Constance Yale. That was one tough broad. He didn't know many skirts that could have handled being nearly torn in two by some freak from a nightmare and then turn around and insist she's ready for more. He knew for the first time in many years that he was honestly attracted to someone—a real person and not one of these dames that regard a mirror as their best friend.

Liz put her robe on after hearing Connie start her hot bath. She looked in the mirror and didn't particularly care for the woman who looked back at her. Her eyes were sagging and her hair was a mess, enough so that she wasn't in a hurry to go out and face Frank. She quickly ran a comb through it and placed two bobby pins on the side in a successful attempt to get her hair up off her neck. She looked at her glasses and decided against putting them on as they would magnify the fact that she tossed and turned all night, just as she knew Connie had done in the bed beside her. With a final look she opened the door and stepped out of the bedroom. Before she closed it behind her she heard Connie humming something and knew that their new client was feeling much better about facing this new day.

Frank and Stevie were sitting at the small yellow table. Frank had a cup of coffee in front of him and was reading the morning addition of the *Times*.

"Good morning," she said as she tied her robe off in the front.

Stevie's eyes widened as he had never seen Liz in anything other than a practical dress or business suit. He had to avert his eyes before Liz moved them with a sharp whack.

"Hi Doll, want some Joe?" Frank asked.

"Don't get up Galahad, I'll get it," she said as she made her way to the cabinet. "Anything news worthy?" she asked as she retrieved a cup.

"Well," Frank said sitting back down and spinning the newspaper headline on the tables top so she could read it, "You might say we have some news, it seems we've become quite popular overnight."

Liz was just about to pour her coffee when she saw the headline:

HOME OF ABDUCTED GIRLS BURNS OVERNIGHT IN ELYSIAN PARK, ARSON SUSPECTED. POLICE ARE LOOKING TO QUESTION THE ELITE SUNSET DETECTIVE AGENCY IN BLAZE.

"Oh, shit, have you called Sam yet?" she asked.

"He called about twenty minutes ago to check on us, he's on his way over now, he had me call Charlie and tell them not to go into the office. He said we'll all meet up later."

"This isn't good," Liz said as she read the rest of the article.

Connie stretched out easily in the large tub. She realized now that Liz was right, she was tense and needed to relax. She hummed an old song that she couldn't remember the name of but was sure it was a Tommy Dorsey hit sometime back. She eased her sore arm under the hot water and then allowed her shoulder to slip under. She closed her eyes as the hot water started doing its business of relaxing her sorely tested muscles. She left her eyes closed as she felt the warm embrace of the water. When the lights went out it was several moments before she realized it. As her eyes fluttered open she was stunned to silence when the shower curtain screeched across its mounting rod, effectively closing her off from the bathroom.

She started to scream when she felt an invisible hand close over her mouth. She kicked and managed a few loud splashes before she felt a massive weight settle upon her legs. She tried kicking free from the tremendous pressure but knew it was futile as it felt as if her legs were getting crushed. Even though it was pitch black in the windowless bathroom, she knew that whatever was in the bathroom with her was invisible, just like it had been the day before in the office of John Rainbird, just as she knew beyond all doubt it was the creature from last night that had invaded the bathroom.

Sam pushed the buzzer and Frank cracked the door, then quickly removed the chain when he saw it was Sam.

"Hey, boss. How's John?" he asked as he quickly scanned the hallway before closing the door.

"Sleeping like a baby, either that thing is hurt and leaving him be, or it's busy with other things."

"You saw the morning headlines, Sam?" Liz asked as she retrieved another coffee cup from the cabinet over her sink.

"Someone must have spotted one of the cars there last night. You can be sure the cop's won't be far behind the *Times* on this one, I have a feeling their normal ineptness may go by the wayside where we are concerned."

"What'ya mean, you think the cops have been got to?" Frank asked.

"Not all of them, but maybe just the ones that count," Sam said as he nodded at Liz in thanks for the coffee. "Today's going to be hard, Liz you have to get to Pickfair and get Mary and the kid and her parents out of town. I don't care how you do it, we don't need LA's finest to find them just yet, they'll ask questions we can't answer, and see if you can get Charlie and Doug to go with them which shouldn't be a problem. I think they've had their fill of this case. Coop will lay low, he's afraid of women right now. Speaking of women, I have a call to make on a certain Count and Countess, and they're going to answer some of my questions."

"You got it; you want me to take Miss Yale along?" Liz asked.

"I may need her, she's connected to her sister and may be of help," he said as he looked around at Stevie, Frank and Liz. "Where is she by the way?"

"She's relaxing in the tub, believe me, she needed it," Liz answered shaking her head.

Connie couldn't breathe. She fought with her good arm but to no avail. She felt herself being lifted from the tub, she couldn't scream as the unseen hand tightened around her face. She used her good arm to relieve the pressure by grabbing the assailant and pulling upwards, her head felt as if it were being twisted off her neck as she was placed against the pink tiled wall. With her legs now free of the massive weight she kicked out but struck nothing but the loose shower curtain. She felt her chest being groped by a large hand and then felt the roughness course down her abdomen and stop at her pelvis. She turned her head in fear and frustration. She felt the hot tears form in her eyes as she squeezed them shut. She kicked out once again and once more she only succeeded in striking the dark shower curtain. Her right leg was caught and the rough hand ran up her calf to her thigh and then between her legs. She whimpered and tried to cry out as she hit at the unseen hand around her throat and mouth.

"You are mine woman, anytime I wish it so," the voice whispered in her right ear.

Connie twisted her head from side to side as she felt a sharp object, possibly a claw touch her, almost to the point of penetration.

"Your sister is dying and soon I will have no need for her entertaining voice. Contrive to have Dalhart step away. Tell him there will be another time, for now I have my work, later we will finish his chapter," the claw partially entered her. "Convince him, or I will not allow your sister to go on her way, I will keep her as I have kept others, a child of the dark."

Connie didn't fathom what the beast meant by his threat. She released her hand and with both her good and bad arm she started swinging. She hit nothing but the hot air around her. She managed to take a hold on the shower curtain and then she pulled. The plastic started popping off of the steel rings and the rod broke free of the wall with a loud clang. The shower curtain fell off and that was when she saw that it covered an invisible shape. Her vision was fading and she knew she couldn't force another breath into her closed throat. She thought she heard some commotion a hundred miles away, but even that came to her like an afterthought. Like a dream she heard a scream and men shouting and then the world was shattered by loud explosions. Then mercifully she passed out, closing her eyes against a sudden burst of light, and then there was nothing but the blankness of unconsciousness.

Sam was the first to move when he heard the crash of the shower curtain rod. There was loud splashing coming from the bathroom and he moved quickly. The door was locked from the inside and he placed his shoulder to it and pushed. He stepped back and hit the door again, this time he heard a cracking sound as the small deadbolt gave way and then one more lunge and he was through.

Frank and Liz, with Stevie close behind all crowded into the small bathroom. Sam reacted first as Liz screamed and Frank yelled something no one really understood. The shower curtain was floating above the tiled floor and Connie looked as if she were nailed to the tile wall. Her head was thrashing about as her naked body became limp. The curtain was billowing up and down and it was Sam who figured it out first. He quickly drew his thirty-eight and fired three times into the floating shower curtain, aiming his fire carefully away from Connie, the bullets penetrated the tiled wall two feet to the left of the now still form of the woman. There was a roar of anger and not pain as the curtain quickly fell to the wet floor. Sam dropped the gun as Connie started sliding down the wall. He caught her before she hit the water and placed her in his arms. The water soaked through his jacket as his senses caught the smell of rotten meat. Stevie had jumped onto the shower curtain and was tearing through it, trying in vain to find out what it had been covering. Frank holstered his gun and gently pushed Liz toward the door.

"Help Sam, baby," he said as he then reached and pulled Stevie up off the wet floor. "Don't waste your time, kid, ain't nothin' there."

Stevie stopped tearing at the plastic curtain and sat down on the water covered floor and leaned up against the wall. He drew his legs up and wrapped his arms around his knees.

"What are we'z dealin' with here, Mr. Wiechek?" he asked as he finally looked up at Frank with haunted eyes.

Frank didn't say anything as he looked around the bathroom. He knew they were up against something they couldn't possibly beat.

Liz sat on the bed after Sam had covered Connie's shivering body with a thick blanket. She took her hand in her own and said a few words into her ear. Connie opened her eyes a moment and then turned away from Liz as tears rolled down her face.

"I wasn't strong enough."

"You're strong dear, very strong. God knows I couldn't have survived what you have the last two days."

"You don't understand," she sobbed, "It...it forced..."

"Honey, honey, don't say another word, you're here and you're fine," Liz said as she looked up at Sam with a helpless look he'd never seen before from his longtime employee and friend.

Sam walked over to the other side of the bed and leaned over and brushed away a strand of wet hair that had fallen over Connie's face.

"Connie, you have to think clearly now. That thing wasn't here. It was never in the bathroom. Whatever was in there with you wasn't real. It was you; I truly believe it works through John and now somehow through your sister to you. You have to focus on that. It never really touched you."

"The smell, the feel of its skin, the heat of its breath...it was in there with me, it—" She stopped suddenly and opened her eyes and sat up, reaching out and touching Sam on the side of his face. "It wants you to leave it be, Sam. It said for you to leave it alone, that your battle will come some another time."

"Is that right?"

"It said if you persisted it would, would take my sister to the dark side."

"Is that a fact?" he said with anger starting to put an edge into his voice.

Connie leaned forward, the blanket slightly dipping before she pulled it back up.

"She may already be gone so you can't even think about not going after it. I won't allow it, she wouldn't want it either," she said in near panic as Sam lowered her shaking hand from his cheek. "It would kill her anyway, that corrupt bastard would never keep its word, don't you feel it, don't we all feel it can't be trusted, wasn't meant to be trusted?" Connie said in near panic looking from Sam to Liz.

"How about we do both, get your kid sister back and send this thing back to hell where it belongs," Sam said as he stood up. He winked at Liz and quickly left the room. He spoke with Frank and then pulled a small black book from his inner pocket and called a number after lifting the large phone from its hook. He spoke quietly, turning his back to Frank and Stevie, and then he waited.

Frank could see his boss's jaw clenching and unclenching, and then Sam quickly said some more words they couldn't hear and then he quickly hung up the telephone. Sam then gave Frank and Stevie instructions and then placed his fedora onto his head and left.

Sam knew he couldn't involve the others, at least not yet, so he went to the *Alhambra* alone. If he was tossed into the can, he would at least have others still working on the outside. He left Frank instructions on what to do. He was to take everyone to his apartment, and Liz was still to go to Pickfair and make sure the child and her parents were safe and she was to convince Mary, Doug and Charlie to get the hell out of town. He had to answer to the police about last night and the best way to do that was not to answer anything at all. He would put up what smoke screen he could and hope for the best.

As he drove down Sunset he could see that his initial conclusion about the cops finally moving was accurate. There were three prowler cars parked along the sidewalk with two cops on either side of the doors of the *Alhambra* Building. He pulled into the alley and parked. He would go in the back way and use that entrance so he could skip the formality of being escorted to his own office by the police where he would undoubtedly find the officer in charge.

As he opened the rear door he was grabbed from both sides and a hand quickly slid inside his jacket and deftly removed his thirty-eight.

"These gentlemen didn't believe you would be arrogant enough to return here, but I said you didn't know the stupid bastard the way I do," Purvis said as he tossed Sam's gun to one of the policemen beside him.

"Well, I would say I'm surprised but I would be lying, it figures you and the cops would have a close working relationship," Sam said shaking his arms free of the two uniformed policemen. They started to grab for him again but Purvis waved them off. "Come now, I doubt Mr. Dalhart can outrun a bullet." Purvis gestured for Sam to follow. "Come on Dalhart, the LAPD have a few questions about your activities last night and I'm interested to hear your answers as well, and we can begin about your janitorial service, they seem to be a might lax in the way they clean your offices."

"Yeah, we've been having trouble finding good people," he said as he glared at the two cops beside him, "you fellas want the job, might be something you can handle."

"Yeah, well come on smart guy," Purvis said as he started up the back stairs, "I can't wait to hear this story."

Once on the main floor Sam looked through the smashed windows of the front doors and saw a man sitting on Liz's desk. He was swinging one leg back and forth as he looked around the cluttered reception area. Two other cops were at the broken plate glass window that looked out on Sunset and were dusting for prints.

"Well, well, Samuel Dalhart, Private Dick," the man said as he continued to swing his leg back and forth. "You have an explanation for this," he asked waving his hand around the office.

"Hmm, looks like we had a break-in, or do you have another theory, sergeant Finnerty?"

"It's Lieutenant Finnerty, gumshoe, and you bet I have a theory, wanna' hear it?"

"Why not? I love fairytales," Sam said as he moved into the office and slowly removed his hat.

There were no lies between him and Finnerty. Sam had known him since the academy. They had come up through the force together; their only difference between them was the small fact that Sam had always been clean, whereas Finnerty was dirty before their rookie year had been up. Sam could even smell it on him now. The new suit, the expensive shoes and the barbershop shave.

"Special Agent Purvis is here as a guest of the department, he says he has a special interest in you and a few of your, shall we say, more colorful clients."

Sam looked at Purvis who stood by the door with a smile on his face. The man purposefully unbuttoned his coat and allowed his two holstered .45 automatics to gleam in the overhead lights.

"I knew someone had to be holding your leash, Finnerty," Sam said as he eased himself into one of the reception chairs. He looked at his watch, hoping Finnerty's theory took a while.

"What I think is that you and your so called associates may have been caught with your hand in the cookie jar Dalhart. It's obvious to a trained eye you had trouble here last night, trouble that may have started out in Elysian Park. Ring a bell?"

"You sure it isn't a case of janitorial technician transgression, Lieutenant?"

A confused look momentarily crossed Finnerty's features; he looked from Sam to Purvis and then slid off the desk, losing his cool.

"Okay smart guy, what were you and the Indian doing out at the Rodriguez's house last night? You know—the one that you burned to the ground to cover up your involvement!"

"You should write for the movies, but then again I forgot, you can barely spell cat."

"You're going to find a shortcut to my fist Dalhart, you were seen, and that puts you right in the middle of arson and possible kidnapping. An arson that now links you to the kidnapping of two young girls, coincidentally after it was discovered as a fact that you were in the employ of a man that Mr. Purvis here has a suspicion that may involve this actor gentleman and foreign nationals in the disappearance of another young girl—a certain Charlie Chaplin, how's that for a fairy tale, Dalhart?"

"I'm just surprised you could string so many words together without stumbling, but then again I guess you could always follow a script that someone else wrote for you," Sam said as he looked from Finnerty to Purvis, the real author of what the cop was saying.

"You son of a bitch!" Finnerty said as he started toward Sam.

Dalhart was about to calmly lash out with his Florsheim shoe when there was a voice from the doorway that stopped Finnerty dead in his tracks. Standing beside Purvis and looking at him like he was a bug was Louis B. Meyer, and beside him with a serious scowl on his face was Talbot Leonard, who Sam had called just before leaving Liz's place and now stood with his hat in his hand taking in the scene before them.

"I'll ask again, what is going on here?" Meyer asked sternly, his small bowtie working up and down and his eyes penetrating through his small round glasses.

Finnerty looked from Sam to the most powerful man in Hollywood, speechless for the moment.

"We're questioning this man for his possible involvement in a double kidnapping of two young girls," Purvis offered with a sneer.

"Is that right?" Meyer asked as he stepped inside the office, his tightly controlled and coached demeanor on how to speak to hireling's clearly evident. "And you are—?"

"Purvis, formerly of the FBI, now in private service," he answered with an arrogant tinge to his voice.

"I see, and your jurisdiction in this matter is—?" Meyer asked with a deep scowl.

"I'm an observer and I—"

"In other words, you have none. Now you," he said as he turned to Finnerty, "may I see your badge please?" Meyer asked holding his hand out.

Finnerty swallowed and removed his badge and identification and handed it over.

"Lieutenant Finnerty, Vice?"

"That's correct, last night this man—"

"Last night this man did a service to the community and it's for that fact that I brought these gentlemen and ladies down to ask him about," Meyer said as he nodded toward Talbot Leonard who walked over to the stairwell and waved the people who had gathered there up onto the floor.

As Finnerty and Purvis stood silent and stunned, about thirteen reporters ran up the stairs and squeezed past Purvis and into the office.

"Ladies and gentlemen of the press, I'm sure you know Samuel Dalhart of the Sunset Detective Agency," Meyer said as he backed away allowing the press to get a good look at Sam.

"Sam, Harvey Bennett of the *Times*. Is it true you have recovered the younger of the two girls kidnapped from Elysian Part and that she is alright?" was the first question asked.

Sam was totally taken back. How had the press gotten wind of what happened last night? He looked at LB Meyer who just raised his eyebrows and almost imperceptivity nodded his head toward the waiting reporters.

"It's true, we found the little girl, Adria last night in the park, her kidnappers had released her unharmed. After we were hired by the Rodriguez family to investigate the disappearance of the two girls, it was this agency that just happened to find her after her release."

"Where is the girl now?" Mary Sinclair of the *Herald Examiner* asked, pencil poised over her writing pad.

"She is under protective custody until such time as we can arrange a safe turnover to the Los Angeles Sheriff's Department."

"Sam, you're accused of setting a blaze at the Rodriguez house in Elysian Park, do you care to comment on that allegation?" another reporter asked.

"Yes, I'll comment, we at the Sunset Detective Agency disavow all knowledge of any fire that may have started at the house."

"He's lying," Melvin Purvis said under his breath, but loud enough that the gathered group of reporters heard it.

"Care to comment on Mr. Purvis's accusation, Sir?" Mary Sinclair asked before the others could shout out the same question.

Sam smiled. "Well, I will tell you what I saw last night just before the girl was discovered in the park. The Police Department had just initiated a riot in the street just moments before the house started on fire. There are a hundred witnesses to this fact, so maybe your question ought to be answered by the officers who were there last night, now I have no more answers for you today, if you'll excuse me."

The reporters turned on Purvis and Finnerty who were busy staring angrily at Sam and were being pushed out the doors by the mob of reporters. Louis B. Meyer caught Finnerty's eye and tossed him his badge over the heads of the questioning group and winked.

"Good luck Lieutenant," he said.

"Thanks LB, I owe you one."

"For you my boy, any hardship is not too great, you've saved us quite a few embarrassments to ignore a call for help. The reporters just happened to be out front, I didn't call them. Now, explain the trouble you are in."

As Sam told the fantastic story of the last two days, Meyer listened without comment. After hearing about the attack this morning on Miss Yale, Talbot shook his head and went into the back to make coffee. This case was taking on dimensions that were well beyond their boundaries and Talbot Leonard for one was getting very scared.

When Sam had finished he waited for Meyer to comment but instead of doing so the portly studio head stood and accepted a cup of coffee from Leonard. He nodded his thanks and then finally turned to face Sam.

"You know, I'm considered a dirty rotten son of a bitch by those people who work for me and a back stabbing opportunist by those who don't. But I'm a business man in the end Sam, it's that simple, profit and loss, that's the bottom line. What's your profit in this my boy?"

"None, I only wanted to find out what happened to these girls and to help my partner regain his sanity, and stopping the thing that's bringing so much misery to people around here." He looked from Meyer to Talbot and then lowered his head. "There's more to it than just missing girls, I feel it LB, this thing, man, whatever you want to call it has a plan, it has to."

"It sounds as if you may be in over your head here. After all, you're not even sure if the authorities are really turning a blind eye toward this, are you?"

"I could never prove it, but let's just say for the sake of argument that they're dragging their feet somewhat."

"I can't believe the things that you've told me my boy. I'm a realist, I see black and white and there is no land of make-believe, other than the town we work in, hell, I own make-believe. There has to be another, more plausible explanation for these occurrences."

Sam started to say something as Meyer took a sip of his coffee.

"Easy Samuel, I believe you are in a bind and I feel I must assist you in any way I can," Meyer handed his cup over to Talbot.

Meyer reached into his coat pocket and brought out a small date book. "If he knew I was sending you to him for something like this he would come to my office and kill me, which would make half this town ecstatic and the other half remorseful that they couldn't have done it themselves," he said as he finally found what he was looking for and then walked to

Liz's cluttered desk. He saw a splattering of something that had a greenish tint to it and avoided it when he pulled over her notepad and started writing. He finished, tore the paper free and gave it to Sam.

Sam accepted the note and then looked up at Meyer as if he had lost his mind.

"I'll call ahead to make sure she lets you in her door, she's rather eccentric, but don't be put off by that, she's the best for providing the information you're looking for. It's my understanding that Tod Browning, the whiz kid over at Universal used her for his research on those horrid Lugosi films and she fought him every inch of the way on them. She seems to believe in something that's similar to what you're describing." Meyer smiled and patted Sam on the shoulder. "She's just someone who can advise you on what steps you may possibly take in your investigation, because above all else you have to know what you're fighting before you may formulate a plan for victory," he said as he placed his hat on his head and then stared at the floor a moment. "Because you may be right about one thing, I feel we're heading into dark times, and I'm one of those old Jews who don't like most things you run afoul of in the dark," he looked up and smiled. "Go and see her. Oh she'll huff and she'll puff, but the old hag *will* help you. Now, if your man Talbot can drive me back to the Metro lot, I have to fire someone, don't know who yet, but I have the urge. Besides, I have to make things ready for the president's visit and fund raiser tonight at USC."

Sam didn't say anything as Talbot escorted Louis B. Meyer from the office. He looked down at the sheet of paper and shook his head. Written in Meyer's scraggly scrawl was five words; *'Madame Yvonne Grakstoffo Boueveree-Smith.'*

Sam looked up, one of the most ruthless men in all of Hollywood was sending him to see the queen of all the gypsies on the west coast.

PART 2

A TIME LONG FORGOTTEN

✌ TWELVE ✌

The countess was back to normal after a rough night of nightmares, tossing, turning and little actual sleep. The count eased the service tray easily in front of her as she stared at the far wall, voiceless as she had been all morning; she managed a smile for her husband.

"You saved me last night, my love, don't think I didn't notice through all of my pain," she said as she carefully eased a strand of her long black hair behind her right ear.

"Nonsense, I only did what any husband who loves his wife dearly would do," he said as he seated himself across from her in the dining area of their suite at the Westerly.

"I have been so unfair to you, the filthy way I have been carrying on with Karl; it is completely unforgivable to one as loyal as you."

The Count took her hand and smiled.

"It was Karl who said your wound was not mortal, he eased you back into your beautiful-self and I will be forever grateful to him for that."

"Von Railing is a pig of the first order. Through my pain I saw the way he treated you, it was as if he were angry at the intrusion," she said as her green eyes flared.

"Well, its past and we'll soon be shed of the dangers of this backward country. I was hoping that maybe we could—," he started to say but was interrupted by a soft knock on the door.

He smiled and patted his wife's hand again and stood and handed her a silk robe, and then as she stood slowly and put it on he walked through the large suite to the ornate door.

"Yes?" he asked through the door as he looked through the peephole. He saw a uniformed hotel employee whose body was mostly blocked by a large bouquet of roses.

"Sir, I have a floral delivery for the Countess," the unseen man said.

The count turned and looked quickly at his wife and she shrugged.

"Is there a card on the arrangement?" he asked.

He saw the man dressed in the maroon uniform of the hotel raise a ticket.

"Yes sir, a Mister Karl Von Railing."

"He's lying; Karl would never send roses or any flowers that have an ounce of life in them. Especially roses!" she hissed as she ran for the large bathroom.

"Go away and take the roses with you, the Countess refuses the delivery!" he called through the door.

Suddenly a loud crack and the door flew inward, smashing into D'Sarcuni's face and chest. The delivery man was the first through the door, quickly followed by eight other men. As the count tried to get up off the carpet, something clear and cool was splashed into his face. The water hit him and he acted as though acid had struck his flesh. He howled in pain, trying in vain to cover his eyes, but he was too late as they were inundated with water and he felt his eyes melt to almost nothing as he scratched at his orbital sockets in a vain attempt to wipe them clear. As he writhed on the floor, two of the large men took the door and haphazardly placed it back on its frame after checking for onlookers in the hallway.

"I must assume we have your attention?" the man who had delivered the flowers said loudly.

The count hissed and struck out blindly at his assailants. The claws were out and a full six inches of sharp death clawed out in an attempt to impale. The count hissed again and transformed, becoming somewhat sleeker as his teeth grew and his stubby arms muscled. Four men held him at his arms; they bucked up and down trying to keep the tremendously strengthened D'Sarcuni from getting free to strike at them, even blinded they respected his power. There were four more holding his legs in place as he kicked out. The count's robe had flown open and the men could see the white, deathly pale skin beneath working as his agonized cries went unheeded.

"Your wife Count, where is she? Von Railing, the Scotsman? You know who we came here for, where is Phaltazar?" the man said to the blinded and subdued Count as he dribbled more water onto his chest. The Italian screamed as the holy water seared a path down his chest, oozing first blood and then pus. The smoke was nauseating to the attackers but they still held the count's flailing body.

"God in heaven help me!" the count hissed through his agony filled voice.

Major Paul Lansdorf lashed out with his heavy shoe, catching the Count in his ribs; it seemed to have no effect other than to hurt the German's foot.

"You abandoned God! You gave up your right to any humane treatment you monster!" the Major cried out, knowing he was being unprofessional. "The water was specially blessed by the man you once worshiped as Pope, and next I will make you drink it! Now where is your Master?"

"I can't," D'Sarcuni hissed and snapped in anger at the German major. He was starting to turn animalistic in his attempts to shake free. The men were being lifted clear of the floor as they watched in horror at what was being done to this changeling they were restraining.

"Then we will most assuredly ask your lovely wife, and I guarantee it will be in the harshest of terms you bastard! I will personally stake her to the fucking walls!"

"Nooooooo," the count shouted as he gave a mighty pull with his arms, bringing the four men across his chest and smashing them together with a smack. Then the count was almost free, but the major threw himself onto him and used his own weight while the soldiers quickly recovered. Major Lansdorf was only inches from the jagged teeth of the Count as they closed and opened, snapping relentlessly as they tried to clamp onto his face.

"Leave my wife be, leave her be, I beg you!" the thing under him cried. "I'll tell you, please, I'll tell you!"

The men looked on in triumph as the count said the words they wanted to hear. But their joy was short lived as the bathroom door and wall surrounding it exploded outward. Through the swirl of plaster and shorting of electrical wires the Germans could see a most hideous sight as the countess made her appearance. Her arms were outstretched and her long claws and sharp, filthy fangs barred as she waded into the room with a speed that caught the German soldiers off guard. Through the flash of the on and off electrical lights the major saw the hideousness of her features. Boney and sunken cheeks, the long and ill aligned front teeth and the hissing and growling as spittle flew from her purple tinted lips. Her mouth was three times its normal size as it slashed at the major, driving him through the already damaged door and into the hallway, hitting a credenza and then he fell to the floor. She then lashed out at the two men holding her husband's right arm, the claws catching the first man across the face, tearing the flesh away from the muscles beneath, leaving him with a meat mask. The man fell away screaming. The second one never made a sound as his throat was sliced cleanly through, allowing his blood to gush over the count as he threw the other two men holding his left arm easily off of him.

"Hold him!" the major screamed as he reached for the bottle of holy water that had fallen from his hand.

The countess then turned her attention to the four men at the count's feet, she lashed out with lightning speed and one man quickly fell dead as the other three rolled clear of her attack. Then instead of continuing to strike out at their attackers, she reached down and stared into her husband's red eyes, her green eyes were full of fire and betrayal.

"Why? Betrayer!" she screeched as she reached down and slashed his throat as fast as any animal had ever struck. She reached back, ready to strike the death blow and that was when she felt the searing pain of holy water strike her back. She screamed as she reached back, trying to tear away the material of the flapping robe where the water was soaking through. Then she turned and in a split second calculated her long odds of surviving this attack and moved, flying as though on a current of air toward the glass enclosed balcony, smashing through them and out into the early day. She knew that Phaltazar would have to be warned.

The men once again threw their weight onto the writhing Count. D'Sarcuni. Dark blood spurted from his opened jugular as his blind eyes failed to make the tears he felt at his betrayal of all that he had loved. Finally the major approached and went to his knees.

"Salvage your soul with your final breath, Count, tell us where we may end the nightmare you have helped to create?"

D'Sarcuni weakly lashed out, but his strength was all but gone as the major caught the shrinking hand. The claws were already curling and yellowing away to nothing, but the major saw the look was still a fiery one on the man's features, even with his red eyes burned away, his wife's killing blow had awakened the fool to his treachery and he would no longer be willing to give up his Master. He looked toward one of his men who no longer was needed to hold the counts legs and nodded. The man stood and quickly moved to the large bouquet of roses and pulled several of the blood red flowers from their stems.

"I damn you to hell for what you have done," the major said into the counts shriveling face. The skin was going sallow and wax-like. "For what you have brought to the world's doorstep your punishment will be for eternity," with those words he stuffed the roses into D'Sarcuni's mouth, smashing the counts front teeth with his gloved fist.

D'Sarcuni bucked harshly as the rose petals took their toll. Then the Major blindly reached back and an Ash stake was thrust into his hand by one of his surviving men. With possibly their last hope of finding the Arch and his minions before they had a chance at ruining the rest of the world, the major shook his head and then thrust the stake into the chest cavity of the Count D'Sarcuni.

Major Lansdorf stood and turned away from the horrific sight as the count writhed in momentary agony as the flames ate him from the inside. The rest of the major's men could swear there were a thousand voices crying out and singing their praise as the fat man burned alive.

The Major walked over to a vacant chair and sat down hard. He knew he would have to tell the colonel that they had failed in their one chance at finding the beast. He slowly removed his gloves and lowered his head. The world was doomed to a horrible darkness that would envelope them all.

"Armageddon is upon us," he said to one but himself.

As Mary Pickford, the sweetheart of all America and most of the world, looked out of her study window at the small child who was being helped into the pool in the backyard of Pickfair. She smiled, but was sure to wipe it from her face as she turned to face the two cowering men standing and waiting for the wrath of God to fall upon them.

"I do not for one moment believe a word of it, and you can ask Mr. Dalhart to verify this all you like, I won't buy it from him either. You two *gentlemen,* and I use the term in the loosest possible sense, were on some sort of gin-induced nighttime spree that may or may not have included Gary Cooper, I've yet to see him to get his version the story."

"But, Mary, my love," Fairbanks began.

"Don't you do it Douglass, not now, don't you dare ask me to take your word for anything, Vampires. You know. I blame you, Charlie, you have his head so mixed up with your mind bending stories he can't think straight any longer."

"But Mary, that's not entirely—," Charlie started but stopped when she raised her eyebrows. After all the years he had known *Miss Ball Crusher* she never failed to silence anyone with those plucked and painted brows when raised.

"Now, if this child is indeed who you say she is, the police must be notified immediately. I will not be scandalized this way. I have United Artists to think about since obviously my partners do not."

"But my love, Samuel said to keep away from the police."

Those brows again and Doug immediately shut up.

"I will handle the child—who is a doll by the way," she batted her eyelashes, "and her parents until I can think of what to do, you both admit I have the best solutions to odd situations, don't you?"

Charlie looked at his shoes and Doug looked toward the bar and all the pretty bottles sitting there.

"Now, I'm angry at you two and don't want to see you for the rest of the day. You are dismissed, and don't think you can go and skulk around the tennis courts and hide from me, I'll know it. Go and play with Coop and Sam, go and continue your Vampire game, just leave me out of it and don't get into any more trouble, or I'll give you both something worse than any make-believe vampire, something you *won't* walk away from. And do not forget the reception and fund raiser tonight, either of you." She smiled and tilted her head. "Now, be good boys and behave yourselves, and tell Sam the girl and her parents are in good hands."

On the way down to the first floor from the second floor study, Charlie slapped Douglass on the shoulder, making him wince.

"I told you, you fool, you always do that!" Charlie said as he stopped on the winding staircase.

"Must I be brutalized by you too, wasn't last night enough, Charles?"

"Now you got us kicked out and she has control of the child, after Samuel specifically said to watch her, take her away. Hell old boy you may just as well have given her over to the damn Gestapo, action star my balding ass!"

"Now see here, Mary's a lot of things but comparing her to the—"

"You're right," Charlie said as he reached out and turned Douglass on the stairs to lead him down. "I should have compared her to Hitler himself!"

Mary Pickford watched them go from the upstairs window. Charlie was animatedly speaking and her Doug was hanging his head as they climbed into Charlie's car. She didn't tell them that she had called the police an hour before and she expected them at any time. As she watched her companion and Charlie from this distance she smiled. Doug was a drunkard and a constant irritant in her life, but she truly loved him. She loved Charlie too for that matter. She just couldn't stomach him sometimes the way he constantly had Douglass in trouble. Where they came up with these wild stories she would never know. As she watched the child in the pool it made her pause. Oh, she had no doubt that Sam has something to do with getting her back from her abductors, she read that much in the *Times* morning addition, but for them to claim that fantastical story? She decided that she would give Samuel Dalhart a piece of her mind also.

There was a slight knock on her door and her butler, who never smiled at any time in the years she had known and employed him, told her she had a phone call. She nodded and accepted the gold handset.

"Yes?" she answered.

"Miss Pickford, this is Senator Emile Farnsworth's office, would you please hold for the senator?" a female voice asked but didn't wait for her to answer.

"Miss Pickford? Senator Farnsworth here," a gruff, Midwestern sounding voice stated.

"Yes, this is Mary Pickford," she said demurely into the phone.

"Imagine, America's little sweetheart, I didn't think I would be speaking to you today—"

"Senator, I'm an extremely busy woman, would you mind getting to the point of this call," she said, arching her evil left brow.

"Yes, yes, of course. Well Ma'am, we were informed at this office that you had the abducted child in the Rodriguez case sheltered at your home and we—"

"And may I ask who it was that informed you of this fact Senator?"

"Yes, of course you may," the voice said, but she could hear a hesitancy in it, "A Mr. Samuel Dalhart, I believe he was instrumental in recovering the child, he informed us she was with you."

"I see, what can I help you with please?"

"You are attending the reception for the president tonight at the university, are you not?"

"Since I am the organizer of the event, you could say that, yes."

"Yes ma'am, I am aware of that, my polio foundation is making a presentation to Mr. Roosevelt, it's on the agenda, are you not aware of it?"

Senator, I don't mean to be rude…well; yes I do as I do not have the time to go over every minute of the function tonight, so if you would please get to your point."

"As you know the child has polio and since the president has followed this case so closely in the newspapers, we thought it would be a wonderful idea to have the child…this Miss Adria Rodriguez, present the president with a welcoming bouquet."

Mary thought about this as she stepped to the window and watched the parents of the girl as they tried to coax her into the water. Mary's face grew concerned when the small girl didn't respond, her small legs outstretched before her with her leg braces. Mary choked back a tear and then decided.

"I will broach the subject with her parents. To ease your mind Senator, at least on my behalf, I will recommend it, only because she's such a brave child and deserving of the president's attention."

"Excellent, this is so wonderful. I can't adequately express my gratitude, Miss Pickford."

"I still want this child protected before and after the reception."

"I have already dispatched LA's finest to your address. They will let no one get remotely close to the child, I assure you, Lieutenant Finnerty and his men will be there shortly and thank you again."

Mary hung up the phone and watched the poor child from her window. There was no telling what the girl went through at the hands of her abductor. *This will be good for her*, she thought

Farnsworth hung up the phone and waved Finnerty and his men out of the office. Then he stood and walked toward the adjoining door that led to a private sitting room and entered.

The man was sitting in a chair facing him with his driver standing beside him.

"It's arranged, by none other than Miss Mary Pickford herself. There's no way the President's men will keep this girl from presenting him with a bouquet of flowers. It was very fortuitous that Finnegan is on our payroll, and was as informative and forthright as to the child's whereabouts."

The man smiled and nodded and moved his hand, dismissing Farnsworth who frowned but turned and left anyway.

"I can't believe after last night that anything would have worked correctly, but the Master was right, while Dalhart and his men concentrate on the impossible, they would never notice the mere improbable. He will be pleased his little ticking time bomb will be sitting upon Roosevelt's very lap." He chuckled and shook his head and then stood. "Come; let us be among the welcoming fools for the President's train, shall we? I want to see the man who will not be here to thwart the darkness coming from the east."

With those words, McDougal followed Karl Von Railing out of the senator's office.

The clock that would foretell the moments of light left to mankind had started ticking, and a moonless midnight was fast approaching.

❧ THIRTEEN ❧

Sam stopped and made his phone calls. He felt inside that time was running out and he couldn't figure out why his gut instincts were telling him that. He had just spoken to a very angry John at his place, still fuming for the much needed sleep he claimed he hadn't needed at all, but his partner soon calmed with news that at least for the moment, they weren't wanted men after last night, but as fortune may have it, just the opposite, they were considered heroes for rescuing the girl. He quickly gave John the address where to meet him after he was to swing by and pick up Connie and Liz. As for Pete and Willis, he wanted them to stake out the Westerly Hotel where the Count and Countess were presently staying. Frank and Stevie were to find Charlie and Doug and find out where it was they took Mary and the Rodriguez family. As long as they were out of the way of the press, their freedom and safety should hold true for a while.

It took Sam twenty minutes to climb Kellogg Hill and drive to the address Meyer had given him in Pomona. The sun was out and it looked to be a perfect day before Halloween in Southern California. The fall rain had washed the small town's filth away and it actually seemed as if it were a normal day, but Sam knew it was anything but normal, and also guessed that when it went dark his world and the world around them would turn far more menacing than it had been even the night before.

Sam finally located the out of the way house just two blocks from Ganisha Park on White Avenue. The large white house was one of those old stone monstrosities that were built just after the World War. It seemed every twenty feet the roof had a different pitch to it and shot off at impossible angles. If you wanted to describe a haunted house in one of those old novels you would choose this one to do it with. If Sam had the money it took just for the windows in this place he could have retired a year ago. He pulled his Chevy across from the house and looked the place over and waited.

Down the street he saw several girls cross White Avenue and walk into the park with its sloping hills and green grass, blissfully unaware that according to his fact sheet, two young women had disappeared from this very park three weeks past. He watched them until they made the playground area where they sat on a picnic table and started talking whatever girls talked and giggled about. He turned toward the house and thought he saw one of the large curtains in the wide plate-glass window move, and along with the motion he had the feeling he was just being spied upon. He hoped LB Meyer had called and forewarned this Madam Yvonne that he was coming.

Sam didn't notice the car pull in behind him and almost jumped out of his skin when John lightly tapped on his door, making three hollow *thunking* sounds.

"Well, you drug us all the way out here. To tell you the truth *partner,* I'm damn well surprised you wanted company at all," John said, obviously still mad for having been left behind this morning.

"Damn it," Sam said closing his eyes.

"Hey you're really spooked, this place isn't that bad—it's Pomona for crying out loud."

"I always hated these old places," Sam said as he climbed from the car. He immediately noticed Connie and for some reason he felt better for seeing her. Liz exited the car first and stood before Sam, blocking out his view of Connie Yale.

"Sam, I really need to be working on cleaning that office up and getting it back to working order," Liz said as she looked at him above her pointed and false diamond sunglasses.

"Yeah, well can it. No one goes near the office or back to your place again, it knows those places." Sam said sternly as he turned and started across the street toward the tall, intimidating house.

"Don't look now but the neighbors are looking at us," Connie said as she stepped faster to catch up with Sam and take his arm.

As John, Sam and Liz looked on casually, they did see several people with their faces poking through parted curtains. Not that the houses were close together, they weren't, and what was funnier, they didn't believe the neighbors cared if they were caught looking.

There were three extremely wide front porch steps made of white painted cement, Sam could see that they had recently been scrubbed, so whoever Madame Yvonne was she kept a neat porch at least. The veranda was as wide as the front of the house and had a porch swing, also painted white.

Sam stepped up to the wide double front doors and saw the buzzer to the right, but just before he pushed it a voice stopped him dead in his tracks.

"Get the fuck away from my door!"

Sam looked at John and he smiled in return.

"Sounds like Mary Pickford doesn't it?" he said jokingly.

Sam ignored the remark and leaned toward the lace curtained leaded glass.

"Ma'am, I believe L.B. Meyer called you about me, Sam Dalhart, I'm a detective out of—"

"I've heard of you Dalhart, big hero aren't you, you and that Indian fellow. I don't like Dicks, never have," the craggily voice said through the solid door. "I'll tell you like I told that fat SOB Meyer, I'm not at home today, so get the hell off my porch!"

"Madame Yvonne, my name is Yale, my sister has been—"

The door opened a crack freezing Connie's statement before it was finished. They all saw two old eyes as they peered at them from the darkened entranceway beyond.

"Taken," the old woman said finishing for Connie.

"Yes, how did you know?"

The door opened wider and they saw a woman of about seventy, well dressed in a soft red dress with white pearls about her neck. Her gray hair was done neatly in a tight bun and her aged hands were well manicured.

"My Dear, why do you think you were sent to me, for my research prowess for those stupid horror films? I'm a gypsy goddamn it, now you may as well come in, you managed to get the sympathy vote, it was a goddamn low blow bringing a missing girl into it though, girlie."

Sam watched as the door swung wide and Connie started to step through.

"After you girlie," he snickered and Connie hit him with her elbow as she smiled at the old woman.

The woman looked to be anything but the Queen of the Gypsies in Southern California. Sam had heard only rumors about her. She was also known to the Hollywood community as the best source of information on old-world facts. However, she was also known to police departments from Chino to Sacramento for her shadier activities. Rumors of grand-theft and even murder followed her many Gypsy devotes.

Madame Yvonne Grakstoffo Boueveree-Smith, was about four feet eleven inches and about ninety-two pounds in both Sam's and Rainbird's estimation. Her face was heavily made up with cosmetics, but was tastefully done. Her attire was immaculate and she was a far cry from the gypsy portrayals that Hollywood had poisoned audiences with the world over.

The old woman waved off her maid who came in from what they assumed was the kitchen wiping her hands.

"A day late and a dollar short, as usual Melanie, now back to making lunch," she said with a quick wave of her hand. "But bring us coffee first."

Sam saw the maid-cook roll her eyes and turn and head back through the large swinging door that obviously marked her slave quarters, or kitchen as this case may be. He turned away and followed John, Connie and Liz into a large parlor that was more of a library he saw after he entered. There were shelves upon shelves of books. There was even a small ladder attached to those shelves for reaching books on the highest shelf. Sam was duly impressed.

"Please, have a seat," she gestured to two couches and a love seat.

Sam waited for the ladies to seat themselves—Liz on the love seat and Connie on the couch. She demurely looked at Sam and her eyes said it all. She swallowed and patted the couch cushion next to her. John noticed as well as Liz, but Sam didn't care, he sat next to Connie and immediately felt relaxed, except for the lingering eyes of the old gypsy, who looked from Connie's innocent face and then toward Sam. She sat in a high backed chair that fronted the dead fireplace and placed her hands over one knee. She smiled and arched her eyebrows.

"Now, if I may ask why am I being disturbed at my lunch hour?"

"We need information—"

Madame Yvonne cut Sam off. "Excuse me young man," she said and then looked toward John who quickly removed his fedora, forgetting his manners, but that wasn't what the old woman was looking at him for. "You're an Indian?"

"Yes, Ma'am," he said, wanting to get the hell out of the creepy old place.

She patted her right hand over her mouth several times, making a very insulting Indian call, "That sort of Indian and not one of those head-towel wearing, Peacock rearing people?"

"Northern Cheyenne, Ma'am," John said holding eye contact with the old Gypsy.

Madame Yvonne clapped her hands together twice and smiled broadly. "Oh, Dear, my late husband, Mr. Smith, was Sioux, you know of them young man?"

"Yes, they are our neighbors," John said looking nervously from the old woman to Sam without moving his head.

"Yes, yes, we met at what we used to call a "Dirt Road Carney. You know, a carnival that never did the big towns and cities, but stuck to the dirt roads for…well, let's just say we kept a low profile in those days as we didn't like the police and local sheriff poking around."

She smiled and seemed to drift away for a moment.

Connie glanced at Sam with a little unease.

"You know, people think I resent it when they call me Mrs. Smith, but it's not because I didn't love my husband, or that he beat me or some other foolishness like that, it was because in the end, I didn't think I was worthy of the name. You see, he made a life for a small girl who was shunned by almost everyone, he gave me all of this," she said as she waved her hand around the large room, "after saving all the money he could over the years. All the nickels and dimes from those horrid readings I used to do," she said and then her smile slip somewhat as she looked at John. "You remind me of him young man, and I sense your troubles, they're dark and you try and block them out but you cannot."

"Ma'am, Mr. Meyer said that you would be able to help us with—"

"He's a fat piece of shit that treats people badly. Mr. Louie B. Meyer will get his one day," she said cutting Sam off again. "You know he owes me money, so does Universal?"

The group was quiet as they looked at the old woman.

"LB says you think a vampire's come-a-visiting the City of Angels, is that true?"

"Yes, and he has my sister," Connie said. She couldn't help it, she was in no mood to hear about carneys and the like, or about how well-off the woman's husband left her.

"Yes, my Dear, that's the only reason you are now guests in my house," she said crossly, her European accent coming through only slightly in her rebuff. She looked at Sam. "I know what's come to America, and," she started laughing, and then stopped abruptly, "Well, it's not a vampire. Oh it looks, smells, and probably tastes like one, but that's its game. It wants to make you think precisely that. It may have a Vampyre or Nosferatu, as my Great Grandmamma used to call them, protecting it during vulnerable times, but a Vampyre it is not."

"Then, what is it?" Sam asked.

Instead of answering she looked at John. "You dream of it, don't you?"

John closed his eyes and when he opened them a moment later the old woman was still looking at him.

The maid entered and placed coffee before each of the guests and then moved off without saying a word. The old Gypsy watched her go with a slight shake to her head.

"And the beast has come to you, physically come into your life, but then again, it wasn't really there?" She then looked at Connie, her eyes fluttered and then she closed them. "You also, the beast has, has," her eyes opened and she still looked at Connie, "Why would it do that?" she asked with a confused look on her face.

"That bastard has my sister and for some strange reason has not killed her like those other poor souls."

Madame Yvonne closed her eyes a moment and her right hand went to her neck as she toyed with the pearls there. She opened her eyes and looked from Connie to Rainbird.

"I am sensing that neither one of you is its target, it fears only his," she gestured her manicured hands toward John, "ability to appear where he is not wanted. But it does not fear you for no other reason than the lone fact that you may be harboring someone that *can* harm it." She stood and tuned toward the fireplace. "The concept here is easy, where there is a seer, there is a knight. For good, there is evil, always opposites. There are always two, at least God gave us that much."

"I'm not following at all," John said shaking his head.

She turned away from the fireplace. "No offense young man, I am like you, *I see*. While he," she looked directly at Sam, "is the one person it fears. My husband was as you Mr. Dalhart, he had the ability to see a wrong and make it right. I suspect you were once a policeman, but found corruption and politics not to your taste. Am I correct?"

Sam reached out and picked up his coffee and took a sip and placed the cup slowly back into the saucer. Connie watched him for a reaction to the woman's comment but Sam was stoic and not committing any position.

"Yes, I am correct. God is never one to interfere in this universal chess match. Oh, he sometimes places his strategic pieces to block, maybe even challenges the dark pieces on his board, and I suspect you and your employer, Mr. Rainbird is God's move, his challenge as to what is happening. What you do with his chess move is entirely up to you."

"And just who's playing on the other side of this board?" Sam asked as Connie eased her hand into his own after he placed the strong coffee back on the table in front of him.

Madame Yvonne smiled and clapped her hands just once.

"I so rarely get to tell this story," she said as she sat in her chair opposite her guests. "I was first told it in the old country when I was but six or seven, and I have remembered every word of it since, she said and then leaned forward in her chair ever so slightly. "But I must tell you, before we do what has to be done this day, I am afraid I will have to cancel my lunch, which will thrill Melanie ever so much," then she leaned forward, again conspiratorially. "She is really a terrible cook, but who am I to complain, I was quite used to hotdogs and meat sandwiches with popcorn as desert in my day with the carnies."

"Ma'am, maybe we have bothered you far too long," Sam said as he started to rise, knowing now for sure the old woman was about a cherry short of an ice cream sundae.

Connie eased him back down while smiling at the old woman. Then Liz shot him a look that said to Sam in no uncertain terms that he was embarrassing her and the others.

"Let's hear her out Sam—I mean, what could be stranger than what we've already been through?" John didn't look up from the knot he had made his fedora into.

"Young man, your skepticism will not be helpful when the time comes, and it is coming very soon. You will be called on to make the move for your side of the board, and it must be a good one, because it will affect every other move in the nearest of futures, this game will go on and all we can do is delay the inevitable. And don't give me the same attitude toward the real Nosferatu Tod Browning and those fools at Universal did. They thought that other fool, Bram Stoker wrote the goddamn bible on the damn things, and the truth be known, that idiot didn't get but a few of the old legends right in his limited research."

Sam looked from face to face. The only realities he ever knew was what he could face down with a gun or his fists and maybe in the end his wits, not what he had to seek out in the darkness. But looking at the others right now with their curious dispositions and hope, he decided he owed it to them to sit and listen. When that was done, then he would do things his way. As he relaxed, a flash of memory—a quick picture of Rainbird saving him that long ago night, how Frankie Brill had come moments from cashing in his ticket, and he knew he owed his friend everything. So with a final look at John, he nodded and relaxed, but he still held Connie's hand.

The old woman smiled at Sam and then glanced at Connie's and his hands between them and nodded, seemingly pleased somehow.

"Mr. Indian, Mr. Dalhart, as I said, you are pieces in a game. Not big pieces, but strategic ones to say the very least. But the opponent you face is out to win. Win at all costs. The beast is insane, has been for century upon century upon century. Its anger and hatred knows no bounds. It's out to win and you are out to block that win and it's too bad the beast has not played the way that would allow you to win, but that's God, you can battle to a draw and only play again, maybe not you two and your people, but others that will be chosen. Who can understand the mind of that crazy bastard upstairs?"

Liz adjusted her position in her seat, becoming a little uncomfortable with the old woman's words. John merely looked at his shoes and Sam and Connie kept still.

"I can say that I've earned the right as my husband died in the Great War, saving a French family from being shot by the Hun. After being awarded the Bronze Star, his earthly reward was to be shot by an Arizona State Policeman outside of a small town called Apache Junction, Arizona, for arguing a fine imposed on the carnival for a zoning violation. I've paid dearly in this little game of his. Now, the beast you face is not Nosferatu, nor Vampyre, but an Arch, it's *The* Fallen One."

"You mean Lucifer?" Liz asked, remembering her religious upbringing.

Madame Yvonne smiled and lightly shook her head as she rose from her chair and went to the largest of the four giant bookshelves. She half-turned and looked behind her and then satisfied there was no one spying her movement she pulled out on a small false-front incorporating five regular sized books. She pulled out another, much larger volume and then closed the small and secret door. The book looked ancient and delicate. She opened and carefully eased her way through the pages, stopping and then turning a few more until she found the page she wanted. Then she passed the thick book to Connie.

"Show your friends my dear. That picture is only reproduced in this book, and there are only sixteen copies known to be in existence. I really should have it in a bank somewhere, but I'm too old to care much about the battles of men anymore."

Connie leaned over and placed the book half on Sam's lap happily rid of at least half the weight and half the horrible feeling she got when she touched the rich leather of the binding. Liz stood and so did John to see what the book revealed.

"This book is a book of angels. It was copied from papyrus script that is well over five thousand years old by a man known as Kallcus Gallium of Rome. The original is no longer in existence. The last known place of that original papyrus was rumored to be in the Great Library of Alexandria, where it was told that Gallium, a Roman soldier at the time, copied it and the other five volumes. This, as is the others are but a poor recreation of that original. The rest were believed to have been collected by the holy Roman church and destroyed."

The picture they were being shown was one that looked as if it had been painted in the pre- renaissance period. The colors were striking and all was hand painted. It resembled the last supper, only they were angels gathered around the great bearded figure of God, depicted as a not-too old deity who benignly sat amongst all of his archangels in heaven. Below them and through the clouds you could see the dawn of man depicted as Adam and Eve as they played in the green gardens of Eden.

"The celebration of Jehovah's greatest creation, that of mankind—a creation that supplanted the Archangels power in heaven. They lost face when God no longer trusted them because of their jealousy. See Lucifer on the right hand of God?" The old finger shook as it touched the ancient rendering.

In the painting, a mild faced young Archangel stared longingly at the face of God, while the others, save for one, stood to the left of God and looked down upon man with smiles.

"The Archangel to the Lord's left hand side, according to the ancient texts and the book of Angels, is Phaltazar, the favored of God, the only angel to actually live in God's presence."

"I thought the old legends said Lucifer was God's chosen favorite?" Connie asked.

"The betrayal of the Archangel Phaltazar was so much greater than that of Lucifer, his name was struck from all the old writings of man, and the name was never spoken of again in heaven. You see Lucifer tried to take away the kingdom of heaven, while Phaltazar, who was insane even then, usurped the war with God from Lucifer. Unlike the dark heart of Satan, Phaltazar did not want the rule of heaven; he tried to destroy it because of his insane jealousy of mankind. Phaltazar and Lucifer were the only two actual brothers in the kingdom of heaven. They were siblings."

John, Connie, Liz and Sam listened to the statement without saying a word. The picture on the opposite page shown in black inks depicted a brutal battle for heaven. Angels were impaled on long golden spears, many were decapitated, and all through the horrible picture there was the smiling visage of Lucifer at his height. The brother, Phaltazar, was Lucifer's avenger, his Berserker. But the brother didn't stop with the killing of the soldiers of Gabriel and Michael; it soon turned on the followers of his own brother, Lucifer, until there were but a few hundred of God's Archangels left. In the end of things they subdued Phaltazar. The insanity pictured in the brother's eyes was horrifyingly real. The artist had captured true hellishness in its features.

"You mean this angel Phaltazar, Lucifer's brother, was worse than the dark one himself? But wasn't Satan's punishment great, being sent to reign over hell?" John asked.

The old woman laughed and gently removed the book from Sam and Connie's laps and closed it.

"God disfigured Phaltazar and condemned him to a life upon this earth as the lowliest of creatures, that which preys upon the dead and innocent—a beast that would be forever hunted and persecuted by mankind. It owes not its allegiance to its brother, nor will it ask for forgiveness from God. It's doomed to forever try and take our world from us—it's only life, is to *take* life."

"But yet after all these thousands of years, it's still here?" Sam asked.

Madame Yvonne walked to the book shelf and placed the large volume back in its secret spot and closed the false-fronted volumes and then turned and walked slowly to her chair and sat; she straightened her dress and then looked up and smiled.

"God failed to foresee the hatred of this Archangel. He was so hurt by this Phaltazar's treachery that the Lord was blinded as to how powerful it had become. Throughout the centuries weapons have been provided, the most recent of which was two thousand years ago," she said and then reached over to a small table and picked up a small plaster figurine that sat upon its own knitted doily and tossed it to John. Rainbird almost dropped it but gained control and looked at it. The piece was a small spearhead made of plaster and painted gold. Overlaid on the spearhead was a band of copper for protection. John turned it over in his hand and then passed it to Liz, and so on down to Connie.

"That is a replica of the Spear of Destiny—the very spearhead that supposedly pierced the side of Christ after his crucifixion. It was the last weapon that the church officially sanctioned that could kill Phaltazar. It was actually blessed by Pope Nicholas II in 1059 AD, expressly for that purpose as passed down through the church by Peter, the Fisherman himself, who was told the story of the *Great Betrayal* by the rabbi from Nazareth before his crucifixion. Did you notice the pouch hanging from Phaltazar's neck?"

John locked eyes with the old woman, it was if he knew from a long dead memory of his people what the pouch signified.

"You know don't you?" the old gypsy asked, holding John's brown eyes with her own.

"Well, do you mind clueing us in?" Liz asked.

The gypsy finally broke eye contact with John after the scene became somewhat uncomfortable for the rest of her guests.

"That pouch was used as a payment, more than once throughout history, and every time Phaltazar retrieved it for use against the weakest of man." She smiled and then just as quickly lost it.

"Forty coins—gold coins," John said. "The very same coin the bible tells us was used as payment to the man responsible for the betrayal of Jesus of Nazareth."

The old woman just nodded her head and reached for her cold cup of coffee.

"You are bright aren't you my Sioux friend. The coins he recovered from the cold body of Judas."

"This pouch, does it have significance other than a corrupt talisman. Is it still in existence?" Sam asked, having an idea that maybe the pouch would play a role in this nightmare.

"I've seen it Sam. He wears it in my dreams. I actually hear the rattle of coin when he moves," John said turning and facing away from the group. Why the subject of that pouch bothered him he did not know. He turned back and his eyes fixated on the object Connie was holding. He desperately felt the need to get off the subject of the pouch and of Judas.

"Where is this spearhead now?" John asked, standing up and retrieving the plaster replica from Connie and looking it over.

The old woman smiled again, this time it was a sad smile as she shook her head. "No luck there either I'm afraid. The last people to have had it, well, could be the only people that would benefit from Phaltazar's power over man."

The others waited while Madame Yvonne stretched it out forever. Impatient Sam cleared his throat, this woman had worked in Hollywood too long because she most definitely had flair for the dramatic.

"The spearhead was discovered and retrieved by Adolph Hitler and the Nazis in 1932, before he came to power. At least that is the rumor in my…my gypsy circles. Where these evil men came to know its whereabouts is a big mystery in the field archaeology and to us gypsies and Jews, but they did come into possession of it. Ask yourselves why—why would a leader of a major power want the only weapon known in existence that could stop an Archangel that has been trying to destroy mankind throughout history? The answer is simple. It's because they need each other, and the Nazi's having no wish to destroy their patriarch, keep the spear hidden."

Sam stood and walked to the front window that looked out onto Ganesha Park. He could never fully believe in the Bible and its many stories. He found it hard for any thinking, educated man to believe it. But the pieces fit and he was one who *did* believe in following the bread crumbs to its logical end, no matter how strange the conclusion to that ending became. He turned.

"Why the girls?" he asked.

A saddened look came across the old woman's face as she placed the cold coffee down on the table.

"Vanity, sheer vanity—I suspect he is the loneliest creature in existence. I think it's only a loving touch with anything close to human are the girls he murders and keeps alive. He can't love his servants, his Nosferatu, his watchers, they're even colder of skin than he," she smiled again, bowing to her guests, "The Vampires, Phaltazar, every ancient legend from the old world stems from this creature. Understand, stories are linked by time and incident and put down as different beasts of the darkness, but they all stem from one, and only one."

"How does it keep these girls alive after he takes them?" Connie asked, horrified by this train of information.

"Dear, he is an Archangel, and has the power of reanimation, it is a power called upon many times throughout the bible, and that is why you must be ever so careful in your fight ahead. It can animate anything that once had life in it. Anything that had living cells it can bring back. Its soldiers can be an endless stream of the recently or the ancient dead, thus, Vampyre, Nosferatu, the undead."

"So do you have any suggestions?" Sam asked turning back to face Madame Yvonne.

"For a price, after all I will not be here much longer; it is *you* that will have to live in its world, not I if you fail in stopping whatever its plans are."

"And that price is?" Sam asked, waiting for the catch.

"Get that low-life son of a bitch Meyer to pay me my two hundred dollars he owes me."

John smiled and looked at Sam. "I think we can get that for you."

"Now, you have the weapon that can defeat him and you don't even know it. But before I tell you what that weapon is, you have to know, you must find out what it is doing here, it has a plan, it always has a plan. You must find out and stop it because it's a piece of the puzzle you see, a piece that fits into the big picture, and without that piece, his plans will take longer, who knows, you may thwart it altogether if you strike well and with thought. But remember the pouch. He will use that talisman against someone he thinks is corruptible."

John swallowed but didn't ask any more details about the pouch and he hoped the others would either.

"What weapons do we have that can help?" Connie asked.

"The same weapon you have been using since this started. The beast has been helping you learn how it can be destroyed and the slimy bastard didn't even know it."

"His nightmares," Sam said looking from the old woman toward John.

She just smiled and rocked in her chair with her eyes closed, face toward the ceiling.

"Have you ever wanted to fly in your dreams and then did it? Have you ever thought of a person in your dreams and then the next thing you know, there they are, a visit, a phone call, a letter?" she finally asked.

"Yes," Connie said, figuring it out before the others.

"There is danger as I'm sure you have learned from your earlier encounters. Before you dream walk, the beast has to be occupied in the waking world, then the dreamer can perform anything he, or she, wants; fly, create allies, anything at all. You can even invoke other worldly entities. Remember, Phaltazar has made many enemies through the centuries." She raised her brows, "Do you understand? In order for the dreamer to try and attack in his sleeping world with his mind and have the time to do it, the beast must be confronted in the waking world with danger to itself," Madame Yvonne said, finally lowering her head and then looking straight at Sam and holding his blue eyes.

Connie stood up suddenly.

"The only way Sam can do that is to have that thing try to kill him!" she said, never even considering that anyone else would do the confronting, like everyone in the room, she knew it would be Sam.

"Thus is the job of a seer," she looked at John and then raised her eyebrows at Sam, "And the destiny of heroes."

✤ FOURTEEN ✤

The rest of Sam's reluctant army was sitting across Wilshire Boulevard looking at the coming and going of policeman in and out of the Westerly Hotel. Frank Wiechek looked over to his right at Talbot who was just sitting and shaking his head.

"What do you suppose is going on?" Frank asked.

"Can't be good, the coroner has been in there a long time and that's the second covered stretcher they've brought out. We have to find out if whatever it is involves those Italians." Talbot was about to open his door when little Stevie grabbed shoulder from the backseat.

"It'll do no good to get the coppers asking you questions, Mister Leonard, Jeez Louise, after last night, that's all we would needs!"

"The kid's got a point, Tal. We better find some other way," Frank said holding Talbot's arm as well.

"Let's bypass the cops and ask some hotel employee, they'll gab for sure," Willis said from the backseat next to Stevie.

"That's not bad, knobby," Frank said making fun of Willis's lumps.

Suddenly a loud banging sounded on Frank's driver's side window and they all jumped a foot in their seat. Frank shot around and there, framed perfectly in the Ford's window glass was Gary Cooper. His hair was uncombed and his white shirt was un-tucked and filthy. His eyes were wild as he was gesturing for Frank to roll down his window while at the same time trying the locked door handle.

"Hey, it's Mister Cooper," Stevie said.

"Shit, is it? Look at him, he looks crazy!" Willis added.

Frank quickly rolled down his window. "H…hey Coop."

"Let me in, for God's sake let me in!" he cried as he pulled on the door handle again. "Come on Goddamn it, I'm not kidding around here!"

Willis swallowed when he saw Frank was at a loss for what to do, so he opened the back door and Cooper shot around the open door and practically dove into the seat across first Willis and Stevie's laps.

"Go, go, go and don't let the cops see, go Goddamn it!"

Stevie felt Cooper's chest heaving in gasps and was afraid to move as his arm fell into the floorboard. Stevie shook him, thinking maybe he was dead.

"Hey, you's okay Mister Cooper?" Stevie asked wide-eyed and afraid to really shake him.

"If you have any mercy at all, please drive away from here," he said into Stevie's leg.

"I think's you better goes, Mr. Wiechek, I think Mister Cooper's fainted.

As the Chevrolet drew out of the lot across the street, a black Mercedes took note and one of the three cars that had been watching the men from the Sunset Detective Agency followed close behind.

They had made sure there were no surprises waiting at the office for them before they took the back way in. Sam had instructed them not to come back here, but they had no choice as it was the closest place to the Westerly Hotel where they could get Coop to in a hurry. Willis held the door for Frank and Pete, as Stevie ran to the elevator. The doorman had come on earlier but had been chased off by all of the reporters that had been there to grill anyone in the building. His note to that effect was on the gold-leaf doors.

Stevie pushed the up button several times, slamming his hand onto the brass plate. He watched as the arrow set above the doors moved slowly from six, to five, to four—he heard the approach of Pete, Frank, Coop and Talbot. As he looked up again the arrow just struck one and the doors opened and then Stevie screamed as if he were a small girl at the two figures standing there.

"Ahhhh," Stevie screamed.

"Ahhhh," Charlie and Douglass echoed in immediate response.

Talbot and Frank dropped Cooper and Willis drew his gun as the others tried to mimic his action, but were caught off guard as they struggled to remove their own weapons.

Chaplin and Fairbanks hugged each other for protection and Stevie turned away and cursed himself under his breath. He immediately turned back and angrily stepped inside the elevator.

"It's okay. It's Mr. Chaplin and Mr. Fairbanks, who aren't supposed to be here kneader," Stevie called out.

Frank and Talbot leaned over and retrieved Cooper and with Willis helped him into the elevator.

"Good lord, what now?" Chaplin asked as Stevie pushed the button for floor six.

Two minutes later inside the smashed offices, they had to use smelling salts on Cooper to get him to respond and as he did he saw a glass full of amber liquid next to him and immediately grabbed for it and took it in one gulp. Then held the glass out to Stevie and called for another. He sat up and looked around the reception room and at the frightened faces staring at him and then he really noticed his surroundings and exactly where they had brought him.

"When I said get me out of there, I didn't mean back here!" Cooper said looking at almost the same faces he had left inside this very office last night.

"We had to come here tough guy, you fainted," Frank said taking the refill from Stevie and held onto it. "Now, what in the hell were you doing at the Westerly?"

Cooper looked embarrassed as he ran a hand through his dark hair, putting it back into shape as much as his fingers would allow. Then he held his hand out for the shot of whiskey Frank had seized.

"Give me that first gumshoe and then I'll talk."

Frank, against his better judgment, handed it to the lanky Copper.

He drank and then wiped his mouth. He shook his head and then looked at the expectant faces around them. "Say, where's Dalhart and Rainbird?"

"They're out, now what do you have?" Frank asked.

"Come on Coop, you cut us short on what we were supposed to do at the Westerly," Talbot said as he lit his pipe.

"And that was?" Copper asked rubbing his face.

"To keep an eye on that Italian Count and his wife," Talbot said, pausing the match at the mouth of his pipe.

"And I'd like to know why you're not there."

They all started and jumped as they turned toward the smashed door. Sam was there with Rainbird and the two women. He removed his hat and stepped into the office and they could tell immediately he wasn't real happy.

"And I thought I told you two to get the girl and her parents to safety," he said with an angry glance at Chaplin and Fairbanks.

"Well, they're all safe old man, they're with Mary, and so in truth they may as well be in the bosom of—"

"Cut it Doug, this has gotten a little more serious in the past hour."

"You can say that again," Cooper said as he stood and faced Sam.

"What do you mean by that?" Connie asked as she and Liz walked over to her desk.

"I…I went to the Westerly this morning, I wanted to…well I wanted to see if the Countess was really—"

"Goddamn it Coop, after what you went through last night you still can't control that libido of yours?"

"Well, I was thinking that maybe it wasn't her, that maybe, maybe—"

"What happened?" John asked throwing his hat onto Liz's desk.

"I was just coming out of the elevator when I saw this group of fellas standing at the Count's door, the next I know they smash it in and that's when I thought it would be best to get out of there."

"Did you get a look at these men at least?" Sam asked with his hands on his hips.

Cooper just hung his head and sat hard into a chair next to Charlie and Doug.

"Oh you're good," Chaplin said, looking from Cooper to Sam.

"Don't you say anything Charlie, you had one job to do and you didn't do it. Now is the child and her parents out of this town or not?"

Charlie looked at Douglass and quickly decided on the small lie. "Yes, Mary took them with her to an engagement," he looked at his watch, "where we are supposed to be going at this very moment. Look what time it is Doug, and we still have to dress."

"You're not heading anywhere right now, you have to—"

"I've got it!" Cooper said loudly.

"What?" Sam asked turning from Chaplin and facing Cooper.

"I heard those fellas speaking German, yeah, it was German!"

Sam turned and looked at John.

"Sam, I was in the alley going to my car when I heard the most God awful scream and then I heard a window above me crash and…and, that thing, that woman, the Countess I guess, come flying out, and I mean flying, she flew to the next building over, dug those horrible claws into the brick and then scrambled over the roof, and that was the last I saw of her."

"Are you convinced now you horny bastard?" John asked while standing and walking toward the window.

"Yeah, I don't want to ever see another foreign woman again," he said looking up and then noticing Connie, he smiled just as if he had never mentioned women in a bad light. She just rolled her eyes and shook her head. He looked deflated and lowered his gaze. "Sam, I saw them carrying that fat little count out of the side doors and into an ambulance. He was deader than a doornail."

"The German's…killed him?"

"Hey, that isn't the way it's supposed to work," Connie said looking from Sam to the back of Rainbird.

"How what's supposed to work?" Talbot asked with the same questioning expression that was now on Franks, Willis's, Doug's and Chaplin' faces. Stevie was too busy looking inside the coat closets for any more surprises. Cooper just stared.

Sam told everyone to take a seat and then gestured for Connie to tell them the story that Madame Yvonne had told them.

She spoke for close to an hour, just long enough for the sun to start setting over the Pacific Ocean and for the unexpected dark clouds to cover what remained of the day.

The last night was starting to unfold.

Sam waited for Connie to finish. He had allowed her to repeat the tale that had been told to them by Madame Yvonne for the express purpose of allowing him time to contact some friends of his at the *Times*. He had learned that three bodies had been recovered from the Continental suite at the Westerly Hotel. One was as Coop had said, the Count D'Sarcuni. Although the preliminary coroner's report hadn't been made public, it was rumored the count had died of multiple injuries suffered in an apparent assassination attempt by foreign nationals. The other two men had not been positively identified but they were thought to have been German because of paper money found in their possession.

While Connie was speaking to the group, Sam waved John into his office and explained what had been discovered at the Westerly. It fit with the tale Cooper had passed on.

"What about the German element in all of this? Isn't this opposite of what the old Gypsy told us, isn't this Phaltazar and the German's supposed to be working together?"

Sam pushed his chair away from the desk and stood. He buttoned his vest and while he did he looked at John. He was thinking about something and didn't know if his partner was going to like it.

"I don't have the faintest idea what in the hell is happening with this German group. Maybe that thing wanted the D'Sarcuni's eliminated for some reason, I don't know. But there's one thing for sure, let's just assume the German's are who the old woman said they are; we can't trust them, right?"

"Absolutely," John said as he watched Sam walk over to the coat rack and put on his jacket. "What's up?" he asked.

Sam looked at John a moment and shook his head. "I don't know yet, but when I do you'll be the first to know buddy."

Connie and Liz looked at the others who stared back at them and each one was utterly speechless. Frank held Liz's eyes and gestured to her as if saying, *you're kidding, right?* She raised her left brow and placed her glasses on and just looked at him, her expression of truth etched on her face unchanged.

"If you fellas could have seen this creepy old book she had, you wouldn't be looking at us like that," she finally said taking her eyes away from Frank.

"What does Sam have to say about the tale the old woman passed on?" Talbot asked.

"I think we have no other option than to at least follow her warnings, because my gut has been telling me all along that whatever this thing is, it wasn't just here to snatch young girls off the street. And we owe it to Connie to carry this thing out to its conclusion," Sam said as he stepped into the reception area followed by Rainbird.

"Then what's our next step boss?" Frank asked.

Sam looked at what he had for his small army. He had his men, Pete, Willis, Frank, Talbot and Stevie. Liz and Connie, two actors, one a comedian, and silent film star who was almost dead of virtually every ailment on the books. It wasn't much to do battle with the forces of evil with. He closed his eyes a moment and rubbed the bridge of his nose. He was tired, and if a man's tired he's sure to make mistakes, so he had to run his ideas at least by other tired people and try to get a consensus. He opened his eyes and turned and looked John who was casually leaning against the doorway.

"I think what we have to do is two-fold. We have to find out where this creature is at, and then we have to find out what its plans are. John you said that in most dreams you start at the kitchen door and you have the option most times of turning and running, or you go through the door to the subbasement, is that right?"

"Usually, but the last few have been straight down into that hell hole."

"Now, when you did go into the subbasement, you said that in the candle lit area before the darkness began there was sort of a shrine—papers that had been placed on the basement walls, like clippings of some sort, do you have any idea what they could be?"

"I don't know, but my gut, like yours right now, is telling me they're important to finding out what this thing is after."

"Then you also know what has to be done, don't you?"

John pursed his lips and thought a moment and then slowly nodded his head.

"Wait a minute Sam, that's not fair to put this all off on John," Connie said standing up, "to ask him to go back inside knowing what that thing is, is suicidal."

"I don't think we have a choice if we're to stop this thing because your sister's life may depend on it," John said as he straightened and then reached into his coat pocket and tossed Sam the same small bottle of sleep juice he had used two nights ago.

Sam smiled. "Didn't fool you a bit, did I? You knew all along what we had to do."

John just winked and started removing his coat.

"Gentlemen, I must say this is madness," Fairbanks said, finally standing up on shaky legs.

"Here, here. Our Indian friend is a stone faced, straight forward man of ill humor most times, but to send him off to possibly die at the hands of this, this, malcontent angel, why, it's absurd!" Chaplin added.

"Charlie, Douglass, didn't you say you were going to meet Mary for some function or other?" John asked as he turned and walked back into the office area.

"That can wait, I'll not leave while this foolishness is happening," Fairbanks said starting to follow Sam and John.

Chaplin swallowed and began to fall in line, as did the others. John may be going into the depths of his nightmare alone, but he now knew that everyone present would have gone with him if they could.

As Sam handed John a small glass of water with only two small drops of the amber sleeping liquid in it, the others watched him and most actually opened their mouth as if they too tasted the medicinal tasting water.

The chairs and main conference table had been pushed aside. Gary Cooper, Charlie Chaplin, Douglass Fairbanks, Talbot Leonard, Frank Wiechek, Pete Sanchez, Willis Jackson, Stevie Kratzenheimer, Liz and Connie all watched from standing positions as Rainbird sat at the foot of the couch they had brought in from John's office. Sam was on one knee and he looked at his friend. He held out his hand and showed him another small brown bottle, it was ammonia.

"It may burn a little but it should bring you around real quick if you find yourself in a bind."

"Let's just hope you'll know when to use it," John said as he lay back onto the leather couch.

"I can't believe this is happening. Is there nothing we can say that would change your mind in this madness?" Chaplin asked, grasping Douglass's shoulder.

Stevie looked from the nervous Chaplin toward his boss and then stepped up to the couch. Sam was going to stop him and then thought that the kid had earned his right more than anyone here after taking John's abuse these many months to have his say. Stevie took off his golfer's hat and twisted it in front of him.

"Mister Rainboyd, I knows I'm forever givin' ya's grief, but I wish you would recon…recon—well, I wish ya's tink' about what's ya's doin'."

Rainbird sat up half way and winked at the kid. "Don't worry, you ain't getting rid of me that easy," he started to lie back down and then stopped and looked at Stevie. "If I had a choice of all the people in this room to take with me kid, it would be you."

Stevie twitched out a half smile as he watched John lay back and close his eyes. He placed his hat on his head and looked at Sam who just raised his eyebrows. He walked back to the conference table and leaned against it. It was Frank that leaned over and whispered to him.

"He probably means it too kid, he found out a minute ago that the cheap coffee urn you bought quit working already, so yeah, he probably did want you to go with him into never, never land so's he could throw you to that monster when the goin' got tough," Frank said as he placed a toothpick in his mouth and nodded his head up and down when the kid looked at him worriedly. Frank smiled until he saw Liz staring at him over her glasses with murder in her eyes. He removed the toothpick and looked away.

"Alright, he's under," Sam said as he stood and walked over to where Connie was nervously twisting a Kleenex in her hands. Sam removed the tissue and looked at her. "He knows to check on Jeannie first—if he has any control left."

She just nodded her head and leaned into him.

On the couch John's eyes started to move rapidly under his eyelids. He had started to dream.

This was different; it wasn't the kitchen, or the basement of the old house. He was on a snow covered piece of rough looking landscape and he felt as if he were lost. He heard his mother calling him from a great distance away and John knew immediately he was on the reservation someplace. He looked down and he saw that he was dressed in the same clothes he had laid down onto the couch with, but he remembered he had removed his suit jacket and now he regretted it. He looked up into the setting sun and into the cold blowing wind, trying to catch in what direction his mother was calling from. He tilted his head as he crossed his arms over his chest in a vain attempt to protect him from the dipping temperature.

"Mama?" he called. Then John caught himself a moment after the words had cleared his mouth. He quickly looked around and saw nothing but flatlands as far as he could see, but he felt he wasn't alone. As he watched the barren landscape he heard his mother's voice calling out to him again to come home, that it was getting dark.

He wanted to call out so badly but he knew he had to stay—he just had to find the house, people depended on him to do his job, but he couldn't. He started to call out to his mother but he just didn't know what was listening to him out there on that wind-swept plain.

As he bent over into the strengthening wind his mother's voice came again, as if she were right in his ear.

"John, there's something in the dark with you—*COME HOME!*"

John opened his eyes and saw only darkness. The smell from before was there but not as powerful as before. He tried to look into the blackness around him and felt that the girls from his previous dreams were now gone.

He sensed no dead in the room with him. What was far more disturbing to him was the fact that he felt the beast wasn't there either.

John closed his eyes tightly as he didn't know if he should be happy about that or more nervous. He opened his eyes and moved to his right, touching the last foot of stair banister as he did. This should be the right direction toward the far foundation wall where he had seen the clippings. His foot clipped a box and he felt his shoe push deeply into it. He knew without looking it was a wet cardboard box and he didn't really care to know what it was wet from. He had gone several feet, his shoes bringing up little unseen puffs of dirt from the earthen floor when he heard a noise behind him and knew that he was not alone any longer. He almost panicked when the hand fell on his shoulder.

John went down to his knees knowing hope was at an end.

Von Railing didn't like the darkness of the library. He looked at McDougal and then at the Countess. He thought about seeking out Phaltazar who had made its first ever appearance in the house proper since their arrival. The beast was sitting in a large, thickly cushioned rocking chair. The leggings covered only half of his enormous legs and the leather vest only a fraction of its chest. It was still for the most part as its yellow eyes slid over the form of the countess D'Sarcuni, who couldn't bear to look its way. Von Railing felt that the beast at any moment would spring from the chair and end their existence. But instead Phaltazar chuckled.

"So our German friends dispatched the hog of a man?"

"He was loyal—,"the Countess started to say and then thought a moment about lying, then told the truth. "He betrayed you to the German's. He would have told them the location of your lair if I hadn't struck him first, so no my Lord, it wasn't the German's and their resistance element that killed my husband, it was I."

Von railing watched the exchange taking place before him and was amazed that the Master took it so well that one of their numbers had been cut down by one on this, the most important night in history.

"All is well woman, the girl child is where she needs to be and the Count is where he is well suited to be, in hell with brother Lucifer," the beast laughed again.

"Our numbers are short my Lord, what if Dalhart comes for us?" Von railing finally asked.

The yellow eyes narrowed and the crunch of wood could be heard as the beast crushed the handrail on the large rocking chair, then the eyes relaxed, opening all the way.

"The magician has performed his trick, and there is nothing Dalhart can do about it. They know nothing, they had me thinking they were different, but they are not. If they were they would have shown themselves here, but again they have not, they—"

The beast stopped in mid-sentence and its eyes widened. It stood to it full eight feet of height and it brought the black satin cape up to cover most of its face as it looked around in near panic.

McDougal stepped back and behind the Countess who tilted her head as she watched the strange behavior of Phaltazar. Von Railing had a look of near disgust on his face as he watched his Master look around the library.

"My Lord, what is it?"

The cape went flying and the large mouth cried, slobber and spittle flew from its mouth and its eyes closed as if in mortal pain.

"HE'S HERE! FIND HIM!"

"Who is here?" Von Railing asked, stepping away from the swinging claws.

"THE RED NIGGAR, HE HAS INVADED MY HOME! FIND HIM!"

John turned to see the white form of Jeannie Yale. She eased her hand away and tilted her head. John tried to concentrate on the few helpful things Madame Yvonne had passed on to them. The comment about wanting to fly in a dream and making it happen. He concentrated on seeing better in the dark. He closed his eyes and then opened them quickly, not liking the feeling. When he did he saw the candles that had lined the walls in his other dreams had been lit, by him or the girl, he couldn't be sure. But as the face of Jeannie Yale became more clearly defined, he saw that she was indeed dying. Her eyes drooped and the dark circles had become black. Her hair was matted and her hands, feet and arms were filthy. The stench coming from her was from excrement and other bodily wastes. John tried to smile and then he reached out and took the girls hand.

"We will come for you," he said in a halting voice. "I promise."

The girl tilted her head again, seemingly to tell John she didn't understand him. Then she released his hand and pointed to his right. There on the wall, stuck to the mildew and slime of the stone was dozens of newspaper articles. Jeannie seemed to have known what he was there for. He looked from the clippings to the girl—she tried to smile but the only change to her face was a lone tear that coursed down her cheek from her reddened eyes. John took her hand again and lightly pulled on her so she may follow him to the wall, but just as he did he heard loud banging coming from the house above them. As the girl looked up she yanked her hand from John's and fell to the floor and scrambled away, raising dust as she did until she struck the wall were she curled up into a ball and watched.

John heard the scrambling coming from the floors above and then he heard a sound that froze him in place.

"How dare you!"

He closed his eyes and froze, unable to even travel the remaining few feet to the wall to at least look at the clippings. He started trembling as the walls shook around him as he heard the large door that led to the basement above from the kitchen splinter and then the sounds of pounding footsteps, or rather the sound of hoof beats on the thick wooden stairs above. He felt the girl move but couldn't open his eyes. He tried the trick Madame Yvonne had told him about and he willed himself to move, saying that he could move, will move. But he couldn't. He was frozen in place like no other dream he had had before.

Suddenly he was touched as the crashing and pounding on the stairs above came closer. Jeannie had risen from her spot against the wall and had grabbed him by the hand and was pulling him toward the stairs and out of the candle light. He felt first his left hand being pried open and felt something shoved into it. He felt himself strike the same sodden box he had when he first entered the cellar. Then he willed his eyes open with a final mental push. As he did he saw Jeannie on her knees scrambling to the box he had just struck again with his foot and started throwing papers and envelopes in all directions. Then she seemed to find what she was looking for and shoved it into John's left hand just as the door separating the basement from the cellar below crashed inward and he could see the beast above standing on the landing. The animalistic roar threw John against the far wall, knocking Jeannie backward into the darkness. John tried and this time managed to scream. He stood with his hands at his side and screamed again it felt so good. Phaltazar roared back as it leaned forward and launched itself from the landing toward the candle lit cellar below. The black cape flying outward and its claws extended. As John watched in horror he knew that he had become such a substantial part of the nightmare dreamscape around him that he felt he was more real than ever before and knew beyond any doubt that those claws would sheer him right in two. The yellow eyes locked on him and he cringed from the awful stinging smell that was crowding up his nose as he screamed.

Anxious faces were watching John as he writhed on the couch. The women were yelling for Sam to bring him out of it. Chaplin and the others were mute as they saw and heard John scream and scream as if the hounds of hell were chasing him.

"God help him!" Fairbanks cried.

Sam actually spilled some of the ammonia on John's upper lip as he waived the small bottle under his nose again and again. Connie ran to the couch and as Sam continued to use the ammonia she started slapping John across the face.

"Wake up, wake up, wake up," she screamed over and over again as tears started welling in her eyes as the screams emanating from Rainbird became more desperate.

Finally his eyes opened, closed and then opened again. His eyelids fluttered as Connie froze and Sam moved the bottle of ammonia away. His eyes focused on Connie who fell to him and hugged him crying, and then he looked over her shoulder at Sam who had closed his eyes and handed the small bottle out for Liz to take. The liquid spilled as both Liz and Sam were shaking.

"Oh, thank God, is he alright?" Chaplin asked.

Frank and the other detectives gathered around. Talbot actually had his thirty-eight out and with shaking hands placed it back into his shoulder holster.

Connie straightened and smiled at the confused Rainbird. He looked from her face to Sam's who wasn't smiling.

"That son of a bitch almost got you didn't it?" he asked.

"How long was I under?" John asked still lying still.

"A minute at the most, but it seemed like an hour trying to get you to wake up," Sam said as he stood and ran a hand through his hair. "Not near long enough to find out anything."

John half-heartedly smiled at Connie and then sat up. He started to rub his left hand across his face and was stunned to see he held something, not only in his left, but his right hand also.

"Well, thanks to Jeannie, I came out with something."

Sam turned and saw that John was holding out an old and damp looking envelope.

"I guess the previous owner had stored some things in the cellar and Connie's sister made sure I took something from an old box," he said as he looked at the old envelope and then passed it to Sam.

Sam took it slowly and looked at it. "D.W. Griffith, 6789 Somerset Drive, Pasadena, California, it's a bill from the power and water district."

"D.W.'s place? The old mansion out in....why, we've been there Charlie, years and years ago. Remember that old redwood monstrosity?" Fairbanks said standing and quickly taking the old letter out of Sam's hand, looking it over.

"Yes, it was a bleak old thing, even when new. I thought that place burned down years ago," Chaplin said as he looked over Doug's shoulder at the bill. "The beast has actually made this place its lair, no wonder John is terrified of it."

Suddenly Rainbird stood up and almost fell back onto the couch. He was looking at something else. He held it out toward Sam who took it.

"Jeannie also placed this into my hand," John said staring off into space and then taking Connie by the shoulder and then lowering his head. "We know its business now," he mumbled.

Sam looked at the crumpled up newspaper clipping. It wasn't old or yellowed, but looked as if it had been freshly clipped out of the *Times*—

'PRESIDENT ROOSEVELT TO VISIT CITY OF ANGELS; WILL MEET WITH HOLLYWOOD ROYALTY.'

"Its strategic move," Sam mumbled.

Charlie reached out and took the clipping and read it quickly along with Doug. The headline fell from his grasp as he and Doug realized at the same time what was happening.

"My God, Mary!" Douglass cried

"The child!" Charlie added.

It was then that Sam realized just what Hollywood function Mary Pickford had gone to and he realized with dawning horror that she had taken a ticking time bomb with her to meet the President of the United States.

The game pieces were irrevocably moved on the part of Phaltazar, and Sam Dalhart knew the game may well be over before it had even begun.

The one word raced through his mind; Checkmate.

Von Railing watched as Phaltazar stormed back into the library as its massive claws scraped furrows into the wall as it roared, and the voice of unreason brought the Countess and McDougal to their knees in terror. The beast tried to focus but it was close to being out of control. Von Railing braced himself for the thick claws to swipe at himself, but instead Phaltazar calmed—almost instantly it became stock-still and the thick lips started moving as if it were speaking to itself. The muscled legs straightened as the beast rose to its full height and then brought both arms straight up until its claws raked the ceiling and then it lowered them as it closed its eyes, shutting out the library and the three occupants. Then it cried out, chanting something that Von Railing knew was ancient Aramaic, but then the speech pattern changed and the language altered to the most ancient tongue of all. As he listened he realized it was angelic in nature, something his mind couldn't fathom. To try would bring on insanity and so he turned away and covered his ears as the beast started reciting the strange sounds and started turning in slow, purposeful circles.

Connie leaned over and gave Rainbird a glass of water and he accepted it gratefully. He drained the glass.

"Can you tell me anything else about Jeannie, John?"

John nodded and looked at Connie. "She's still alive, she made sure we knew where to find her, she's still a thinking young woman, but we do have to hurry."

The lights blinked on and off.

Sam straightened up from where he was talking with Charlie, Douglass and Talbot and he pulled his thirty-eight and waited, looking from the window to the front door.

"Stevie, get in here," he said.

The lights flickered again.

"It's coming," John said as he stood and moved Connie away from him and gestured for her and Liz to get behind the wet bar.

Stevie came through the reception room door and was looking behind him.

"It got cold out there Mister Dalhart—real cold"

"Where are Pete and Talbot?" John asked.

"The last I knew, they were going to check the buildings doors down on one," Fairbanks said, looking nervous for their safety.

"Sam, do you feel it? The cold's spreading—it's not like it was in Liz' bathroom, or in John's office, this is different," Connie said as Liz reached out and pulled her closer.

Charlie stood and started frantically looking around. Frank moved closer to the conference room door and kept his eyes on the reception area as just then the lights went out and then back on and then slowly dimmed to almost nothing. The entire office was almost chocolate in color as Sam moved to the door beside Frank.

"This isn't your normal blackout, Frank volunteered, it's like the power's being sucked up before it reaches the office."

Sam looked out into the hallway and then half-turned. "If it's coming, it's coming after you, John. Willis, stick with him."

"Right," Willis said moving toward Rainbird.

Sam moved quickly into the hallway and looked down toward John's office. The door was closed and secured. The hallway was deserted so Sam moved to the door separating the offices from the reception area and peeked around the corner. He looked toward the large broken window that looked out onto Sunset and was surprised to see that the jagged pieces of glass that were still lodged in the frame were starting to frost over. He slowly pulled back the hammer of his thirty-eight knowing that if it was their visitor the gun wasn't going to do much good. He stepped into reception. The lights grew brighter, and then went low again, this time even darker than before.

"THIEVES!"

Liz yelped and Charlie took hold of Douglass. Frank came very close to firing off a round and Willis cautiously stepped in front of John when the voice boomed out. The booming voice seemed to come from every direction.

"I thought I would reciprocate!" the voice said loudly, then seemed to lower and relax. "Only I will steal something that is maybe a little more valuable to you and to your pet Indian, lawman."

"I never had a chance to welcome you to our office the last time you visited, Phaltazar," Sam said as he moved to the center of the office, using himself as a target after the threat was made and not knowing what the creature was going to do when its name was called out for the first time.

As Connie leaned around the edge of the wet bar, she noticed her frosty breath for the first time.

"God, it's like the bastard is more, more physically here this time," she said as she couldn't see Sam through the door so she closed her eyes and leaned back.

"We have been doing our schooling, who is the teacher I am wondering?" came the softened voice.

"Someone who knew an awful lot about you," Sam said as he moved quickly to the broken double doors and pointed the thirty-eight out of the door frame.

"Thousands have known about me, it's those who have survived any meeting with me that is few in number, Dalhart."

"Regardless, five or six of us know now. Why don't you show yourself instead of hiding all of the time? Was our last face to face meeting a little too hot for you?"

This time his remark was greeted with laughter. "Yes, yes, that was a good guess on one of my weaknesses. It took me all of half a day to feel much, much better."

Sam watched the stairs for a moment and then looked over at the elevator that was still indicating it was on the sixth floor. He wished Pete and Talbot would hurry up.

"I have tolerated the red savage because he was an interesting visitor, but now he has taken advantage of my hospitality and stolen from me," the sentence this time ended with a soft growl.

"And what was it he stole?" Sam asked, looking back into the office hallway.

"It matters not." The voice swirled around Sam, bringing with it a stench of corruption.

The lights went completely out and that was when Sam heard the elevator start its descent and in the dark he could barely make out the large arrow at the top of the doors move downward. Someone had pushed the up button on the first floor. That meant that the elevator was on a different circuit than the lights. As Sam was thinking this he moved to the stairwell and cracked the door open slightly. He immediately heard heavy footsteps walking on the stairs far below.

"Tal?"

There was no reply.

"Talbot? Pete?" he called again.

"Coming up, slowly, but coming up, what happened to the lights?" Talbot called from somewhere in the stairwell.

Pete must have taken the elevator while Talbot covered the stairs. He shook his head in the darkness that permeated the stairwell.

"No, Tal, stay put down on one, and then as soon as Pete comes back down, you two get out onto Sunset and stay there."

"Yeah, okay—"

There was a loud moan and the mixed screaming of hundreds and hundreds of what sounded like lost souls.

"Sam, Pete, is that you?" Tal called out.

Sam ran through the stairwell door and looked over the railing. "No Tal, it's not me, get the hell out of there and get outside!"

The moans and screams filled the air as Sam strained to hear if Talbot was retreating from the stairs. Individual voices were pleading in his ears for salvation from the beast.

Sam steeled himself and then started taking the steps two and three at a time.

"Tal, Tal answer me Goddamn it!"

"God, Frank, it's so cold, I can't hear Sam anymore, you have to go out there and help him," Liz cried through cacophony of sound.

Frank was joined by Rainbird as he pushed by the protective bulk of Willis as they both met at the door, but as they did a thick scream of pure hatred filled the air and a blast of cold air mixed with ice crystals slammed into both men. They were thrown back so hard that Frank hit Willis who was attempting to join them. Rainbird hit the carpet and rolled into Charlie's and Doug's feet.

"NO!" the beast cried as the voice shattered bottles behind the wet bar, making Liz and Connie scream.

Rainbird was pulled to his feet by Charlie and a white faced Fairbanks just as the outside reception room door slammed shut and then the conference room door quickly followed and then the opaque glass in the window iced over. Stevie reacted first, as scared as he was he took a chair, raised it and struck the ice covered glass. The wooden chair shattered in his hands and caused nothing but ice to fly from the door.

"It's separating us!" Connie screamed over the noise of the dead.

"It's using a lot of energy, look at the lights!" John said as he ran again for the door.

As they looked up the overhead fixtures were getting somewhat brighter.

Frank, Stevie, Willis, Charlie and Doug joined Rainbird at the now ice covered door and started battering at it, making the beast use more and more of its concentration holding them in so Sam and the others could have a fighting chance outside.

Sam was dangerously close to missing steps and taking a hard tumble down the remaining flights from three. As he slammed into a landing wall to slow his descent before taking the next staircase, he tried to make the turn and slipped in something wet and slid down four risers before he could arrest his fall. As he spun and landed on his back his eyes saw Talbot in between the first and second floors suspended over the well. His hands and feet had been broken as they had been slammed into the plaster and he was left spread-eagled in midair. His neck was broken and his face was turned away from Sam, his head was twisted opposite of where it was supposed to be.

"Goddamn it!" Sam cried aloud as he tried to gain his feet in the blood soaked stairwell, slipping as if in a nightmare, unable to find traction. He crawled, stood, slipped and crawled until he gained his feet to head back up to the sixth floor, while all around him the screams and cries of people long since gone swirled in every direction.

The men hit their fists against the frozen door to no effect. Finally John turned away screaming, spittle flying from his frustrated efforts to get out. He quickly grabbed a small end table, knocking a carafe of water and several glasses off onto the floor and raised it over his head and slammed it into the plaster and wood slatted wall. Large chunks flew off into the air as he raised the chair and slammed it again, and again. Plaster and wood flew in all directions. Connie saw what he was doing and what the beast had overlooked, while sealing them in with ice forming over the door, John decided that he would just go through the wall. Finally, John threw the small broken table away and used his large frame to crash through the final slats of wood and into the outer wall's plaster and then into the hallway where he fell against the opposite wall. The others quickly followed and started working quickly to punch a hole in the reception room wall.

Sam cleared the sixth floor landing and ran for the elevator around the corner. A new sound reverberated off the walls as he rounded the corner, the beast was laughing.

There was loud banging coming from somewhere to Sam's left as he turned and faced the elevator just as John and the others broke through the already damaged office doors. The elevator doors were closed and the car was headed back down to the first floor. Sam hit the doors and tried to get his fingers into the minute slit and started to pull the doors apart. The two triangular windows set at head height were frosted over. With John's help they managed to get the doors open an inch, and then two and then three. Willis grabbed a broken table leg and shoved it into the small opening and started prying them open wider. Connie and the others stood at the office doorway and watched anxiously as the men worked.

Suddenly the screaming and noise stopped. The heat started returning to the building and the strange wind started to die down until it was again silent.

"ADVANCED PAYMENT RENDERED, WE WILL BARTER STILL MORE AT A LATER TIME. The coin is for the red man, without him I could not have tracked you easily," the voice said as it slowly diminished in strength as the sixth floor landing lights came back up to full power.

The doors slid open and Sam pulled apart the cage and almost fell into the open elevator shaft, but John grabbed him by his vest and yanked him back. Liz screamed and Connie turned her head away.

"Oh, my God," Charlie said as Douglass stiffened beside him.

Stevie fell on his backside and pushed himself away from the open elevator pit until he could catch Willis's legs and then turned and held onto them. John held Sam as tight as he could.

Caught up in the elevator cable and coming up the shaft as the car went down was Pete. He was wrapped like he had been inserted in a large human sized spring. As the car descended the cable went tighter until Pete's body was deformed beyond recognition, and then it just came apart as it was sliced in ten different places. The only thing John and Sam saw that was recognizable was the leather pouch full of coin that was tied around Pete's neck.

Liz started screaming the agonizing sound of a woman close to the edge and Connie took her into her arms and guided her away from the gruesome scene.

John still held Sam and felt it when he stiffened up and didn't move. Rainbird knew for a fact Sam had just kicked into another gear.

"Let go of me," Sam said quietly.

John and the others heard the menace that was laced into those four words. Rainbird released Sam but knew better than to say anything as Dalhart pulled down his vest and ran a hand through his hair. John looked from his friend to the leather pouch that dangled inside of the elevator shaft. He angrily reached out and pulled it free of the entwined cable.

He looked at the other men who were standing there watching him. Their eyes never wavered as Sam's bored into theirs. They had never seen their boss look like he was looking now. Charlie, who knew he should have been frightened to death seemed to be drawing strength from Sam as it was rolling off him in waves, and he knew he had never felt anything like it before, he turned and took his friends hand and as he did he knew

Douglass was feeling the same energy flowing out of the man standing before them.

"Don't say anything stupid, Sam, you can't keep us out of this," Willis said with tears in his eyes. "That Mexican was my best friend, and you don't come across those very damn much where I come from."

"Here, here," Douglass said. "As the evil witch Mary would say, fuck it old boy, shall we be off to do battle?"

Sam looked from face to face, his features set into a mask of hatred as he straightened his tie and started walking toward the smashed office door, the menace in his voice nearly scaring all who heard it.

"Yes, let's do."

PART 3

THINGS THAT GO BUMP IN THE NIGHT

❧ FIFTEEN ❧

The University Club Association was an all-male faculty club whose mere name irritated Mary Pickford to no end. She nodded politely at the faculty members from USC but tried to talk very little. She looked around and was at least pleased to see these chauvinists had invited their female colleagues for this one occasion. She would have to remember to endow some money over here and equalize this uneven situation.

Her attention was caught by a man waving at her from the front of the main conference room where the reception was to be staged. She nodded and then walked a few feet to her table where she leaned over and spoke to the Rodriguez's. They were resplendent in the new suit and dress she had bought for them and far more relaxed with knowing that nice detective Finnegan was here with them tonight. Mary smiled at Adria who sat and sipped a cherry soda looking like a fallen angel. She was glad the new, long dress hid those awful braces. She looked so nice it was going to be a pleasure to introduce her to the president, a polio victim himself. She and

Senator Farnsworth would present the surviving daughter of that most horrible kidnapping to Franklin.

The good senator Farnsworth was extremely happy because he had admitted to Mary earlier that he and Roosevelt were quite the adversaries. He for keeping out of the conflagration starting up in Europe and Roosevelt who couldn't warn people fast enough about it. The senator was hoping this fund raiser for the awareness of polio would be a nice gesture of goodwill toward the president. And speaking of the devil, Senator Farnsworth was there, smiling broadly and holding a gorgeous bouquet of at least two dozen roses.

"Hello there, I thought I would fill you in on what's going to happen. The little girl will take the roses—"

"Her name is Adria, Senator," Mary corrected him as rudely as she could.

"Ur, ah, right, right, Adria, well, she'll accompany you to see the President on the stage just before his address and will present him with this bouquet, then you will of course be granted your five minutes at the podium and then you will introduce the president by saying, ladies and gentlemen, The President of the United States."

"I understand who he is Senator, and I know protocol" Mary snapped, looking at the radio producer waving frantically from the door. She took the roses and handed them to Adria, then thought better of it and gave them to her mother for safekeeping; after all, she didn't think the small girl could carry a bouquet that large.

"Well, uh, that's fine Miss Pickford," Farnsworth said looking nervously at the bouquet. "Be sure little Adria gets the bouquet to present, it's a wonderful photo opportunity with the girl having polio and all."

Mary's eyes flared at the man until he smiled at the Rodriguez's and started backing away. He only turned once as he went to the podium and checked on the chairs there.

"I'm really not liking that man, he's kind of a...well, he's a nincompoop, isn't he," she said taking Adria by the chin and winking. "I'll be right back you three, I have a radio man waving at me like some street corner hook..., I mean, I have to do an interview. Having fun?" she asked regaining her composure after almost calling the radio producer a hooker.

Mr. and Mrs. Rodriguez felt out of place, but they were grateful for having their minds on something else besides their other missing daughter. They politely nodded and Adria smiled with a straw stuck in her mouth and then lightly touched the cellophane wrapped roses.

"Good, if that no good man of mine shows up from his latest adventure, would you tell him and undoubtedly his friend in crime, Mr. Chaplin, that should be right back?" she said smiling, but as she turned away she mumbled, *"that dirty, lying son of a bitch."*

"It's a guest list of who's who of Hollywood entertainment here tonight ladies and gentlemen, on this momentous occasion to meet and greet the President of the United States and to sit down to a two hundred dollar a plate dinner benefiting the American Polio Society from right here in beautiful downtown Los Angeles."

The announcer was tall and lanky and was dressed in a white dinner jacket. He had a pencil thin moustache as he held a microphone in front of his face that looked as if it had been borrowed from one of the sound stages at MGM. Mary rolled her eyes as the radio man pronounced Los Angeles as *Los Angalez*.

"We were lucky enough to have the founder of the Polio Society stop by to chat before the President arrives and the festivities get underway, so ladies and gentlemen in our listening audience, it's my pleasure to introduce America's Little Sweetheart herself, Miss Mary Pickford," he said loudly as a few of the gathered star gazers applauded the announcement from the man from *KMPC* radio.

"Thank you, Johnny; it's always a pleasure to stop by, especially this evening for this marvelous benefit for such a great cause."

"Tell me Miss Pickford, just how many of your famous friends will be here tonight?"

"Well, I hope we'll see the cream of the crop out to greet the President and help fund this marvelous charity," she said smiling into the bright lights that were on for the newsreels cameramen and the still photographers.

"Will your marvelous counterpart, Mr. Douglass Fairbanks be attending tonight?"

Mary kept smiling for the briefest of moments and then gave a small laugh, "Well, he better," she said through clenched teeth.

"And your friend and partner, Mr. Chaplin is due to attend I am told?"

Again Mary kept smiling, but the smile never made it to her lovely eyes. "Why, yes, Charles should be here, well, let's just hope he is," she again said through clenched teeth. "Thank you, that's all the time I have right now, I adore you all," she said as she blew kisses to the fans that lined the ropes outside of the University Club.

"Those two bastards better get here or I'm going to castrate them both!" she mumbled as she turned and smiled and waved one more time before entering through the front doors.

'Smiling' Johnny Danes of KMPC radio smiled even broader and then turned away from the closing doors. He tried not to look stunned because Mary's threat was heard by the soundman and he was praying it hadn't gone out over the air. Johnny Danes just continued to smile as he lowered his suitcase-sized microphone.

"Jesus Christ, I wouldn't want to be in their shoes."

"I just want you two stupid bastards to know if anything, and I do mean anything happens to the president or that little girl, well, I just wouldn't want to be in your shoes," Frank said as he looked in the rearview mirror.

They had split up into two teams, the first destination for both was the campus at USC and then the University Club where Sam and John were sure Phaltazar would make his move. The first order of business Sam had told them was to get to the reception and get the girl before she could do anything to harm the president and then they would confront the beast and its minions in Pasadena. It was a good sound plan that Frank knew would go wrong at some point. Connie almost had to be restrained when Sam had said the president came first. The look in her eyes was horrible at the suggestion she was to leave her little sister as a secondary priority. It was John who had calmed her down by saying it had been Jeannie who had taken the chance to give them this break because the girl knew what was about to happen and wanted it stopped. Connie just broke down and cried and then decided there was nothing she could do about the situation and then calmly informed Sam that she and Liz would stay behind, out of the way until they were done. They would await their call before they went to Pasadena.

Frank was having a horrible feeling as he drove out of the back lot of the *Alhambra* for the drive to the USC campus with Chaplin, Fairbanks, Willis and Gary Cooper crowded inside. He hadn't liked the look Liz gave him as they left. Her and Connie wouldn't possibly go out to Pasadena alone with only Stevie as protection would they?

Sam looked down at Connie before climbing into his Chevy. She couldn't look at him and he knew she was fuming.

"You know why this has to be done first, don't you?" he asked.

She finally glanced up and nodded as her eyes were still boring into his, and then her features relaxed and then she reached out and hugged him, wrapping her arms around his waist under his coat.

"Just be careful, I need you to help save my sister after you save the world, okay?"

"You got it, and we *will* save her," Sam said and then leaned down and kissed her on the forehead and then turned and got into the car. He looked out of the open window and said; "Stevie will help keep you company, be nice to him, he's a little peeved he ain't going."

"We'll calm him down," Connie said in all seriousness. "He'll be a big help to me and Liz."

Connie watched Sam and Rainbird and the rest drive out of the long alley. The look on her face was one that was set and determined as her left brow arched and she turned toward the waiting Liz.

"You ready?" she said as she showed Liz the thirty-eight revolver she had just lifted from Sam's holster at his side knowing that he carried as a spare.

"Yep," Liz said as she removed a snub-nosed model from her purse.

They turned as Stevie stormed out of the backdoor of the *Alhambra* building with two guns stuck in his drooping pants.

"Leaves me outta the action, why, I oughtt'a—" He looked up at the two women. "Mister Dalhart can kicks my ass if he wants ta, but I ain't no coward," he said and then looked around the empty rear lot. "One of you's ladies have a license?"

Both women looked at the frazzled and self-conscious Stevie who kicked at a non-existent rock in the parking lot.

"Well, we's don't drive much in Brooklyn."

As the two cars pulled out of the lot of the *Alhambra* the lead vehicle in a procession of five others that had been watching the Sunset Detective Agency from across the street in the diner parking lot, and the same men who followed Gary Cooper and the others, pulled out onto Sunset and followed the two cars of detectives. The occupants were hoping that after tonight they could return home with good news for the men in their country who knew what black deals had been struck and the same men who sent them on such a strange mission for their homeland and for their world.

The yellow eyes watched the festivities taking place across the road from high above. There were two large spotlights lighting the sky and numerous police vehicles lining the roads of the campus not far from where the beast was perched. The eyes narrowed as it spied a long column of cars led by a police escort as it traveled down Figueroa toward the south end of the USC campus. Sirens and lights were blazing as the object lesson for the evening approached.

Phaltazar adjusted the way it sat atop the old landmark. The flame burned brightly behind it as the torch was perpetually lit. The Los Angeles Memorial Coliseum was dark as the wind freshened and brought the night smells to the beast. It turned its head again toward the gala and watched as the motorcade pulled up to the front of the University Club. Again it stepped lightly away from the Olympic torch and dropped easily to the cement ledge just below.

The squealing of tires brought its massive head up as it sniffed the night air. Its eyes locked on two cars that were speeding down Exposition Boulevard. The Archangel smiled for the first time that day after the intrusion of the seer into its home. The trap for Dalhart would be sprung in moments, and Von Railing would make sure nothing interfered with the presidential reception.

The beast tore the satin cape from its thick shoulders allowing it to catch the wind and soar into the open and columned end of the Coliseum, and then for the first time in years Phaltazar spread its wings. It stretched them out to their full thirteen foot length and then flapped them twice, allowing the wind to cool its body. What were once white, pristine feathers were now a sickly gray and brown as several loose ones flew into the night wind. The beast jumped and gently glided down to the cool grass below. The night of nights was upon them, and no matter the outcome its ancient game was at least afoot.

Sam took the turn as quickly as he dared and started searching for the University Club. Cars were parked everywhere making it impossible to see where the buildings started and the street ended. He was about to make the turn onto Figueroa when the car was suddenly struck from the side.

Sam fought the wheel and then covered his head as the car tipped beyond recovery. The accident happened so fast that they had no time to voice anything dramatic as the Chevy went over on its right side. Frank who had been speeding behind couldn't react in time and his Ford slammed into the underside of Sam's car, sending it careening into a grassy area just off Thirty-First Street and sent Frank off into a tree, the loud crunch of metal rebounded off the campus buildings.

Sam fought to right himself as he lay on top of Rainbird. He finally reached out with his right leg and started kicking at the door which opened but fell back. He was about to kick again when the cars door was yanked off its steel hinges with a screech. In the darkness he heard men screaming from a distance away as something reached into the car and pulled him out by the leg. Sam was upside down as he tried in vain to reach for his gun. Then he felt himself lifted and brought higher and the next thing he saw was a face that was unrecognizable as human.

"We meet again Dalhart!" the voice hissed through teeth that were at least five inches long in a mouth that was set in a menacing smile.

Without really recognizing the malformed face, Sam knew who his assailant was. The German, Von Railing. The muscled form hissed and threw him onto the grass and then hopped down from the side of the overturned car and started marching for him. Sam tried to get his breath as it had been knocked from his lungs. He rolled onto his back and his eyes widened when Von Railing came into view. The size of this version of the German surprised him, he had grown at least a foot and was bare-chested as the Vampyre reached down and brought Sam to his feet none-too gently. As Sam finally drew a breath he heard breaking glass as the others scrambled from the two smashed cars.

"It was very impolite of you to send your man to my house to steal from us!" Von Railing screeched as he tossed Sam ten feet and watched him land hard. "For that I will split you like a piece of chicken!"

Rainbird pulled himself free of the smashed windshield and then reached behind for the shotgun that had whacked him in the head in the rollover, then he spied the leather pouch with the forty silver coins inside. He grimaced and then snatched that up also. As he stood he saw Frank, Chaplin, and Fairbanks, who was limping noticeably, Willis and were Cooper running toward him calling out both his and Sam's names. Frank collapsed and fell to the ground. John managed to finally stand and then he ran to him and knelt beside him. He quickly ran his hand along Frank's head and it came away slick with blood. He eased Frank to the ground and then looked up at the others.

"Charlie, take Coop, Willis and Doug and get over to that reception, do what you have to do, but get the girl away from the president—go!"

"What about Frank?" Cooper asked.

"Frank's not going anywhere right now, now get!"

Charlie took Fairbanks by the arm and Cooper took the other and they limped west led by Willis along Figueroa toward the lights of the University Club and the arriving Presidential motorcade.

Sam felt like he was a rag doll under assault by an enraged child as he rolled, trying desperately to get behind a tree. As he did he felt his jacket for the shoulder holster, hoping the thirty-eight hadn't freed itself in either the car crash or his more recent flying lesson, but just as he felt the satisfying lump of the gun he was grabbed by the leg again and brought upside down to face Karl Von Railing.

"I forgot, you don't have wings, do you Dalhart?" the thing said as he lightly tossed Sam again, this time he landed on his back and again knocking the wind from his lungs.

Sam was getting the impression that this Kraut was enjoying throwing him out like an opening day pitch.

Through the trees Charlie saw the large motorcade pull into the drive of the University Club and redoubled his efforts. He saw military and police cars and then he saw the president's car as it was wedged in-between.

"Lord, Charles, it's the President," Douglass said as they hobbled along. "Leave me, go do what needs doing!" he cried out.

Cooper, against Chaplin's wishes and by the pulling of Douglass, steered them toward a large and very thick-bodied Eucalyptus tree and eased Douglass against its cool bark. Cooper patted the old man on the shoulder and turned. Willis called out for them to hurry and that was when Fairbanks had to push Charlie away.

"Go, old boy, go and be a hero, I highly recommend it."

Charlie smiled at Fairbanks. "I always wanted to be you old friend," and then Charlie turned and followed Cooper and Willis who were watching his back.

Charlie was running for all he was worth, regretting every martini and cigarette he had ever smoked in his life when Gary Cooper just vanished. Chaplin came to a stop and looked around him. The darkness was full of rustling sounds that unnerved him. His foot hit on something and saw he had kicked a Eucalyptus branch that had been broken from one of the large trees. He reached down and picked it up and held it out like a cricket bat.

"Coop?" he called. "Willis?" he said with a loud whisper.

All he heard was cursing and gurgling from somewhere ahead. Then he saw Cooper as he was being throttled by that horrible visage of a woman who had assaulted them at Sam's office. She raised her right hand and was about to strike the death blow when Chaplin screamed and ran full speed at the creature. The Countess looked up and around at the last second just as the tree branch struck her across her face, sending her reeling away with little whiffs of smoke trailing behind her. Francesca screeched and grabbed for her face. She looked at Chaplin and hissed while bright red blood coursed through her long, thin fingers.

"You little bastard, I've had quite enough of you!" she said as she lowered her hand and started walking toward him with her thin dress trailing behind her.

Cooper who had fallen on his back when the Countess was struck by Chaplin reached out and picked at one of the rose bushes that ringed the trees of the park. The first one he grabbed was full of thick, pointy thorns, but it was long enough so he broke it free and then rushed forward, striking the Countess across the neck from behind, the thorns struck deep and held firm in the sallow skin for a moment before pulling free.

"That's for not being a real woman!" he screamed at her for no apparent reasoning other than he felt he needed an excuse to strike a lady, even if she were a vampire.

As she screamed in pain and anger, blood gushed from a wound Cooper had opened in her throat. Even then she turned on her assailant as the gash was started to close with the blood flow diminishing as she hissed and smiled. That was when out of the darkness Willis smashed into her whitish body, taking her to the ground, his fists were flying so fast in the dark that they couldn't be discerned through their speed by either Cooper of Chaplin. Francesca screamed in outrage as blow after blow struck her in the face, neck and chest. Willis had turned into a wild man, his motivation was Pete, his best friend dead back at their office. As he brought back his right fist for another strike, Francesca reached out and slid her long clawed fingers into his chest, slicing cleanly through his clothing, skin and bone and directly to his heart. Willis froze as she ripped his still beating heart from his chest cavity.

Cooper and Chaplin saw him wobble and then slide to the right and onto the ground. The vampire seemed to float back to her feet as she smiled at Chaplin and with her long fangs bit harshly into the dying heart. With blood running like a river down her face, she threw the heart away as if it were nothing more than a half-eaten apple and then hissed at Charlie. She crouched and was ready to spring, but before she could take a step, Chaplin whipped the tree branch across her face from behind. The blow took her to her knees. Then Douglass was by Charlie's shoulder taking the tree branch from him.

"Leave you two alone for a moment and all you can think of is meeting women, now get going before the President is harmed, go!" he cried as Charlie just stared for a moment, and then the spell was broken and he rushed toward Cooper who tossed the long, and now broken rose stem to Fairbanks and ran away.

The Countess wanted to chase after them but Doug maneuvered his injured body in-between her and the two retreating forms.

"I guess, it's you and I my dear," he said in his self-taught cultured brogue as he bowed at the waist.

"You fucking idiot, you wish to play make-believe with me?" the Countess hissed, "Then by all means, let's play!" she screeched as her shoulders hunched, transforming into huge muscled caricature of her once fluid form. Her teeth, if one could fathom it, grew even longer and her thin bony fingers shot out another three inches.

Fairbanks could see she had lost all self-control, which he knew would be his only advantage, but as he was thinking this she shot out and backhanded him to the grass.

"No stunt men here, Mr. Swashbuckler," she cackled loudly.

Douglass felt the old surge of adrenalin as he first kicked out with his feet and then in one fluid motion placed his shoes under him and shot up into a standing position.

"My Dear, you have been sorely misinformed, I did all of my own stunts, now, on guard me lady!"

The countess hunched over at the waist but was ill prepared for the attack of Fairbanks as he lashed out with the thin branch, striking her across the cheek and laying it open to the blackish bone beneath. Fairbanks smiled as he knew that injury wasn't going to heal in just a few moments.

She screamed her pain, her anger, her defiance as she whipped her head back toward his assault, slinging fresh blood across Douglass and onto the grass, which if it could have been seen, withered and died from the contact with her blood.

"I will eviscerate you!"

Douglass got a shocked look on his face.

"Is that even a real word?"

As fireworks lit the sky around the University Club, Rainbird cut loose with the twelve-gauge shotgun. The thick lead pellets struck Von Railing in the lower back and it roared in pain. The impact knocked the Vampire from its feet and slammed him into the ground at Sam's feet. When it looked up smiling, Sam lashed out with his foot, catching it in the mouth. Von Railing's head shot to the right as Sam used that time to gain his feet. He saw in the exploding fireworks the pure hatred on the Germans face as it quickly flew ten feet into the air and gracefully turned in mid-air and that was when another load of buckshot hit Von Railing center chest and sent it into a nearby tree trunk with a thud. The large man merely rebounded and landed on its feet between Sam and Rainbird. It crouched as an animalistic instinct took over and its eyes darted from one adversary to the other. Sam knew the longer it kept them occupied the longer they could do nothing to help Charlie, Doug and Coop.

Von Railing hissed and spat and then wiped the blood from its chest and slung it toward Sam.

"Do you know how many men have tried to kill me?"

Sam wasn't going to waste one ounce of breath trading words with this thing. He quickly brought up his spare revolver he had recovered from his ankle and fired three shots into Von Railing's head. The bullets struck two in his right cheek and one took out a large chunk of its nose. That was the one that made the German scream and grab its face. Sam had figured that if a punch in the nose can make a grown monster of a man tear-up, a bullet just may do the same to the undead. Besides, what did he have to lose? Rainbird took that opportunity to eject a shell from the shotgun and fire his last round into the side of its head, and then as the creature was thrown off balance, John attacked with the other end of the twelve-gauge, using it as a club he commenced to strike the Vampire over and over until the wooden stock broke into three large pieces.

Von Railing struck outward with a clawed hand and hit John in the upper chest, sending him reeling backward and pin wheeling his arms in a vain attempt to keep his feet under him. Sam then emptied his thirty-eight into the German and watched as it turned on him and started walking with horrifying directness toward him.

"This ends now!" Von Railing wailed.

That was when Sam saw it, lying on the ground just two feet in front of him where it had landed—a large, sharpened piece of the walnut stock from the broken shotgun. But as his eyes locked upon it, Von Railing laughed and placed his boot on it, grinding it into the ground.

"Foul thought I would say," Von Railing cackled.

The side door opened and the small quartet started playing "Hail to the Chief," which was almost a comical version of the tune most related to marching bands. The first man out of the stage door was the president's press secretary and he was quickly followed by an U.S. Army major. Then the gathered guests stood as President Franklyn Delano Roosevelt was seen on the arm of his eldest son James for support. The applause was overpowering as Senator Farnsworth made it over to Mary's table while applauding.

"Are we ready for the big moment, Miss Pickford?" he asked smiling and showing stained teeth that Mary had a hard time looking at.

They were interrupted by the army major that had preceded the president. He had to speak loudly because of Hail to the Chief and the thunderous applause around them.

"Miss Pickford, Miss Rodriguez," the army man asked looking from Mary to the small child who now just seemed to be staring off into space with a blank look on her face. She was humming along with the song that Frankenstein had liked and had Jeannie teach her. "I'm Major Cobb; the Press Secretary has asked me to relay to you that your presentation will come after the president's speech, not before. He felt it would have a better impact at that point—more poignant."

"I presume you will signal us when we are to greet the President?" Mary asked, making the Major feel uncomfortable with her disapproving eyes and smile that never reached those eyes.

"Uh, yes ma'am, that's right, it's only a twenty minute speech."

"Very well," Mary said over the noise.

The major bowed to Mary and winked at the very strange little girl and then left. Senator Farnsworth frowned and then looked over at the emergency exit at the policeman, Lieutenant Finnerty, who raised his hands in a questioning manner. All the senator could do was shrug his shoulders, smile and leave the table.

"What's the problem?" Finnerty asked angrily when the senator approached him. The dirty cop was quite anxious to be on his way.

"It's only a delay, some nonsense about the old cripple making his speech first, don't worry, I saw the girl, she's getting in the right frame of mind as we speak.

As Finnerty looked from Farnsworth to the little girl only twenty feet away, he saw her with wide eyes as she toyed with the bundled end of the two dozen roses. He just hoped she didn't drop them and allow everyone to see the special surprise that was planted inside that special bouquet.

Douglass swiped the tree branch like a sword thrust from one of his old swashbucklers and caught the Countess across the arm. The recently alive wood furrowed a deep cut down her arm. She screamed and grabbed the bleeding wound. As she did Douglass swung again like in his old film days, only instead of a sword, he was using a Eucalyptus tree branch, and enjoying every minute of it.

"You fucking old man!" she cried as her red eyes looked up in pain.

"I have the advantage here Countess Francesca D'Sarcuni," he said as the name rolled off his tongue. He was enjoying doing the one thing he was tossed unceremoniously from acting for, speaking, and speaking eloquently. The Countess's name was like music to his ears, between his very own talkie and his magnificent sword play, he was only sorry about one thing—it was all without audience.

"Your friends left you alone to die old man, they ran like the cowards they are."

Douglass smiled. "My stalwart friends my dear, are off to foil your evil plan, and the advantage I have is not one of numbers, but one of not fearing death as so many of my friends do. My advantage is the fact that death is my constant companion, while you on the other hand are terrified to meet your ultimate fate, which is hell, and that is exactly where I intend sending you!"

Francesca's eyes widened as the foolish old actor actually charged her with his sagging branch high over his head as if he were in one of his silent films. She covered herself waiting for the painful but non-killing blow from Fairbanks, but as a second went by there was nothing. She removed her arm and saw Douglass lying on his side clutching his chest, the tree branch a foot from his grasp.

"Ha ha ha," she shrieked in laughter. "Fool, you old bag of bones you can't even—"

Her eyes widened as she saw the stake pierce her chiffon dress. She staggered a step and tried to pull the offending piece of wood free of her body but when she touched it, it burned her hands and she couldn't even scream the pain was so great. She looked down at Fairbanks who had rolled onto his side and was looking up at her. Her eyes rolled into the back of her head as she stumbled and almost fell. Then her eyes locked upon three men standing to her rear, they looked intent on her plight but she knew there would be no help there as another one of the men stepped forward and with a determined strike he punched another stake through her chest cavity.

"Oh, GOD!" she yelled as she started to smolder and burn.

"Bitch," Fairbanks said as he rolled away from the flame sputtering woman.

"Swine," one of the men said with a German accent.

The Countess went to her knees and that was when Fairbanks saw the long saber as it was removed from a sheath under one of the men's coats. Without ceremony he spat at the burning countess and swung the sword, instantly cutting off her screams as her head was severed from her neck.

Another man in a black trench coat ran forward and leaned over Douglass.

"Ve cannot stay and assist you, Herr Fairbanks—we must state zat we admire your heroism, Auf Wiedersehen," the man said as he stood and motioned his men forward, chasing after Charlie and Cooper.

"This country's going to hell in a hand basket. There are foreigners everywhere," he said and then closed his eyes and fainted.

Gary Cooper took Chaplin by the elbow and tried to pull the out of shape actor along as best as he could as the bright lights of the University Club shone brightly through the trees as they were finally in shouting distance.

The last of the fireworks were set off some distance away and a bright plume of silver and red sparks burst bright colors through the park-like setting as they ran, but as the descending shower lit up the area they both saw the figure standing in front of them as clear as if it were daytime. Phaltazar flapped its oversized wings twice as the two men slid on the slick grass in an attempt to stop. Charlie went down and Coop quickly tried to get him to stand.

Phaltazar watched contently as the two men hurried to stand and flee. The yellow eyes grew brighter as the dying fireworks display faded from the sky.

"I see that the great hope of man has been reduced to a fool and an actor, such a sad note to end this Passion Play on, is it not?"

"The bastard's actually waxing poetic on us now," Charlie said as he finally gained his feet and leaned on the stronger and much younger Copper.

Cooper pushed Charlie ahead of him and started skirting to the right. He had to turn his head to make sure of their path and when he looked back the beast was gone. He was near to panic as an unnatural wind sprang up from the sky around them and the tree branches started to bend and sway.

"Go Charlie, that thing's above us somewhere!" he said as he urged Chaplin on through the dark.

"Coop, we must split up, that way it has two targets it must get to and then—"

Cooper and Charlie felt the long sharp claws of the beast grab them by their shoulders and coats and lift them free of the ground. Charlie yelled in anger at their failure to do as Sam requested. Then he thought of an old gag he had pulled in several of his films and knew that the time for using it was fast ebbing away as the creature climbed higher into the sky. He quickly hunched his shoulders together and felt the pressure ease on his right shoulder as the beasts claws came free, he gave a quick glance over at Coop and even in his own struggles saw what Charlie was doing and yelled above the noise of the flapping wings, "Do it!" With that Chaplin let his body shrink by hunching and then placing his shoulder blades together and raising his arms high over his head as he had done several times in film to escape the clutches of make-believe policemen. He closed his eyes when he felt his arms start to slide from the sleeves of his coat. The beast felt the movement and tried to reach out with its large hand but only felt the weight loss as Chaplin slipped free of its grasp.

"Lost one, you son of a bitch!" Cooper laughed out and then yelped when the claws sank through the fabric of his coat and into his skin.

Sam crouched as low as Von Railing and they started to circle each other, the German knowing Sam had no weapons and Sam knowing he only had John behind the German. Von Railing slashed out, catching Sam across his coat and shearing it in three long tears.

"Hey, that's a Newberry's jacket!" Sam said as he held out the hem of his coat and looked at it, and then his eyes fell on the small but deadly weapon in his inside pocket.

Rainbird attacked from the back with his large fist but all he managed to do was partially turn the Vampires head as it swiped at him and knocked him to the ground with a thud. Then he reached out with an elongated foot and held John down by placing his clawed toes onto his chest.

"I suspect that your next of kin will purchase you a better one for your funeral, Dalhart!" it spat.

"Not my family, they shop through mail-order, strictly Sears and Roebuck."

"Cease this futile attempt; if you get through me, you have the lovely Francesca, then the Master himself."

"Goddamn, I bet you don't get many women on nights when you look like this do you?" Sam said as he chanced a look at John who was battering at the greenish leg with his fists.

"I have been in his service since the time of Frederick the Great," he said through the thick lips and long teeth. "And I will be with him still when your kind is eating rats for your nourishment!"

"That'll be more than you'll be eating, you son of a bitch, your Master don't know it yet, but he is facing his last night on earth for killing my friends," Sam said as his eyes narrowed.

"Your friends? How about whole nations of friends, do you for a moment think small man that is why you are defeated before the real fight begins?"

"John, are you ready to take notes?" Sam asked.

John was still battering at the white haired leg and didn't slow as he glanced quickly at Sam, not understanding.

"First rule of the agency as you've told Stevie a dozen times, don't trust your memory, write it down, so use that old number two you have buddy—use it now."

Von Railing didn't understand what Dalhart was saying, so in anger it started placing pressure on Rainbird's chest, the claws of its toes penetrating his skin through his white shirt.

Sam didn't wait for the dawning of understanding in John's eyes, he quickly reached into his inner pocket and brought out a long, freshly sharpened number two pencil and ran forward, not letting Von Railing see his small weapon. Sam saw a flash of movement at the creature's feet and then a look of confusion again on the German's horrible features as John brought his own number two pencil up and down again into its shin. Its red eyes widened in pain and shock at the unexpected pain of the assault. The pencil penetrated the thick bone and then snapped off as Von Railing raised his leg in the air just as Sam struck it with all the force he could muster. The sharpened end went straight into the right eye of the German who, choking on a scream fell backward.

"Help me hold him John!" Sam shouted as he threw himself onto the writhing body of Von Railing.

As Sam hit the hot skin and tried to grab the protruding pencil, two bat-like wings burst from the back of the German and flapped once against the long grass. Then again, and again, finally flapping out and knocking Sam from its chest. Then Von Railing cried out, not in anger but in sheer terror of dying. The wings flapped again, and again, each time getting stronger. The creature rolled over to its knees, careful of its eye and forgetting its leg as the wings flapped again, then again, this time faster, so fast and hard was the last wing beat that it knocked John back down to the grass. Then as Sam watched in stupefied wonder, Von Railing's body lifted free of the ground. With four powerful strokes it cleared the trees and then disappeared with its wounded leg dangling free.

John rolled over and looked at Sam and tried to stand. Dalhart helped his friend to his feet and they stood there facing each other.

"Just think, buddy," Sam said scanning the sky.

"What about?" John asked breathlessly.

"That was just the second team, now we have to find the first string."

"You don't think he would just quit do you?"

Sam slapped Rainbird on the shoulder just as they heard the screaming man and looked up in time to see Phaltazar set against the rising moon as he had either Charlie or Cooper in its claws and was flying toward the Coliseum.

"This isn't good," Sam said as he bent at his knees catching his breath. "We need an army to stop this bastard."

That was when they heard Frank's voice calling from the darkness.

"Sam, John, reinforcements are here!"

As they looked into the night, they saw Frank being helped by ten men as they crossed the grass toward them. They heard quietly delivered orders and the men started to spread out as Frank and two other men approached.

Frank looked at the two men and nodded. His head had been hastily bandaged and he bent over catching his breath and then looked up.

"Sam, John, this is Colonel Erich Raedal and Major Paul Lansdorf of the Seventh German Army Corps, they're here to help."

As Sam and John looked on in amazement, the two German's clicked their heels together and bowed at the waist.

"Herr Dalhart, we have been ordered by our superiors to offer you the assistance of the German Wehrmacht in your pursuit of the fiend known as, Phaltazar," the Colonel stated as he stepped forward.

Sam looked from the two German's to John and just shook his head.

"It's still better than telling the LAPD or the FBI," he said.

They heard more shouts as another figure came running at them through the trees, and this shouting man had a silverish firearm pointed their way.

"Now who in the hell is this," Frank asked holding his head.

Again Sam shook his head and turned away and rubbed the bridge of his nose. He was getting a massive headache and knew it was going to get worse before it got better. The man was telling everyone in front of him they were all under arrest.

John checked his gun and started loading it with extra rounds from his pocket and answered the question; "That Frank is former Special Agent, Melvin Purvis, late of the FBI."

Charlie knew he was going to break both legs as he hurtled to the ground below. In daylight he would have been able to see the onrushing ground and would be able to brace for it, but in darkness that option just wasn't there. As his eyes widened in an attempt to see the ground in darkness, a tree top rushed at him and he hit the first of the brittle top branches of a large tree. He felt the harsh wood shred his jacket and grab at his skin as he careened down the trees trunk. He fell free for a moment and then struck a large branch, knocking the wind from him and then he was spinning, waiting for the inevitable crash into the grass below. And did he hit. Flat on his back, forcing what little breath he had at the bottom of his lungs out. He was now not only in pain from at least three broken ribs, he was gasping, trying desperately to force air into a system that just wasn't accepting business at the moment. He rolled onto his stomach and he buried his face into the cool grass and that helped a little.

As he lay in the grass knowing his death from oxygen deprivation was near, he suddenly felt himself lifted free of the ground, and someone was shouting at him to take it easy, try to breathe through his nose first. As he listened and tried on the strange orders that seemed to echo in his mind, precious air found its way past the closed door of his throat.

"That was a tremendous jump old boy, tremendous! I have never seen the like, and to think it was you that performed it—I'm astounded!"

Charlie managed to open his eyes as he finally took a deep breath and focused on the face in front of him. Then he blinked as he recognized his best friend.

"You look bloody awful!"

Fairbanks hugged his friend. "Yes, yes. But you were magnificent in your escape from the clutches of that horrid beast old boy."

Chaplin pushed Fairbanks away and looked at his friend as he spat out a mouth full of blood.

"Stop it Doug, you look ghastly! What happened to you?"

Fairbanks still kept his arms on Charlie's shoulders and slumped only a little.

"Oh, a heart attack is the best bet, old man. Playing with that woman back there didn't help my health situation."

"Look Doug, you have to sit down and take it easy, if you die, Mary will absolutely kill me. Now please old friend, let me go into this thing not having to worry about you."

"I'm afraid my mind says no, but my body has betrayed its master, so go Charles, continue on your way, I'll follow along as best as I can."

Charlie didn't have time to argue with Fairbanks, he just nodded and turned and fled into the ground lighting of the University Club.

ভ SIXTEEN ৬

"**S**o in closing my friends, we're at war with this horrible disease, not for the old such as myself, it's for children like little Adria Rodriguez whose agreed to be here with us tonight even after her horrible experience of the past few days. Courage knows no bounds with this brave child, and for every Adria there is another ten thousand Infantile Paralysis victims, and believe me my fellow Americans, they are just as brave," the President said as he grasped both sides of the large podium for support as the applause rose for the fifth time in his speech.

"We have to attack these debilitating, horrible, spirit robbing diseases just as we have to confront the growing evils in our own world today. We cannot and will not turn our back on these children just as I know we won't ignore the cries of our friends in Europe and Asia. The people of America will never abandon the fight against disease and poverty and never abandon the fight for freedom, thank you and goodnight."

The attending stars, producers, faculty and invited students stood as one and applauded loudly as the president stood as stately as ever and just smiled, nodding his head like a tolerant father. One of the only unsmiling faces was that of Senator Farnsworth as he pushed away from the side of Finnerty and moved through the crowd toward Mary's table.

The President waited for his son John to join him at the podium and then waived to the attentive audience as he was guided to a large chair just beside the dais.

"Well, let's present the President with those nice flowers shall we?" Farnsworth said to Mary while smiling at Adria who looked at nothing at all. Her father noticed she wasn't paying attention and reached out and placed his hand on the side of her face.

"I don't know if she's up to it," Mary said looking concerned.

"Up and back, we'll make it that quick," Farnsworth said as he was having difficulty holding his smile.

Mary looked from the Senator to Adria who was smiling at her father with a distant look.

"Adria, shall we go?" Mary asked.

Adria had no hesitation about her as she quickly stood, using the table top for support, she reached out and took the large bouquet of roses. Mary quickly moved around the table, squeezing past her fellow actors as she made her way to Adria. On the way she caught sight of the familiar face of Paulette Goddard and she mouthed the words, *Where are they?* Mary just grimaced and hunched her shoulders, basically saying *your guess is as good as mine.* She caught herself frowning at the thought of Douglass and Charlie and instead smiled down at Adria.

"Let's go meet Mr. Roosevelt, shall we?"

Adria placed the large bouquet in her left arm, covering her completely and held her right hand up for Mary to take and then moving at a slow pace in deference to Adria's braces, they started up the aisle toward the stage.

Adria wasn't seeing or feeling anything as she walked with Mary Pickford, she wasn't even in the University Club. In her mind she was in the basement singing *Jesus Loves the Little Children* to her friend,

Frankenstein, and he was whispering something to her and smiling with his large teeth. She stopped singing to him and smiled back and nodded her head as she clearly understood everything her friend told her. After all, why wouldn't she, she had straight A's in school and that's why she was chosen to help her new friend.

As the child held the bouquet, she could feel the handle of the weapon at the base of the roses. And she smiled at the thought of the horrible act she was about to commit.

In three minutes time, the President of the United States would be lying in an expanding pool of blood and then Adria could go live with her new friend forever and ever.

The new dark ages described in history books was about to turn the page into the modern world.

"Don't you have better things to be doing than running through the park waving those movie prop guns?" Sam asked.

"You just stand still Dalhart and tell your Indian pal to put that weapon on the ground!" Purvis ordered as he took in the four men standing before him. His chrome plated .45 automatic pointed at the most dangerous person as Purvis figured it, Dalhart himself. The other waved over the others.

"We don't have Charlie with us at the moment; he's off trying to save the President."

"Can the crap funny man and get those hands up, you too," he said waving his aim toward the Germans.

They slowly raised their hands as they watched the comical white-suited agent.

"And just who are these fellas?" Purvis asked.

"They're Germans, new friends of ours," John said as straight faced as he could.

Purvis looked from Rainbird to the two large men and scowled. "That wouldn't surprise me at all, perverts, Krauts, Communists, it just doesn't matter to you two does it. Now, who in the hell are they, are they helping you hide Chaplin, or have you just graduated to treason?"

The night was filled with bolts being thrown forward, a sound Purvis knew all too well from his days chasing Dillinger and Pretty Boy Floyd. It was the sound of submachine guns being charged.

"Herr Purvis, we are Germans and Mister Chaplin is indeed off to save the president of your country, but we have no communists, that should answer all your inquiries, so please, lower your weapon, and do it now," the taller of the two men said as he stepped forward and held out a gloved hand.

Purvis didn't respond at first but knew he was totally surrounded by forces unknown. "You'll go to prison for this Dalhart," he mumbled as he handed over both of his .45's.

"Okay, we'll go wherever you say, but only if we survive tonight, fair?" Sam asked as he removed his thirty-eight and checked the cylinder to make sure it was reloaded.

Melvin Purvis watched as eight more men joined them from the surrounding trees, all were dressed in workers garments and each carried a bleak looking submachine gun. The German major waved them forward toward the Coliseum using the two .45's he had just taken from Purvis.

"Look, we have a real bad man out there who is responsible for all those missing girls and we can't spare a man to stay here and baby-sit you Purvis, we need you and those two fancy guns of yours," Sam said as he holstered his own thirty-eight.

"Why are they here?" Purvis asked as he nodded toward the Germans.

"They've been tracking the same killer as you and us, and let me tell you Melvin, it's not Charlie at all."

"Okay, but if there's nothing out there and I come up empty, you're coming in with me and you'll give me your full cooperation, is it a deal?"

"My word on it, now if you don't mind, there's a real bad one out there we have to get to," Sam said as he turned and followed the German soldiers toward the towering monolith of the coliseum, and the darkness of Exposition Park that surrounded it.

Major Lansdorf bowed at Purvis and then when he straightened he tossed him his two shiny .45's.

"After you, Herr Purvis," he said with a small grin.

"Stop Charles," Fairbanks said as he let his weight alone bring Chaplin to a stop just as they stepped from the trees. "This will never do old boy, look at us, it's as if we just went twelve rounds with Gentleman James Braddock."

Charlie released Doug and looked at his clothes. The tennis whites were filthy and grass stained. His hair was traveling down roads he would just as soon not think about.

"Bloody hell, they'll never allow us in looking as we do!"

"You're supposed to be the quick witted one, think!" Doug said as he watched a few of the policemen that covered the front door.

Charlie turned away and placed his hands over his face. He turned and looked at Doug. "We'll just have to rush the door, Doug old boy."

"Wait, isn't that Menjou right there smoking a cigarette?"

Charlie stopped pacing and looked. "Yes, yes it is," he said as he left Doug's side and crept into the parking area in front of the University Club. He went from car to car, ducking as he went, finally settling on the one closest to Menjou.

"Psst," he hissed.

Adolph Menjou was lost in thought as he lit his cigarette and tossed the match away.

"Menjou old boy," Charlie called out as loudly as he dared.

Menjou finally looked up and squinted into the darkness. "Who's out there?"

"It's me, Charlie," he answered, daring to stick his head up above the trunk of a newer model Ford.

"Charlie who?" Menjou called out, trying hard to peer into the night.

"Oh, for Christ's sake old boy," Douglass called out loudly from the tree line. "Menjou, it's Fairbanks and Chaplin, would you please come over here!"

Charlie stuck his head up as his mouth fell open and watched as Doug walked over toward his hiding place, but he didn't complain as he watched Menjou toss his cigarette away and start toward him also. He glanced at the policemen who lined the walkway and doorway, they didn't even glance over.

"What are you two jokers doing out here? I heard you were supposed to be on the lam, that Dalhart told you to get lost and stay lost?" Menjou said as he rounded the car and confronted Chaplin. He turned and watched as a white faced Fairbanks joined them.

"No time to explain old man, needless to say we have to get into that reception and in our state we couldn't get by a group of boy scouts," Doug said as he placed a hand on the trunk of the same car Charlie had been hiding behind.

"Any word on my niece?"

Douglass looked at Chaplin and nodded his head. "The beast that's responsible for your niece's disappearance is attempting to kill the President as we speak, as Doug said old man, we have to hurry."

"What do you need?"

Charlie pursed his lips in thought and then reached out toward Menjou. "First I need your coat and hat," he said as he removed Menjou's fedora and crumpled it up and then leaned over and found the bumper of the car and ran his hand along the edge. "Yes, that will do nicely," he said as he placed the hat on the sharp edge of the chromed steel and pulled it along, putting a neat cut along the brim. Then he straightened and started tearing.

"Say, that's a new hat!"

Doug just shook his head in exasperation and then started to pull the coat from Menjou's back.

"Hey, hey!" he protested but spun out of the coat anyway.

Charlie finished with the hat. The brim was but a three inch ghost of itself as he punched at the inside, breaking the crease and puffing out the top.

"Doug, get me that tree branch and peel the leaves from it, will you old man?"

Fairbanks limped back toward the trees. Charlie watched him for a moment and just knew his friend wasn't going to be able to recover from this night.

"Say, he's not looking at all well," Menjou said as he handed Chaplin the coat.

Charlie put the coat on and it was as he thought and hoped. The sleeves fell six inches short of his wrists. He smiled for the first time that day. Then he quickly put the hat on and then reached behind the rear wheel of the Ford and ran his fingers along the axle, then he brought his hand up and with two fingers wiped the grease in two straight lines right under his nose. He looked at Menjou and wiggled his upper lip.

"Oh, I see, the Little Tramp!"

Doug slowly made his way back and as he did he was plucking the small elongated pepper leaves from the three-foot branch. He smiled as he looked at his friend and nodded his head.

"Good plan old man," he said as he gave the Little Tramp his walking stick.

Chaplin took the offered branch and broke the end, the green branch snapped but the wood didn't break away as he figured it wouldn't. He bent it over and then hooked the end around his hand and spun the makeshift cane as he had a thousand and one times, then he waddled with his legs together and his feet stuck out like a duck.

"Excellent!" Menjou cried.

"Let's just hope it is good enough for a ticket into this bash."

The three men hurried toward the front door.

Inside the University Club the applause was dying down as the small girl in her heart rendering leg braces and accompanied by Mary Pickford, started to climb the riser leading to the stage and the smiling President of the United States.

The creature swooped low over the running men and actually knocked two of the pursuing Germans down with the dangling feet of Cooper before he could raise them up. Phaltazar laughed loudly as the large wings propelled it and Gary Cooper back up into the sky.

"What in the hell is that?" Purvis yelled as he ran beside Sam and Rainbird.

"That's your bad guy Junior G-Man," Rainbird said as he ran.

"What's that it's got in it arms?"

"Gary Cooper," Sam said.

Melvin Purvis, the single most humorless man in the country laughed as if something in his head had just broken—and Sam Dalhart knew that it might not be fixable after tonight.

As the men covered the ground from Exposition Boulevard toward the Coliseum, the moon rose to its apex. The beast swooped again toward the center of the running men. Sam instead of dodging the swinging feet of Coop then faked right and then held his ground. The creature over-compensated and was shocked at the sudden extra weight as Sam grabbed the two dangling feet. He almost missed, knocking one of Cooper's shoes free and then Rainbird grabbed for the sock covered foot. With two men hanging from his long legs Copper yelled at them to pull. He screamed in pain as the beast's claws dug in deeper as it tried to pull away with several powerful movements of the large wings. Feathers started to dislodge and float away and down upon the men as Purvis joined Sam and Rainbird in the effort to dislodge Cooper.

Three Germans un-holstered their Lugar's and sighted quickly and fired. Four rounds hit Phaltazar's wings and one hit its shoulder, jerking its hand free of Coop's coat and that gave the hanging men the leverage they needed to free him. He flew down on top of Sam, John and the shocked Purvis.

The creature flew straight up and then before any of the men could react, swooped back to earth and quickly dispatched two of the shooters with quick swipes of it long claws. They fell lifeless to the grass. They were now down to twelve men, including Cooper. The creature shrieked in pleasure as it shot back into the sky with powerful strokes of it wings.

"Look, its set down on that building, what is that?" The major asked.

Sam gained his feet by pushing the mumbling Gary Cooper off of him. He looked up just as Phaltazar was settling atop a glass dome. It just watched them. It spread its wings and shook them rapidly and then folded them in toward its body. The yellow eyes narrowed as it laughed.

"The Natural History Museum," he answered.

"We cannot allow it to go in there!" the Major said as he gestured for his men to go forward.

"You have new friends I see. I sense the old world; could they be my old countrymen?" Phaltazar boomed mentally from its perch.

The words were entering their heads, but they knew the beast wasn't voicing them as far away as it was. Purvis shook his head as the speech echoed in his mind.

"What in God's name are we dealing with here, Dalhart?"

"God has very little to do with this thing, at least not anymore," Sam answered as he helped Copper and Rainbird to their feet.

"Why, what's in there that would help it?" Sam asked.

"Allies, Mr. Dalhart, allies."

The policemen were laughing as they watched Chaplin waddle up the winding walk swinging the improvised cane. He removed his hat and wiggled his greased upper lip and bowed. The police clapped and laughed.

"Gentlemen, I am sure you will find my name and that of my two friends on your list of invitee's, a Messier Fairbanks, Douglass, and Menjou, Adolph, actor extraordinaire!"

A burly sergeant looked at a clipboard while he wiped his eyes of tears, he was still laughing as he waved the three men in.

"My Keystone friends, I thank you," Charlie said as he spun the hat and allowed it to roll down his arm to his hand and then he placed it on his head. He waved Menjou and Doug forward.

The three men entered the building just as the applause died down. Charlie waved the valet away and looked around, almost in a panic, then he grabbed the valet by the arm.

"You recognize me son?" he asked quickly.

The man laughed as he took in Chaplin. "Yes, sir, I'm not blind."

"Good, I am running very, very late, is there a back way onto the stage?"

The man was still laughing and it took Fairbanks to shake him to get him to stop. But he continued and could only point at a side door.

The three men ran for the door and opened it and ran into a long hallway.

"What is your plan Charles?" Doug asked, slowing down and running his hand along the paneled wall.

"I don't have one, this is what you would call winging it old boy," he answered and then noticed Fairbanks wasn't with them. Oh, God, Doug!" He turned to see Fairbanks collapsed against the hallway wall.

"Don't, don't stop, go, go," Fairbanks said as he waved them on.

"Addy, old man, take care of him, I must continue on," Chaplin said to Menjou.

"You got it, do what you have to do."

Chaplin swiped a tear from his eye as he watched his old friend slide down the wall until Menjou caught him in his arms. Charlie turned and ran down the long hallway with new determination.

Finnegan moved into the wings of the stage and nodded at Senator Farnsworth, who smiled broadly and clapped his hands as Mary and Adria slowly made their way up on stage to the left of the seated president who had his ever present cigarette holder placed in the corner of his mouth and was clapping his hands as the small child made her way up the six steps. Farnsworth made his way to the stringed quartet and slipped the violin player a note.

"For the President's guest," he said loudly over the growing applause for Mary Pickford and Adria.

The violinist looked at the note and nodded, and then he passed the note to his group. They didn't need the sheet music because each one of them had grown up singing the song themselves.

"Oh, look at this heavenly child, why, the bouquet is much larger than herself!" the President said to the men gathered around his chair. "How marvelous!" he said as his eyes went to Adria's leg braces. He stopped laughing and leaned toward his son, John. "And this child was kidnapped not two days ago?"

"Yes, Dad, she was just recovered by a private detective last night."

"Sounds like a man I would like to meet, saving a sweet child such as this one, see if you can arrange it will you?"

"Yes, father, I'll see what can be done, but as you know, most private detectives are sort of shiftless and lazy, this one is probably no different."

Sam sprinted toward the Natural History Museum but he knew what was going to happen before it did. He cursed when he saw Phaltazar stand and then dive through the glass dome of the museum. Sam stopped running and placed his hands on his knees as the others caught up. He made Coop set down on the first steps leading up.

"Well, we have to get in there," he said waving everyone up the white steps. He called back over his shoulder for Cooper to stay put.

He took a couple of deep breaths and then ran up the stairs after the others. He arrived just as the lights inside the building went out and the emergency, battery-powered lighting came on, in other words, they would be hunting the creature in the dark. He reached out with his thirty-eight without hesitation and smashed the glass window in the wooden door. Several other windows were broken down the line as other doors were breached by the Germans.

As they entered the museum, they saw a large banner stretching across the foyer announcing the newest exhibit; *Los Angeles, 12,000 Years Ago!* Sam and John had read about the newest showcase for collections from the LaBrea Tar

Pits. Thirty-five new examples of the animal life that had been caught in the tar when Los Angeles was a barren plain, full of vicious wildlife now long extinct.

"This place is too big Herr Dalhart, I suggest we divide into two teams," the Colonel suggested.

"You know whatever the hell that thing is; it has the advantage of cover in this joint, right?" Purvis volunteered as he made sure he had his extra clips in his coat pocket.

"This is one of the reasons it has chosen this place, Herr Purvis, that and the fact it has many friends here," Colonel Raedal said as he pointed to four men and waved them forward. "You men are with me and the Major, you two men, stay with Herr Dalhart and his men, we will meet in the center of the building, Ya?"

"Yes," Sam answered and nodded at the others to follow him as he trotted off into the exhibition wing of the museum.

The Colonel and his men headed in the opposite direction toward the Dinosaur Hall and museum offices.

The laughter brought Sam and the others to a sliding stop. The moonlight filtering through the skylights gave them just enough light to cast a million menacing shadows in the massive room.

"Sam," John said as low as he could.

John was kneeling by the headless body of one of the museum's security guards. The body lay prone on the marble floor, his flashlight held tightly in his dead left hand, his thirty-eight still in its holster.

"Damn," Sam said as he shook his head.

"Not getting squeamish at this late time, are we Dalhart?" the beast asked, its thick, coarse voice was clearly in the massive hall somewhere in the darkness ahead.

Sam looked around. "Frank, grab the flashlight," he whispered.

"The fight is not a fair one; you have introduced more pawns into the game."

"Look, Charlie's stopped your little game over at the University Club, so why don't you just head on back home, the Germans have even arranged an escort for you," Sam called out into the surrounding darkness.

There was silence for a moment, and then a chilling, hoarse chuckle filled the hall.

"The clown has failed; I hear the music that has signaled his ineptitude."

Sam closed his eyes and mouthed the word *'fuck.'*

Rainbird turned toward a noise that came from behind them. Frank followed suit after hearing the same, strange creaking. He turned the light on and showed the beam around.

"Dalhart, is there something else in here with us?" Purvis asked.

"Is there something in here with us?" The beast's voice mocked. "There is always something with you in the dark. In the closet, under the bed, I am in all places, and so are the creatures that haunted the lives of your monkey-like descendants. "

Another noise from the far end of the hall screeched like rusty hinges, making Frank shine the light in that direction. They saw strange animal shapes as the beam hit the exhibits.

Purvis held his two .45's in the ready to shoot position as he saw the pedestal in front of the group of men. As Frank played the flashlight over it, they saw the gleaming bones of the long extinct skeletal remains of a Saber tooth cat. The bulk of the skeleton was massive. From foot to shoulder the animal was as tall as Purvis and the fifteen inch incisors as long as his forearm.

"Jesus Christ," he said as he moved his aim from the cat toward the next exhibit, the large skeleton of a Wooly Mammoth. The curator had posed the animal over the cat with its giant foreleg raised in defense against a long ago attack.

The screech sounded again cutting off whatever Purvis had planned to say next; Frank shined the light back at the Saber-toothed cat.

"I could have sworn that thing was looking the other way a moment ago," Frank said, the light shaking minutely.

Sam and John who were examining the deep shadows along the high walls turned and looked at the large skeletal cat. As they did the neck bones of the Saber-tooth creaked and squealed in protest as the massive head turned toward the men just as the large mouth opened and it hunched its front shoulders and lowered its head. As it moved, plaster replacements that the museum staff had used to replace missing parts of the animal that hadn't been recovered, fell free and were shaken off by the cat. The Saber-tooth tilted its head and roared in all the impossibility of the situation shaking the men to their very souls.

The laughter of Phaltazar was deep and rich.

"Now you will know why you have always feared the dark!"

On cue the cat roared and started to spring and at the same moment screams echoed down the hall from the other direction as another roar shook the very foundation of the museum just as men started screaming in agony. The cries of pain and horror came from the Dinosaur exhibit where the German Colonel and Major had taken their men.

Sam reacted first and brought his gun up and fired, but he was too late as the skeletal Saber-tooth was upon him.

Charlie opened the door and quickly stuck his head in; his eyes widened as he surprised two policemen who were there to guard the left wing of the stage. Charlie thought quickly and wiggled the makeshift grease moustache.

"I take it this is where I'm supposed to be?" he asked stepping through the door. He spared a glance at the stage and saw the President sitting with three other men, most likely from the University, smiling and clapping his hands with his cigarette holder stuck in the corner of his mouth. Mary was helping Adria step easily along, only feet from Roosevelt.

"Hey, you're not supposed to be back here at all," the larger and dumber looking of the two said as he stepped toward Charlie.

"Hey, Jimmy, you know who this is?" his partner asked, hitting him on the elbow.

Charlie knew this would be tricky.

"Oh, dear, you mean I came to the wrong wing?"

"It's Charlie Chaplin, I've seen every one of your films," the smaller policeman said with a large smile on his face.

Charlie bowed and wiggled his moustache again, grinding his teeth as he saw Mary and the child were now only three feet away from the president.

"Gee whiz, Mr. Chaplin, we have orders no one enters from this side," the same cop said as he smiled at the smaller Charlie's facial antics.

"Oh, my, that foolish man at the door sent me here, it looks like I'll miss my cue," he said as he looked over the larger cop's shoulder at Mary as she stepped up to the President with small Adria beside her with an impossibly big bouquet.

"Well, if you were supposed to go to the opposite side, there should be no harm in letting go on from here."

"Hey, no way, we have our orders, no one—"

"This is Charlie Chaplin, and he's here to entertain the President you dope, what do ya think he's gonna' do, pull a gat on him? You mug," the smaller of the two said looking from his lummox partner and then he smiled at Charlie. "Go ahead, Mr. Chaplin, knock'em out."

Charlie wanted to reach out and kiss the little policeman but knew he could not spare a second.

"Thank you, you're a prince," he said as he tilted his makeshift bowler forward on his head and stepped out onto the stage.

Mary smiled her Academy Award-winning smile and curtsied to Franklin Roosevelt. He applauded and then nodded his head in the fatherly manner he had perfected over the tough years of his terms in office. Just as Mary eased Adria in front of the President and Roosevelt reached out to scoop the girl into his arms, the crowd erupted in laughter and applause, stopping the proceedings in their tracks. Mary pulled Adria back and looked to her right and saw Charlie Chaplin duck-walking in that stupid style of his and twirling his cane and his body moving from side to side.

"That son of a bitch!" Mary mumbled under her breath and then turned and smiled at the crowd, "I'm going to castrate him," she continued saying under her breath as she reached out and picked Adria up and placed her in the President's lap.

Only the people in the front few tables could see Chaplin's eyes widen as Charlie saw what Mary had just done, he sped his walk up almost into a run, making the secret service agents in the front of the stage take notice. Mary stepped forward to greet Chaplin as the applause grew as the stringed quartet hadn't realized what was happening yet and still continued playing *Jesus Loves the Little Children.*

"Where is Doug you bastard," Mary hissed as Charlie raced by her as quick as he could while maintaining his Chaplin waddle. Pickford was embarrassed as she started to turn and follow, that was when she saw Douglass and Adolph Menjou moving up the aisle in between tables as fast as they could go. Menjou had Fairbanks around the waist and Doug was white as a sheet.

Charlie swooped up to the President as Adria started sliding the handle out of the bottom of the bouquet. Charlie saw what was happening and his mind was screaming that he wasn't going to make it. My lord, the child has a knife!

The President was laughing loudly and not watching the movements of the child in his lap, but had his eyes on Charlie as the celebrated clown stumbled hilariously and almost fell.

By the exit door Senator Farnsworth pushed Finnegan into action as he saw that Chaplin was about to ruin everything. Finnegan was hesitant but then he quickly realized if he didn't get Chaplin off that stage a whole lot of shit was about to hit the fan and he was standing right in front of it. He darted through and around three tables and for no reason in the world he tripped and went flying through the air as the crowd started standing and cheering even louder at Charlie's antics. As Finnegan hit the carpet and rolled over he looked up into the grimacing face of Mr. Rodriguez who had quickly figured Charlie was up there for a reason and that reason could very well be something Mr. Dalhart had sent him to do.

"You son of a b—"

That was as far as Finnerty got when Sanchez reached back with all his strength and kicked Finnerty right in the jaw, knocking him completely out.

Farnsworth had lost sight of Finnerty in the standing crowd and was wondering where he was when he saw Chaplin finally reach the president.

Adria, eyes as blank as an empty chalkboard and seduced by the music which was only just now breaking apart because of the antics on stage, almost had the twelve inch knife out of the bouquet of roses.

The President was laughing uproariously as Chaplin stumbled again and lunged toward him comically waving his arms, his feet seeming to fly on every direction except the one in which he wanted to go. For an instant, he righted himself, his eyes glued to Adria's hand as it slowly removed the knife from the bouquet of roses. As he neared the President, Charlie reached out and snatched the child up and spun her around in his arms, the bouquet of roses fanned out like a carousel of color and Adria's tiny leg braces catching the spotlights as they were forced out by Chaplin's spinning body. He hugged the girl to him and started dancing with her, one hand around her waist and his other outstretched with her own small hand in his. That left him a hand short as the girl removed the knife the rest of the way and under the cover of the roses stabbed Charlie in the upper chest. He grimaced as the pain shot up both arms and he felt his heart race. He started to reverse his dance steps and headed back toward the center of the stage, twirling and dancing as he went.

"Ho, ho, ho marvelous!" the President called out as he laughed and slapped the leg of his son who was shocked at the change in program.

Mary met Chaplin as he spun comically up to the president and easily and flawlessly sat Adria back in his lap and spun away with the bouquet covering the protruding knife. He started stumbling as he became dizzy and the crowd erupted even louder than before. He bumped into Mary and reached out to her as he deftly reached up with the hand holding the roses and removed the knife from his chest just to the right of his shoulder. He quickly slid it inside his coat and then tossed the roses away, all that is but one as he placed it in Mary Pickford's mouth just as she was opening it to cuss him back to the stone age, he then wrapped his arms around her and took her hand in his and then danced away toward the stage wing and the policemen waiting there and laughing along with the rest.

"You mother fucker," she tried to say through the clenched rose in her mouth.

"Mary, for God's sake, shut up, I'm dying here," he said weekly as he laid his head on her shoulder as they finally spun into the wings and out of sight of the audience.

Doug and Menjou quickly shot up the steps to the right of the stage and through the curtain.

On stage the President was laughing as the stringed quartet struck up For he's a Jolly Good Fellow, and Adria batted her eyes as they focused on Roosevelt. She blinked and blinked even more as she stared at the president.

"That was absolutely stupendous, my child, how long did you and Chaplin work on that little number? It was marvelous, simply marvelous!"

Adria looked at Roosevelt and smiled, coming out of the strange trance she had been in the past full day, "You laugh like Frankenstein," she said and laughed along with the president.

Charlie became dead weight as they smashed into the two policemen who were so caught off guard they all four fell to the floor. Menjou leaned Douglass against the far wall and tried to separate the struggling mass. First he pulled a cursing Mary from the pile and spun her toward Doug. Then he lifted Charlie up and helped him over to the wall where he slid back down. The two cops scrambled to their feet still unbelievably laughing at what had just happened.

"Would you gentlemen excuse us for a moment, we have business here," Menjou said in his rapid fire voice.

The two cops moved away into the further reaches of the wing, just happy to have been a part of the show.

"Chaplin, you okay?" he asked and then he heard Mary curse and start to scream when she discovered she had blood on her dress.

Douglass placed a hand over Mary's mouth and she struggled to remove it.

"For once my dear, you'll shut your mouth and pay homage to the man who just saved the life of the President of the United States."

Mary looked around and finally managed to remove Doug's hand from her mouth.

"Charlie, Charlie, oh lord," Menjou said out loud, "he's been stabbed."

Douglass struggled to get off the wall that seemed to hold him place, harshly pushing Mary away as he went to Chaplin's side.

"How did I do old boy?" Charlie asked as his eyes focused on Fairbanks.

"Remember in that big monkey picture where the big ape saved the children from the burning orphanage, old man?"

"Yes, RKO wasn't it? Mighty Joe Young?" he said as he grimaced when Menjou placed a handkerchief over his wound and pushed.

"Well, you topped the monkey you clumsy, crazy Limey!"

"Now I know what you felt like in all those films, you dashing bastard."

"Yes, but I suggest next time you use a stuntman old boy."

Sam's shot went wide of the long dead animal, and as it jumped it had left several plaster pieces behind as they had never had the rich blood of the cat flowing through them. Sam placed his arm in front of his face as the skeleton hit him. He heard Frank, John, Purvis and the Germans shouting all at once as the tremendous weight of the long extinct beast crushed him to the floor. Sam had his forearm pinned under the rough jawbone of the impossibly strong cat as the long Saber-like teeth snapped in furious rage at being kept from its prey. Sam quickly brought his left arm up to take some of the pressure off his gun hand and maneuvered his wrist and fired the thirty-eight just as the large mouth clamped on his arm. This time the large bullet struck the right foreleg of the Skelton and the nightmarish beast went down, taking a lot of Sam's jacket and skin with it. As soon as Dalhart was clear, Purvis started shattering petrified bone with .45 rounds. The skeleton tried to stand, but other rounds from John, Frank and the two Germans kept hitting it with bone shattering fire.

The head of the once great cat went down and finally fell silent; its ghost screams still echoing in the great hall. They quickly reached down and pulled Sam to his feet, but just as they did Sam yelled; "Duck!"

Suddenly and before they could react to the warning, a long snaky skeletal trunk, held together by bailing wire and plaster, came out of the darkness and wrapped itself around one of the Germans, his swinging arms and legs knocking both Frank and John to the shiny floor. As Sam scurried out of the way, a giant bony foot crashed into the tile exactly where he had just been. Frank rolled and brought the flashlight up and to their amazement standing before them and holding one of the German soldiers out with its trunk stood the prehistoric Mammoth from twelve thousand years before that had been on display for the last six years inside the museum. They could hear the ghostly trumpet of the beast as it threw the German in its grasp to the floor and then quickly brought its right foreleg up and stomped the man to death, the skeletal foot crushing his head completely.

"Goddamn it Dalhart, what in the hell are we dealing with here?" Purvis screamed as he helped Frank to his feet.

"I'll try and explain later, for now let's see if we can outrun this damn thing."

Shots were echoing all over the Natural History Museum as both Sam's group and the Colonel's fired upon ancient beasts that were now stalking and hunting them—if they once had blood flowing through them, no matter how old and petrified now, they could move and kill, thanks to the power of the Master of Darkness.

As Sam ventured a look back into the darkness of the great hall he saw the Mammoth coming for them, its large skull struck the small arch of a doorway and tore the mahogany lined arch apart. Its fifteen foot long, curving tusks smashed out one of the great windows as it trumpeted and charged after them. They ran into the great rotunda where they had entered the building and Sam could only hear the charging bones behind them when John screamed for them to look out. As the detective fell to the floor, Phaltazar swooped out of the great beams of rafters above them and clawed Frank on the back, careening him into a display of fossilized eggs, smashing the glass and then falling to the floor. Phaltazar continued on and picked the remaining German up by his head, the soldier's weapon firing rounds everywhere, one even taking five inches of sleeve from John's coat. The beast shot back into the air with its victim, all the time laughing deeply and insanely until it twisted the head of the soldier and dropped him a hundred feet to the floor.

Sam stood and fired his last four shots into Phaltazar. Two went completely through its left wing and the other two struck it in the side. The creature just laughed and landed somewhere up in the darkness of the second floor.

Suddenly the Mammoth crashed into the foyer, slipping and sliding on the tiled floor and screaming as it again swiped it trunk at the crouching men. Pieces of fossilized frame flew off in all directions from the force of its attack. Plaster and bone fragments struck Sam and Purvis, making the G-Man's shots go wild.

"This is too open Sam; we have to get out of here!" John called as he and Frank crouched and fired into the Mammoth causing sparks as several of the bullets struck the heavy gauge wire holding the beast together. All the while they could hear Phaltazar somewhere above them laughing maniacally.

Somewhere to their left they heard the scream of a man as he careened into the great hall from the Dinosaur exhibit. As he smashed into several cases of ancient arrowheads, he righted himself and fired over his shoulder, the flash of his large caliber handgun lighting up the horrific scene before them. Sam saw it was Colonel Raedal and he also saw that the Colonel was alone. Not one of his men was trailing behind him.

But as the men moved in a group firing as they did so, they heard the creature that was chasing the Colonel, the building started shaking and several thick glass panes broke free of their frames as out of the darkness a roar filled the great hall.

"Run, run!" the German Colonel shouted.

Sam and the others froze for a moment and even the moonlit white frame of the Mammoth turned its attention to the new threat heading their way. The beast trumpeted as it turned from the cowering men and started running for the archway separating the great foyer from the central exhibition hall. The Colonel skirted the charging skeleton as it ignored him and kept up a skidding run for the arc.

"Now," Sam cried and they all stood as one and broke back through the opposite arch from where they had emerged from only a moment before.

Sam slowed and turned as the Colonel ran by. "Where are your men?" Sam called out.

"Dead, all dead," Raedal cried out as he followed Frank and Purvis.

"Come on Sam, Goddamn it!" cried John.

"You've got to be joking!" Sam said loudly as he stared at the monstrosity coming at them.

As he watched the Mammoth struck something huge as both extinct creatures hit the archway at the same moment. The mammoth hit the creature before it, lodging one of its large tusks into the other animal's ribcage which elicited a surprised roar from the beast. It was hard to make out in the darkness, but Sam saw the Mammoth as it overshot on its attack and crashed into the side of the arch and then it hit with a shattering crash, sending broken bone skittering in all directions on the polished floor.

Sam's eyes widened as he saw that the tusk that had buried itself in the giant animal now clearly outlined in the moonlight filtering in through the glass sunlight's in the roof was pulled free by the largest set of jaws in the history of the world.

The Tyrannosaurus Rex snapped at the tusk until it had its black fossilized teeth locked onto it and then pulled it free of its boney ribcage with a deafening squeal of bone against bone. The giant beast tossed the tusk aside and then slowly stepped up to the struggling remains of the Mammoth which was now legless as it whipped its wired together trunk from side to side. The skeletal T-Rex simply bent at the waist and crushed the giant skull of the animal, creating an explosion of dust from bone and plaster. The great skeleton crunched bone and with none of it lodging in its empty mouth, it caught the scent of something else. The great head with its eyeless sockets looked up right in the direction of Sam and John at the other end of the grand foyer. It tilted its head and the mouth opened and Sam could just imagine a long ago tongue as it would have slipped from that mouth. Then the beast straightened up, slamming its head into the archway above it and then took one step, then another and then another toward the two men.

"This isn't good," John said as he pulled on Sam's shoulder from behind as he had become mesmerized by the sight of the remains of the great animal.

"Do you like my pets, Dalhart?" the voice boomed from above. "There's more waiting in the dark."

Sam stood his ground as the T-Rex charged through the emptiness of the foyer toward him. But Phaltazar's words had ended so abruptly that Sam knew it had been caught off guard by something.

"NOOOOOOOO!" it cried from high above.

The T-Rex slid to a stop and wobbled comically as it slipped and fell. As it tried to stand, one of its small bony arms fell free and crashed to the floor. Then as it attempted again to stand it fell back and shattered into pieces and then lay still.

"Phaltazar's lost concentration!" Sam called out. "Something's happened and it's mad as hell," he said as he turned toward John. "Charlie did it, Charlie must have stopped the assassination!"

They heard the slapping of flesh against flesh as Phaltazar flapped it great wings. Then as they started backing away they saw the beast light right before them and start walking with murderous rage in its yellow eyes. John reacted first and emptied his thirty-eight into the chest of the beast who reacted as if nothing more than a pea shooter had assaulted it. Yellow eyes locked on Sam, it marched forward, the massive claws at its side and its face a mask of rage.

"Do you think this will stop the carnage that will happen? It is far too late for that, the world will be mine!"

Suddenly the front doors flew open and several flashlights lit the foyer and Phaltazar was caught in the middle, it hissed and swiped at the offending light and then with one last look back at Sam and John it leaped into the air and then crashed through the glassless skylight above.

"Samuel? Samuel, are you in here?" a familiar voice called out.

"Charlie?" Sam asked as he stepped from the archway.

Chaplin and a coatless Fairbanks, who was holding onto the arm of Gary Cooper, and the two policemen from the stage of the University Club, were standing at the doors and were gaping at the scene of destruction before them.

"Charlie," Sam said again, "Adria, where is she?"

"She's on her way to Pickfair with Mary and her parents and Ad Menjou, we stopped her Sam, the President never knew a thing. Sam, your man Willis, he's dead, he saved us and he and Doug, well, they gave us the time we needed."

Sam looked back at John and then leaned over and placed his hands on his knees, thinking he was going to be sick. First they had lost Pete and Talbot, now Willis Jackson. His boys were gone because he couldn't protect them.

"I don't know how, but we've got to make that bastard pay," he said as John holstered his thirty-eight and placed his hand on Sam's back.

Purvis, Frank and Colonel Raedal slowly made their way out of the darkness. Purvis saw the two policemen and stepped up to them and flashed them his identification. On the way past Charlie he eyed him up and down and then shook his head. Chaplin flinched, not knowing what to think.

Sam thought if anyone could explain this mess it would be Purvis, so he straightened to a standing position and stepped up to Charlie and tried to smile. He then took in the very ill looking Fairbanks and patted the old man on the shoulder and in turn looked at Coop.

"You three really came thru tonight."

"I wouldn't have missed it for the world, but that will not ease your mind about the loss of your brave boys," Douglass said as he placed an arm around his oldest and dearest friend. "We did it for you and for them, but it was really all the work of this quick thinking clown, Sam old boy. He delivered a masterful performance and you would have been as proud of him as I."

Sam took in Charlie and just nodded. He looked over their shoulders and saw that Purvis had finished speaking with the two policemen and then turned and walked back to the group of men, sidestepping several large pieces of petrified bone.

"Well, the museum won't be too happy about the break-in tonight, and the senseless deaths of several German tourists and museum guards by the perps, but it should be enough to keep the local police off of you for at least a while."

Sam nodded and then looked at Charlie.

"Purvis, don't ask me to explain what happened here tonight, but I hope you now realize that there are blacker evils in the world other than this man," he said as he grasped Charlie's shoulder.

Purvis nodded and simply held out his hand. "You may have trouble from Director Hoover, I can't control him, but as far as myself, you belong right here in this country."

Charlie swallowed and then looked at Sam who just nodded his head and then the small Englishman took the offered hand.

"Now you three go home, and thank you, you were superb tonight," Sam said to Doug, Coop and Charlie. Then he turned to John and Frank. "We better call into the office and let Liz and Connie know we're headed out to Pasadena."

Douglass grimaced, still having difficulty breathing. "Oh, we tried to call, but there was no answer old boy."

Sam nodded and then his features clouded and then he looked at John who was thinking like his partner. "You don't think—"

"Yes, I do and all they have is Stevie with them. I knew it was like allowing the cat to watch the canary, goddamn it!"

"What, what are you saying?" Frank asked, knowing full well what was happening but refusing to believe it.

"Maybe the failure of its small puppet Adria wasn't the only reason Phaltazar flew out of here in a rage, maybe it was because it was having unexpected visitors at its home," Sam explained, feeling ill again.

"Oh my god, no, no, no, no, Liz," Frank said angrily as he bolted for the front door.

"Sam, you have to let us come along," Charlie said pleadingly.

"No, go home, we're ending this thing tonight."

With those words, Charlie Chaplin and Douglass Fairbanks watched Frank, Sam, John, the German Colonel and Melvin Purvis run into the dark night. As they turned and left the museum, Charlie knew he would never see most of them again.

"Goodbye, Samuel," he whispered so low only he could hear.

Above in the night sky, the first of the black rain clouds crossed over the moon, blotting out what light there was. Now it was up to the remains of the Sunset Detective Agency to make sure the world didn't go dark as well.

The battle to stop the beginning of the End of Days was about to take place.

PART 4

THE BLACKEST SHADE OF EVIL

❧ SEVENTEEN ❧

Liz put the parking brake on and then leaned back in the seat of John Rainbird's purloined Chevrolet Coupe. Connie stared out of the window at the long and winding drive at 6789 Somerset Drive. The city of Pasadena was below them just south of Highland Avenue which made it seem like it was in another country—a country of humanity compared to the neglected property she now looked upon. There were no cars to speak of this high up and they knew they were as alone as three people could be.

The driveway wound around past a tree lined field and that was where their view ended as the gravel tapered off to nothing around the bend.

"Well, I'm not waiting here," Connie said as she looked at Liz who was biting her lower lip and looking out of the front window. Stevie was chomping his gum in the darkness of the backseat at a high rate of speed as he shifted to the right side of the car. "You guys don't have to do this, but I do."

Liz slowly turned her head and looked at Connie and then removed her severely pointed glasses and let them dangle from the gold chain around her neck.

"There is no way we would let you go in there alone, so get that out of that farm girl head of yours right now."

Stevie leaned forward and placed his elbows on the front seat.

"Ladies, I can't get out unless you's open the door, we're waistin' time here," he said as he chomped his gum for emphasis.

Liz closed her eyes a moment and then opened them and held out her right hand toward Stevie. "Give it to me; I'm not going to get bit by any Vampires because you can't keep from working your jaw muscles."

Stevie looked hurt, but allowed the gum to fall from his mouth and into her hand. Liz opened the door and tossed it out and then closed the door and then quickly released the emergency brake as if any delay would cause her to falter. She pulled the car off the drive and into a line of trees and then shut the motor off.

"Okay, let's go before I wise up and wait for Sam and the boys," Liz said as she opened her purse and brought out her small .32 automatic and pulled the slide back and chambered a round.

Connie smiled nervously and nodded. "Okay, let's go."

They climbed from the car just as a slight breeze sprang up and made the branches of the trees move and whisper. Stevie pulled the black slab of a .45 Colt automatic out of the back of his pants.

"This is my momma's gun, and if these things can be stopped, this'll do the job. And, I'm blastin' anything that ain't a girl," he said as he held up the pistol for the women to see in a silent challenge to them to try and take it away.

"Deal, just watch for Jeannie, everything else is on the menu," Connie said as she was the first to start up the long drive toward the unknown.

It took a twenty long minutes of stopping and starting, watching and then moving to make it to the head of the long winding drive. On the way they must have heard almost every animal that roamed these foothills. Several times Liz had to cup a hand over her mouth as a jack rabbit sprang from holes along the tree line and almost made her faint. Stevie came close to blasting something that hooted and then flew low over his head. Connie had to explain to him that it had just been an owl. He silently explained that there weren't too many owls in Brooklyn as a way of explaining his nervousness, and it was a damn good thing there were no owls because they would have been extinct by now.

As they started to wonder if there was a house here at all, the first of the wooden gables that lined the roof came into view between the trees. As they slowed and came closer foot by foot they could see how enormous the old mansion was. The dead grass lined the sides and the half circular drive and long dead rosebushes looked as if they had once climbed the front of the Redwood estate. Connie counted no less than four chimney's protruding from the high sloping roof. The immense front porch would have been homey in an old western movie as it could have easily accommodated a hundred milling guests. The wide steps leading to that porch were bent and warped from neglect. The large pane glass windows in the front were dark and stared at them as if daring them to approach the house.

"Who in God's creation would have built something like this?" Connie asked.

"Obviously you haven't known many of the Hollywood types around here; the bigger the better is the local motto. And old D.W. Griffith was a God in these parts."

"I don't see any cars," Connie ventured as she raised her head as far as she could to look at the house and the surrounding area.

"Yeah, well maybe cars don't mean a whole lot to the people who live there, Ma'am," Stevie said from her side.

"Yeah, I guess you're right."

"Well, front door or back?" Liz asked as she cringed at the thought of using any door at all.

"I don't like the idea of going back there, at least we can see what we have here, so I say front," Connie voted.

"Me too," Stevie said. "I mean, if we's have to run, it's a straight shot out to the driveway," he said looking at the stern visages of both Connie and Liz, "well, ain't it?"

"Yes, and quit that, you don't have to explain everything, your idea's aren't bad all the time. I think we'll follow your lead tonight, Stevie, okay?" Liz said.

"My lead, oh so you can tells Mister Dalhart it was me's that screwed up?"

Liz looked at Connie and shook her head.

"She means because you're the only man here, so we'll follow you, that's all," Connie said in explanation.

"Oh, well, I knew that, come on if we're goin'," Stevie said as hitched up his pants and shoved his hat forward and put the gun out like he was strolling to the O.K. Corral.

Connie took a deep breath and fell in right behind Stevie, Liz, looking behind her at the breeze blown trees, followed. The house seemed to be getting larger as they approached and Connie looked to the large windows and thought she saw something but figured it was only the moon gleaming off the glass. She swallowed and tried to pray—pray that Jeannie was still in there and alive. She silently apologized to her sister for mounting such a feeble rescue attempt.

"Oh, Sam, where are you?" she said as she looked up at the gables which returned her stare with accusing eyes of their own. It was if the house was waiting at long last for company. "Well, fucker, we're coming," she said a little louder than intended.

Stevie led them across the center of the drive, which once must have been beautiful with its large pool and fountain that had filled with leaves and other debris over the many years of it vacancy. They left the fountain behind and eased their way through the crunching gravel of the drive that fronted the house. Every footstep brought them closer to being discovered and they cringed with every one of those steps. Stevie turned back and smiled and winked at the women. He had made it to the first riser leading up to the ancient looking porch. They could see old furniture, some of it upright, but most in a state of deterioration. An old porch swing was hanging from one chain while the other end rested on the porch; the pad that had lined the seat had long vanished.

Stevie started up the steps and the two women followed. As he gained the top step he held out his hand for them to stop as he moved the gun from one end of the porch to the other. Then he gestured for them to come up.

"There's too many shadows, there could be a whole army of them neck munchers out here and we's wouldn't see'em till they was on us."

Connie knew exactly what he was saying. Long and blacker than night shadows appeared as they left the moon behind. The old wicker porch furniture looked like it was a hiding place for any and all black, evil things.

Stevie quickly stepped up to the large redwood double door entry. He nervously stepped to the left side and waived for Connie and Liz to get behind him. Then he leaned out and took a quick look into the left window that ran the length of the door. The small curtain only covered the center of the leaded glass so he could see some of the dark interior. Stevie hissed and then leaned back and closed his eyes.

"What is it?" Connie asked, while Liz who didn't know what was happening pointed her small gun in all directions.

"I swears to God, I ought'a take this gun and blow my own brains out," he said as he opened his eyes and looked at Connie. "Did one of you's even tink to bring a flashlight?"

Connie stared at him wide-eyed and Liz just grimaced.

"Dat's what I taught," he said as he looked into the window again. "Hey, we may have caught a break here; I see some candles and their lobbras just sittin' on a table."

"Yeah, candelabras will work," Liz said.

"I just said 'dat," Stevie answered as he reached out and tried the cut-glass doorknob closest to him.

They all three wanted to just turn and run when the door simply popped open.

"I don't think 'dis mugs really afraid of us."

Stevie swallowed and stepped in front of the door and lightly pushed it open. He expected a horror movie creak but it moved as if on recently greased hinges. The first think to hit them was the smell of decay—not only of the house itself, but of other things that they didn't want to think about.

"Oh, god, that smell," Liz said as she followed Connie inside.

"Now come on, John said this place was lousy with smells," Connie whispered, "Just breathe through your mouth," she thought back on all her experience on the farm, having to hold her nose as she cleaned out the pig sty and chicken coop. But she knew she was only lying to herself. Those simple and living smells were perfume compared to what this house reeked of.

Stevie quickly stepped up to a small table just inside the entrance way and retrieved the large silver candelabra and passed it back to Liz so he could keep his eyes focused on the darkness of the house. He was shaking badly because he knew they were being watched.

"Hurry, Miss Wheeler, I think someone's in here wit us."

Liz placed her small gun under her arm; the steel hadn't warmed any in her sweating hand and was quite cold. She fumbled in her jacket pocket and brought out a box of matches. She slid open the case and took one out and dropped it. She tried again and this time she actually managed to strike it, creating a momentary flare of light, and they all missed the movement that passed by the kitchen doors. Liz tried again but this time the matchstick broke and fell from her fingers.

"I'm sorry," she cried in frustration. "I'm so goddamned scared I can't function."

Connie sympathized with the tough woman, she knew because she was terrified as well, but when she reached out to take the matchbox from Liz's hand she pulled it away and swiped at a tear at the same time. "I got it," she said as she again struck a match with more determination. Finally it flared up and Stevie closed his eyes against the killing effects of his night-vision.

Connie breathed a sigh of relief as Liz put match to wick, first one, and then another and finally the third candle flared to life.

"Finally," Stevie said as he opened his eyes and looked into the entryway. As he did, he thought his eyesight had failed him because standing there fifty feet away and down the entryway in front of a large swinging door was a tall man in a black suit. His eyes were those of an escaped mental patient and he was glaring right at the three intruders.

Connie and Liz looked up at the exact same moment and both, although reluctantly, screamed.

In front of the kitchen door, McDougal started forward with murderous intent. He tossed a small tray he had been holding away and water, bandages and a bottle of whiskey slammed into the wall.

Connie, Liz and Stevie froze. Connie felt the blood rush to her heart as the man moved toward them with large strides taking up precious feet between them. And then their hearts went to their throats when he pulled a large kitchen knife from somewhere under his coat, and then with his black hair flying in all directions started speaking in a language none knew. Stevie brought his gun up again and aimed and pulled the trigger.

Nothing happened.

Melvin Purvis was having the most difficulty with their situation. Here he was sitting between Frank, and for all he knew, a Nazi spy, in the back seat of a car that was screaming through Los Angeles on the way to Pasadena where they may or may not be facing Vampires and a fallen Angel. So instead of bombarding Dalhart and his Indian friend with a bunch of questions, he held onto the only two things that made sense to him—his two chrome plated .45' Colt automatics. They were real, tangible tools of his violent trade, not the whisperings of the club of madmen around him of which he had so readily volunteered to become the newest member of.

Sam had pulled over in one of the many motor courts and placed a fast phone call, the others could see him yelling animatedly into the phone, gesturing wildly and then he slammed the phone down and returned to the car and sped off.

"Who was that?" John asked.

"Someone I felt we needed, but I don't know if they'll help."

"I think you're going to need me in there, damn it, not taking a nap out in the car!" Rainbird protested as Sam threw the gearshift into second as they gained Highland Avenue and fishtailed around the corner heading east.

Sam grimaced and then chanced a look to his right. "You remember what the old woman said, you have to be dreaming while we're in there, and I think she's right, you're the one that's going to do this, we're just going to be moving targets that will give you a shot at....at...well, whatever."

"What if she's crazy and I can't just summon up any damn thing I want, what if—"

"There's a million what ifs, John. We won't know until it happens. But one thing I'm thinking *is* for sure, if that bastard gets out of here and heads back to Germany, I believe we're in for a whole lot more trouble than we already have. I don't think this will be his last attempt at thwarting his plans in Europe."

"We cannot allow that to happen," the Colonel said from the backseat. "It will prolong whatever agonies the world is going to go through."

Sam, without taking his eyes off the road reached over and slammed his hand against the glove box. It popped open and he reached in and felt around until his hand closed on the small bottle.

"We don't have much time, take as much you think will be necessary to put you out," he said as he flipped the small brown bottle to John.

"Goddamn it!" he said as he unscrewed the cap and swigged the remainder of the bottle and then slammed it onto the floorboard. He didn't look at Sam but turned instead toward the window and the passing scenery on Highland. His eyes looked over the real-life settings around the street, the small motor courts and service stations that were the only buildings from here to Pomona, and then he saw his own tired reflection in the glass. He watched as if from another body as his eyes grew heavy.

"Fuck you Sam, I feel like a shit-heel."

"Just do what you can buddy, our asses will be hanging in the wind in there."

"He's going to sleep? When this is over, you guys have some explaining to do," Purvis said as he slid his last clip into one of the .45's.

Sam ignored him as he looked over at his big friend as he slowly rested his head against the window. He reached over and squeezed John's shoulder.

He hoped it wouldn't be the last gesture he ever made to a man he had come to admire and respect, John Rainbird was his best friend, and in this day and age, especially in this town, that said a lot about a man.

Stevie realized too late he had left the safety on and as he struggled to thumb the too small lever, McDougal punched him in the head with his ham hock sized fist. Stevie immediately saw stars and felt himself falling into darkness. McDougal kicked him again for good measure when the kid hit the floor.

"You son of a bitch!" Connie said as she brought her gun up, but McDougal who was so close he just slapped it from her hand.

Liz swung the candelabra at him and only succeeded in losing the small .32 automatic she'd been clutching under her arm and only succeeded in slinging hot wax into the face of the Scotsman. He quickly grabbed Connie by the hair and then reached for Liz, grabbing her by the face and hitting her head against the wall where she cried out briefly and then slid down the wall.

"You fucking cunt!" McDougal said, hissing the words between his teeth as he lifted Connie up by the hair. "I was told to expect men, not a boy and two bitches, this is too easy!" he cried as he tossed Connie into the darkened foyer.

Connie slammed into a rat eaten rug and immediately lost her breath as her back slammed into the floor. She heard the man approach and tried to raise her head. She managed to force her eyes open just as the Scotsman raised his black shoe to smash her head in, but he was stopped by a haggard voice from somewhere in the darkness.

"No!"

McDougal looked up into the torn face of Von Railing who was leaning against the open library door. He reached out and shoved the opposite door open.

"Bring them in here," he rasped and then closed his one remaining eye. His face was actually dripping the whitish looking flesh around a ruined eye socket and the pencil that had contaminated it was still sunk deep into the shriveled eyeball. His body was almost back to its human form, but the wings still hung limp along his back. His still naked body was sallow and sweating. His blonde hair was askew and long, with large patches of gray and even larger swatches missing altogether.

McDougal cursed and then turned and walked back toward the foyer. On his way through, he grimaced and kicked Stevie in his stomach, who failed to recoil from the brutal assault.

Liz came too and looked up at that moment and rage filled her features as little Stevie hadn't reacted to the kick in the slightest.

"You bastard, leave him alone!" she cried out from where she sat after hitting her head.

"If I were you, I wouldn't be worrying quite so much about the dead, and begin worrying about yourself," he said in his deep brogue as he reached out and picked Liz up by her pinned up hair and threw her into the room with Connie. Liz hit and rolled and felt something in her arm give way as she smashed into the still struggling Connie. "Now, get up, I'll waste no more energy on you—GET UP!"

Connie coughed and was able to draw a breath and then she rolled over and touched Liz on the cheek.

"The boy?" Von Railing called out from the library.

"He won't be able to join us, I heard his skull crack like an egg."

"You animal," Liz cried as she reached out and clamped her teeth onto McDougal's leg until she felt her teeth pop through his pant leg and into the salty tasting flesh beneath.

McDougal hissed and then cried out in anger and pain as he started to bring his fist up, but Connie reached out and tried to grab his other leg, sending him off balance and making the big man forget about punching Liz while cart wheeling his arms, fell over onto his side. When he landed he felt the teeth leave his leg and he reached out quickly and punched Liz in the mouth, immediately sending her head back, then he easily kicked out and caught Connie in the side of her face, finally knocking her senseless.

"Having a hard time with the women folk?" Von Railing asked with difficulty from the doorway.

"I want these bitches, they're mine," he screamed as he stood up and was about to kick the swaying Liz in the head.

"Stop! You'll get what's given to you. Now, I've changed my mind, these women seem to be more formidable than I thought. I don't want them anywhere near me, so until I'm right again, take them to where they wish to go, the subbasement."

McDougal, forgetting about his deeply wounded leg, smiled through the pain and once again picked Liz up by the hair and punched her again, knocking her cold with only a small whimper escaping her lips. He threw her roughly over his shoulder and then reached down and grabbed Connie by her thick hair and dragged her along as he turned toward the kitchen.

"I just hope the Master sees fit to leave me a small treat," he mumbled.

Von Railing watched as he slumped against the doorway, his body weak from the wood poisoning. "I doubt if either of us lives to see the dawn," he said as he turned and slowly made his way into the dark library.

Outside the old mansion the first drops of rain delivered from a massive storm front fell onto the dead landscaping and lightning lit up the night sky and revealed the brief flash of a giant bat-like creature as it swooped out of the black roiling clouds.

EIGHTEEN

Sam laid John down across the wide front seat and ordered the others to lock the cars doors. Frank was champing at the bit to get moving because they had parked so far away from the house. Sam explained to him that no matter what happens to them, or Liz and Connie, nothing, but nothing could be allowed to find John. Frank grimaced, still angry, but nodded his head anyway.

"You ready?" Sam asked looking at Purvis, Colonel Raedal and then Frank.

"For my men, for the road upon which this creature has set my country and the world upon, yes, let us end this," Raedal said as he slid a thirty round clip into his machine pistol.

"Come on, Dalhart, let's go kill *something!*" Purvis said as he removed his two .45's from their hidden holsters, so nervous and scared the falsity of his bravado shown through brightly.

"Okay, Frank, you're too anxious, you'll make a mistake, so Colonel you take the lead."

Frank again looked furious but instead of arguing fell in quickly behind the German, not waiting for any other direction from Sam.

"Bet you didn't think you'd be doing this last week did ya?" Purvis asked as he stepped by Sam.

Dalhart didn't say anything as Purvis followed the others, but he did chance a look back at the car and hoped John was close to dreaming because he thought Connie, Liz and Stevie needed him in the worst way. He looked at the dark sky, the moon had completely vanished and the first rain drops drummed off the car and his Fedora. He turned and trotted after the others as the night was ripped apart by lightning and thunder. It was now well after midnight.

Sam just remembered, it was October thirty-first, Halloween night.

McDougal heard Liz cry out as he tossed her unceremoniously onto the dirt floor. Connie he just let go of. The movement of their bodies made the few candles that were burning flicker and almost die, but then they gathered another grip on life and brightened. McDougal spit on Connie's exposed back and then turned and left. Liz heard the horrid man lock the door behind him.

Liz quickly wiped the blood from her mouth and then scrambled over to Connie who moaned as she was turned over. In the flickering candlelight she saw her eyes blink and then her body stiffen as she came fully back to consciousness.

"Oh, God, Stevie—"

"We can't think about that right now," Liz said looking away as she felt the tears well up in her own eyes. "They put us down here for a reason, and I have a feeling that reason is on its way back here."

"God, that smell," Connie said as she started gagging.

Liz placed a hand to her mouth and fought the same reaction. "I guess it's not as bad for me...," she gagged and then breathed through her mouth, "I've smelled Frank's apartment."

Connie sat up and looked around ignoring the brave way Liz tried to ease their dire situation. Her scalp felt as if it had been torn free of her skull and her jaw was throbbing like one of her horses back in Iowa had kicked her. She turned to Liz and took her in as much as the weak candlelight would allow. Her face was swollen from her jaw-line to her eyebrows and both eyes were starting to darken. She was cradling her left arm and hissed when Connie touched it.

"We're a mess."

"Yeah, real rescuers aren't we?" Liz said as she used her good arm to push up from the dirt floor.

"That underlying smell," Connie said as she too stood. "It's the same as in your bathroom; this must be its lair."

"You couldn't have just said its house, you had to say lair?"

Connie tried to smile but she couldn't and Liz didn't even attempt it because when she did the face of Stevie came to mind and she wanted to just set in the dirt and scream until she went crazy.

"We have to find a way out," Connie said.

"Wait, listen," Liz said as she suddenly became a mannequin as she turned her head toward the blackness of the basement. "Something's in here with us."

Connie backed away until she knew she was close enough and then bent at the knees and picked up a stub of candle from the floor.

"This is definitely the basement John described," Connie said as she held the candle higher, not reacting as the hot wax ran down her arm. In the flickering light she thought she saw movement. She swallowed and took a tentative step forward. Liz reached out with her good arm and took Connie's free hand, secretly glad that the tough farm girl was shaking as badly as herself.

"There's no place like home," came the small weak voice from their front. "I would like to go home, but I don't live in Kansas, I live in...live in...Iowa."

"My God," Connie said through trembling lips, "We saw the Wizard of Oz her last night at home, *JEANNIE!*" she screamed and handed the candle to a shocked Liz who took it and she too found herself crying and shaking as Connie ran forward.

The girl was sitting against the damp wall with her knees up to her chin and she was hugging them with her arms. Her gaze was locked on something unseen, maybe her home she had left far behind. Connie fell to her knees, not feeling the skin peel away as she slid to her sister's side. She started to touch her but the distant look in the girls eyes made her hesitate; instead she held her hands just inches from her sister's torn clothes and white emaciated body.

"Jeannie, Jeannie, it's...oh God, its Connie honey," she said, letting the words dissolve into a sob.

Liz swiped at the tears running freely down her face with her broken arm making her wince in pain. She was looking at the lost look of Connie's sister and wondered if it wouldn't have been better if they hadn't found her at all, then she hated herself for the horrible thought.

The girl blinked her eyes and then slowly turned her head toward the sound of Connie's voice. Her dark eyes were ringed with black circles as Connie touched her face. She blinked again and then grunted and fell backward, scrambling away as fast as she could, but to Connie's credit, she was faster and grabbed her pitifully thin leg and pulled herself up to the girl and fell upon her, crying hysterically.

"It's Connie, Connie, Goddamn it!"

Liz cried out in horror at Connie's frustration, tears flowing freely as she tried to cover her mouth with her broken arm and failed, letting it fall back to her side.

The girl stopped screaming and kicking. Connie was still hugging her legs, stopping her from scrambling away from her.

"Are…are…you mad at me," the small and distant voice asked while her eyes looked far beyond Connie.

"Oh, baby, baby, of course I'm not mad at you," Connie said as she released Jeannie's legs and scrambled up and lifted her from the dirt and away from the slime covered wall. Jeannie was almost non-compliant as her sister hugged her to her body.

The candle shook as Liz started crying out loud and couldn't stop no matter how hard she tried.

"It won't let us go home," said an almost inaudible whisper as Jeannie stared at nothing.

Connie looked around and swiped the tears from her face and almost growled as she lifted her sister. "The fuck it won't, we're leaving!"

Liz braced against the pain and used her broken arm and numb hand to help Connie lift her sister as a hard breeze and smell of fresh rain entered the subbasement and just as there came a loud crash of wooden doors.

"Leaving before your host has properly greeted you, I should say not!" said the deep and booming voice from the thick wooden stairs at the rear of the cellar. Connie and Liz both heard the deliberate footfalls as something walked down from ground level, as if it were intentionally building up the entrance.

As they looked into the blackness, the candle Liz held flickered and the light dimmed, just as if the air itself had smothered the flame, or worse, the evil was drawing all light from the darkened basement.

The master of the house had returned.

Sam, Frank, Raedal and Purvis squatted in the shadows of the front porch. The mere size of the mansion had caught them off guard and now they figured it might be a tougher task than they'd first thought to find anything inside this pile old redwood. But they knew they were out of time because on the way in they had accidentally discovered John's Chevrolet stashed in the tree line on the way in, meaning Connie, Liz and Stevie were already inside, and needless to say Frank and Sam were almost beside themselves as they planned their entry.

Sam's plan was blurted out as they double-timed their way toward the door.

"Okay, Purvis, you and the Colonel get around back and try and gain entry there. Frank and I are going through the front door and anything that isn't wearing a dress or Stevie's stupid hat is getting blasted."

"Okay, I'm with the Kraut…, I uh, mean the Colonel, let's go," Purvis said and went to the right following the curve of the overhang.

"I am really finding it difficult to like zis man," Raedal said as he brought the automatic machine pistol up.

"I know exactly what you mean," Sam said as the Colonel took off in pursuit of Purvis. "Ready, Frank?"

"We're wastin' time, Sam."

"Better than blasting our way in there and losing everyone," Sam answered angrily.

Frank put a hand to his bandaged head and nodded. "Sorry."

"Now, let's go get our people."

Sam placed his empty hand on the bottom porch step and looked quickly around and then took every other step on the way up. Frank hesitated as he looked around him for any surprises and then followed. Sam went to the right of the double doors and Frank to the left. Sam then reached out and tried the cut-glass knob and it turned freely in his hand and to Frank's surprise he didn't hesitate but slipped right in the front door. Frank quickly followed his boss into the dark entryway and almost bumped into him as he had stopped and was squatting.

"Look," he said as he passed Frank a small object.

"Shit," Frank said between his clenched teeth. He was holding Liz's small .32 caliber pistol. "Damn it!"

"Yeah, come on," Sam said as he moved and then stopped again as his hand fell into a puddle of something wet. He held up his hand and rubbed his fingers together until they became sticky. He now knew it was blood. He closed his eyes and took a deep breath and without showing Frank his discovery, stood up straight and that was when the lights in the foyer snapped on with blinding clarity.

"Drop your weapons or I'll snap this boy's neck," McDougal called from in front of them.

Dalhart looked up and saw that the tall man had Stevie held by the neck, there was a trail of blood coursing down the side of the kid's face from an unseen wound. Stevie moaned and gasped for air.

"Easy there, we're not here for you," Sam said.

"Put the fucking guns on the fucking floor or I'll snap this child's neck!" McDougal called out in his harsh brogue.

Sam didn't like the odds, but if they put their guns down all would be lost. So he nodded his head figuring he had no choice and pursed his lips and then fired his thirty-eight from the hip. The bullet flew true only inches from the top of Stevie's head and struck the Scotsman between his white lips, shattering his teeth, entering his lower brain and blowing a hole out of the back of his head. Stevie fell like a rock as did his captor.

"Jesus Christ, Sam," Frank said as he brushed by him and ran to Stevie, "So much for no noise."

Sam grimaced, knowing full well anyone that was in the house knew they were here before he had killed the big man in the black suit.

Frank stooped and eased his hand behind Stevie's head and lifted. "Hey kid, you okay?"

Suddenly two double wooden doors slid open and Frank was knocked three feet away from the prone Stevie. Framed in the doorway was Von Railing, seemingly recovered from John's attack from this evening.

"No, he's not okay, as you are not," he said as he glared at Sam. "Now Dalhart, while the Master has fun with your women, we will settle accounts!" he said far too calmly as he stepped over Stevie and started for Sam.

Sam raised his thirty-eight and fired five times but Von Railing kept coming on while smiling the whole distance.

In the impending silence after the gunshots, Sam could swear he heard screaming coming from somewhere beneath him.

John was somewhere he wasn't supposed to be, although he really didn't know exactly where that was. As he looked at his child's hands held out before him, he knew he was young again and in the wrong place. As he blinked and looked about him, he recognized the old Baptist Church that used to be a part of his reservation before it had burned down twenty-six years before. He was then inside a basement, why that was familiar, he wasn't sure. He was sure though that this particular basement wasn't the right one. This was bright with whitewashed walls and had a clean cement floor. He sat as still as he could like in the old days, hoping he wouldn't be asked any questions that he couldn't answer—failures that would cost him a smack on the knuckles with either a pointer or a ruler

"John, John Rainbird! Ignoring me will not make the question go away, now snap to, son."

John looked up and into the small beady eyes of the Pastor Franklyn M. Loveless. That mean it was the fourth Sunday of the month when the Pastor himself oversaw his morning Bible school on the reservation. The pastor removed his glasses and glared at him and raised his bushy eyebrows.

"We wait upon thee, oh child. Now what is the other name for Beelzebub that we have been taught?"

John looked to the other Indian children around him, but as he did he saw that they had no life in their dark eyes. Their once rich, red skin was drained of all color and their arms were lifeless but still folded neatly upon their desks. As he watched, his friend and neighbor Henry Manyguns fell forward and then rolled free of his seat and onto the cold concrete floor.

"You see, young Henry failed to know and he has paid the ultimate price for his savage ignorance."

"We're not savages, we know….we know—"

"Know what, John Rainbird?" the Pastor said as he stomped toward him.

"Lucifer, its name is also Lucifer!" he screamed at the balding white man.

"That's exactly right, John, Beelzebub is another name for Lucifer. Now what word would we not use in conjunction with Lucifer or any of his given names?" the Pastor asked leaning close enough to John that he could smell the whiskey on the man's breath.

"I don't know what that word means," John said flinching at the harsh words thrown at him and the horrid breath smacking him in the face.

"Conjunction, to use with," the pastor screamed.

"I…I don't know."

"Yet you will possibly try to call upon one of those names someday to help your friends and you will fail, John, you will FAIL!"

John looked around the Sunday school class. He looked for his mother who had saved him once from a conversation very much like this one, but as he looked now he knew she wouldn't be there to rescue him this time.

"I won't fail, because even the devil has enemies in his own house, my mother even said so!"

"Blasphemous heathen child," the Pastor reached out and slapped John across the face. "Lucifer is not, nor can he ever be an ally of good! He has no enemies in his own house, just as God no longer has enemies in his!"

John turned his head as an open handed slap was now coming at him and just as quickly turned into a closed fist and he quickly closed his eyes before the brutal punch to his face. He wouldn't give the white man the satisfaction of his crying out in fear, he would stand firm as he realized where he was supposed to be and that this little stop over was a way for his mind to remember. He closed his eyes and without looking caught the Pastor Loveless' hand in his own small one and when he opened his eyes again he saw the Pastor's eyes open wide in surprise as his hand inside of John's became smaller and smaller. John raised his own eyebrows and looked at the man who personified evil when he was but a boy. As he made the Pastor from his childhood wince, the man dropped something he was holding in his free hand—it was a small pouch and when it hit the concrete floor the contents spilled out and several coins rolled free.

"I know exactly what evil is, and what evil is capable of."

Suddenly John was thrown out of the light and into total blackness. He knew where he was immediately as the mixed smells hit his nostrils. The sting from the Pastor's slap was still fresh on his face but John knew it to have been only a dream as the quite righteous Reverend Franklyn Loveless had been found dead by a self-inflicted gunshot wound inside his battered old pick-up truck out on Broad Hollow Road in Fort Collins, Colorado ten years ago. And John was only sure of one thing, he was happy that old bastard was dead. Evil comes home to roost his Ma always said.

John looked around and could see people, three of them sitting on the filthy ground cowering from something that he knew was in the darkness. There was Jeannie, the girl who had helped him in this place once before. He was happy, glad she was still alive. As his eyes moved he saw her sister, Connie and then Liz. They had come to this place he remembered now—they came for the girl. John now looked into the blackness before him.

"You've had a rough night," John said.

"Shaman, you have come at last. I could only hope you would be so bold as to see me off."

John waited and was rewarded with the movement of air. The beast moved forward in the black inky basement.

"With any luck, you won't be leaving this place."

"Is that so?"

John didn't answer as this was going to played his way and he knew all the pieces weren't on the game board yet, his, nor the creatures.

"Have you not lost far too many of your friends this day? You wish to lose more?"

"I am flattered that this subject concerns you," John said as he moved toward the women.

"John? John are you in here?" Connie called out when she understood that the beast was talking to someone.

"SILENCE!" the creature shouted.

"Fuck you asshole!" Liz called out.

John heard gunfire from somewhere above. At first there was a single shot and then moments later, four more distinct shots.

"Dalhart! Tell me you have brought our mutual friend?"

"Sam wouldn't miss this for the world, he's upstairs right now saying hello."

"Your humor in the face of your destruction is an admirable quality, Red Man."

"I have my moments," he said as he finally reached the women. He wanted to reach out and reassure them but knew his power inside of his dream state was limited.

"Move away, Shaman, the women are forfeit. Of all creatures that may leave here tonight they will not be among them, you may count them as mine."

John moved a few feet away as the creature took a menacing step in the direction where the women sat. He looked around him and then thought inwardly if he could actually do what the old woman had asked. He thought he could do it, but he wouldn't know until the moment came.

"I feel your thoughts, Red man. Because of your small victory tonight, you believe you will triumph over me? Do you know how many have thought this? I cannot count the souls that I have dispatched. And even if I could be harmed, the wheels of a dark machine have begun to turn and eventually the world will at least be void of humanness and thus, it will be mine. The failures of my father will be complete."

"Maybe so, but you're not going to be around to see this thing, you'll finally be where it is you have always belonged, with your brother."

John and the three women could feel the change in the atmosphere as the last words were uttered. The creature was unaware of their knowledge of its lineage and was taken by surprise.

"The game is over and I have lost patience with you, Red Niggar!" the beast cried as the air parted as it charged John.

John saw the creature emerge from the blackness but was surprised as the claws reached out and actually made contact with his dream body, slicing a nice neat path down the front of his shirt.

"The problem with you, Red Man is that you believe, and believe too much!" it screamed as the great claws raked down again, this time slicing John's left arm to the bone.

As he fell back he saw the beast squat just to the left of the women, its long arms resting before it and its scaly knees high in the air. The yellow eyes seemed to fix on his exact location and the creature smiled, exposing his browned and yellowed teeth. The gray hair was all but shooting in all directions as it began to laugh.

"The only one that can save you, won't save you, and I can see your disappointment. His decree is my life, for better or worse, I am to reign over your kind, 'tis my punishment as well as yours! Damn you father!" it cried as its massive head looked upward. "My brother reigns in hell and I suffer with you monkeys upon this foul rock!"

John could feel the depth of Phaltazar's insanity once again and each time he did he knew there were doors upon doors of unopened hells that this creature had suffered in its failure a million years before. The loneliness of not even being sent to hell with its brother and the only company on earth was with death, had driven the beast into deep insanity, far deeper than the original sin of its crime against God.

That was when John realized the creature was right, the plan they had wouldn't work unless it had been decreed to work a millennia ago by God himself.

God, John knew, wasn't anywhere near Pasadena tonight.

Sam knew he had had it. Von Railing was upon him in an instant and had transformed in front of his eyes moments before he was grabbed by the throat. Even when Purvis and Raedal broke in and started firing at point blank range into Von Railing's back did Sam know he was about to be history. He fought the strong hands of the last Vampire as the huge creature slammed him from one wall of the foyer to the other, his shoes kicking out a window, knocking a hole in the once expensive plaster walls as the last few bullets flew through Von Railing and struck the front doors. Even when both Raedal and Purvis attacked with their fists, and then a shaken Frank stood from where he had been tossed and helped, the Vampire's concentration was on nothing but the immediate death of his main target. Sam's eyes fluttered as he was battered once again into the hard wall.

Suddenly they heard a scream of outrage from behind and Raedal turned just in time as Stevie ran forward through the swinging kitchen door with a cleaver he had just lifted from an old butcher block. Raedal's eyes widened in horror as he let go of Von Railing and on his way to the floor pulled the grunting Purvis with him. Stevie swung with everything he had, remembering his many hours imitating Dodgers star Duke Snyder's batting style. The cleaver flashed brightly in the overhead lights and connected right at the base of Von Railing's neck. The blow failed to sever the German's head completely, but it did get his undivided attention as it released Sam and swung around and stared with its one red eye at his assailant. Stevie had had it.

The cleaver slowly fell from his hand and the head wound he had gotten from the tall scary guy earlier was taking its toll. He was ready and stood his ground as Von Railing took one more step. Then his mouth opened to say something but no words followed. Then as if in slow motion his head leaned to the right and just kept going until the last vestige of sallow skin that was attached to neck and head stopped it. Then the mouth worked again as the skin finally gave way and his head thumped to the floor, followed soon by his slumping body. Sam was struggling to sit up when Stevie ran to him, sidestepping the slowly dwindling corpse of Von Railing who was a simmering and smoking pile on the rug as he seemingly melted into the old tattered rug.

"You were really cutting it close kid," Sam gasped.

"Geez, Mister Dalhart, when the first five bullets didn't stop it, why didn't you's try something else, don't you fellas ever go's to the movies, nothin' can live without its head."

"We'll remember that the next time, Kid," Sam said as he allowed Stevie and frank to help him up. "How's that hard head of yours?"

"Ah, my Ma hit's harder than that mug," he said but wobbled as he said it, his balance clearly shot.

Sam ripped open his collar so he could get more precious air into his lungs. "Well, let's head to the basement for the final quarter of this screwed up game."

"Ya, it's time, do you feel it?" Raedal asked.

"If by feeling the house shake from somewhere down below, yeah, I feel it," Purvis said, not looking all that well.

"No, I mean the atmosphere, it's getting thicker. Something's coming, Herr Purvis, and I don't know if we should welcome it."

"Our other guests are arriving, I will greet them," the beast said as it swiped at John again, effectively moving him out of the way when he dodged to the right.

The whole basis for their plan was that John couldn't be touched, but the beast had ruined that one with its new ability to hurt him. John looked at his arm and knew he needed a tourniquet or he would soon run out of high-test. He quickly removed his belt and tied it around his arm just below the shoulder and then he quickly moved toward the girls.

"As soon as you see the opportunity, get yourselves and Jeannie the hell out of here," he whispered as he heard a wrenching noise coming from the stairs.

Connie and Liz looked around and were unnerved when they could see John anywhere in the basement.

"We can't leave you, we—"

"Do as I say! You have what you came here for and a lot of my friends were killed helping you, now do what you're told for once!"

Connie just nodded in the darkness, Rainbird's words hitting her like a sledgehammer.

Sam told Stevie to go outside and wait. A groggy headed Stevie started cussing and then Sam told him something Purvis and the Colonel couldn't hear. The kid nodded once and moved out through the front door and into the falling rain and the flash of lightning.

"Okay, let's go," Sam said as he led the way to the kitchen.

They paused only long enough to do what Stevie had suggested; they grabbed anything that would cut; old butcher knives, the cleaver Stevie had used and long meat skewers that had once roasted duck and spitted beef for the glamorous silent era movie stars that had once been guests inside the old mansion.

Sam turned to the locked door John had described and slammed the cleaver down on the old lock three times until the hasp, not the lock, fell from the door. He stepped in and turned on the light and started down, not waiting for Purvis, Frank and Raedal. They took the first flight two and three steps at a time, taking a severe chance of falling and breaking their necks. They came to the door that led to the subbasement and stopped. The evil inside was so strong that it almost physically pushed them back from the door. They knew that the creature was down there, waiting for a final confrontation that it had no doubt it would walk away from. Sam reached out and turned the old knob and the door opened into a darkness he had never seen the likes of before. He saw four steps before the ones that followed vanished in shadow.

"Come on, Dalhart, let's go," Purvis said as he Frank and a reluctant Raedal pushed past him. He quickly reached out and was able to grab the German's collar as he heard first Purvis scream and then Frank, then before he could react he and Raedal was pulled into a black hole with them. They fell forever and Sam felt the floor as a dull thud that made him blackout. The thirty foot fall was broken only by the bodies of Purvis, Frank and then Raedal as they hit first.

As Sam tried to open his eyes he felt the two men under him move, then stop. And then he felt himself picked up and again he was airborne and again he felt his battered body slam hard into the floor and skid to a sudden stop against a mercifully cold wall. He decided along with every nerve ending in his body that the best course of action was to just lay still and not attempt to move, because that could only lead to learning just how bad he was busted up. His trained mind overrode his commonsense and his eyes fluttered open and there at eye level were the cloven hooves of the beast he had come to destroy. Then he figured out what had happened—the bastard had torn the damn stairs out.

Sam was jerked up by the collar and turned to face the beast. It smiled, its features actually glowing in the dark from some inner luminescence.

"Looks as if you fell off the map at the point where it said, *Here there be Monsters,*" Phaltazar said as it laughed at its own sophomoric joke.

Stevie saw a line of three cars drive up one after the other in the strengthening storm. One was a black Cadillac and the others were old and battered pick-up trucks. The car drove to the front porch and a man dressed in Chinos and with a red handkerchief around his head jumped from the front seat. He had an old Winchester rifle and he scanned the area with it pointed outward. He eyed Stevie closely and the kid threw his hands in the air. Then he saw the rear window go down in the Cadillac and the man holding the gun squinted at him and then nodded his head.

"You, boy, you with Dalhart?" the man inside the car asked with a strange accent.

"Yeah, uh, yeah, he's my boss," Stevie stammered.

The rear door of the Cadillac opened and the man reached in and helped the old woman from the car. Madame Yvonne Grakstoffo Boueveree-Smith stepped out and then under an umbrella that another man had waiting. She looked up at Stevie and she didn't bother to smile.

"Is your employer still alive young man?"

"Yes, ma'am, he left me here to tell ya that."

The old woman was dressed in silk pants and wore some sort of fur coat that she pulled tighter around her. The queen of the Gypsies gestured her five well-armed men forward.

"Then take me to him, if he and the Indian are still breathing, I will do what I can, Dalhart's way, even if the damn fool gets us all killed."

Stevie didn't understand what the old woman meant, but if it would get these men inside where the fight is, that was fine with him.

As the men and Madame Yvonne gained the front porch and were out of the rain, Stevie opened the door for them. The old woman turned and one of the men gave her a large book which she handed over to Stevie.

"You take this heavy old thing until I need it boy," then she turned and said something in Polish and the men dispersed into different areas of the porch, their guns at the ready.

"Ain't they comin' in?" Stevie asked incredulously.

"There are enough fools inside; a few more won't make any difference at all, they stay here."

Stevie watched as the old woman passed by him with an air of royalty about her and into the old house.

Sam was finally face to face with Phaltazar and he wasn't caring for the experience all that much. As he looked at the face of a million years, the beast closed its eyes and as the women along the wall jumped and Sam blinked as a thousand candles ignited, first three or four, then in groups of a hundred. They were placed at the base of all four walls and Connie was sure they hadn't been there before.

"You see the years now Dalhart?"

Sam looked at Phaltazar and could discern a thousand small scars— some larger than the others, and also the lines of time that were etched as deep as canals in the ancient scaled skin. The large upper lip ran down to its jaw line and tapered back toward the neck. The nose was almost flat and it too melted into the green and scaly skin of its cheeks. The creature lowered Dalhart and pinned him to the wall.

"I didn't used to be so," it said as it tilted its head and opened its large mouth wide to allow Sam to see its front teeth, the way they hung down eight inches below the other filthy and stained teeth around them and the way they curved inward. "I was once the golden face of Heaven, the envy of my brother and those who would put me down from their jealousy," Phaltazar said as it lowered its head and then tightened the grip on Sam's neck.

"You're killing him," Connie cried out.

"Is that such a bad thing woman of man, to die, to leave this place and journey to the land where I can no longer go? No, that is the merciful thing for me to do. And throughout my existence, through this curse of my God,

I am but here to do just that thing. For my arrogance, my deceit, my insanity, I am given this task, while my brother gets hell beneath us," it said while examining Sam as if he was making sure he listened, then he let him go and allowed him to slide down the wall gasping for air.

John couldn't move, he tried to imagine all things that the old woman said he could conjure, but it wasn't like his normal dreams as it seemed he was no longer in control. If you didn't believe in Lucifer, could you actually conjure him up? And if he could wouldn't that be opening a doorway to something else? No, his mind wouldn't allow him to imagine such an entity as that. His old, disgusting Pastor was right about that, some things were best left out of it.

The beast half turned in the candle light and looked around, not knowing where John was, but guessing.

"The world started dying long before you started dreaming of me, Shaman. My revenge against the God who placed me here in exile will soon be complete and I will reign over a barbaric wasteland where the worst thing possible for your kind will be afoot, the loss of all hope," it turned and looked back at Sam, and from him to Connie, Liz and Jeannie. "The loss of all the heroes, the very substance that gives you hope."

"Your servant's killed my men and you killed those young girl's," Sam said in almost a whisper, "You have to pay for that, your time on earth may come, but it hasn't come yet," he said as he started to stand back up.

"My time is upon this earth, Knight, your leader is old and a cripple and he will only lead a nation that comes to the fight too late to do much good. Darkness is upon the old world and night comes fast to the West. I have always been man's challenge and now you have failed, no miracles, no reprieve," it said as it suddenly swung its thick and muscled arm out and missed Sam as he ducked and allowed the claws to gouge five inch gashes in the old redwood.

Sam moved out into the room, he spared a glance over to the Colonel, Frank and Purvis, there was only moaning and slight movement coming from the remains of the fallen stairs. He moved to the far side of the basement wondering if John was in the room and when he was going to attempt an attack of any kind.

Connie stood and started forward, Liz reached out and tried to grab her but it was too late, Phaltazar reached her first.

"I used to lie with women such as this and once long ago they would slay themselves when they were pushed away from my face, my golden hair," it pulled Connie forward and held her close to his face, this time he had her by both shoulders as it sent its tongue out and licked her from her neck and then up the side of her face. She cried out and turned as far away as her neck would allow. "Now, they shun me, a HUMAN WOMAN!" he cried out in anguish and threw her down.

Sam slowly walked forward and struck the beast with both hands in a two fisted swing, only to hit hard muscle and thick scales. The creature easily extended one of its wings and knocked Sam across the basement.

John closed his eyes and concentrated like he had never done before. Images of his life as a boy, the ridicule and anger, the shame of a drunk father, the way his mother had to explain him away as not the child of Satan, but a boy of the old and forgotten days of their people. He remembered when he believed, when he controlled. He imagined once again. He thought about wood, the Crucifixion of the white man's savior, the horrid image he stared at for hours on end, being forced to think about that awful event. The wood of the cross, small, insignificant pieces of wood, splintered over time and distance. As he concentrated his head was aching, his heart pounding, he could feel the coarse seat of the car under him, as he knew he knew he had just thrashed out in the car and hit his arm on the steering wheel. His eyes fluttered but he must not wake up, he was so close. The coarseness of the splinter, long, jagged, broken into a thousand pieces two thousand years before and now most lost. But not this one, not the one he thought about, dreamed of, an icon, a talisman—a weapon.

John slowly opened his eyes as the beast bent low to smash its claws into Sam, he looked down at his open palm and there it was, eight inches long and pointed at one end. It had a cheaply made brass plate attached with four tiny screws; the etched engraving was hard to read but he knew what it said; An Original Piece of the Cross of Christ. And he remembered his mother scoffing at it to a man in a white coat and straw hat, the place escaped him, but the man was saying it was handed down hand to hand, generation to generation from the old country many, many hundreds years before, and it could be had for the not so princely sum of $7.50. His mother laughed at the man and had pulled him away, but it had been that cheesy piece of made-up wares that allowed him to look at the horrible rendering of Christ on the Cross for all those years of childhood. It made him believe.

He grimaced and then closed his large hand around it and gave out a war whoop that would have made his ancestors proud just as Phaltazar sent its claws on their downward flight toward Sam's face.

Connie thought she heard a yell, a scream of outrage but it went by so fast she thought she was hallucinating. Then she heard the whoops again, seemingly coming from all directions of the subbasement.

Sam heard them too. It was John, he was sure of it, but as the clawed hand started its downward swing he knew he wasn't going to be around to see if the old lady's plan had worked. As he clenched his eyes closed, waiting the killing blow, Phaltazar hesitated and started to turn and at that exact moment it howled in pain and then screeched as it swung backward with the same hand that had only moments before was going to be the instrument that slashed the life from his own body.

John had launched himself, not by running, but literally flying from where he had been against the far wall and used the distance and speed to sink the sliver of wood deep into Phaltazar's backside just below the protruding ribcage and into the deep muscles there. The beast swung back at that exact moment and John didn't know how, but connected solidly with his neck and shoulder, sending him caroming into the pile of rubble that used to be the stairs and onto Frank, Purvis and the unconscious Raedal. Purvis grunted and then lay still as John quickly rolled free as he felt Phaltazar as it turned toward the spot he had come to rest at.

Sam saw the creature reaching for something on its back, both arms swung back and were reaching in a vain attempt to dislodge what had attacked. The beast suddenly turned as if seeing something that was invisible behind it, and that was when Sam saw the protruding piece of wood. The beast cried out in agony as it twirled this way and that until it ran backwards into the wall and then slid sideways, finally pulling the small sharpened piece of wood free. It was still shaking its head wildly as if it was poisoned, the screeching of the beast sent chills up Sam's spine.

"I'll rend you to shreds of raw meat, I curse you niggardly savage, Oh, Lord!" the creature cried. Sam saw the real tears it shed as it swung back toward him.

He rolled as close as he could and reached for the sliver of wood, which lay against the wall, smoking and sinking into the earthen floor. He wrapped his fingers around it and then it turned into a liquid and ran free of his hand and into the dust where it soaked in like moisture in the dead desert. Sam's eyes widened as the beast saw what he had tried to do and grabbed him and threw Sam against the far wall. He hit and his eyes rolled to the back of his head.

"Thou shalt not defile God's creation," the beast screamed as it cried and bent at the waist, the pain it was sheer agony.

Connie screamed and ran for Sam and again slid in the dirt and started shaking him.

John scurried against the wall, not twenty feet away from Sam, he knew he was injured badly but as he reached up and felt his neck and shoulder, he didn't feel any blood. But he knew for some reason that out in the car that sat in the rain and wind, his body was bleeding. It was if he could see the car from a distance but could also see inside. He didn't try and stand, but closed his eyes again and tried to think. The small porcelain piece the old woman had given him had been smashed to pieces in the museum fight and now he couldn't remember what it even looked like. He tried to think of more wood, but knew in his mind he had used the one and only piece, because he had partially figured out the magic—that one piece of counterfeit wood was the only one he had ever come into contact with, real or not, it had worked and he had used the only one in the world, because it was the only one he really believed in from the wonderment of a child's point of view.

"The shaman has hurt me, hurt ME!" the beast cried as its head swayed and then stopped as it looked for Sam. "Come to me Shaman, robber of thought, or your friends will be denied mercy!"

John thought with all his might, but he was coming up short. He thought about one of his father's ceremonial arrows he displayed on the wall of their small home on the rez and as he opened his eyes, the old crooked arrow was there. The touch of the wooden shaft was as real as when he used to take it down and feel of it. His father said it was a medicine arrow and should always be handled with respect, but he knew even then as a six year old his father was a drunk and half out of his mind even by then. But John had that arrow now and he prayed it had magic in its hand smoothed finish.

The creature shook its head and felt the blood coursing down its back and roared. As Sam's eyes again came open, he was reminded of a sound he had heard once long ago by a bear up in Big Bear Lake as a boy. A bear was hurt and rangers had tried to capture it and it had made a noise similar to that the beast was now making. As the yellow eyes again settled on Connie and he, Sam saw the hatred there

He quickly pushed Connie away as the beast took the twenty paces to him in one tremendous leap. The heavy hooves landed only a foot from him and the beast was about to reach down once again when he heard the same war whoops again and felt the air rushing toward him. Then as if from nowhere an old Indian style arrow with worn feathers at its base was sticking from the beast's side. Only nine inches of the arrow had failed to sink into the scaled green skin. Phaltazar screamed and turned and swiped at his invisible enemy and then reached for the arrow.

Connie scrambled back to Sam and started tugging on him until he fell to his right and she started dragging him away from the enraged beast.

Phaltazar stopped screaming and looked at the arrow and then started to laugh, a deep, insane chuckle.

"Toys, is that what you have for me Shaman, toys from your childhood?"

John stood only feet from where the beast mocked his feeble attempt and closed his eyes. The magic of the medicine arrow wasn't real, he never really believed his father when he had said that to him time and again in his drunkenness. He thought about saying this to his mother and the sad way she had looked at him while shaking her head. She was saying something he could hear, but as her lips moved it looked as if she were saying, you shame me. John opened his eyes at the hurtful vision and when he did he saw the beast standing before him with the arrow clutched in its large hand, the yellow eyes looked as if they could see him, and then they roamed to the left of where he was actually standing.

"I feel you red man, I sense your failure and your shame at your beliefs," it said and then laughed sensing not only John's shame, but victory in this unsettling but inevitable matter.

John closed his eyes again and then he remembered his mother's words; "Your father is a drunk, forced there by his own failures, but that does not give you the right to look upon him with accusing eyes about his deep belief in our past. Alcohol has stolen everything from him, but honor was not one of them, believe in his medicine, he speaks truth."

John opened his eyes after remembering things he had long chosen to forget about his father. He had buried him along with all the things he had believed in, and those things became his to disavow, to toss back in his face and memory and claim them to be only the ravings of a drunk. He smiled, his father was a drunkard, but that didn't mean he was a fool, it didn't mean that he wished for the old days, because it was the one thing he had and believed in, and now so did John.

The laughing stopped as the beast reacted as if something hit it in the side. It cried out and stumbled backward clutching the side the arrow had penetrated, it removed the hand and it came away drenched with bright red blood. The creature screeched and then looked at the arrow in its hand. When John believed, the arrow worked.

Sam kicked, scrambling further away with Connie's assistance as the creature dropped the arrow into the dirt and turned away screaming incoherent words from the long-lost language of heaven. John at the same time saw the arrow on the floor and reached for it. He picked it up and without hesitation ran at the back of the beast and sank it to its feathered end. Phaltazar reacted with sheer agony as it again arched its back and screamed, it immediately started shaking and fell to the floor, trying to dislodge the arrow from its back but only succeeded in breaking it off.

"John, it's working," Connie cried out as she pulled Sam into her arms and held him as she reached for Liz and Jeannie.

Phaltazar looked up in anguish at the woman and it seemed to have a questioning look on its horrid face. It shook its head and tried to rise but fell forward. Its chest was heaving in great sobs as blood bubbled from its back. John watched from his dream and knew you had to believe in something, anything to have been able to cause the horrible impossibility of reason now writhing on the ground any harm.

"Father," it cried, sending a large plume of aged dust into the air. "I'm frightened!"

"Finish it, Indian," said a voice from above them.

John looked up in his dream state and at the top of what remained of the stairs stood Madame Yvonne, Queen of the Gypsies, and holding her arm was Stevie who he held an old storm lantern high revealing the blood dried on the side of his face.

"The beast suffers, end it," she called down into the basement; she was looking around, not knowing where John was.

"Father, I beg of you, I know not of being afraid," the creature said in its deep, crying voice and then it gasped and tried to look up, but then its eyes blinked and focused on Sam who was just realizing what was happening. It looked at him for the longest time. "I know not of friendship, I have love for none," it hissed in pain as the blood continued to soak the floor. "I want..., I want my father's forgiveness," Phaltazar laid its massive head on the floor but its eyes remained open. "I wish to go...home."

The old woman reached out and took the large book from under Stevie's arm and turned to a marked page. She took the thick gilded paper in her old hand and then let go of the book and it fell and landed on top of Purvis far below and he reacted with another loud grunt. The page had ripped neatly from the large text and she held it in her hands. Stevie took her arm again and she smiled at him. She folded the page and let go of it, it drifted down to the semi-dark subbasement and landed not five feet from where John stood in his dream.

"The creature must be allowed to bleed out. But I leave it to you Indian how you send it off," she turned to Stevie, "It's over in this dark place young man, I wish to go home, please take me to my car."

With a last look down the broken staircase, Stevie turned and escorted the old gypsy up toward the real world.

John walked over with quite a bit of mental effort, it was again like walking in syrup or setting cement. He reached down and picked up the page and scanned it, seeing perfectly well in the darkness that was only lit by the many candles. The picture was of the young archangel Phaltazar and his brother Lucifer. They lay among friends in the painting and were laughing, but Phaltazar's eyes were on something unseen that the artist left out and the look on his face was one of contentment. Then he figured it out, it was the same picture the old woman had showed them at her house, only it was cropped by the original builders of the book. God was there, but he wasn't there, but in the rendering Phaltazar was oblivious to that fact, meaning at one time he too had faith, friendship and love, for his brothers and for his Lord. John thought he understood now. He took the page and walked toward the dying creature and as he passed its failing body he felt a kinship with it. He didn't understand that part of it, but somehow this creature wasn't a beast any longer, it was truly Phaltazar, the chosen archangel of God once again.

"Leave me to die, Shaman," it said as its eyes started to close.

John saw that the large eyes were no longer yellow, but a shiny blue that caught the candle light and reflected back, and they were once again after a million years, peaceful eyes.

"John," Sam rasped out.

"Yes, Sam," he said.

"Oh, my God," Connie said as the shimmering outline of John appeared before them, he held something in his hand.

Sam smiled. "You okay pal?" he asked as he raised his head from Connie's lap.

"I think I am, might be bleeding all over your car though."

"I'll take it out of your next check," he said as he watched the shimmering outline of his friend.

John smiled and nodded and then knelt down beside Phaltazar. He brought his hand up and hesitated a moment, and then smiled softly and laid his fingers to its cheek. The blue eyes opened slightly and looked at him.

"I am afraid...all of the men, the women...they all await...me."

"Yes, but they are waiting at a place where they wish you no ill will. Phaltazar, you have to believe. Believe that God has forgiven you, believe it."

"Fath—," it tried to say but its voice failed. It swallowed and tried to speak through a dying baritone. "Father...I want to come...home."

John watched the light fade from Phaltazar's eyes and its body exhale its last breath as it became still on the dirt floor inside the filthy basement. John stood and watched as the body of the first angel rose slowly from the floor. He almost smiled because he felt no shock or surprise at this seemingly miraculous occurrence. But he was startled when first one piece, then another piece of flesh peeled away from the creature's skin with a flash of sparks. Each piece soared toward the ceiling and then vanished. This happened in full view of an astonished Sam, Connie, Jeannie and Liz. For a moment, Purvis was watching from the far corner but pain and shock overcame him and he fainted dead away. The scales were now gone and what was left was a silvery vision of a boy.

He looked close to sixteen years of age and as if he was merely sleeping. Then the glowing body spun slowly and rose and then simply faded away.

"Sam?" Liz said as she couldn't take her eyes off the spot above them where the body had vanished.

"Yeah, Liz?"

"I want a fucking raise."

❧ EPILOGUE ❧

Six days after that night of nights, the remaining members of the Sunset Detective Agency sat in the only un-burnt, unbroken chairs left in the offices at the *Alhambra*. They had found the inside suite of offices gutted by the blaze that the fire department said was started by a cheap coffee urn that set off the electrical short that destroyed their offices.

No one blamed Little Stevie. And it was just Steve now; no one could call him the kid anymore. Even though he had bought the cheapest coffee urn possible, no one said a word to him.

They had gathered one last time before Sam took Connie and Jeannie to Union Station for their train back to Davenport, Iowa. Connie sat with her hand on Sam's leg, as if making the final touch before he sent her back to the sanity of her world a lasting one. Jeannie had spent the past five days at the Los Angeles County Hospital where she was treated for being malnourished, dehydrated and for being in a state of shock. Her distant stare finally ceased on her third day. The circles were fading under her eyes and she had even smiled at Stevie's jokes, not understanding most of what he said, but smiling at him nonetheless. She would recover only because she had very little memory of what had happened to her. The child sitting next to her was in the same boat. Little Adria was already back at school and was doing as well as ever. It was her parents that would not soon forget the ordeal of losing one daughter, only to have the happiness and confusion of regaining the life of their youngest.

"So, no charges are being filed by the County?" Frank asked from behind the chair where Liz sat with a small box on her lap filled with all that she could salvage from her desk. She reached up and took Frank's hand, the only thing sticking out of the cast he had received for his fall off the stairs. Liz looked around as if daring anyone to say anything about her holding his hand. They didn't.

"No, thanks to Mr. Purvis here, he was mighty convincing," Sam said nodding at the former FBI man who only nodded his head, easily as it was in a neck brace.

As he looked around the room, his eyes locked on John. He was in a cast from a broken arm he had received while, of all things, sleeping. He didn't remember how he got it, as a matter of fact his recollections of that whole night was a bit scrambled. But he knew something had taken place and he felt he was, for the first time in his life, at peace. While he healed he was planning to go see his mother in Montana. She was getting on in age and he figured he would ease her mind a little by telling her he had finally found himself. Found the faith in his present *and* in his past, enough so that he had come to understand the father who'd had left him so very long ago. Forgiveness was in the air for Rainbird and for the life of him he didn't understand where that forgiveness had come from—it was like a fading dream, the answer being there one minute and gone the next.

As for Sam, it would take him a long while to get over the friends he had lost, Pete Sanchez, Willis Jackson and that old coot, Talbot Leonard. They could never be replaced and so they wouldn't be. The Sunset Agency

Detective Agency was dead for all time, they would never reopen again. But what was left of it would remain together. Somehow.

Before Sam could turn back to his friends, the broken and shattered door opened once more. A small man with horned rimmed glasses walked briskly inside and then stood and nodded to Dalhart. He looked behind him and then advanced into the room. He removed his hat and placed a briefcase onto a broken desk.

"Mr. Samuel Dalhart, I presume?"

"That's me," Sam said as he faced the small man with the drab suit.

"Sir, as I cannot say in mixed company who I represent," he said while glancing at the others in the room, "I am here to offer you a position that you and your team have recently dealt with only recently," he looked around the smashed office and shook his head. "As war grows closer to our shores, there have been some disturbing developments in certain areas of the world, notably from the Axis powers, for their desire to investigate…how do I say this? The occult origins of history? We have discovered the Allied Axis powers are working in certain areas that are more than just disturbing, but very unsettling to the men I work for."

Sam didn't say a word, he just watched the small man as he nervously pushed his glasses up on his nose.

"Some of this material you have dealt with," he looked again at the smashed office, "as I stated before, only recently." The man opened his briefcase and took out a file. "This document is authorizing a new unit of the State Department, it is known as Office 66-6. You are to head this office and we will funnel you mission parameters, and you will seek out these dealings of the Axis powers and thwart them wherever possible. You will be paid in the grade of full Colonel, your associates, whatever degree of rank you prefer."

Dalhart took the sheet of paper and looked it over as the man closed his briefcase and then adjusted his hat.

"Thank you for your time, we expect you in Washington no later than the end of next week as we have a mission scheduled for that time. He gave Dalhart a business card. "Go to that address when you arrive. Thank you again for your time."

The man turned to leave as Sam called out to him.

"Look, we've had just about enough mystery for one day, who in the hell sent you?"

The small man turned to look into the office. His eyes settled on Rainbird and the rest who stared at him as if he were a bug.

"These people will be with me, so you better spill it government man, or you can take your offer and shove it where the sun don't shine."

The small man smiled and then removed his black hat.

"Okay Mr. Dalhart, I'll break policy this one time. The name that isn't on that sheet of paper, the very man who authorized this office, is Franklin Delano Roosevelt, I expect you've heard the name before?" The smallish man placed his hat back on and then smiled again. "Good day, Mr. Dalhart, your first mission is described in the package. As you can see, the president wishes you to work for him. I suspect it would be better than awaiting a draft notice that will most assuredly be coming in the next few months when war breaks out."

The small man left.

As everyone got up and started to head out of the office for the last time, confused as hell as to what was to become of them, Sam stayed behind and looked at several empty chairs in the reception area and smiled. They were perhaps reminders of friends that weren't there that day—his boys and his Hollywood friends, Charlie, Doug and Coop. The three stars were loved by millions who worshipped them for what they could do on the screen. He was proud to know that they were that rarest of creatures in Tinsel Town—men who were as good off the screen as on.

Sam would not be around when the fate of his friends came calling...there would be no goodbyes as they would soon lose Doug

407

Fairbanks to the cancer that riddled his body in December of that same year of 1939. Charlie Chaplin would be devastated at the loss of his best friend, and Mary Pickford would never get over losing the old swashbuckler, even though she would never come out and admit it.

As for Charlie, he would go on to create one of the most iconic film characters of all time with his motion picture; the Great Dictator, and would be hailed as one of the few men of the free world that warned early on of Hitler and his true intensions. Charlie Chaplin was finally chased out of Hollywood in the late fifties because he was accused of being a communist during that maniac McCarthy and his hearings. Anyone that knew Charlie Chaplin knew exactly who and what he was, and a communist wasn't one of them. He loved ordinary people far too much. As for Sam and the rest of the agency, it was closer to love and respect than just business for the Little Tramp. Charlie would die in 1977 and many believe that a large part of the world also died that very day.

Sam took a last look around and shook his head from the memories he would take with him of the Sunset Detective Agency's last case.

"Yes, sir, it was one *hell* of a case to go out on."

ABOUT THE AUTHOR

David L. Golemon was born and raised in Chino, California. He comes from a family steeped in military history, from the Civil War through to Vietnam. He has raised three great children: Shaune, Brandon and Katie Anne. After spending many years in Loveland, Colorado, he now makes his home on Long Island, New York.

Besides his bestselling EVENT Group series, David is the author of The Supernaturals: A Ghost Story and its upcoming sequel, In the Still of the Night.